Cryptic Spaces

Liz –
Hope is NEVER more than a heartbeat away –
Deen Ferrell

Book Three:
Dark Edge Rising

Deen Ferrell

Curio Creative

American Fork, UT USA

Cryptic Spaces
Book Three: Dark Edge Rising
by Deen Ferrell

Copyright © 2017 Deen Ferrell
ALL RIGHTS RESERVED

First Printing – April 2017
ISBN: 978-1-68111-179-7
Library of Congress Control Number: 2017938490

Printed in the U.S.A.

0   1   2   3

Ray Bradbury once told me that writing, for him, was an adventure. He would often find himself running behind his characters while they shouted, "Hurry! Come on! Catch up!" Writing Cryptic Spaces has been a bit like that for me. The characters have a strong sense of where they want to go and how they want their story to unfold. Sometimes, I try to tell them, "Hey, no, wait—you're going the wrong direction!" They just laugh and keep going. So, I've learned to trust my characters and just sit back and try to enjoy the adventure. But as always, there are times in writing a book when you need outside help. Sometimes, it's just to keep sane—writing a book, especially a series, is a huge commitment and challenging undertaking that tests you in many ways. I have been fortunate to have lots of family and friends to thank for helping me. I would like to take a moment and thank several others that deserve to be mentioned. I gained added insight about St. Petersburgh from my friend Moses Podoxik. Disney animator Thomas Leavitt created the images for the dragons Mac and Beth. Leah Finkelstein shared her enormous musical talents in bringing Sydney's lyrics to life—check out "Just Another Lonely Kid Like Me," on YouTube. (Then purchase it from iTunes—Sydney would approve!) I also received editing notes from several professionals and friends, including Sherry Wilson, Jeff Gilbert, Andrea, Ashley, and Melanie. Many thanks to each of you.

OTHER BOOKS BY DEEN FERRELL

Cryptic Spaces: *Foresight*, 2013

Winner, "The Book Pick" 2013, BookBundlz.com

*Winner, "Best Sci/Fi, Time Travel" 2013, The Dante Rossetti
Young Adult Fiction Awards*

*Honorable Mention, Young Adult Science Fiction category,
Reader's Choice Awards, 2014*

Cryptic Spaces: *Eight Queens*, 2015

Finalist, "The Cygnus Awards" 2015, Time Travel Category

DRONE VIDEO, CAMERA #MNC7701
TRANSCRIBED FROM VIDEO:
Subject: St. Petersburg break-in
Location: Senoya Enterprises, Interior office,
Date/Time: March 19, 2012, 8:13 PM
CLASSIFIED: **HIGHLY SENSITIVE**

AIYITO: *(Aiyito is a youngish Asian man, slender, well dressed, with dark hair and dark eyes. He appears in the camera frame and looks toward someone out of frame.)* You must be mad! What do mean, coming here, especially tonight?

PERSON OF INTEREST (Designate **#A1129**): *(Only one shoulder, a smattering of neatly trimmed white hair, a small patch of pale skin at the neck, and the crinkled tip of an ear protrude into view. The voice has a notable European accent.)* Why is tonight special? Ah, you mean your daughter's performance. All of St. Petersburg is agog with anticipation. She will be looking for you, you know. Why did you not leave earlier, Aiyito? Your plane has been standing by for hours. The level of your failure as a father astounds me. So, why am I here? I come and go as I please, and there is nothing you can do to stop that. Let us not waste time with absurdities.

AIYITO: *(He wipes his forehead, walks behind the desk, and pulls a bottle and a glass from a credenza. The label on the bottle identifies it as Sake from Asahi Sake Brewery.)* You didn't say why you're here? I gave you what you wanted.

#A1129: *(still out of frame)* No... You gave me what *you* wanted.

AIYITO: *(As he pours a drink and gulps it down.)* What do you mean? I gave you information. That's what you asked for. Are you telling me you don't want it now?

#A1129: I am telling you that I do not have what I seek. I instructed you, Aiyito, to tell our good friend the Director *everything.* I instructed you to gain his confidence, to get him to talk. You did not tell him everything. Nor did you get the information I need. Do not forget how I found you. It is completely up to you how I leave you.

AIYITO: *(After hanging his head for a moment, he looks up, pours another glass of Sake from the bottle and throws it down in one gulp.)* I didn't need to tell him. He already knew.

#A1129: Really? How?

AIYITO: *(Pouring a third glass, he holds it out toward the pale-skinned man, still barely in frame. A1129 makes no effort to take it. After a long moment, Aiyito shrugs, gulps down the contents of the glass himself, and slams the glass to the desk.)* I don't know. He's like you. He just knows things.

#A1129: I seriously doubt he is like me. Perhaps he is just very good at watching you. Your security is woefully lax. He could be recording us now.

AIYITO: No. I have this room swept daily. We use the best system money can buy.

#A1129: Ah… I forgot—your technology is so impressive, and his can only transport people through time.

AIYITO: *(He glares for a long moment.)* What do you want?

#A1129: *(He steps fully into frame now.) What do I want?* Oh, there are lots of things I want, Aiyito.

AIYITO: We cut a deal.

#A1129: No. *You* cut a deal. I do not cut deals. I merely… cut. *(The figure stops, turns slightly, and lifts his head, managing to keep his face hidden.)* So, here is what I propose. I make you a suggestion, and you be a good boy and follow it. If you are good enough, I let you and your family, such as it is, live. I suggest you get me what I want. Do you think you can do that Aiyito?

AIYITO: *(He walks hesitantly to his desk, puts the bottle away, and steps behind his high-backed chair.)* You think you own me, don't you?

#A1129: Yes, I own you. I own you, how do they put it— lock, stock, and barrel. You know that as well as I.

AIYITO: *(He steps around and eases into his chair.)* Perhaps I don't care. Perhaps your threats don't scare me anymore. Perhaps I am finally willing to face my death.

#A1129: Perhaps. But then, you and I both know there are things so much worse than death. Why, some of my most useful associates beg me daily for death. Then there are those sad and horrible things that can happen to those we love. If you were gone, who would be left to care for that precious daughter of yours? Oh yes, she does interest me. She is talented in ways you do not even understand. What if something happens to her mother? What if she...*changes* somehow? I can make people change, Aiyito, you know that. What can you do to protect them?

AIYITO: *(Slamming both fists onto the desktop.)* You promised me! You said you would stay away from her! You promised you would not harm her or her mother!

#A1129: *(Giving the hint of a soft chuckle.)* Oh, but 'harm' is a matter of perspective. I may not have approached your family—yet—but I am never, *ever* far away, Aiyito. I guard my assets closely. Did you ever wonder that you met your estranged wife mere weeks after I found you and offered you asylum? I *intended* for the two of you to be together. I *intended* for the two of you to have a child. You tried to keep the relationship from me, to separate yourself from them in order to protect them. But you see, I am always watching. Now, I have made an investment in you. You will either pay up, or just *pay*. I told you I wanted you to infiltrate Observations, Inc. I've helped you rise to your present position. If you do what you are told, there is a chance—a small chance—that everyone comes out of this okay. I would hold onto that chance, Aiyito. I would pray for it. That is, of course, if you are a praying man.

AIYITO: Really? I don't think God is interested in me, and I have no intentions of praying to you.

#A1129: *(The man lets out a cold laugh.)* As if that would help... Frankly, this conversation is beginning to bore me.

AIYITO: No doubt you have other things on your mind. Tell me, is it true? Not even a day after the break-in, and already, you have had to personally take control? You had enough information. Your team should have been able to find what you needed, and by the way, if you really are '*all-seeing*,' why do you need me? Why can't you find the artifact yourself? The incompetence of your team is not my concern.

#A1129: (*The man is still for a long moment, then slowly, deliberately, he approaches the desk and leans over, turning again to hide his face from the camera.*) You amuse me, Aiyito. You are brazen and foolish, but you have moments of being *very* funny. Perhaps that is why I keep you around. I suggest you not push your luck. Incompetence is everyone's concern. The information for the break-in was incomplete. It resulted in a considerable loss of life and property, and still, I have no artifact.

AIYITO: *You* killed those people!

#A1129: (The man raises his hand into frame as if to strike Aiyito.) *I? I* killed? (His voice booms with power. A strange shimmer glints in the air near the hand. As quickly as it appeared, though, the shimmer vanishes. The man lowers his hand and his voice.) It was you Aiyito—you provided the old and erroneous information that cost those men their lives. (He seems to stare Aiyito down, causing him to quail and then visibly flinch. When Aiyito finally looks away, A1129 continues.) Now, do you want to continue to revisit the past or move on? What is that exchange from *Alice in Wonderland*? The cat says, '*We're all mad; you're mad, I'm mad.*' The naïve Alice asks, '*But how* *do I know I'm mad?'* The cat answers, '*Because, you are here...*' (The man slowly straightens, remaining in front of the desk, his back visible on screen. He is wearing a long, black trench coat.) Whether you like it or not, Aiyito, *you are here...* You and your family are neck deep in this. (*His voice takes on a discernible menace.*) So, I suggest you stop trying to run.

AIYITO: (Still looking down.) What if H.S. really doesn't have the artifact?

A1129: Then he knows where it is. That is why I have you. I want to know everything he knows. It must be found, and you are going to help me find it. Do we understand one another?

AIYITO: Why won't you tell me what it really is?

#A1129: Above your pay grade.

AIYITO: (*He heaves a heavy sigh, running a hand through his silky, black hair.*) I've told you what I know. Yes, he said there were clues, but that's all he told me. I'm not part of his time traveling buddies. I'm simply the financier. I'm on the board because I bought myself there. You—

(*#A1129 throws up a bony hand again, stopping Aiyito in mid-sentence. He turns away from him, allowing us a momentary view of his face. His eyes are sunken, but bright. His cheeks are pale and scarred. The corners of his mouth are turned down and pulled tight.*)

#A1129: I am not interested in your excuses, Aiyito. You disgust me! You are not fit to be a father, a business leader, an associate. Perhaps it is time I take another tack—perhaps it is time that I start directly mentoring your daughter myself.

AIYITO: *No! (Aiyito appears to melt.)* I'll... *(He drops his face into his hands. When he looks back up, there is sweat beading on his brow.)* I'll keep looking. I'll find it, or I'll find where H.S. believes it is. I just...I just need more time.

#A1129: (The man sighs.) More time...Everyone needs more time, Aiyito. You have what time you have. I suggest you be wiser in how you use it. *(A1129 pauses, and then spins and leaves the room.)*

AIYITO: *(He stares after the figure for a long moment and then picks up the phone, wiping a hand over his face and eyes.)* Sonshi, did you get the flowers? ...Right, to the dressing room, and the note? Thank you, Sonshi. Make sure she gets home safe. *(Aiyito looks out the window, his eyes peering down, then he turns and pulls the Sake bottle back out. He pulls out the stopper with his teeth, spits it onto the floor, and takes a long swig from the bottle.)* Safe... (There is a string of unintelligible mumbling, mostly in Japanese.) As if there is such a thing...

1

GEPP

As a cry, raw and piercing, broke the dawn silence, Willoughby felt a momentary chill. He peered into the jungle, searching the dark shadows carefully. He saw nothing. It was probably a primate, high in a tree somewhere, a lone watcher, anxious for that first glimpse of morning light. Strange how wild things seem to sense the light even before it is physically seen. Was that why he was out here? Had the wild things inside him—the tangle of his incessant thoughts—betrayed him? Had they driven him out into this open air to search a black horizon for some brightening of hope? He glanced at his watch. It read four-forty-nine AM. This was complete madness, to be out on the edge of a jungle in northwestern India, staring up at a dark sky, trembling at the cry of some lone primate.

Yet, here he was.

He rubbed a hand over his face. It was never really quiet here at the GEPP, or Gujarat East Primate Preserve. First of all, the preserve housed nearly a hundred monkeys. Most were gray langurs, but with a few troops of toque macaque and gibbon monkeys mixed in. The high, state-of-the-art habitats were seldom without some kind of activity. Second, the preserve was nestled into a hilly

1

section of jungle. The huge trees, thick with vines, teemed with life, and anchored a raw energy that hinted of ancient, even primal, times.

Willoughby's ears pricked. A tense quiet had suddenly descended on the air around him and he thought he saw the sky lighten ever so slightly. Jungle shadows froze. Willoughby looked up, peering toward the spot where he expected the horizon to be. Like a developing photograph, the low hills faded into view--slowly at first, but then with more conviction. The sky was becoming noticeably bright. With an almost unanimous reverence, Willoughby sensed a thousand eyes trained on the far spectacle. Life, it seemed, was steeling itself, preparing for that moment when bright, hot light spilled in hues of molten gold across the jungle.

A point of sky behind one of the taller hills began to brighten faster than the rest. Fuzzy hints of yellow-white brought clarity to the jungle hilltop, pushing Willoughby's mind to another time, another place. *Hints of yellow-white reflecting out from a vibrant sunset...*

It was early spring in his own yard. Sydney was there, shining and brilliant in her own way. Rays of sunlight played upon her silky, black hair as strands tousled in the breeze. She stood with her violin tucked gently under her chin. They were behind the garage among growing stalks of sunflowers, marveling at how the broad face of each flower had turned to follow the soft glow of the sinking sun. Willoughby could hear his mother in the kitchen a short way off, clinking dishes, and the ting of the porcelain seemed to meld with the ting of Sydney's bracelets. She honed her focus and raised her bow. Music circled in the air—beautiful music, soft like the singing of angels.

Willoughby's half-sisters exploded with giggles and claps of delight as they danced in and out of a row of waist-high corn. The oldest of the girls, Densi, was studying to become a violinist as well, and she and her sister, Cali simply adored Sydney. They reveled in her status as a world-renowned musician with a pop-star-like following. They also loved her music. They would not let her leave until she played for them at least two or three tunes. Often, it was a fairy tune, or an adventure chase, or an angel's song. This late summer evening, they had wanted to hear angels…

Another shriek, this one louder, bringing his mind back to the GEPP, to his visit here to India. A low cascade of rumbling shook the branches of the trees as unseen critters jockeyed for better views, deep blue turned to powder blue. Streaks of white gold began to shoot up from the hilltop. Then, in a moment, a heartbeat, the morning broke. Rays of sun shot over the jungle canopy, highlighting the dark greens of the treetops with new edgings of gold. The jungle sang. Screeches, and hoots, and whistles, and roars burst out in one brief moment of pure ecstasy. It was a welcome cry. It said, "*The dark is gone! The long night is over!*" The effect was not unlike that of hearing the wail of a newborn, hung upside down, startled by the sensation of cold breath being slapped into its newfound lungs. Willoughby thought of a line from a poem he had memorized in tenth grade; *To Morning*, by William Blake: "O radiant morning, salute the sun, Rous'd like a huntsman to the chase…"

He stared, spellbound. He couldn't turn away. Smell was palpable. A thousand odors rose and mixed to form a pungent, tangy scent, crisp in the morning air. It was a magic moment, very like the moment with Sydney. He breathed in slowly. *What would it be like to live in such golden moments forever?* But that is not the way of time. He had come to understand that now. Time is not a book, dusty on a shelf, or a picture hung on a wall. Time is liquid, and like a river, it can only be observed within a context of motion. We may reach for moments, but in the end, we find them impossible to hold. Even as we cling to each second of joy, we see it slip, like flowing water, through our fingers. The key to appreciating time, Willoughby mused, is less about stopping the moment, and more about finding beauty in the rhythms of its flow.

Standing perfectly still, Willoughby let his eyes move over the jungle canopy to a small, mountain village, barely visible on a hill in the distance. He was facing away from the tidy buildings and the carefully manicured lawn of the GEPP. The Gujarat East Primate Preserve was one of the dozens of facilities which were secretly owned and operated by Observations, Inc. Dawning sun warmed his face as his eyes traced the curve of a deep ravine, cutting through a small clearing to his right. It snaked lazily through the jungle vegetation. A dirt road bordered it, leading up to the village, white against the dark greens of the scraggly hill.

The drama of the sunrise complete, Willoughby let out a sigh. He walked to a low, wooden bench. He sat, content to wait for the sun to clear the treetops and its warmth to spill down his lanky frame and thaw his chilled bones.

Even though he was still facing the jungle, his thoughts turned toward the preserve. It was divided into three segments. The first set of low buildings housed the dorms, a state-of-the-art lab, an animal hospital, and various public areas (including a research library). A second set of domed buildings housed a few local breeds of spider monkey and a toque macaque troop. The third, or central, habitat held the bulk of the monkeys. Overall, the facility was one of the more brilliant facilities designed by the secret organization of which he was a part, which was saying a lot as the organization had proven itself to be a master in the art of disguising its facilities. Like others he had visited, the facility was really a façade used to hide the true purpose of the complex. Ingeniously hidden beneath the center habitat was a functional time door, designed to take advantage of a natural weakness, or *hole* in the fabric of time and space.

Willoughby frowned. It had been just under two years since he discovered this secret organization. They called themselves Observations, Inc. They had allowed him to find one of their time door facilities, then had promptly whisked him off to another time using technology he only dreamed could exist. The promise of adventure, of time travel, the ability to unravel mysteries, spending time with a team of like-minded geniuses—it had seemed so alluring. Then he had learned that there is a dark side to adventure. He had come across a being in the grid, one who called himself *Beelzebub*. The demonic creature took an interest in the fact that Willoughby could sense the time grid and was brilliant with mathematics. Suddenly people were dying all around him. He learned that his birth father, Gustav, had run from this creature almost his entire life. He had left Willoughby and his mother one dark night without any explanation. That was before Willoughby was even three years old. As he grew into his teens, he had dreamed of finding his father and bringing him back—of knowing the truth about what had happened to him. Now that he knew, it hurt even more. He had to face the fact that his father was gone and would never come home.

Willoughby thought of his friend Antonio, who had helped recruit him, and had been the architect on many of the Observations, Inc. facilities. When the Director of the organization, a formidable man who went by the initials H.S., had been brutally killed, Sydney's father, Aiyito, had officially taken over the secretive organization. That had been a little over a year ago, and during that time, Willoughby had rarely seen the man, despite several contacts with Sydney, Antonio, James Arthur, and a new member of the team, Hauti. His family had met and grown to trust his whole team, viewing them as fellow victims of the unfortunate incidents on their "educational" excursion on the *Absconditus*. In fact, Antonio had somewhat framed the current invite to GEPP as a way to "put the terrible tragedy of the *Absconditus* behind the team." His parents had been a bit reluctant to let him go, but he was seventeen going on eighteen, and they had grown to trust the team—especially Antonio.

Frankly, Willoughby suspected that Antonio was the real power behind the scenes at Observations, Inc., despite Aiyito's title. It was he who reached out about a month ago, and agreed to visits and discuss the trip personally with Willoughby's mom and step-father. He had framed the excursion as an "educational tour of India."

Willoughby still wasn't completely sure why Antonio had invited the team to India. He had been a bit vague about the purpose of the gathering, saying only; "*There are issues we must discuss my friend—together, and in a safe location.*" The only thing that made sense was that Antonio had found a clue nearby, a lead that could help them find a missing friend. Antonio had been searching relentlessly to find her—a Princess, first lost from her own time, and now lost somewhere in the time stream. The late H.S. knew her. Just before he was killed, he had confessed to being a man out of time himself. The tale had to do with a city out of fable, the lost city of *Atlantis*. The Princess had confided to Antonio that she was much older than she looked. She had claimed that H.S. was much older than he looked as well. She had become stuck in her late teens due to the odd effects of time displacement. H.S. still looked to be in his fifties, despite being in at least his hundreds. When Willoughby met her, the Princess had gone by the initials T.K. She was a Cabin Girl on the ship that was to take them to France on their first mission together as a team. She had the bluest eyes Willoughby had ever seen. They had become friends.

He sighed to himself. Antonio had not arrived at the GEPP facility yet. They had been told that he was busy setting up some sort of expedition to a nearby set of ruins, one recently discovered under a couple of hundred feet of water in the Bay of Cambay. Wiping at his eyes, Willoughby tried to let the memories go. So much ground to cover when trying to think over the past two years of his life. So much he had tried to not think about, to block from his mind. His superior in the organization, H.S., had been a teacher, a mentor, and a father figure to him. Even after a year, he struggled to cope with what had happened, with the man's brutal death. H.S. had seemed larger than life, invincible--a window to wonder, to the secrets of science, a guide to the pathways of time itself. Willoughby had begun to imagine that H.S. alone could stand against the demonic Beelzebub and the edge of darkness that had descended upon all in the organization. His step-father, mom, and half-sisters knew nothing of what he was going through. Sydney's father had stepped in after their disastrous first mission. He had invented a plausible natural disaster, and on behalf of the educational organization that had sponsored the excursion, had personally offered his apologies, lauding Willoughby's bravery.

The real story was that the mission had ended with their beautiful ship, the *Aperio Absconditus,* being sunk after hijackers had killed most of the crew. The main team had barely escaped with their lives, diving into a dysfunctional on-board time door that flung them out across multiple time lines. That had been only the beginning of the adventure. After facing a frozen mummy on a mountain top where he almost froze himself, an attack from hungry plesiosaurs, and a desert witch with an army of snakes and skeletons, Willoughby had struggled to put up a façade of normality to assure his family he was okay. He knew the danger was still out there, though— somewhere; waiting, watching him.

A low hooting sounded from the complex behind him and quickly rose to the pitch of a staccato cough. Willoughby knew without looking that something had startled the gray langur and toque macaque monkeys. The cry of the langurs in particular was hard to mistake. It was probably Sydney. She was usually up by now, and seemed to enjoy going into the monkey habitats to practice her violin, playing a lively mix of classical and original violin compositions. The monkeys made a fuss about her encroaching upon their domain, but in the end, they gathered around her and quieted, watching with rapt attention as she played.

One particular male toque macaque monkey found Sydney quite intriguing. He seemed to have taken a shine to her and watched her every move. His chosen methods of attracting her attention included clicking his teeth together whenever she looked his way and rummaging through her things when she did not.

Willoughby listened for the crystal-clear tone of Sydney's Stradivarius. When it came, he smiled to himself. The preserve was familiar territory to her. She had spent a fair amount of time here with H.S. In fact, she had known H.S. much better than any of them. The Director of Observations, Inc. had been more than a father figure to her—he had been a true second father. She rarely saw her own father Aiyito, and her mother had left long ago to pursue a dancing career, so she had clung to H.S. and his secretive organization.

What was she feeling? There had to be memories of H.S. flooding back to her. It had been almost a year now, and she still refused to really talk about it. There had been no funeral for H.S. Aiyito had made sure that the man simply disappeared, listed among those lost when their ship had been hijacked and sunk. None of the team had been able to openly discuss the loss of the *Absconditus* captain and crew, or H.S. It had been too painful, and Aiyito had been adamant that they could not afford anyone asking too many questions. So, the fabricated stories were supported, and the whole affair had been swept under the rug. But that didn't keep them from grieving on the inside.

Willoughby leaned forward, resting his elbows on his thighs. He looked up, out toward the jungle. At times, it seemed that his course was set, that he had a path he *had* to follow whether he liked it or not. What was it the Roman general, Julius Caesar, said as he crossed the Rubicon, defying the demands of the Roman Senate and inciting civil war? *"The die is cast..."* That's the way he felt now. He wasn't sure what demands he may be asked to defy and certainly hoped he wouldn't incite any wars, but he couldn't shake the feeling that he was locked into a chain of events he had little control over. He knew something was coming, but what? When? The waiting around was eating away at him.

So, he had come outside in the early hours of the morning to watch the sunrise over a wild domain and it had been beautiful, magical. They couldn't take that away from him.

Or could they?

At least if it came to confrontation, he wasn't without talent. He *knew* things, he could see things, mathematically, in the air around him—equation strings that let him track weaknesses and human traces in the time grid. He had learned to manipulate these weaknesses, allowing himself to physically move while time stood still. H.S. had believed he could chart his own destiny, that he *could* face the challenges ahead and even change things. Was he right?

Leaning back, he gave a great yawn and stretched. If he allowed himself to think too long, or too hard about his predicament, he knew the strain would cripple him. So, he tried not to think about it. The team was back together, on some sort of Observations, Inc. business and he couldn't ignore the sense of dread that he felt. *What was it?* He couldn't name it, he couldn't put a finger on it, but it was there, there in the jungle itself—a primitive feel, an unnatural silence. It forced him to face and take note of the shadows in his past, but even more than that, there was also something else...a presence, a darkness, waiting, watching, wanting to awake.

The sun trickled down through the edges of the high canopy working its way down the ravine. Maybe Antonio sensed something here as well. Maybe that's why he had called them all to this place. As brilliant, yellow shafts of light finally reached the tops of the GEPP habitats, the hooting exploded into a cacophony of shrieks, whoops, and chatter. The troupe of langur monkeys were giving their own welcome to the sun. The shadows in the ravine began to soften and lighten. Willoughby let his head drop back. He felt something touch his shoulder and jumped, spinning his arm around with his hand curved in a karate style. He checked the blow mid-swing. It was only his old limousine driver, the captain of H.S.'s yacht, Sam. The dour-faced man looked down at the poised karate chop with a raised eyebrow.

"Am I to defend myself, or just cry out in terrible pain?"

"Oh," Willoughby said, dropping his hand. He relaxed his shoulder and plopped back against the bench. "It's just you." He motioned for Sam to join him on the bench.

"Yes, it is just me." The man, still standing ram-rod straight, gave no hint of a smile. He stepped to the side of the bench but did not sit.

"I swear, Sam, you sneak up like a ninja." Willoughby complained, forcing a crooked grin. "You about got what I'm sure would have been a crushing blow."

"Lucky for my larynx that reason prevailed." Sam looked over, his steel blue eyes beginning to twinkle.

"Hey, I'm serious. I've been working out." Willoughby started to flex his arm, but then thought better of it.

Sam squinted up at the sun's rays. "It is a bright morning sun, is it not? I would prefer you to stay away from those trees before daybreak. There is… something about them." He paused, then looked down. "Did I really startle you?"

"Yeah. Didn't you notice? I about jumped to those trees. If I didn't know you better, I'd say you planned it that way." He flashed Sam a quick smile. "You *are* fortunate that I was able to check my killer instincts."

"Yes," Sam said, studying him for a moment; "very." He turned back toward the thick, green canopy, his back still perfectly straight.

After a long moment, Willoughby broke the silence. "Was there something you wanted, Sam?"

The tall man smiled. "You mean other than testing your *killer instincts*?" He turned back toward the jungle. "No. But what do you make of the view?"

Willoughby frowned. "I, uh… I wasn't really thinking of the view. I was…" He seemed suddenly unable to finish the sentence. He glanced over at his chauffer, his confidant, and his long-time good friend. Sam's face had not wavered. His eyes were steady and penetrating, as if they were trying to pull truth out of him by sheer force. Willoughby blinked. "I was, uh, just thinking about H.S. What—" he looked back at Sam. "Why did…" He looked away. "Never mind. It's not important."

Sam pursed his lips. "It is important. Things that you feel are always important, Willoughby. Never forget that. When feelings become unimportant, actions lose their solid bearings… Besides, I miss him too." He narrowed his eyes. "Something about this place, this jungle reminds me of him, but not in a happy way. I'm not sure I can put my finger on it. Do you understand?"

Willoughby looked back over the vines and vegetation. "Yeah, I think I do. The jungle, the wildness of it—I don't know, it seems to pull at you, especially in quiet moments. It seems to want to, to sort of swallow you whole." His voice became almost a whisper. "Kind of like what happened to H.S."

Sam was unique. He reminded Willoughby of a meerkat, standing alert, sniffing the air, ready to react to the slightest danger to protect his charge. He acted as if he hadn't even heard Willoughby. But then, that was Sam's way. The man was uncanny in his ability to cut to the chase and read between the lines. He always seemed to hear what people *didn't* say.

"H.S. loved this jungle," he finally responded. "I never did understand why. I feel that even he would have found those trees oppressive today. They feel sad." After a long moment, Sam turned from the jungle, looked squarely at Willoughby, and lowered himself to the bench. He seemed to struggle for a moment with how to say something, then just looked up. "I think he would have wanted us to go on, to find and accentuate a more vibrant side of life, one less shrouded in shadow. H.S. was always an intensely alive man."

They sat in silence for a moment until Willoughby spoke. "I thought I'd have more time with him, you know? When you think about it, I barely got to know him. Yet, it still hurts. He was more than a friend. He was the one who seemed able to make sense of—of all this." Willoughby gestured wildly in no particular direction. "Now, everyone is looking at me like I'm supposed to know what's going on. I'm the one who sees numbers. Yeah, I can navigate a time-stream—sort of—but that doesn't mean I have the first clue of where to go. Then there's knowing that *he's* out there, watching and waiting with all his zombies and witches and whatever his weird agenda is. Sometimes I swear I can *feel* him breathing on the back of my neck, you know? He'll come again, I know it, and this time I don't have H.S. to help me face him down." He choked back the sudden throb of emotion that quivered in his voice, blinking his eyes rapidly.

Sam didn't say anything at first. He just watched. He was good at watching. Finally, he looked back toward the complex. "All of us, at times, feel alone, Willoughby, but we seldom really are. You have us—friends who would never consciously abandon you. Antonio considers you almost a brother. You have Sydney. You have James Arthur, the girl Hauti, and you have me. You also have your family. You have a faith in that power inside you, the power of all that is good. You have the full support of the remaining structure of Observations, Inc., for what that's worth. Think about it Willoughby. Together, that comprises a pretty formidable team. You have skills. You have surrounded yourself with talented people who are determined to help you, but you decide whether or not to allow them. If you are determined to approach this bully alone, you play right into his hand. That is exactly what he wants you to do."

Willoughby rubbed his forehead. "You don't get it, Sam. I *don't* want to approach him. But it doesn't matter. *He finds me.* He has *real* power. He can make sure you guys aren't even around when he approaches, and he knows there's nothing I can do to stop him. I'm just some punk kid to him—an upstart."

Sam considered this. "What is *real* power, Willoughby? In my experience, power follows power. Perhaps this…being sees more in you than you see yourself. H.S. believed that you could be more than Beelzebub's equal. He believed that you could beat him at his own game. Do not sell yourself short. Ever."

Willoughby listened to the words without any reaction. Sam had tried to step into the void created by H.S.'s death. He had been a friend, a confidant, an ally. But Willoughby had spent two years seeing Sam as only a limo driver, and then as a driver for H.S., and Captain of his yacht. It was hard to think of him in terms of teacher, strategist, or more precisely, a protector.

Before he had decided how to respond to Sam, the moment was interrupted by a riot of screeching from the habitat. Sydney was at the heart of it. She had stopped playing and had let out a low curse in French. Willoughby didn't speak much French, but he caught enough to know that he didn't want to be anywhere around the toe of her antique boots about now. The monkeys were scurrying higher into the trees with a chorus of low hoots.

"*You thief!*" Sydney screamed again, this time in English. "Give that back!" The monkey chorus grew louder. "You have no right to take it. I said give it back *now*, or believe me, you'll be sorry!" A single monkey screech rose above the sound of the others. This screech seemed different—it had an altogether different tone and cadence. It was obviously one of the toque macaque monkeys, perhaps the one who liked to shadow Sydney. The monkey appeared to be the one who had led the charge to the top of the trees. Sydney yelled up again, and then played a long, piercing wail on the violin. Even at this distance, Willoughby instinctively threw his hands to his ears. Both sets of monkeys went ballistic this time, shrieking as if in pure agony. Finally, the violin wail stopped and the chaos died down.

"*All* of it!" Sydney yelled. "I want to see every last sheet."

Sam caught Willoughby's eye, and gave his head a slight twist. "I would not want to be in *that* monkey's shoes about now."

As if to punctuate the comment, Sydney played another excruciating volley of discord on the violin. It continued for a good two minutes until the cries of the monkeys fell into a series of low, pleading whimpers. The violin stopped. "Serves you right," Sydney huffed as the monkeys continued their pitiful chorus. "You try that again, and I promise you, it *will* be worse!"

Sam gave a crooked smile. "I think she secretly likes the young rogue."

"The toque macaque, you mean? She's started calling him CW."

"SW," Sam sighed, "short for *Sun Wukong,* the mischievous Monkey King of Buddhist tales."

Sydney hit another painful note. Willoughby winced, seeing a single monkey scampering back up into the trees. "Don't even think about it," Sydney said.

The hooting and whining of the troupe lasted a good five minutes this time before Sydney returned to her playing. Willoughby gave Sam a smile. "Well, the name sort of fits. That monkey seems to stay up all night coming up with new ideas to torture her. So far, today is better than yesterday. At least he's still in the habitat."

Sam let out a low chuckle. "Yes, but the day is young. She has yet to attempt to exit."

Willoughby realized that he was grateful for the distraction. "You think the rascal has a crush on her?" He was quiet for a moment, thinking of Sydney. He glanced over at Sam who had a concerned look, peering out into the thick vines and brush of the jungle. Slowly, the smile faded from his own lips. He followed Sam's gaze. "You feel it too, don't you? You feel something, someone out there, watching us. Do you think it's him?"

Sam frowned. "I feel—something. I can't say who or what I believe it is. I can say I'll be glad when we can leave this section of jungle."

Willoughby and Sam stood in silence, listening to the sound of Sydney's music, the chatter of a waking jungle, and searching the shadows, alive to a sense of menace at the edge of the darkness, just beyond the bank of thick trees.

2

Alpha 7

Tainken Keilhar was no fool. The girl, who often went by
the initials T.K., had lived for over seventy years, though
she looked more like twenty. Once daughter of a ruler, and
Princess of the fabled city *Atlantis*, she was now lost in a
dim tomb of scrolling time equations. It frustrated her. It
made her angry. Yes, H.S. may have saved her life, but for
what? To rot here in this cold, Spartan control hub? She
sat moodily on a marble incline against the inner wall of
the structure. How long had H.S. been searching for this
Prime Hole Facility? Well, she had found it, or, more
accurately, it had found her. When imminent danger
presented itself, H.S. had panicked, initiating some sort of
automated return mechanism. He had combined a sort of
crystal pendant with the crystal necklace her father had
once given her, and *presto,* she was here. The auto-return
function certainly worked.

She looked around. The facility was in lock-down.
She couldn't get out through the exterior doors and there
were no windows. The walls were a heavy titanium alloy,
several feet thick. An atomic bomb probably wouldn't
penetrate the hull of this facility. Besides, if what Antonio
told her about H.S.'s suspicions were right, she could be

buried under miles of rock and ice. On top of that, she had no clue how to use the main bank of controls to operate the time walls and get out that way. About the only thing she had managed to do so far, in the many weeks she had been here, was to boost the lighting to full strength, and get the heat up to a tolerable temperature (though it was still *way* too cold for her liking). She had found some mostly stale food stores and there was plenty of water. H.S. had probably known this when he sent her. She remembered her father discussing once that there were key food stores in certain time depots throughout the history of the planet in case the city ever had to be evacuated. This must have been one of them. Perhaps this had been where the full council contingent planned to weather any crisis. There had been, how many on the council? Twenty? The stores were enough to keep a group of that size alive for at least twelve months.

She had tried everything she could think of to make the east gate doors—the doors that had once led to her beautiful city–open. She could not. They wouldn't budge. So, for the last ten days or so, she had been obsessed with the time walls. She faintly remembered from her childhood that scenes of other places had shown on them. She had a vague recollection of jungles, and deserts, and the craggy peak of a green island. She had once seen a man choose one of these and step through the wall into it—at least, that's how it had seemed to her as a small child. The walls were cold and hard now, though. All she could get to appear on them now were number strings.

She had found a bit of a journal, written in ancient *Atlantian* and had been able to decipher most of it, despite the fact that her *Atlantian* was beyond rusty. The journal told how, when the rains and storms continued and the

Council became convinced that the city would be destroyed, plans were put in place to allow the city's residents to slip away in small groups into various time corridors. Before the plans could be fully implemented, though, something catastrophic happened. It had seemed to catch them off guard. The last entry in the journal was rushed and sketchy, and far from complete. She was able to make out that some people had escaped, but only a very few. The entry ended with the words, *"The doors are now being sealed."* That's it.

Whatever happened, the facility from the inside was mostly level and intact. She tried to remember everything she had ever learned about the Prime Hole Facility. It had been central to *Atlantian* life and their work here on planet earth. The hope had been that, someday, they could restore the connection between the prime hole of Earth and the prime hole on her people's home world. The connection had been lost many generations ago. She never understood why. She had heard different people express various theories, but none of them made much sense to her. She did recall, however, that the Prime Hole Facility was built to be virtually indestructible and that it was self-supporting. She thought she remembered a conversation where her father told her the facility had a cold-fusion generator. Its construction had been one of the Council's crowning achievements. As the current head of the Atlantian Grand Council, her father had shared pride in not only the facility, but the work that was done at the facility. Her people were historians and used the time walls to document every age of Earth to the present. There had even been some talk of corridors to the future of the planet, but her father had been against those. He'd felt that, instead, resources should be focused on re-establishing the link with their home world.

She thought she remembered that H.S. and his family had disagreed. They felt that something awful had occurred to the home world. Why else would they have failed to reach out to the outpost when the link had been lost? She thought she remembered someone saying that there was strong evidence suggesting that the place where their home star had been located was obstructed now by a black hole.

Anyway, she had visited this structure a half-dozen times as a young girl, the last time being the fateful night when she and her brother had found their father murdered. Her brother had seen the killer and given chase. She had tried to stop him, but ended up following, tumbling after the assassins through a time wall. She had not seen where they were going, so intent on catching her brother, and next thing she knew, she was splashing to the surface of a body of briny, sulphur-infused water in a dim, Jurassic Era cave. A pack of plesiosaurs had attacked as they tried to pull themselves out of the water. Her brother had sacrificed himself to save her. Needless to say, this facility was not a place of fond memories and she had a certain reluctance to ever walk into a time wall again. But she couldn't stand the silence and loneliness of this tomb. Sitting alone, in this sterile facility, a haze of images haunted her: her brother, her father, her life before that ill-fated day when her world had changed forever. *Ghosts...* That was all they were—hints of faces—whispers from lost moments of time.

With a heavy sigh, she pushed up to go grab lunch—or was it dinner? It's hard to keep track of time when there is no day or night. The wrapped cakes that made up each meal were dry and tasted like ground tree bark, but at least it staved off hunger. She also grabbed a container of water. She had plenty. There was at least a four-year supply of both food and water in the storage area, still perfectly edible and drinkable. Of course, she hoped she wouldn't be around that long.

To the left of the storage and kitchen area, a small bath allowed her to clean herself, and she had a huge supply of dry clothes, though it was impossible to put enough layers on to stay warm in this tomb. She had a control that raised the temperature from freezing to a setting of 60 degrees, but that was as warm as it got. She wondered if the control was broken, or if it was some sort of safeguard to conserve power. She had no way of knowing. Whatever the reason, the result was that this place was *always* cold.

Being alive, but alone in a frozen tomb with her memories was almost worse than death. She thought back on the Jurassic cave where she lost her brother. She had thought only two people escaped the cave that first visit—a man named Haubus Socees, and herself. She had learned that a third man, a schemer named Belzar, had been attacked by the beasts, but had managed to get away, losing only the full use of one leg. The three swam into an underwater time hole and she had come out gasping and cold in a murky body of water she later learned to be the Scottish lake, Loch Ness.

For years, she had lived for one reason and one reason alone—to find Haubus, who she believed killed her father and was the reason for her brother's death. She thought she had found him when she uncovered a man who calling himself H.S., one who ran a clandestine organization with futuristic technology. Then everything went wrong. The ship she was serving on was hijacked. In trying to help some of the team escape, she found herself thrust back a second time to the Jurassic cave of horrors—this time with a Spanish-American man named Antonio. This visit to the cave, however, proved different from her first visit. For one thing, she was older and able to face the beasts. For another, she grew close to the brilliant young architect that had been thrust into the cave with her. He was a member of Observations, Inc., the clandestine organization which H.S. had built. Antonio had slowly unraveled the layers of her secrets. He had come to know her for who she really was. He—*could she admit it to herself*—he had seemed to fall in love with her, and she, had she fallen for him as well? She thought herself incapable of falling in love with anyone. *But had it happened?*

They had found a way out of the cave into an Observation facility Antonio's organization built. She had learned the true identity of H.S., and had finally come face to face with Haubus. The man was dead now. H.S. probably was as well–a plesiosaur had been breaking through the observation window and she and H.S. had gotten trapped on the wrong side of the facility safety wall. She thought there was no escape, but she had been wrong. There was an escape, but only for one of them. She closed her eyes trying not to think of H.S. She pushed toward Antonio. *Had he survived? Had the safety wall held against plesiosaur attack? Was he out there looking for her now?* She had to believe he was. It was the only thing that kept her going.

She looked down at the crystal necklace, back around her neck. She had separated it from the pendant as soon as she arrived at the facility. She had worn the necklace for many years and felt somehow naked and empty without it.

The special necklace was the only keepsake she had from her father, from her life as a princess. H.S. had known things about the necklace that she had not. What else had he known that could have helped them possibly locate the ruins of Atlantis, or possibly other survivors who had escaped the city's destruction? She looked over at the pendant he had used to send her here. It was lying on a low table a few meters away. It would have been better for H.S. to come here. She could have taken her chances with the plesiosaurs. He may have known how to work the equipment.

She sighed, wiping a hand across her eyes. It was no good to endlessly wonder and debate every moment that had brought her here. The fact was that she was here, and she was alone. She needed to bottle up her emotions and just get on with finding a way to make this place work, of finding a way out of here.

She looked around the bleak, sparse enclosure, taking stock for maybe the fiftieth time. The main room was circular. Not all of the walls were just cold and hard. Pockets of wall space flickered and hummed with odd, sporadic equation strings that she knew to be a visual representation of the time stream. Occasionally, a hazy cloud of color covered the equations for a few seconds, but then it was gone and the walls were unchanged.

If she could ever get the walls to work properly, she could see scenes upon them that she might recognize and muster up the courage to step into them. She knew from experience that jumping into an unknown time could make things worse as easily as better, but what choice did she really have? Die here cold and alone?

Day after day had continued to click by on the wall chronometer and she got no closer to uncovering the secret to how the odd-looking controls worked. But she couldn't just sit around and wait for some miracle. So, right then and there, she came up with a systematic plan of adjusting the controls one at a time. She glanced at the chronometer and date-stamp which were marked in a small line across the top of the center wall. This clock and calendar had been counting since the days when Atlantis was founded. The clock was already old when she was a girl, and yet here it was, hundreds of years later, continuing its slow, precise march.

She let her eyes probe the rest of the space. Against the back third of the wall were three doors. Two led to sparse sleeping chambers. Each chamber had four beds, a desk, two upright dressers, and two closets. The middle door was the small, hexagonal washroom, with a spacious sink, an odd version of a toilet, and an intricate, sunken, marble bathing pool with a fountain that sprinkled down when turned on. That was easily her favorite place in the whole facility. It was the only place where she could actually feel warm. She daily resisted the urge to simply hang out there. To the side of the bathroom was the small eating and food preparation chamber that she called the kitchen and the entry to the storage closet, a wide space that ran the full length of the living quarters and carried rows of supplies on shelves. At either end were large water tanks, each about 400-500 gallons.

The control room held a dais in the center with semi-circular bank of control panels. The systems in the facility seemed to be operating in some sort of low-power automated mode. She knew from bits of conversation she overheard as a child, that any technology considered critical to Atlantis was built in a redundant mode with a redundant repair drone functionality built around the core technology. The bulk of Atlantis technology was powered by cold fusion, geothermal energy, or cleverly collected sun, wind, and tidal energy sources. She began again to adjust the controls. The markings were strange to her, and if she inadvertently hit a wrong button, she might turn off the lights, or the life-support systems, so she had to carefully document every adjustment she made and check for any change to the facility. It was tedious work—move the dial slightly, check for results; move the dial slightly, check for results. *There!* Had the walls just flickered? Not just the small sections where the number stings were scrolling, *but the whole wall.* She backed the dial up, and tried moving it forward ever so slightly again. *The walls had flickered!*

She moved the dial again. This time the walls displayed a soft spray of color. She jumped to her feet, excited by the change. She was half-way across the room before she stopped herself. The view was still just hazy color—nothing distinct. She closed her eyes. *Stick to the task*, she thought. She returned to the controls. She needed to be patient. If she could figure out how to work these controls, if she could document it, she could maybe find her way back to civilization. Then, at least, she wouldn't be alone, and she might possibly find a way to signal Antonio through the timeline. She knew he would be looking for her, hoping for some clue. Perhaps *knew* was too strong a word. She *strongly suspected* he would be looking for her. If he had been the one to fall into the time grid, she knew she would be looking for him.

As she worked, her eyes fell to the teardrop necklace she wore around her neck. Her father had told her that it was their world, their people. She had not understood what he meant. Then, H.S. had told her that the necklace and pendant together formed a powerful computer that held a record of Atlantis and the race of people who built it. *Could this computer offer some clue to how the controls worked?* What H.S. hadn't told her was how to use the thing. She had tried reconnecting the two pieces again and giving it verbal commands. Nothing. She had tried looking for any buttons or switches on the crystal itself. Both pieces of the alleged computer just seemed like polished crystal with spidery arcs of colored light illuminating their interior from time to time. She didn't get it. Was it password protected by fingerprint or something? The auto-return feature had initiated the second she'd touched it. Why didn't the computer react to her touch now?

On an impulse, she grabbed the pendant portion of the crystal computer. She stood. The thought occurred to her that somehow, this mechanism connected back with the Prime Hole Facility, pulled her into the nearby time grid, and brought her here. *Had she gone back in time?* She wasn't sure. It was obvious that something had happened to the facility or else why was it locked up tight? If she had gone back in time to her day, to her home, Atlantis would be just outside the door, teaming with her people. Technicians, scientists, politicians, all would be hurrying in and out of the facility. Instead, the place was cold, empty, and operating on low power. That meant she must be in a time after the destruction of her city. *Could it be that she was back in Antonio's time?* She had been thinking about wanting to visit his home and his barbershop when they thought they had escaped the cave. Had those thoughts somehow surfaced, somehow directed the point in time that the crystal computer had chosen?

She paced as she thought. What if this computer was the key? What if it could somehow unlock this facility—if it was somehow a part of the facility, somehow tied to it as well as being tied to her? Her mind was racing now. The fact that the computer had an auto-return function that brought her to the facility indicated that the two were connected at least on some level. It had been a phenomenal feat to pull her physically through space to this place in the blink of an eye, and had to have required way more power than the little crystal computer could hold. If it was somehow connected to the internal brains of the facility, and could access the facility's power grid, didn't it stand to reason that it might know how to operate the controls? She walked to the center of the long, curved control dais. She held the crystal pendant out over the edge of the right-most panel of controls, slowly working her way left, holding the computer for several moments over each individual control or read-out, looking for any slight change or reaction.

By the midway point along the dais, there had been nothing. She felt a bit like an idiot, like some sort of mystic with a divining rod, but she refused to quit. She started down the arc of control panels toward the far-left edge. She came to a large, green indentation that seemed to be lined with emerald stone. As she passed over the center of the indentation, she felt a tug. Heart pounding, she moved her hand slowly back. There was definitely a resistance here. It was as if the indentation wanted to somehow align the pendant. She carefully let go of it. The crystal twisted, floating in air, and re-aligned itself, the tip of the pendant moving slowly around until it pointed up at the ceiling. It hovered and began to rotate length-wise, like a slow-spinning top. Spidery streaks of light inside the pendant increased in frequency and then fired, quick arcs of lightning striking the green stones below. The necklace, still around her neck, had also started sparking and floated up, pulling against its chain, as if also wanting to align or connect with the pendant. She unclasped it and let it glide perfectly into position, connecting itself just as H.S. had connected it.

Suddenly, a thick arc of white light shot up from the green crystals and connected with the pendant. Almost immediately, the walls changed. T.K. found herself looking out, as if through glass walls, at an early stone city of some kind. There were crude towers with long steps leading up steep pyramidal structures. It reminded her of pictures she had seen of the ancient temples of the Mayan, only with a distinctly Asian flair. The screen highlighted a young woman. She was outlined in a sort of white sheen, and text to her side gave her name, as well as other information about her. The script was in a more formal, scientific form than the journal entries had been, and it had been a long time since Tainken had read this type of Atlantian script, but she could make out some of it. This woman was named Belyan. She had been assigned by the Council to this city, called by the Council, Alpha 7. Tainken even saw her father's stamp—her *father's* stamp!

She bounced on her heels, unable to stay still, as she stared in wonder. The read-out was clear on one point. *This woman was not only Atlantian, but had been assigned to this ancient city when her father was still alive.* Regardless of what time the Prime Hole Facility currently existed in, it still had connections to earth's past timeline—including a time when her city still existed, *when her father was alive!* Perhaps that is what he had meant when he said the necklace was "our world, our people." Perhaps the necklace was key to tracking all of the people of Atlantis, from their origins, to where they served, and possibly even where they died. The view on the screen faded and another came clear. It appeared to be the same city, around the same time period, but this time, a man was highlighted. The read-out determined his name to be Enyondha.

T.K. took a step toward the time window. This was a place she could go! All she had to do was touch the time wall, and the prime-hole would sling her there, much like it had slung her to the plesiosaur cave so very long ago. She could look up her people, explain to them how she got there.

A sudden thought made her stop cold. *These people had no idea what would happen to Atlantis—that it would vanish without a trace.* How would it affect time if she told them, if they believed her? Would her father even recognize her now as a much older daughter, having survived in another time? And what if this city existed before her father, or if he had just joined the Council and she claimed to be his daughter when he, as yet, had no children? Or if she came face to face with her own younger self? Surely any of these scenarios would wreak absolute havoc with history as she knew it.

She looked at the softly spinning crystal computer. There was another problem. She could not leave the facility without her necklace and the pendant H.S. had entrusted her with. What would happen when she snatched the devices away? Would the windows go hazy again? Would she have time to jump into the time hole?

The view changed again. This time, the city was in the distance. Men were working in a quarry surrounded by jungle. Another man was highlighted, this time an older, bearded man. T.K. headed toward the supply room. She had to find paper and some sort of writing utensil. She needed to record who these people were and try to determine where and when they were. Then, she needed to determine where the best place to enter the city was, and what she would immediately need once she got there. If she was careful, she was sure she could keep anyone from finding out anything that would affect time. She would also be free of the deathly cold, and silent, incessant boredom of this facility. One day, she would come back to it, and study it, but preferably when she had Antonio and his team with her, and warmer clothes.

Blood pounded in her ears. Maybe she couldn't tell those around her the truth, the whole truth, but at least she could be around people, *her people*, again. This was more than she had hoped for. She had a plan, now, and it did not entail dying a lonely death in an automated tomb.

3

The Sunken City

Just as Willoughby and Sydney sat down to lunch inside the beautiful atrium at the center of the GEPP facility, one of the maintenance staff approached. The staff member was female, blonde, and quite attractive. She whispered in Willoughby's ear that both *young master* and his *personal accompanist* were wanted in the library by one who called himself *the most fantastical barber*.

Willoughby grimaced, looking over at Sydney, who had raised an eyebrow.

"Well, it appears that Antonio is here, and he is flamboyantly requesting our presence in the library." He decided to skip the *accompanist* remark. Such comments had a tendency to result in flying objects, often being flung at him.

"Really?" Sydney held her food poised. Willoughby wasn't sure if she planned to take a bite or fling it. She could have overheard. "Is that what you call it?" she continued, taking a dainty bite of the sandwich. Willoughby sighed with relief. "Is it *flamboyant* to summon your friends, and then keep them waiting for two days before you make an appearance? I think, then, in the spirit of *flamboyance*, we can keep him waiting for a while—at least until we finish our lunch."

Willoughby started to disagree, but then thought better of it. True, he was anxious to see Antonio and hear more about why they had been called here, but he knew better than to argue with Sydney, especially when her morning practice had been less than acceptable. He shoved bites of a delicious walnut, apple, and raisin salad into his mouth, pretending to listen while Sydney started in on a story about a recent April Fools' ruse. This one involved PacMan and Google. He didn't have anything against PacMan, per se, and he did feel that Google often hatched clever April Fools' schemes (*his* favorite was the Google announcement of a flushable device that turned the toilet and sewage system into a giant WiFi antenna), but he was having a hard time keeping his mind on her story.

He realized that Sydney had stopped mid-sentence and was staring at him, waiting for comment. He had no idea what he was supposed to comment on. So, he did what all males did when faced with a similar situation. He improvised.

"Uh… Yeah, you're right! That was a totally amazing story. You ready to go?"

"Sure. Just as soon as you answer my question."

Willoughby narrowed his eyes. "You asked a question?"

Sydney smiled, enjoying his discomfort. "I did."

"Well, of course you did, and the answer is obviously *yes*."

"Obviously. I'll let my agent know."

"Good!" Willoughby forced a smile. "Just…how do you plan to…tell the agent?"

"It won't be hard," Sydney said, chuckling. "I'll just say that my boyfriend has agreed to come on stage with me in Madrid, dance a tango with a rose in his lips, and kiss me so hard that the blood drains from his cheeks. And you're right—yes *was* the obvious answer."

Willoughby turned a pale shade of chartreuse. "Absolutely." He forced a smile, desperately searching for a way out of the commitment. "I just hope my mathematics don't get in the way."

"Oh, do tell," Sydney leaned in conspiratorially.

"Well, it's simple—they call it the *law of diminishing returns*. Getting my body on a stage in front of an audience and keeping it there, much less making it dance or kiss a girl on said stage—no matter how brilliantly beautiful she is—may not be worth the resulting effort expended. There could be massive miscalculations. Simply put, the heart could give out...or the bladder, not sure which would go first. Either would be a disaster to your otherwise phenomenal performance, and ergo, criticism of the fiasco could cause a loss of both revenue and prestige, causing the demand for future performances to diminish." His smile became much more genuine. "It's simple economics."

"I thought you said it was mathematics?" Sydney leaned forward, speaking low. "Careful. Two can play the game of diminishing returns. Still, you did prove light on your feet. I'll give you a B- for effort." She winked.

Before Willoughby had time to respond, or determine if there were ramifications to her response, the attractive young attendant returned.

"Excuse me, but the barber asked me to tell you that lunch has ended."

"He did?" It was Willoughby's turn to raise an eyebrow.

"I think his exact words were," the young lady paused a moment before continuing, "*what is food compared to the beauteous harmonies of inner wisdom*'."

Willoughby gave Sydney a quick grin. "Sounds like our fearless leader has spent time up the road at the Monastery." He rose to his feet with a shrug. "Well, I guess we're done."

Sydney rose more reluctantly. "I think you may be right," she said, turning to Willoughby and smiling at the attendant. "Thank you, Tish. We certainly wouldn't want to keep *the barber* waiting, now would we? After all, he may *do things* with his scissors."

Willoughby bit his lip, trying to keep a straight face.

"With his scissors?" The young attendant asked, her countenance darkening a little.

Willoughby nodded to her. "Yes. His inner quest has always been to bring hair into harmony with inner wisdom." He stated the words sagely, as if they, alone, should explain everything.

Sydney bent her head toward the attendant conspiratorially. "Of course, if you make *the barber* angry, well...Well, let's just say *your* inner harmony may be destroyed for a long, long time."

The woman's confusion turned to sudden concern. Willoughby put a hand on her shoulder. "You have wise hair, Tish. Listen to it carefully." He smiled, then gave a slight wave as he and Sydney headed toward the nearest exit. Sydney tried to stifle a snicker, allowing it to escape as somewhat of a snort.

Once around the corner, she burst into full laughter. "*Listen carefully?* Oh," she tried to compose herself. "That was—wicked."

"Well," Willoughby countered, also coming off of a good laugh, "you started it."

"Yeah, I did," Sydney sighed. "I'll apologize to her later. But frankly, it was deserved." The two turned a corner.

"Why did she deserve it?" Willoughby asked, wiping water from his eyes. "Couldn't have anything to do with the fact that she's attractive, could it?"

"Well, I didn't mean *her*," Sydney shot back as they navigated around a small, sunken lounge. "I meant Antonio deserved it."

Willoughby thought for a moment before giving a curt nod. Antonio *had* kept them waiting, and the *summoning* didn't help. He was affectionately known in the group as *the barber* because he had posed as a friendly, if somewhat eccentric, neighborhood barber for almost two years while observing Willoughby to determine if he would be a good fit for the Observations, Inc. team.

Willoughby paused at the end of a corridor and glanced around, searching for the door to the high-tech library. One of the things Observations, Inc. seemed best at was creating atmospheres that were elegant and inviting, as well as breathtakingly sophisticated. They headed toward an ornate, mahogany door which opened into the library. Dark paneling, walnut shelves, and leather-bound books covered two walls. English inspired landscapes served as backdrop for a grouping of antique, high-backed couches, and lavish padded chairs arranged in a loose semi-circle that faced the wall opposite the door. He knew from experience that the lavish paneling and decor masked hidden 3D projectors, voice-controlled lighting and doors, movement activated computer access panels, beyond state-of-the-art security, and an array of automated communication choices. The library was, hands down, Willoughby's favorite room in the complex.

Antonio did not react when the two walked into the room. Sydney casually grabbed Willoughby's hand. "So...you found her attractive?" she said softly, leaning in.

Willoughby glanced over. "Don't worry," he whispered back. "She's a mere mortal."

Sydney smiled, but her attention had moved to a small lectern near the front of the room. An image floated just to the side of it. It appeared to be some sort of ancient obelisk, rotating slowly. Antonio stepped behind the lectern, highlighting something on the obelisk with gold light. As Willoughby squinted, he could see that the gold light surrounded a symbol. He froze. It was a symbol he knew well, the very symbol that had first drawn him to Antonio's barbershop—the symbol Observations, Inc. used to mark time holes. A spiral of right triangles chiseled above three numbers. The numbers were three-one-three, with the last three turned backwards.

The obelisk was old and weathered and had seaweed hanging from it, as if it had been submerged on a murky sea floor for some time. Sydney continued to clasp his hand and pulled him forward to one of the small couches near the center of the library. The tightness of her grip belied a certain amount of apprehension, even though her face and voice seemed completely calm. *It must come from performing,* he thought. *She has learned to mask internal anxiety with her voice and manner, but her hands speak,* he thought. *She is feeling it too—the disquiet, the discomfort, the feeling of someone, some thing, watching.* He squeezed her hand just as tightly.

"We weren't quite done with lunch, Antonio," she announced as she sat.

"Wisdom is a banquet from which no person is sent away hungry," Antonio said without turning around or breaking his concentration.

"What does that even mean?" Willoughby asked. "Are you still our friend Antonio, or have you become Yoda of the Barbering Shop?"

Antonio let a smile slip as he stepped to the side of the lectern and clicked a few computer keys, minimizing the image. He looked up.

"I am not thinking I am short, fat, and green, my most illustrious mathematician—so much for your keen powers of observation—but, how delightful that you have deigned to join me! If I claim to be your fine friend, can I claim to be wise? I contend daily with such deep thoughts." His smile broadened. "Still, it is good to see you my friends. There are news items we must discuss."

Sydney looked to Willoughby, her eyes wide. "He admits to not being wise," she whispered sarcastically. She turned back to Antonio with a forced smile. "Good to see you too, Antonio. I'm sure you meant to say; *'Ah, our world-renowned virtuosa and her mathematician genius have decided to greatly honor me with their presence,'* but, once again, you failed. I get so tired of having to interpret for everyone what you really mean to say. How do you ever manage when I'm not around?"

Antonio barked a short laugh. "A fantabulous question, Miss Sydney! I shall ponder that puzzle with painstaking deliberation. Speaking of pain, I trust that you did not maim any monkeys today? I have heard such colorful stories of how you *'honor'* the facility here, and how the monkeys, specifically, have become enraptured with you (particularly when you are speaking in French). Thank you for being such an enlightening example!"

Willoughby couldn't resist a grin as he thought of the string of French expletives he and Sam had overheard Sydney screaming earlier in the day. Sydney blushed slightly.

"Oh. You heard that."

"Yes…" Antonio rocked back on his heels and threw Willoughby a quick wink.

Sydney coughed daintily and repositioned herself on the couch, letting go of Willoughby's hand. "Well, they're impossible most of the time. Especially the golden haired one—"

"Sun Wukong?" Willoughby interjected.

Sydney looked over at Willoughby. "I'm impressed. You know of the Monkey King?"

Willoughby gave a sheepish grin.

Sydney narrowed one eye as she continued. "Well, Willoughby is correct. I call the gold one Sun Wukong because he is a mischievous little demon who enjoys nothing more than to drive me bonkers. I believe the staff call him Tarin, but they're probably just being kind. This morning, he snatched my music and took it all the way to the highest branch of the tree. He then proceeded to drop the sheets one at a time just to see them flutter! When I yelled at him, I swear, he actually *laughed!*"

"Yes," Antonio tried to keep a straight face as he attempted a serious tone, "you *did* swear. It would seem, *Amiga*, that you have considerable trouble with the boys."

"The boys?" Sydney looked over at Willoughby. "Sun Wukong is *not* a boy."

Willoughby grinned. "Well, you've got to admit, he *is* male, and he obviously has a crush on you."

"I think, Sydney, that he wants to make you part of his harem," Antonio chimed in. "You do know that monkeys tend to be very serious when it comes their harems?"

Sydney elbowed Willoughby, whispering. "Big help you are!"

"Ouch!" Willoughby rubbed at his arm. "I was just saying you seem to have an effect on males—*all* males, even male monkeys."

Sydney pursed her lips. "Well...yeah. I guess that does make sense."

"Beauty and the beast," Antonio agreed.

"Most males," Sydney continued, "do seem to like me—at least, most mammal males. I mean, what's there not to like?"

Antonio raised his eyebrows; "Indeed, such insight— even to minds outside your species! You are a most effusive ethnologist,"

"Okay, so I get along with birds, too," Sydney continued, seeming slightly confused. She leaned over, whispering out of the side of her mouth; "*What did he just call me?*" Willoughby shrugged as, holding her smile, Sydney continued, her eyes boring into Antonio. "Of course, I haven't been able to get the same respect from insects yet. They seem rather resistant to my charms."

"Just a temporary setback, I am sure, your magnificence," Antonio said with mock surprise. "We wait with baited breath for your triumph!" He started to turn, then, as if having an afterthought, turned back around. "I have it! The perfect way to help," he said, beaming. "I will herd all the insects from my bungalow to yours to aid you in your most noble quest!"

"Thanks, but no," Sydney said, her smile tightening. She looked past Antonio to the small image of the obelisk, still hovering near the lectern. She was obviously done with this line of conversation. She pointed. "So, when are you going to tell us why you called us here, our *most illustrious* barber? I assume it has something to do with the symbol on that obelisk." She glanced around, drawing attention to the fact that the room was empty except for the three of them. "Have we finally decided to move on without our resident Best-Seller?"

Before Antonio could answer, there was a commotion at the door. James Arthur strolled in, sporting sunglasses, a tweed jacket, a clip-on earring, and rings on every finger. "Thank you for the gracious introduction Sydney. Please, hold your applause, your resident Best-Seller has arrived," he called out. He held his hands out, as if welcoming his adoring fans.

Willoughby leaned forward to give Dr. J a fist bump.

Sydney knitted her eyebrows. "What's with the get-up?"

Before answering, Dr. J stepped forward to meet Willoughby's fist-bump, then took a dramatic step back, and gave a wide, sweeping gesture with his arm to usher Hauti into the room. "Behold, my tailor and new PR Director," he announced. Hauti was in traditional Hindu dress, with a red dot on her forehead. Sam was the last one to step into the room and he quietly shut the library doors.

Hauti strode confidently to the same small couch where Sydney and Willoughby sat. She hugged them both, like an executive host gloating over a corporate take-over, before seating herself on their couch, squeezing in tightly between Willoughby and Sydney, much to the irritation of Sydney, though she pretended to ignore the show. Dr. J sat in one of the high-backed chairs across from the couch after giving Sydney a peck on the cheek. Hauti glanced over at Willoughby with a shy smile. She touched the dot on her forehead, pointed the finger at Willoughby, and then mimed blowing on the barrel of a smoking gun. Willoughby gave a tentative smile and nodded, not knowing what else to do. He then looked forward, edging slightly away from his old Hillbrook Academy friend. Sydney, who was chatting with Dr. J., didn't catch the exchange.

On one hand, Willoughby was glad to see Hauti getting back to some semblance of normal. She had been through a rough time—all of them had—with the sinking of the *Absconditus*, and she had also lost her father. He knew exactly how that felt. On the other hand, why wasn't James Arthur the target of her interest? Of course, maybe he was. Dr. J had introduced her as his tailor. Maybe she was that way with all guys. He turned his attention back toward James Arthur.

"Yeah, but you look like some sort of hip-hop groupie," Sydney said, somewhat amused.

Hauti jumped in. "He said he wanted to look like Michael Jordan, so I did my best. Give me a break—look what I have to work with."

Dr. J smiled broadly. "Success must look like success." He looked over at Willoughby. "So, how's my favorite bean counter? Still hanging out with beautiful women, I see. Have you kept our resident pop artist out of trouble?"

Sydney didn't seem sure whether to smile at being called *beautiful*, or frown at being referred to as a *pop artist*. "James," she finally said, "as I'm sure you are well aware, Willoughby is a brilliant mathematician, not a bean counter, a term usually reserved for money lenders and accountants. Secondly, I am a serious musician, not a pop artist. I just happen to have millions of adoring fans."

Dr. J tapped his chin. "Yes, I feel your pain, Sydney." His smile returned. "But as for our resident mathematical genius," he said, looking back to Willoughby, "beans is beans, I always say."

Sydney stared, her eyes narrowed for a moment. When she spoke, it was with guarded tones. "For your sake, James, and because I consider you a mostly intelligent person, I'll try to find some sort of logic in that string of words."

Sam padded quietly to a high-backed chair next to James Arthur and directly opposite Antonio and the lectern. Antonio, who had been busily typing on the lectern keyboard, picked up a wireless mouse and clicked, once again bringing the image of the obelisk to its full size, hovering beside him.

"First," he began, "it most definitely does my heart good to see everyone. Thank you, my friends, for coming. As you know, I forbade our most illustrious mathematician from jumping into the time stream, even though his help could be valuable in our quest to find T.K. He was not able to complete his training with H.S. and it is my humble opinion that we, as a team, have witnessed far too many casualties in far too short a time. I think you know I developed—feelings for the princess during our time together in the Jurassic cave. While I was not ready to look at the time stream as a way of trying to find her, I have continued to search every conceivable avenue for some clue as to where this Prime Hole Facility H.S. spoke of could be hidden. I have found little, even though I have searched the notes of both H.S. and Dr. O'Grady. So, I began researching the trail of Atlantis itself, and I have uncovered something very interesting."

Antonio turned to the hovering image. "This obelisk was recently found by the National Institute of Ocean Technology. The site is located in the Gulf of Khumbhat, specifically in the Bay of Cambay, which is not far from here. The NIOT was mapping what they thought to be canals carved by inland rivers that no longer exist, when they noted certain square and rectangular features on sonar scans that did not seem to be natural in origin. Upon closer inspection, they unearthed an entire city, about twenty kilometers from the present coast. The excavation has become, shall we say, controversial."

He turned away from the image and looked at the small group as he leaned forward onto the lectern. "I say controversial, my most esteemed colleagues, due to the nature of the find. The city predates Indus Valley Civilization by several thousands of years. It spans over nine kilometers, and scientists have now carbon dated the ruins to roughly 9000 BC. As I suspect Willoughby and Sydney have already noted, the obelisk is adorned with a symbol familiar to us."

He walked around the lectern to point out the symbol of the triangle over three-one-three with the last three turned backward. He clicked on the mouse control. The image of the hovering obelisk changed to the scene of an exhibit table on which rested a stone box. "This box, my friends," he began, "was recovered from a small compartment in the obelisk. Observations, Inc. paid a great deal to the excavators to allow us to, shall we say, take the box for safe keeping." He paused, looking over at the still life scene hovering in the air. "This strange box and the obelisk that housed it were found inside one of the dwellings of this amazing archeological find. It is most interesting. It is the only box ever found to be entirely sealed using an odd, previously unknown type of wax. Scientists have suggested that it may have come from a form of giant insect that had become extinct by the time recorded civilization arrived."

Antonio clicked the small control again. The image changed to a close up of a stone tablet. Willoughby found himself letting out a low gasp. An image had been carved into the stone—an image they all knew well. It was the image tattooed on the necks of the dark brotherhood who were in league with Beelzebub—the same ones who, a little over a year ago, had attacked their ship, the *Absconditus,* and murdered the crew.

"Yes. It is the same mark H.S. introduced to us on the *Absconditus.* When I was trapped in the cave with Tainken," Antonio continued, his eyes sparkling with the far-off memory, "she told me this mark also has significance with her people. It was known to the original time travelers who built Atlantis and was part of a body of information that was known only to those at the highest levels of the Council. Her father had given her a brief history of the marking when he had asked her to wear a tear-shaped crystal necklace that appeared to hold genealogical data about her people, among other things. You may recall, when H.S. prompted her to connect the necklace with his crystal pendant, T.K. disappeared. We believe the connection opened a time hole somehow.

"Of even greater interest, however, are the other markings below this one. Look at the pictogram just below and to the right of the symbol." He directed a thin beam of laser light onto a set of carved images that appeared to be two sea serpents fighting. The serpents had long necks, large flippers, and snake-like heads. Below the pictogram, chiseled smaller than the symbol, was what appeared to be three lines of ancient script.

"What does the script say?" Sydney asked.

Hauti stared, mesmerized. "It looks like a form of Hindi."

"Yes," Antonio agreed. "Perhaps it is the language Hindi is based on. I asked a Hindi specialist to give me his best guess as to what it says. He said the closest match was a question—an odd question." Antonio's voice trailed off.

"What do you mean, *odd?*" Willoughby pushed to the edge of the couch.

Antonio pursed his lips. Finally, he spoke, his voice barely above a whisper. "Judging from modern Hindi, the specialist guessed that it says something like, '*Where is my barber?*'"

Sydney's eyebrows rose. James Arthur narrowed his eyes, but did not say anything. Only Hauti seemed clueless as to the phrase's true meaning.

"What?" she said, looking over at Dr. J.

The good doctor pushed slowly back in his chair.

4

Pigs and a Blanket

Tainken watched with fascination as a series of cities and villages rolled across the time wall, from a variety of times and geographies, each with one or more of her people identified by the sidebar script. She began to make sense of the words her father had told her so long ago when he gave her the crystal necklace: *"This was your mother's. She wanted you to have it. Always keep it around your neck, Tainken. It is our family, our world, our people…"*

She tried to table the thought. She had choices now, but how should she choose? Ironic, it seemed, to be within grasp of so many points of time, and yet to be clueless of the context of what she was seeing. She could usually guess what she was seeing—a hut, a village, a jungle, a tundra, a mountain. Which would give her the best chance to find her way back to her friends, back to Antonio? She had decided against returning to Atlantis. It would be too dangerous. There would too many ways she could affect the time stream.

While the walls continued to click through various scenes, she turned her attention toward pulling together resources she felt she might need. She tore through closets, finding dress garb that at least faintly matched the attire she had seen people wearing on the time walls. She packed small bottles of water and bright containers of food, many of them filled with dry, bark-like cakes. She found a few containers with a sticky, honey-type pudding that brought back long-suppressed memories of her time as a young princess. *No time for that*, she thought, pushing the memories aside. She paid particular attention to her socks and grabbed a pair of slipper-like boots that laced up. She had no idea how far she would have to walk, or how long she would have to live on her own before she could learn the language and get herself established.

Turning once again toward the projections of the time-wall, she noted an image of a wooded village, Nordic in design and set against huge mountains of ice and snow. She shivered. This village did not appear as ancient as some of the cities, but it looked cold and foreign. She was not equipped for the cold, nor did she have desire to jump to a snow climate. She watched for a few more hours, seeing the time wall move to desert cities, the dwellings of some kind of Celtic tribe, and what appeared to be a rather crude castle somewhere in the near-east. Every once in a while, the wall would glitch, showing nothing but dark earth, or bits of rock, or views from somewhere high in the sky, or nothing at all. She imagined that these were time holes that had moved or disappeared, or connections that the Prime Hole Facility had somehow lost.

As she thought back over the cities and locations she had seen, the first ancient city stood out in her mind. The climate had seemed warm, with both jungle and ocean visible. Then, there was her father's stamp. She had seen many of her people, the people of *Aert Olaneous Tis*, or *Atlantis*, spread across time and across the globe. Only the once, though, had she seen her father's stamp, and it was in the first city. Perhaps the data on the crystal uploaded or populated the walls from the most recent entry backward. That would make sense. Her father had given the crystal necklace to her only a few weeks before he was murdered. *Had he suspected his death? Had he known?* This was a new thought.

She pondered it for a moment before turning back to the time walls and to the problem of finding a doorway out of this ever-flickering tomb. She thought again of the first city she had seen when the time walls had burst into full life, of the kind face of the woman who bore her father's stamp. She decided with finality that this was the city where she would go.

How could she get back to that city, though? Since showing it, the walls had moved on. They had shown dozens of other geographies and locations. How could she rewind the mechanism?

She studied the controls again, but was unable to discern a rewind button or knob. She decided she would have to remove the crystal computer to reset the order of the presentation, and then be ready step through as soon as it started up again. The image on the time-wall had changed to a Celtic community in thick forest. She thought back on the turquoise blue waters of the first city. The resources she had noted as her people were highlighted one by one certainly placed it back in a time when Atlantis may have also existed.

As she removed the aligned pendant and necklace, she noted the walls did not immediately wink out. They sort of faded over maybe a fifteen or twenty second window. She steeled herself, practicing removing the two crystal pieces at once, grabbing them just below where they attached. She counted the seconds until the image on the time walls faded.

Twenty seconds was not a lot of time. She would have to have everything but the crystals tied to her back. *Should she leave a message here for Antonio and the team should they track the Prime Hole Facility down?* She took time to grab one of the scratchy paper-like rolls she had found, and using a stylus and a red dye she had also found, stacked in the corner of the supply room, she copied down everything she could remember about the city where she planned to go.

She scribbled two copies, one to leave in case anyone found the facility, and one to take with her. She got a long drink of water and made a brief stop at the starkly lit and impeccably clean hexagon washroom near the sleeping quarters. Then, taking a deep breath, she replaced the computer, watching it slide into alignment again and hover over the indentation surrounded by emerald stones. It started rotating. She drew in a sharp breath and tensed her legs, preparing for her dash. There was nothing left to do now but go. She looked around the dim, silent facility. When she had visited it with her father and the Grand Council, it had been a place of awe—their hope for unlocking the secrets of this world and finding a way back to their true home, a world hidden among the stars, a world that seemed to have forgotten them. Now, this place was just a cold, empty tomb that reminded her of everything she had lost in her life.

She waited patiently until the city finally reappeared across the walls. She let the image of the woman flash up and waited until she saw the stamp of her father. When it finally flashed across the sidebar, she sprang into action. From the moment she snatched the crystal pendant and necklace away from its hovering cradle, to the second she jumped into the time wall, she only let herself suck in one breath. She took no more than three or four seconds to plunge into the wall, eyes closed and arms outstretched.

She felt the same sickening tug she remembered from the first time she had left the Prime Hole Facility, when it had hurdled her toward the dark plesiosaur cave. For just a moment, she had an irrational fear, like someone jumping from a high dive platform without looking down. She had done that once, back in England. She remembered how her mind had suddenly grabbed hold of a fear that somehow all the water had been drained from the pool in the few minutes it had taken her to climb up and walk to the end of the platform. Her fear now was that somehow, the time wall would not take her to the city she had chosen, but send her back to that horrid cave.

With a jerk, her fears faded. She landed with a splat in something warm and somewhat soft, but horribly putrid. As the sickening odor assaulted her senses, she was jolted to her new reality. She pushed up to her knees, stuffing the pendant and necklace still in her fist into a free pocket. She then tried to push up onto her feet, but they were still a bit wobbly, and she fell, slipping in the mud. She felt her hip graze something hard, and throwing her arm out, was suddenly submersed on one side up to her shoulder in freezing water. The water was only a few feet deep, keeping her from banging too hard upon the rocky bed of some sort of trough.

She pushed up, pulling her arm and shoulder out of the water, and saw that the trough had slick sides that were roughly the same level as the mud. As she finally righted herself and sat up, the strong odor assaulted her for a second time. She wiped at the water that had splashed on her face and peered around. She was sitting in some sort of walled pen. Mud and muck covered the ground. When she had tried to stand, she slipped on the side of the stone trough and fell, shoulder first, into it. She began to push to her feet a second time. The trough was roughly three feet wide and about ten feet in length. Her ears now registered protests—a series of grunts and squeals that, coupled with the smell, helped her quickly discern where she had landed.

"Pigs," she muttered. "Really? You send me to the middle of a pig pen? That sounds about right for our illustrious *Prime Hole Facility!*" The low grunts and squeals from behind her came closer. She turned to see perhaps two dozen pink and black bulges in the mud regarding her with what appeared to be irritation and distrust. The squealing ones seemed young, and one absolutely terrified. This one took one long look at her before high-tailing it to one of the largest and meanest looking pigs of the group. The large pig nuzzled it, and then turned protectively, grunting a warning. "Mama is not happy," Tainken intoned to herself.

Mama pig dug her hoof at the ground, flinging up a splat of mud.

"So," TK said, pushing slowly, if unceremoniously, to her full height. She stepped out of the trough and into the stinking mud, feeling it squish up and around her toes. She addressed the biggest pig. "Your little one must have been drinking from the trough? My sincere apologies. My, your little one is so—"

Mama wasn't buying it. She had lowered her snout and started grunting loudly. T.K. had been edging with soft squishing noises toward the stone wall side of the pen, "Uh, I'll just be going."

Mama bolted. She was having none of this. Her huge bulk tore through the wet mud, moving with amazing speed. TK barely had time to turn and throw herself awkwardly over the low stone wall. The pig's razor sharp teeth snapped, catching the bottom edge of her once white tunic. A short wrestling match ended with her tunic ripping off just below the knee.

"Ah!" T.K. shouted, looking back over the wall at the still agitated pig. "And what are you going to do with that? Eat it?" The pig was whipping the bit of cloth back and forth as if trying to kill it. Other pigs had descended upon her backpack, ripping it open and tearing into the containers and bottles. T.K. sighed looking down. She was covered in stinking mud, bleeding, and her nice outfit was now partially in rags. She groaned disgustedly, turning away from the pen. "What is it with me and clothes?" she mumbled. "What is it with me and time?"

As she began to walk, she noticed for the first time that it was raining. Rain drizzled down on her as she looked around for shelter. Luckily, there were no people in sight. The pig pen was located behind a row of low structures that appeared to be barns of a sort, judging from the grunts and bleats that echoed from them. Behind the stone pig pens—and she could see now that there were at least a dozen of them—lay thick jungle, quieted somewhat by the rain.

She made her way slowly around the barns and found herself on a mud path winding up toward a bridge that crossed a shallow stream. One of her sandals had torn beyond repair, and she also had a rip in her tunic just below her left shoulder. She looked around for a place to clean off the pig stench still coating her. She saw a stone bridge and made her way to it. She followed a rocky slope down the side of the bridge to a stream. There, she waded out into a trickle of cool water and spent a good half hour washing the mud and gunk from her feet and clothes, and cleaning her cuts as best she could. She never saw a single soul the entire time.

Climbing back up to the bridge, she shivered slightly, even though the air was fairly warm. It had been a long few months. After fighting plesiosaurs, escaping sure death by only seconds, and hanging out in a sterile, time-hole facility for weeks, she had landed in stinking mud, fallen in a water trough, and been attacked by a crazed mother pig. She was emotionally and mentally exhausted.

With the stench mostly gone and the muck cleaned from her clothes, she crossed the bridge and began to work her way along the muddy path on the other side. She could smell the smoke of fires ahead, and guessed the city would not be too far away. Limping a bit on the foot that had no sandal, she had gone maybe a hundred meters when there was a sudden flash of light. She was thrown sideways by a rough bundle that slammed down beside her. It had seemed to fall straight from the sky. The bundle was stacked high on the back of a tall, dark-haired man. The rough feel of the woven tarp pushed against her skin. She could see it was wrapped tightly around a bundle of goods. She pushed the man and his bundle away from her, rising to her feet while sputtering and slapping wet leaves and grass from her somewhat cleaned tunic.

"Thanks. The ensemble is totally ruined now. Do people always drop out of the sky here?" She looked to the spindly man who had rolled over and was getting to his feet. The man's smile was nauseating, and his head was bobbing like a pecking chicken.

"So sorry, so sorry. How not fallen for long time," he said with an oriental accent. Tainken wasn't sure if he was asking a question or making a statement.

"*How not*—wait, you speak English?" She tried to make sense of the man's sing-song words. The man's smile widened, as did the frequency of his head bobbing.

"Yes to English, no to How Not! I am How *Loa*... How *Not*—he from other side of family. We no speak of him. How is special name. Now, to funny way How fall. How not so good at this, this strange activity... He try to land on feet, but twist and flail, and you get in way! Practice, How say, practice, practice!" He turned and started to pull the bundle back onto his shoulder. "Hurry, chip-chop! You good customer! Boss like to see good customer!"

The man reached into his pack and pulled out a beautifully woven blanket. He threw it to her. "Here! How bring for you! Make you much warm! Always get cold when you drop so much through too many times!"

"Who are you?" T.K .said. "You're a time traveler, aren't you? You're obviously Asian, but you seem to know English." She looked up. "Where did you fall from?"

"Ah, good question! How know English very fine. Fall from time to time. Same as you, only, no like pigs."

"How did you know I fell in with the pigs? Have you been following me? Were you watching me?"

"No," How said, "right now, I just smelling you. Hurry, hurry! I think you be good, fine customer. Boss like to see good, fine customer!"

The strange man began his way up the muddy path, motioning for T.K. to follow. She wasn't sure about the odd man, but she was still shivering, and felt suddenly hungry. She stood, wrapping the blanket he had thrown around her shoulders. It was nice and warm, and she had to admit that she did enjoy hearing another voice after being alone in the Prime Hole Facility for so long—even a strange, sing-song voice like this man's. It was better than being left to slog alone on an unfamiliar mud path. So, she attempted to smile back at the spindly man, who was now dancing to some snappy tune only he could hear.

5

Dwarka (Krishna's City)

The monastery was impeccably clean, though hints of the building's true age settled on every wall, every table, every window, and every furnishing like so much fine dust. Willoughby had to work at keeping his focus on their gracious host and not give in to the temptation to wander the room like a wide-eyed tourist.

"Yes," the monk said softly, in somewhat clipped sentences, "we believe the ruins in the Gulf of Khumbhat to be the ancient city of Dwarka. Some estimate it has been submerged for over 20,000 years. Carbon dating indicates a city that is, perhaps, not that old, but certainly over 7000 and possibly as old as 9500 years. As these claims continue to be refined and verified, it is becoming more and more likely that the Sanatan Vedic Dharm, the civilization we believe built the ruins, is the oldest civilization in the world."

Willoughby watched Antonio bow his head slightly and take a ritual cup of tea from the monk. He followed suit, but only sipped at the tea. Dr. J and Hauti both took cups, also bowing graciously, though James Arthur, after one sip, threw Willoughby a glance that indicated pure torture as he forced himself to drink the rest of the cup down. The small group was seated in a circle around a low table. The room had high ceilings and ornate furnishings. They sat in an archway that opened onto a wide porch. The high-ranking monk was known as Swami Baba Samarth, named after two of his predecessors in the Samadhi Mandir–Garudeshwar Temple, both of whom were believed to be incarnations of the deity Lord Dattatreya. The Langur Preserve was not visible from the Temple, though it was only a dozen or so miles below them, nestled behind a low range of thickly wooded hills.

Dr. J forced a smile and placed the teacup down. "So, why did they never find this city until now? What do they think sunk it?"

The older monk looked up with startling bright eyes. His eyes were his most notable feature, despite a shaved head and 1950's style black rimmed glasses. He considered the questions.

"The site was only discovered when NIOT, the National Institute for Ocean Technology, began using a high-powered sonar to conduct pollution studies. They noted regularly spaced geometric structures. During follow up visits, they discovered artifacts and wood fragments that carbon dated to 7500 BC. That is when speculations began as to the identity of the city. Dwarka, or the Golden City as it was referred to by writers and poets, was one of the seven Holy Cities of ancient India. The others were Ayodhya, Mathura, Haridwar, Benares, Kanchi, and Ujjain. It was founded by Lord Krishna, who is said in cultural and religious histories of India to have been its first Emperor and King.

"As for how it sunk, we do not know. The archeologists are still sifting through the ruins. It is generally believed, however, that something happened to the whole Western coast of India around 1500 BC. That is when many believe Dwarka disappeared. It is described by Vedavyasa in the Mahabharata. I have a copy. Here, let me find it for you."

The monk stood, pulling his yellow and red robes around him in a graceful gesture. He left the room.

Dr. J leaned over and whispered, "I think this tea is made from sugar, licorice, butter, and maybe a little cow dung."

Hauti gave him a disgusted glare. "That's Assam Tea, one of the most popular teas in the world!"

James Arthur shrugged. "Well, it wasn't so popular at my family reunions."

Willoughby grinned and had just opened his mouth to offer a retort when the monk returned, carrying a very old-looking, leather-bound book. He was paging through it and paused for a moment to sit. Willoughby glanced at Antonio, who was sitting strangely quiet, looking back toward the reserve and the jungle.

The monk cleared his throat. "Ah, here it is. It says, 'Rain fell and fell. The great sea rose. It began beating against the shore like beats upon *dun dhobi*." The monk looked up. "*Dun dhobi* is one of our most ancient drums. It is made from earthenware and can be very loud." He turned again to the book. "Suddenly, the waters rose so high they broke the boundary imposed by nature. The sea rushed into the holy city of Dwarka. Water ran through the streets, growing higher and higher, until waves completely buried the city. I saw the beautiful buildings submerged one by one. In a matter of one day, the waters swallowed all the surrounding coast as well. Then, as suddenly as it began, the rain stopped and the waves settled. No more were they climbing higher. The holy

Dwarka, however, was gone. In the blink of an eye, our great city had become only a name, only a memory in an old man's dream'." He carefully, reverently, closed the book.

Antonio had turned around, taking a sudden interest. "You say, my friend, that the calamity that happened to the city was around 1500 BC?"

The monk was still skimming pages in the book. He glanced up. "That is the estimate archeologists give."

Antonio considered a moment and then turned to the others. "The word 'India' first appears in Greek writings in the 5th century BC. The word, as you may know, my friends, was derived from the Indus River. Do you see what I'm getting at?" When no one reacted, he continued. "India and this region were known to the Greeks almost 100 years before Plato wrote of Atlantis. What if Plato never actually saw Atlantis? What if his writings were based on legends that were much older—legends that may have come from plundered ruins, like the submerged city in the Gulf of Cambay? What if the whole civilization of Atlantis is much older than we have believed? If Atlantis and her people were destroyed around the same time as this ancient city, buried under water or earth, perhaps a majority of the coastal people were wiped out at the same time. That may be why there is so little to whisper of Atlantis' existence."

Dr. J leaned back on his cushions. "Now, that's an interesting theory. Plato was famous for borrowing ideas from other places without exactly quoting his sources. What if he found something, but kept it secret, or destroyed it, to protect the claims of his story?"

"Well," Willoughby chimed in, "there is a building body of evidence that sophisticated societies existed long before recorded history indicates. The ruins in the Gulf of

Khumbhat may represent the oldest organized city yet identified, but there are indications that complex cultures existed long before current recorded history suggests. The internet abounds with speculation about a master race that preceded the Egyptians and spread its science and culture around the globe. Carbon dating of the great pyramids has been inconclusive—some dating a few of the pyramids to as early as 8000 BC, a time long before the emergence of Egyptian culture. Sydney and I uncovered this while researching obscure references to the *Library of Souls*. Of course, there are plenty of wild theories out there. One claims that a race of giants once ruled the world and built the oldest pyramids and the original Sphinx. Another claims that a secret society is trying to keep this hushed up, and anyone who brings the evidence to light should fear for their lives. I'm not saying I hold to either theory, but even serious archeologists are having to completely rewrite the book on human history every few decades, it seems."

The monk had looked up from his book at the mention of the *Library of Souls*. He had followed Willoughby's words with some interest. "I do not know much about giants or Atlantis, but we Hindus believe that there is much to the history of our world that is yet to be discovered or understood."

Antonio, who had seemed lost in thought after James Arthur and Willoughby spoke, finally brought his focus back to the present. He looked at the monk as if embarrassed, as if he had forgotten the man was even there. "My friend, you have been so kind to invite us in and to offer us refreshment and share your knowledge with us so freely. It has been an honor to make your fine acquaintance. I only—"

Before Antonio could finish his comment, he was interrupted by a sharp intake of breath. He looked to Willoughby, whose face had gone ashen white. Antonio waited for an explanation, but Willoughby gave none. He simply stood and said, "We need to go… Now."

Antonio threw a concerned look at James Arthur and Hauti. He then turned to the monk. "I must beg your forgiveness," he said quickly, "but our friend is feeling suddenly ill. May we beg your leave, my friend?"

The monk watched Willoughby curiously. He looked to Antonio, pulling his lips up in a hesitant smile. "This, I think, is no sickness. Our Temple invites enlightenment of many kinds. I, too, sense the urgency. Go in peace. I send my blessings with you. One who kindles the light of awareness must sometimes walk in the heat of the flames." He bowed.

Willoughby had already bowed to the monk and was moving back toward the entry door, toward the jeep they had borrowed from the preserve. It waited for them at the foot of a cascading stone staircase. He hesitated only a moment at the door, as if listening to something, then hurried down the steps. The others bowed respectfully and followed. No one said anything as they ran through a light drizzle and climbed in the jeep. Antonio started the engine. The windshield wipers punctuated the lack of chatter as they moved away from the temple.

Once they had left the immediate parking area, Antonio turned to Willoughby. "Okay, I sensed something, but what? What's going on?"

"I don't know," Willoughby said. "Something. I heard Sydney's playing, as clear as if she was standing beside me. She's a dozen miles away, Antonio. *I shouldn't be able to hear her.* There was also something in the tone of the music—a tentativeness, a nervousness. It was like a plea, a cry for help. I think she's in trouble of some kind." He looked over at Antonio. "What did you sense?"

Antonio narrowed his eyes, sloshing around turns at top speed and speaking loudly in order to be heard over the wipers, the rain, and the whine of the engine. "I don't know. Something. You think he is here?"

"Yeah," Willoughby said, staring out the window. "I think he's here. It started this morning and the feeling has grown. The whole feel of this area, the fact that we're back together again as a team—everything, it all fits. It's his style, his signature—he seems to attack whenever we try to make a move, and usually, his brotherhood, or cult is not far behind. You're thinking the same thing, aren't you? I know you are. That's why you kept looking at the jungle, wasn't it? That's why you stopped so abruptly when you heard me catch my breath. None of this is a total surprise to you."

Antonio pushed the jeep to its limit. "I, I feel something, my friend. And it is not friendly. We must make sure Sydney is safe. Then discuss what to do. If you are right—our defenses are, indeed, weak. Staying at the preserve has become too great a risk."

James Arthur leaned forward. "Then, where are we going to stay? We only just got here. Hauti and I flew halfway around the world, and for what? For a fireside chat and a strange cup of tea?"

Willoughby glanced back at Dr. J. His glare was intense. "You haven't met Beelzebub, James Arthur. You don't want to meet Beelzebub."

James Arthur shrank back into his seat. "No, you're right about that. Meeting the man's handiwork was plenty enough for me." He looked over at Hauti and said with a tight smile, "Don't worry, we do this all the time. *Just think frequent flyer miles.*" When she raised an eyebrow, he turned back to Willoughby. "So, you think he's caught up with us? We released his witch. I'm sure that didn't make him too happy. We knew that, sooner or later, he'd come looking for us."

Willoughby didn't respond. His eyes were fixed on something beyond the windshield of the car, something out there in the jungle. His ears strained to hear above the roar of the jeep and the grind of the gravel. *Don't fight him, Sydney*, he pushed out with his mind. *He WILL win.*

6

The Deadly Den

Little was said the rest of the drive. As Antonio turned onto a layer of fresh gravel that led to the complex, Sydney's music assaulted Willoughby again. This time, he slammed his eyes shut and bit his lip. The violin strains were perfectly played, yet they screamed in his mind, as if marking pure desperation with a series of musical tones.

Antonio must have seen the concern on his face. "I am hurrying, my friend," he whispered. Willoughby didn't answer. His heart was beating wildly. *Could he do this? Could he face Beelzebub and his associates again?* The jeep swung around a final bend in the road, tires spitting gravel to the side. They bounded into sight of the complex.

"Stop!" Willoughby shouted.

Antonio skidded on the brakes. The car fishtailed to a halt, throwing up a wave of gravel and brown sludge. For a moment, there was no sound but the slap of the worn windshield wipers. Then, they all heard it. From somewhere within the tangles of jungle, came a muffled scream.

Willoughby threw the jeep door open. *Had the scream cut off?* Was someone trying to contain the sound? He spun around, prepared to tell the others to stay with the jeep, knowing they would reject his command. But there was no need. No one in the car was moving. No one in the car was *breathing!* The windshield wipers had stopped. Even the raindrops, he noted with dread, were no longer falling. They hung, motionless, like suspended beads, in the air. All ambient sound had ceased. *It was a junction!* Had he done it again? Had he somehow created an intersection of timelines, a point at which all time stops? The exact moment of intersect lay frozen before him like a display in a wax museum. It went on for as far as the eye could see. He couldn't have created this.

It was Beelzebub. He knew it. The demon was here!

Somewhere in this vast still-life scene, the creature he had first met in a time junction, back before he knew that time travel technology even existed, was waiting for him. The gaunt figure had first appeared from a rip in the fabric of time. Since then, there had been other visits, none of them pleasant.

Willoughby slid sideways and hopped out of the jeep. Of his team, he alone had an ability to move within a time junction. He could sense time, see its equations, even manipulate it as Beelzebub seemed apt at doing and was probably doing now. He wasn't sure where his skills came from entirely. His birth father also had talents. His birth father also dealt with Beelzebub. Willoughby scanned the landscape for evidence of time holes nearby. He was able to sense the presence of weaknesses in time, or time holes, seeing them as number strings that floated like clouds around specific pockets of space. He could navigate the holes, moving between timelines, and repositioning himself in space, with only the limited aid of technology. He had even created time junctions like this one. He seemed to have a natural connection with time. Beelzebub claimed that he had a hand in this. He claimed that his genetic experiments while with the Third Reich resulted in his becoming the scientific father of Gustav, which made him a sort of Grandfather to Willoughby.

Moving quickly over mounds of gravel and thick ruts of mud, Willoughby noted that the ground remained rigid and rubbery, not soft and squishy. He sensed a mesh of time holes, but none large enough to create so vast a time hole. This puzzled him. He looked down. The mud did not register his footprints. He felt raindrop beads brush against his face and hands. They did not burst when he pushed through them, but rather, bounced off of him like gel pills, sliding back into place after he passed, as if they were curtains of soft beads, suspended on invisible strings. He moved warily toward the pocket of jungle where he had heard the scream.

"We both know you're here," he said coolly—not too loudly. There was no need for him to shout. This was a junction. Sound reached its borders effortlessly. "When are you going to show yourself? Is this another game, another *test?*" Willoughby moved quietly, cautiously, his eyes darting across every inch of the jungle ahead. His voice circled back on itself. A junction was a vacuum, and with no other sound within it, there was nothing to degrade the natural vocal tone.

"This is no game," came the crisp reply. True to his experience with sound in previous time junctions, the voice seemed to come from everywhere. It was a dry, no-nonsense type voice—one with a slightly European accent. "I advise you to keep walking, Willoughby. There is a sight you will want to see. *Is it a test?* You can call it what you will."

Willoughby made his way through the undergrowth, alert for any movement, any hint of color in the shadows around him. "Okay. So what do I call you?" he spoke softly; "Do I call *you* what I will? Murderer? Prince of the Demons? Aribert Ferdinand Heim, Nazi butcher of the Third Reich, and perhaps best known as *Dr. Death?*"

The words seemed to have little impact. "I told you when we formally met that I had many names. You can call me what you like."

Willoughby continued speaking, trying to discern where the precise verbiage was coming from. "Tell me this, Heim—do you ever even think of the thousands of lives you've taken? How many innocent Jewish people became just specimens to you? Do you feel any guilt at all for working to exterminate an entire people?"

The voice appeared uninterested by the question. "Really? We are going to have *this* conversation? What are a few million Jews to you?"

"They're people," Willoughby said. "They're human beings, just like my mom, my sisters... I don't see a religion, a color, a race, a gender. I see people."

Beelzebub considered the response.

"If it makes you happy, I was not the one to order the extermination of the Jews. Yes, I found the situation convenient. There were tests that had to be done. The tests required live subjects. The extermination order was handed to me. It fit my purposes. It was relatively simple. The Jews were a generally mistrusted people at that time. There were *many* who willingly complied with my orders. It is much easier to turn a blind eye to suffering when the one who suffers is not your friend. What I needed, what I was attempting was—well, complicated. Clearing prostitutes from the streets of London was time consuming. Working with the odd murderer or rapist was tedious. But responsibility over a whole ethnicity, even the *chosen ones*, God's own, a people with prophesy that warns them they will suffer?" Beelzebub stepped suddenly out of thin air. He fell in step with Willoughby, matching his strides as he smirked sardonically. "Well, *that* was the ideal."

Willoughby glared with disgust. Beelzebub didn't seem to mind. His eyes were focused ahead, as if he were gathering his thoughts. When he spoke again, it was with a purely academic tone—as if he had no concept of the horrible consequences of the holocaust.

"It is easier than you think to orchestrate a genocide. Take a people who keep to themselves, who are secretive, even Zionistic. If they happen to be undeniably successful and shrewd, all the better. In the early twentieth century, the Third Reich was not alone in its quest to resolve the '*Jewish issue.*' In addition to peculiar customs, there were whispers at high government levels of wild treason and decadent plots. It does not matter if the whispers were true. They did their damage—that is what matters. Doubts were planted. *Could these people be trusted? Were they a threat?* Then there is the matter of intolerance in their own ranks. How do you justify their own bit of murder? They wanted to blame the Romans, but history, in the end, was too detailed in describing the death of Christ. One more nail in a coffin that was all too easy to build."

"You think you can justify that? You think anything you say will justify the slaughter of thousands of innocent people to me? You're a sick being."

"Am I, really?" The being smiled. "You think you are so holy, so good? The Guardian Angel—Gabriel incarnate? I saw a chance and took it. But you, of course, you would never do the same. Yet, you are here *because* I took that chance. You and your talents are a result of my...experiments. Ironic, isn't it? You stand here defending fallen ghosts whose very sacrifice led to your power, and ultimately, to your very existence. I've waited a long time, Willoughby. You will have your chance to decide—will you take your advantage when it is presented, or end up just another fallen ghost yourself? Whether you like it or not, you are destined to unlock the final gateway in the annuls of real power. It can be your destiny to unlock power like no human has ever imagined. One way or another—willingly or not—you *are* the one I have waited for."

Willoughby wanted to spit at this thing beside him. He wanted to run. But he knew it was no use, and besides, Sydney was in some kind of trouble. So, he just glared at the tall, angular man, with his black trench coat, his dark boots, and his carefully pressed slacks. He could easily imagine Aribert Heim with his crisp uniform and the insignia of the SS.

"I would never unlock anything for you," Willoughby finally said, his voice low and threatening. "I look forward to disappointing you."

"Well," the gaunt man said. "Never is a long time," he peered down his pointed nose at Willoughby, "but you may find it has a tendency of coming much quicker than you expect. We are connected, you and I, Willoughby. You *will* help me, but believe what you like for now. That is your charm—your inability to see the big picture. *Whether* you help me is not in question. You have no choice. The game has already selected you. I am simply endeavoring to help you become less of a pawn and more a player. That is the choice before you."

Willoughby looked away. A stab of fear pricked his heart, though he was determined not to show it. Could this be true? *Could he betray himself, his friends, his family—the ones he loved?*

Aribert Heim smiled. "Keep walking," he urged. "You have so much to learn, Willoughby. For one thing, you should never let your girlfriend wander off alone, especially not in a jungle. Jungles are such dangerous places." The man turned, clasping his bony fingers behind him. He peered toward a patchy area where the trees seemed to thicken.

Willoughby maneuvered around a particularly thick Jujube tree so that he could see what the man was staring at. His heart pounded and his blood ran cold at the sight. It was Sydney. She was frozen, twisting in an odd dance, sudden terror on her face. Her gypsy frock had flown out toward one side, as if she had frozen in the act of a quick spin. Her bangles and bracelets also seemed to indicate rapid movement, appearing jumbled and disoriented, as if in mid-jangle on her arms. Her white, cotton Capris were stained green and her matching bamboo sandals were caked in mud. Her Stradivarius was in one hand, while the bow in her other was arching down, like she was slashing at something. Willoughby leaned forward, craning to see what the bow was aiming at. He gasped.

Aribert Heim enjoyed the moment. "Yes, a singularly interesting predicament. I am not always so precise in the moment of my art, but this time, I captured it perfectly."

Willoughby took in the full impact of the scene. A huge king cobra, easily six feet in length, was frozen in the act of striking, its wide, yellow mouth and three-inch fangs less than a foot away from Sydney's thigh. Willoughby ran the calculations in his mind. A mature cobra strikes at a speed of up to two-and-a-half feet per second. It would take Sydney at least a half a second to twist enough to hit the striking cobra away with her violin bow—and that was if the bow and the slash were strong enough to knock the snake's fangs clear of her body. It was not enough time. The snake would connect. Unless Willoughby could come up with some idea, the snake would bite her. There was no getting around it.

"If you look carefully," Beelzebub said with calm detachment, as if describing a point of stage blocking for an interesting play, "you will see that the obvious striking cobra is not the *only* striking cobra."

Willoughby's eyes scanned the dim growth and low ferns. He saw an even bigger cobra just to the left of Sydney's dipped shoulder. It, too, seemed to be rearing back, preparing to strike—its fangs already extended. Letting his eyes carefully study every inch of the area around the twisting girl, he counted five other snakes for a total of seven. Two of the others were also king cobras. The largest of all was positioned about five paces in front of where Sydney must have been looking as she played. The snake had its hood spread out, and was fully upright. From ground to tip, it almost matched Sydney's height.

"Is this another of your associates?" Willoughby angrily snapped, remembering the cobra cave under the ruins of Petra where he had saved James Arthur. He had released another being there, a deadly creature under the control of Beelzebub who the locals called the Desert Witch. This creature had shown an affinity for snakes, especially cobras.

"Not this time," Beelzebub said abruptly. "I had nothing to do with creation of this bit of human drama. Just as I had nothing to do with the death of your friend,

H.S., and little to do with the meltdown of the team who seized the *Absconditus*. I am an opportunist, Willoughby. I don't kill just for sport. No, your friend here created this predicament on her own. I only preserved the moment for your benefit." He glanced at Willoughby, his eyes gleaming in the dim light. "I continue to try to help you, Willoughby. Why, I cannot say, but I do."

The man turned, a smile twitching at the corners of his gaunt face. Willoughby could just make out his pointed teeth. He did not believe for a moment that Sydney had run through the rain into the jungle, through the mud in her white outfit, and into this den of cobras on her own. What was the man's game this time? He stared at the being who called himself Beelzebub, who his father had known as Aribert Heim.

"I won't help you—even to save her," he said, his voice lacking conviction.

"Oh, you can't help her," the man replied. "This is a junction. You can't move or change anything. Should you try to sacrifice yourself--pushing her aside the moment the junction collapses and allowing yourself to be bitten—well, I am afraid that, as noble a gesture as that is, time is not on your side. You would likely allow her to get bitten, and get bitten yourself in the process, and then who would be able to get the other out of here? It would take many long minutes for your friends to decide to come looking and to find you. By then, the cobra venom will have done its work. You do know how fast-acting cobra venom is, do you not? It starts affecting your nervous system almost immediately. Your vision will become blurred, you will experience dizziness and vertigo, and within minutes, you will fall into an ever-deepening paralysis." The being looked again at the frozen scene, as if studying it. "You might try knocking one of the snakes away, but what of the other one? If you do not fling it far enough from you, you won't have time to collect Sydney and get her out of harm's way before the snakes are back. They are tenacious things when riled."

Willoughby's own mind was churning. Sweat poured down his forehead and stung his eyes. He thought through scenario after scenario. How long would Beelzebub hold the junction? What would the being do if he dashed forward to try to eliminate at least one of the snakes? Could he even get there in time?

"You are right about one thing," the demon-man added conversationally. "Snakes do have an interesting talent. It is what draws me to them." He took a step closer to Willoughby. "You see, they can sense time fluctuations. Even the faintest hint of a fluctuation, shall we say, the passing of a soul, catches their attention. You will often find them around death, especially cobras—even when they didn't cause it. You will also find them around time holes." He gestured at Sydney. "It is my opinion that she did not just happen upon this array of cobras. I believe she called them—with her music. She is special, Willoughby. What you do with your mind and your understanding of mathematics, she does with her music. She instinctively transcends time barriers with her equations of sound. I find her quite a fascinating creature."

"Then, help me save her!" Willoughby shouted, his patience waning and panic setting in.

"Well, are you asking for my help?"

"*Yes!*"

"Why would I consider helping you? What do I get in the bargain?"

Willoughby was silent. He had known the trap was coming, and still, he fell into it.

"I thought so," Beelzebub said with a wicked grin. "You are the archangel. You would *never* let your chance for advantage dictate your *choices*. So, I leave it to you. This is your mathematical problem to solve. Five snakes— three in the very act of striking, and you cannot move a single thing on the stage." He studied Sydney for a moment, and then turned again to Willoughby. "Does time have a sound? Can you sing it to me?" He said softly. He turned back to Sydney. "Ah, but my rare beauty, how we could have danced…"

Willoughby felt a surge of anger explode inside him. He needed a plan and he needed it now! But, he didn't have one. He grasped for something, anything. *Music?* Beelzebub seemed to believe there was power in Sydney's music, a connection with time that went beyond the simple notes. Willoughby thought back to the first recital he had heard Sydney play. It was on the *Absconditus*—a recital with island players. He had seen and felt remarkable things, but he had blamed it on the bowl of Kava Sydney had given him as part of the evening ceremony. Was it possible that what this demon lord could hear in Sydney's music, *he could see?* He thought of the phrase he had heard back in Sunday school, "*They have ears, but do not hear; eyes, but do not see.*" He felt a sudden ache in his mind. *What did this have to do with anything? How could he save her?* He glared back at Beelzebub, his eyes holding a mix of fury and hatred. "What do you want, Heim, or Beelzebub, or whatever you wish to call yourself today? Why did you really bring me here?"

The man blinked. "I didn't bring you here. I did, of course, know that you would come." He stared down at

Willoughby, a hatred barely disguised beneath the skin on his face. "I, as you see, am giving you the courtesy of a warning, the chance to react, before letting disaster take one of your own. That's more than you did for me."

Understanding dawned on Willoughby. "The Desert Witch…"

Beelzebub turned slightly. "Yes. You released my Desert Witch. I wasn't done with her yet. She could have been more—useful."

"As I recall, you sent her after me," Willoughby said, never letting his eyes leave the gaunt figure. "Besides, you did not own her."

"Oh, well, ownership—that is a word that has much to do with perspective," the man said. "From my perspective, I found her, saved her, and sustained her, which gave me certain rights to determine what happened to her. I introduced you because I was interested how you would react to her and she to you. I underestimated you, Willoughby. I thought you had no chance against my *associate*. I would not have let her kill you, she knew that. Neither would I have freed her into a pointless abyss. So. We are even. But mark my words, young Willoughby—I will never underestimate you again."

Willoughby felt a rage inside that he couldn't quiet. Who was this being that thought he owned people, who believed he could use innocent lives to complete an experiment or even a score?

"If you had your way, your Desert Witch would have killed my friend," he said, barely concealing his contempt. "Luckily, she proved to be a greater being in the end than you."

The man studied him again, before conceding the point. "You really do not like me, do you? Ah, well. It makes what is to be that much easier. Consider this just a taste, Willoughby; a taste of things to come."

Willoughby was done with conversation. It was time to act. There was little that Beelzebub said that he accepted as true anyway. He began to edge cautiously around the being, moving toward the striking cobra. In a swift movement, he jumped forward, grabbed the cobra's head, and tried to force it, to angle it in a different direction. It was like solid stone. It would not budge. He heard Aribert laugh.

"As I told you, Willoughby, this is a junction. You can't change anything that existed before the timelines were crossed—unless you know when the timelines are and can change something before the junction occurs."

Willoughby gave up, stepping back from the snake. He looked up. "If I'm holding her when I create a junction, or I create it specifically around her and not the snakes, I can move her out of harm's way."

"Yes," Beelzebub agreed, tapping at his chin. "But you would have to work in nanoseconds to accomplish something like that before at least one set of fangs sink home. Do you really think you are up to that task? It is all about probabilities, is it not? You may find a way to disable one snake, but there are three. If you could disable two, or want to risk her life on how quickly you can manipulate the time grid, well, then, maybe she only gets bit once and you can get her to the complex. There they can find and administer the anti-venom, but will it be fast enough to save her? Maybe. That is the thing about probabilities— the more factors involved, the less sure you can be about outcomes."

Willoughby's eyes darkened. He moved away from Sydney and the snakes. "You know I won't let her die. I'll find a way. *What is the point to this?* Do you just want to see her suffer—to see *me* suffer?"

The man flashed his pointy teeth, turning to face Willoughby. "I want you to know what it feels like to lose something you care about. I didn't cause your little dilemma here, but I have no hesitation in using it to teach a fool! You have a lot more to lose than just a girlfriend, Willoughby—*a lot more.*"

"*Teach?* You don't teach anything! You reward and punish—like a bully who's spent too long at the top of the playground hill!" He turned away, fuming. "Just get out of here. You sicken me."

Beelzebub's face contorted. He moved faster than Willoughby thought humanly possible, grabbing him by the neck and slamming him back against a tree trunk. "Be that as it may," he hissed, pressing Willoughby's head against the vine-covered trunk, "I am not one to be dismissed out of hand. You may benefit from knowing what is coming or you may not. But know this my young friend, there will be much which you *will not* be able to control and you *will not* be able to stop. Not without my help. You better remember that."

Willoughby felt the bite of branches cutting at his cheek, his arm and his back.

The demonic figure's voice was low and menacing. "Now, with you or without you, I will find that crystal computer. I will track down the Prime Hole Facility. You have no concept of what is really going on here. It would be so much wiser, so much better for you and your '*team*' if you do not rush into rash statements and judgments."

The being smelled of old, rotting wood. His hands were rough and hot to the touch. When he moved, his skin crinkled, and there was a faint humming, as if great stores of electricity coursed through his veins. Willoughby managed to spit out a response.

"You can already move through time. Why do you need the crystal computer or the Prime Hole Facility?"

The bony hand let go of the boy, though the gaunt man did not step away. "You have no idea what this technology really is, do you?" He straightened, stepping back slightly.

Willoughby let his eyes drop. He bent down, spitting and gasping. The close contact with the creature had left him feeling strangely depleted and ill.

It was the cool, collected voice of an SS doctor that kicked in now as the being answered. "The technology gives more than a mere ability to manipulate this small world's timeline. With access to the prime hole, I tap into the power upon which the fabric of this universe is based—a power beyond your wildest dreams. The ancients of Atlantis were fools. They had no idea what they had stumbled upon. They used it for archeology, for education and recreation. They had lost the view of the bigger picture. You have only bits and pieces of the story, Willoughby. It's a long one, an ancient story. You, me, they—we are all embroiled in a continuing battle that started well before time began." He stepped away as Willoughby rose. Looking toward Sydney, he mumbled. "The technology will not elude me again."

Willoughby gulped in a few more quick breaths, trying to calm his nerves and stop his hands from shaking. "You're at war with everyone, aren't you?"

The man turned and moved closer.

Willoughby held his ground.

"War is what we do, those of us who wish to survive." He reached up suddenly. When Willoughby flinched, he grinned, but he did not grab or hit this time. He, almost tenderly, brushed Willoughby's cheek with a finger, tracing a trickle of blood that had fallen there.

"Do you know, Willoughby, why war exists?" He rubbed the blood between his fingers. "War is good for the economy. War trims the family tree—less mouths to feed, less minds to control. War provides an opportunity for the fittest to do what they do best—*keep on keeping on*. It is one of the most predictable aspects of your world. We carry into mortality the concept of war—war against the elements, the new, the frightening, the unknown. We reinvent it over and over again, but in short, it is always there. Heroes are born. Villains arise. War creates chaos. Chaos creates the need for control.

"War is a means, Willoughby. All the power on this puny planet is nothing compared to what exists out there." He pointed toward the sky. "Out there is power to crush planets, to build universes, to summon something out of nothing, and reinvent it over and again. Out there is the real war. Here we are but children playing with toys. So, I choose war—I choose a chance for real power. Why should I not?" Beelzebub moved several feet away. He brushed down the creases in his coat sleeve. "Now, I believe that you and I are about done here."

Willoughby felt a sudden resurgence of panic. He gripped the damp bark of a tree. He had heard one of the assistants at GEPP refer to it as a strangler fig. He tried to dig his nails into a damp sheen of moss that covered it, to jerk some piece of wood away, something he could use as a weapon. He had to keep Beelzebub talking. He had to give himself enough time to come up with a plan. He fought to steel the tremor in his voice.

"Who, exactly, are you at war with?"

Beelzebub seemed pleased with Willoughby's discomfort. The demon broadened his smile, turning his head toward the nearest snake. He wiped Willoughby's blood onto the snake's open lip. "A story for a different time...Your father knows little of the story. He thinks he knows more. He knows only what those fool friends he plays with have told him. But they were not there. They have no understanding of the full story." He turned back, seeming amused. "Oh, and yes, I know you are trying to stall. You have no idea how to save your girlfriend."

"No," Willoughby admitted, "I don't. But you do. And you're going to tell me."

Beelzebub laughed. "Oh, of course," he said, letting out a long, slow breath. "Do not imagine you have any chance of manipulating me, boy. I was there when Cain murdered Abel. I was there at the side of Agamemnon when he sacked Troy. I rode behind Attila on his merciless sieges. I helped destroy the code of the Samurai. I was given a sword of gratitude from Napoleon, then used it to kill the only doctor that could have cured him."

"Why are you telling me this?"

"To give you a time reference," Beelzebub said flatly. "In this human form, I can slow time, but not stop it. I have found it necessary to step outside of my junctions enough that my form has aged beyond its usefulness more than a dozen times now."

Willoughby's eyes narrowed. "You have the ability to jump to other bodies, to possess them?" While he was speaking, his mind was searching every bit of information around him for some plan.

"Not possess," the gaunt man said. "I am more a symbiont, but then so are you, so is all humanity. Let us just say I have perfected a way of recycling myself when needed—with the proper help, and of course, I always seem to find proper help. I have been gaining power on this planet for millennia, and now, I believe it is time to rewrite certain parts of history."

"H.S. told me that time won't let you change history."

"Well, H.S. knew what H.S. knew." There was a long pause while the gaunt figure made a point of showing off the yellowed points of his teeth. "His understanding was limited. He never dealt with someone like me. I am anchored in one human form, but connected across time to key variations of myself. I am what you might refer to, Willoughby, as a *living* junction—a being in which time, itself, flows like blood. You cannot kill me because I'm not really alive. That makes me indestructible."

Willoughby wasn't really listening. He had bent over and was trying to pick up a stick. Once again, it was frozen fast to its place on the ground.

"Keep talking, Willoughby," Beelzebub said. "If I find the conversation stimulating, I suppose I could give you another moment or two. I see that you are sweating. But your talk has to interest me."

"You said your origins, how you came here, is a long story," Willoughby said, trying to sound calm. "I'm listening."

The tall man turned and started away from the frozen panorama. "I will give you a two-minute story. Are you familiar with the concept of the singularity?"

It took Willoughby a moment to focus on the man's words and stem the paralyzing wave of fear that gripped him. His voice shook as he answered. "Uh, it's a point where a mathematical object is not defined, or fails to behave in a standard way."

The being continued to speak as he walked. "So, how did life, existence begin? As a singularity, of course—a point at which nothingness began to behave in a non-standard way. You could call that God if you wish, for singularities are infinite and eternal, without beginning or end. For the sake of our discussion, let us call our singularity *intelligence*. Intelligence has always existed. It is neither created nor made. It simply is, and by simply being, it becomes a useable unit—a unit that can be multiplied or divided. Eternity, Willoughby, at its simplest, is a framework for equation."

The being was twenty feet away now and continuing to walk. "Nature is all about multiplication and division. It sparks, it shines, and its light strengthens as it divides itself, and multiplies." He said this as if sharing some great secret. "I suppose you can recite Newton's Third Law of Motion?"

Willoughby hesitated, again looking at Sydney and the snakes. He couldn't use a branch or rock or anything. He felt too rattled to count on creating a junction fast enough—he simply hadn't done it enough. *I have to use something on me, he thought. What do I have? A belt!* He began stripping off his belt, considering how to best use it. He became aware that Beelzebub was waiting for an answer. He couldn't afford to have the junction shut down just yet. "Uh," he began, trying to remember the question. "To every action is an equal and opposite reaction."

"Correct."

Willoughby could still see Beelzebub, but the being continued to walk, slowly weaving in and out of the foliage and trees. Willoughby approached the closest snake, the one only inches from Sydney's thigh and fell to his knees. He began to wind the belt around the snake's mouth so that its fangs were covered and it would be unable to bite. *One down*, he thought.

"To every singularity," Beelzebub's voice took over now, "there is an echo. To every multiplication, there is a necessary division. Intelligence conceives light—its antithesis crushes with the deepest darkness of void. Push, pull; something, nothing; order, chaos; the balance and counterbalance—the countering equations wheel through infinity in a grand, macabre ballet. And we? Where do we stand in this eternal operetta? We, my young friend, stand on the knife's edge, the border between chaos and order."

Willoughby had moved to the second snake. He began to strip off his shirt. With the distance, the voice got softer and quieter.

"Intelligence likes to think it is ruled by order. Order is what multiplication and division are all about. Matter, time, they are merely equations to explain motion. Organized motion—highly stylized patterns of structure refined for and tied to a singularity—can seem to create *something* from *nothing*. Only, it is a lie. Motion, as it turns out, *is* a 'something.' Substance, existence, you see, is no more than the physical display of infinity in motion."

Good thing this guy loves to hear himself talk, Willoughby thought. He cocked his head ever so slightly. He didn't know how, but somehow, he was able to follow Beelzebub's sing-song soliloquy, despite his distraction with the snakes. He remembered the Desert Witch—the creature James Arthur had managed to heal—also speaking of a singularity. "*I am my own singularity now*," she had said.

"Void is the antithesis of mathematics," the voice continued, moving to a whisper. Willoughby was running out of time and Beelzebub wanted to make sure he knew it. "Void, you see, is a domain of infinite chaos, the random disruption of motion, the ripping apart of any and all pattern into the blinding potential of incomprehensibility. You sense that I speak truthfully, do you not? What do you know about the transfer of energy as atoms decay?"

Willoughby had a harder time with the second snake. It had only opened its mouth part way, and he had a hard time trying to force his shirt behind and around the fangs. He shouted out an answer to Beelzebub, even though in the junction he didn't need to. He was determined not to let the demon lord know he was rattled. "The transfer creates heat."

"Yes, the heat of hell...You note that I used the word '*potential.*' Nothing comes from nothing, you are taught, Willoughby. As I stated earlier, that is a lie. Potential comes from nothing, and all something is built from this peculiar singularity—*raw potential.* This is the real singularity of power, you see—*potential* built through the mathematics of organized motion. And not just built— there is also great potential found in the deconstruction of organization. In fact, the force of deconstruction is more easily accessed, and more readily tapped for those of us who know its dark secrets."

The being was silent for a moment. Willoughby had decided to tie the shirt around the head of the snake so it couldn't open its mouth wider. Finishing, he looked around. Beelzebub had said there were three snakes striking. *Where was the third?*

"Too bad, Willoughby. You have run out of time. I gave you a sporting chance, even though you gave me nothing. In roughly eighteen seconds—just enough time for me to get to my exit, the junction will be released.

Then, in a blink, time will play itself out. I will not control what happens."

Willoughby heard a click of fingers and panicked. *Had the demon lord been lying?* Were there only two of the many snakes Beelzebub bragged about really striking? He spun, once again searching the ground and foliage near Sydney's frozen form. That is when he saw it. It was hidden in the shadows of a huge vine, its fully fanged, wide-open mouth still partially concealed by the vine's leaves. He grabbed Sydney's arm and gripped tight. *If he jerked at exactly the right time, perhaps he could get her enough out of the way that—*

The junction collapsed. Even as he fought to focus, pulling with all his might while registering Sydney's scream, and calculating how he was affecting her momentum, he saw, with full clarity, that it was impossible. The snake head shot forward, as if in slow motion. He couldn't save Sydney. She would be bitten. His only hope was that he had moved her enough to affect the angle so that, perhaps, the fangs would not sink in as deep. The snake with the tied belt had bounced off Sydney's thigh, and while he couldn't see the other, he heard it thrashing behind them. He heard his own scream of frustration as the uninhibited cobra's head sunk down into the fabric of Sydney's swirling blouse. Then, there was an ear-splitting scream and the rubbery sound of fangs striking home. Willoughby's world *spun.*

7

Sun Wukong

Antonio felt that, in his last blink, something had changed. The wipers slapped, the rain fell, *but something had definitely changed.* He sensed more than saw the empty seat beside him.

"*Willoughby!*" he cried out, noting that the boy had vanished. His door was open, but there were no tracks in the mud.

"Where did he go? What happened?" It was the frightened voice of Hauti.

James Arthur put a hand out, afraid she might try to bolt from the car.

"Listen!" Antonio cried.

There had been two screams, or was it three? It was hard to discern. One of the screams came again, high, with palpitations of intense agony. Then, suddenly, the voice cut into an incoherent mumbling, almost a whimpering. The whimpers faded and a horrible silence settled over the trees, leaving only the sound of the rain tapping on the jeep roof as the wipers beat time. When more shouts came, they seemed muted, interspersed with a sound of someone stumbling or crashing slowly toward them. They thought they could make out Sydney then, her occasional cries piercing, then falling into sobs.

Antonio slammed the jeep door open and jumped out.

"Stay here," James Arthur ordered Hauti as he jumped out as well. The two men splashed away, across the uneven gravel through the rain, plunging through the mud and wet grass and foliage toward the jungle. By the time they ducked into the forested undergrowth, they were almost in sync.

The cries from Sydney were getting closer, and they could hear Willoughby yelling, pleading now. A swift if brief series of unearthly howls sounded from somewhere behind them, from the direction of the preserve. It was as if all the monkeys were howling together in one great lament of pain. Antonio caught sight of Willoughby first. He was trying to drag Sydney forward, but she was fighting, hitting him with a broken bow, her violin held tightly in her other hand. She seemed hysterical.

"I've got to go back; I've got to help him!" she screamed.

"It's too late," Willoughby yelled, dragging her on. "There's nothing we can do for him. He's too small. He's already gone, Sydney! Going back there right now is suicide!" He had blood dripping down his face, no shirt on, and seemed over-matched by Sydney's fury.

"*No!* We'll get him!" She jerked away and turned back toward the jungle.

"No," Willoughby said, tackling her to the ground this time. "I won't let you, Sydney. I counted nine snakes—five of them king cobras. *Nine snakes!*"

Antonio ducked around a tree trunk. "What has happened? Are you bit?"

Willoughby looked up, his face creased with concern and fatigue. He was breathing heavily. "Get her back to the facility," he cried, glancing down at the still fighting Sydney, then looking intently up into Antonio's eyes. "James Arthur and I will go back for, for uh, for Sun Wukong… He, he saved her life, appearing from nowhere, pouncing on the striking snake and grabbing it behind the head. It twisted, turning its attack mostly onto the monkey. The fangs—I don't know, it happened so fast—they may have grazed her. You've got to get her back to the Preserve."

"*No, I'm not leaving without him!*" Sydney screamed again as Antonio positioned himself so that Willoughby could roll off. Sydney still struggled, taxing even Antonio's strength.

"Sydney! Sydney! It is I, Antonio… Now, I want you to settle down! Willoughby and James Arthur will get the monkey. We are going back to the jeep. We will go back to the facility. You need medical attention, Sydney. You are not thinking clearly. Willoughby and James Arthur can finish up here."

Sydney made one last attempt to break free, then broke down into sobs. Antonio, still holding her tightly, pulled her to her feet. He put a long arm around her shoulders and began leading her toward the jeep. This time, she seemed resigned to going with him. She did not struggle but continued to sob. She seemed broken now—limp, like a rag doll. Antonio gave one quick look over his shoulder, and then they were gone.

Willoughby, who was still breathing heavily, looked over at Dr. J.

"Where's your shirt?" James Arthur asked.

"Long story," Willoughby said. He breathed in again. "So," he finally stated, "why do I get all the fun?"

James Arthur barked a short laugh. "Just lucky I guess." He reached down, offering Willoughby a hand up. "But what is it with you and snakes?"

It was Willoughby's turn to force a grin. He leaned his head back and looked up, letting drops of rain splash onto his face. "I was just told they are attracted to time holes. Whatever the reason, Sydney stumbled into a den of cobras—I counted nine."

"Cobras?" James Arthur groaned. "It figures." He took off his jacket and offered it, but Willoughby waved it away.

"We'll need that to carry the monkey in." Willoughby looked around. "What we also need are long, strong sticks. We want to make sure we stay well out of the way of anything that hisses."

"Or spits," James Arthur added.

"Or slithers."

"Or turns into a New Orleans beauty bent on toying with us."

This time, Willoughby's grin was weak, but legitimate. "You're still pining after her, aren't you? I don't think these cobras have anything to do with that being, James Arthur. We—you—released her. There is no longer a Desert Witch."

James Arthur gave a slight grin as well. "That you know of. I hope you're right, actually. I like thinking of her as unique, as one of a kind. You've got to admit, she was something, and you never saw her as a girl. Her image haunts me to this day."

The two began to scour the ground nearby. Willoughby carefully studied a group of thick vines toward the bottom of a low branch. "Hauti is nice. A little weird, but nice." He threw a glance over at his friend, knowing the comment may have seemed to come out of left field.

Dr. J didn't seem to notice. "Yeah," he agreed. "We certainly have no shortage of *weird* around us these days." He found the first stick. Then Willoughby found a sturdy, forked one. They began to slowly, cautiously move back into the jungle, picking up two longer sticks along the way.

"So, you going to tell me about it?" James Arthur finally blurted out. "You just disappeared. You were there one moment, and then, *poof*, you were gone. How'd you know where Sydney was? Did you create a, a—what do you call those things?"

"Junctions," Willoughby supplied, and James Arthur nodded.

"Yeah, junctions. Did you create one of those?

Willoughby hesitated a moment before answering. "No. That wasn't me. It was Beelzebub." He shook his head. "Look, let's just start from the beginning. The monkey—the one Sydney called Sun Wukong—must have been following her."

Dr. J gave a tentative nod, encouraging him to continue.

"He apparently escaped out of the habitat in order to follow her into the jungle. Why Sydney felt she needed to go into the jungle to practice I don't know, but she does that sort of thing sometimes. She seemed drawn toward a certain spot, and the snakes were drawn to the same spot. Beelzebub claims it was because there's a time hole there— or a series of small time holes around that area. He claims he was only watching her. When he saw she had stumbled into a cobra den and was about to be bitten, he froze time, allowing me to get there and try to save her."

Dr. J stopped. They had moved about twenty meters deeper into the jungle.

"Oh, he's a nice guy now? You're saying this 'demon lord' froze time so that you could get there and save Sydney?"

"No, he's not a nice guy. He didn't think I could save her," Willoughby corrected. The two moved forward, carefully prodding the ground and scanning the foliage in front of them. "He just wanted me to be there trying to save her when the junction collapsed. I think he wanted me to have to witness her death. It was his payback for our releasing the Desert Witch."

"But I had a part in that too. Why take it out on Sydney?"

"He knows how I feel about her," Willoughby said, "and I'm the one he's been trying to recruit."

"For what?"

Willoughby shook his head. "I don't know. He's definitely up to something—something big, something that could affect the whole world. It almost seems as if he's trying to create some kind of black hole, right here, right at the core of the earth. I think that's why he's so interested in finding the prime hole and controlling it."

"He wants to create a black hole and destroy the whole earth, including himself?" James Arthur said, seeming to find the idea incredible. "Is it just me, or does it also appear to you that this guy is stark-raving mad?"

Willoughby sighed. "I don't know what to think anymore. Yeah, by our standards, I'd say he's completely bonkers. He's very powerful, though, and he has a way of explaining things so that they appear, on the surface, to make sense. Anyway, let's get back to Sydney. She was frozen in the act of spinning away from one of the cobras.

This one was already striking, fangs bared. A second cobra was only a few inches further away, also baring its fangs and striking at her from behind. I was able to distract Beelzebub long enough to neutralize those two with my shirt and belt. But Beelzebub told me from the beginning that there was also a third striking cobra. I couldn't find it until the junction was collapsing. It was hidden under some vine leaves. It was striking straight at her shoulder. As time unfroze, everything happened so fast. The only thing I could think to do was jerk Sydney back. It wasn't enough. The cobra would have still gotten her had Sun Wukong not grabbed it at that very moment. He leaped from somewhere higher up, and his timing was perfect. He grabbed the huge snake, and that, coupled with my jerk, were enough to cause the bite to fall short."

James Arthur knew where this was going. "But Sun Wukong got the raw end of the deal."

Willoughby nodded solemnly. They were approaching the area now where the den was. He motioned for James Arthur to take extreme caution as they probed with their sticks. "These were huge cobras. I'm hoping they're not hanging around."

A motion to the left caused them both to freeze in their tracks. It was the huge cobra Willoughby had tied his belt around. It was still thrashing, trying to break free, and another snake was there, curling around its head as if trying to help pull the belt off. A few feet away lay Willoughby's shirt, discarded onto the jungle floor. Obviously, that snake had managed to wriggle free of the binding. Willoughby pointed to a lifeless lump of matted fur near the trunk of one of the large trees. Upon seeing the size of the cobras, Dr. J's eyes grew wide and his caution increased four-fold. Slowly, cautiously, they approached the still, small form on the jungle floor and carefully loaded him up in the jacket. They did not speak again until they were clear of the thicker jungle and had the gravel road in sight.

"You didn't know the monkey was there?" James Arthur finally repeated, breaking the silence.

Willoughby shook his head. "I don't even think Beelzebub knew. Sun Wukong was hidden from view."

James Arthur considered this.

"So, this guy freezes the scene to give you time to come watch your girl get bit by a cobra? Man, what's wrong with this dude?" He glanced over. "What else did he have to say—I mean, other than that cobras are attracted to time holes and he wants to create a black hole to destroy the world?"

Willoughby looked away. "He said plenty. But I'm tired, James Arthur. I just want to get out of here. I just want to get back to the facility." As he spoke, he noticed he was shivering. James Arthur took one look and nodded. The rain was still coming down as they reached the gravel road and started back toward the Preserve.

Antonio met them only a few hundred meters from the facility. They had just made the final turn, trudging into the facility's mud-sodden parking lot, when the jeep sloshed to a stop beside them. Antonio jumped out and helped load the stiff body of the monkey into the back-cargo bay.

"How is Sydney?" Willoughby asked, climbing into the front passenger seat. Antonio had brought a gray hoodie with the Preserve logo on the front. Willoughby slipped it on gratefully.

"She is not harmed physically, but emotionally..." Antonio began. "Well, what would you expect from such a trauma? She says she went into the jungle for some inspiration while she rehearsed. She started to play, and multiple cobras appeared. She became panicked trying to escape. They seemed to be all around her, and they were enormous. One was striking. She spun to try to dodge the bite, and then suddenly, you and Sun Wukong appeared out of nowhere to save her from the snakes."

"Well, I can certainly vouch for the size of the cobras," James Arthur added, leaning back in his seat and rubbing his neck.

Willoughby said nothing. He just pulled the hoodie tight and tried to stop shivering. The three rode in silence the rest of the trip. As they got out of the van, Antonio pointed at the entry to the Preserve.

"We can take care of the monkey, my friend. Go get dried off and warm, and get some food in your belly. We can talk later. I suppose you will tell all when you are ready."

Willoughby bit back a sudden rush of tears. He wouldn't break down. The adrenaline had faded, and he no longer felt the anger, the intensity that had helped him get Sydney out of the cobra den. Mentally, he felt the loss of the still creature in the back of the jeep who had given his life for his violinist friend, but emotionally, he just felt drained. He felt numb. And above all else, he felt very, very tired.

"Sam wants you to pack your things this afternoon," Antonio called after him as he limped toward the entrance door. "He wants you and Sydney out by tomorrow afternoon, as soon as we bury the monkey. Sydney wants to lay him to rest at the top of the crest on the north end of the habitat tomorrow at dawn. She says he loved it there. At least, I think that is what she said. She was crying quite a bit."

Willoughby turned around, his hand on the door. "So, we're just leaving? I thought you brought us here to show us something significant."

"Yes," Antonio said. His face became suddenly unreadable. "I think, my friend, that I shall ask James Arthur to stay with me on the yacht for a few days. There are, indeed, things I need to share. Sam will escort you, Hauti, and Sydney back to his apartments in London."

Willoughby thought for a moment. "No," he said. "I'm not running any more. If you've found something significant, I need to know what it is. I'll send Sam on without me."

Antonio and Dr. J were both silent for a moment, and then James Arthur spoke.

"You think you're up to telling Sydney that?"

Willoughby sighed, opening the entrance door to the facility. "Yeah, you're right, it was probably easier to face the snakes."

8

Good Customer

Tainken had trudged after the strange, oriental man through a series of narrow, mostly deserted alleyways, stopping at last in front of a small, brick and straw building that opened onto a stone porch. The porch was shaded by a fine-fabric awning, and as the spindly man ushered her inside, she determined from the trinkets and goods laid out that this was a small shop of some kind. The oriental man cried out with excitement when they came upon the building. He stood at least six feet tall once he lowered his pack and straightened. He swept his hand around, pointing out the shelves of odd trinkets on every side.

"This How's shop!" he said in his sing-song accent, clapping with delight. "You find much good bargains here! Much good, much useful for you!"

The journey to the shop had taken them through what appeared to be an empty alcove. After passing through a barely visible gap, the alcove had suddenly widened into a rectangular courtyard. The small shop and porch were set against the east wall of the courtyard. A variety of baskets were arranged with various odd utensils, bits of stone or rock, and types of dried herbs. Past the baskets, inside the dwelling, stone shelves were arranged haphazardly, and the walls of the room were lined with banks and banks of cubby drawers. Tainken tried to take in the merchandise on the shelves. It seemed like bric-a-brac from all different ages of times.

"You look, you like!" The man continued. He had soft blue eyes, white hair, and a long, white beard. She was fairly certain that his face carried features of Chinese descent, with dark, tanned lines and slightly narrow eyes. "I get big boss!" he exclaimed, and turned abruptly, heading toward a large side door. The door was high and rounded at the top. It was made of a dark, beautiful wood, carved with intricate brass-work reliefs that depicted what appeared to be a symbolic landscape. Stars were arranged in a geometric pattern above a jungle horizon. A being appeared to be stepping out from the trunk of the largest, most central tree. Its right palm was extended and rays of light shone out from its hand.

As How Loa disappeared through the door, it closed with a heavy thud, loud enough to startle T.K., who had looked away momentarily. It was almost as if the door were chastising her for being curious. Once her heart stopped pounding, she turned back to assess the shop's wares, roaming absently through the labyrinth of shelves.

Her mind was whirling. *Who was this How Loa?* He was not Atlantian, yet he was a time traveler, and he had not seemed surprised to crash into her. She had said little on the short journey here, but her odd host had chatted non-stop, telling her mostly about his '*business,*' which he seemed very proud of, and about this and that village custom.

The people of the village were highly religious, according to How. He spoke as if he were not one of them, but rather an outside observer—which made sense. He wasn't exactly like the others. He knew English, he had Asian features, which the other villagers she had seen did not. His skin was lighter. Could this whole village be some sort of melting pot for time travelers? She doubted it. How told her that most of villagers were at a festival honoring Sakarais, a god of rain and thunder, and the mythical being who controlled the monsoon cycle, bringing rain back to the fertile plains and villages along the Tapti River. That did not sound like futuristic time travelers.

All she had seen of the village so far seemed consistent with what she had learned of the ancient culture of India from her adopted father, who called himself simply, *the Captain*. Why was she thinking of her adopted father *now?* Something about this place brought out strange feelings, strange thoughts in her. When she and the Captain had first met, her years of living outside her own time and never seeming to age had become suddenly bearable. She had been attempting to track down the murderer of her real father, and her lack of success had been pushing her into a major depression. She had been very close to giving up when the Captain, a world traveler who piloted ships for Observations, Inc. (the secretive organization she had been seeking to learn more about) had taken a liking to her. He hired her as ship's cabin-girl so he could teach her of the sea. He had also taught her about ancient cultures— especially those that his employer seemed most interested in. He officially adopted her two years later so that the two could be discreetly near each other. It was his plan to pass all his accumulated knowledge and wealth to her someday as he had no children of his own. The thought of the Captain and what had befallen him on their last voyage together, on the ill-fated *Aperio Absconditus,* sent a pang of pain through her. She felt tears welling in her eyes. She tried to shake it off, concentrating on the shop goods. *Why was she so emotional all of a sudden?*

The trinkets and knick-knacks filling the shelves were bizarre. There seemed to be no rhyme or reason to the displays, each shelf, or pot, or basket littered with a collection of figurines, ancient artifacts, tools of various kinds, timepieces, herbs and food items, mixed with a variety of crystals and gemstones, polished wood knots and branches, mechanical and computerized devices she did not recognize, and what appeared to be musical items. Tainken picked up a hollowed gourd that had a half-dozen strings pulled tight over its opening. She reached down and plucked one of the strings, surprised by the deep, rich sound it produced.

"Not for you, not for you!" The tall man sang cheerfully, appearing from behind the end of one of the shelves.

T.K. looked up at the man, furrowing her eyes slightly, and then glancing back over her shoulder at the high door. *How did he get the door opened and closed so quietly this time?* He had also kept out of her sight-line, seeming to just appear at the end of the aisle. He would have had to pass around her to get to the end of the aisle. Had she been that distracted?

"You know you not musician," the man proffered with a wide, gregarious smile. "You appear to be somewhat lacking in tone identification. To use proverbial tongue, you not able to carry tune even with bucket."

T.K. peered at him as if wounded. It was true, she was not very musically inclined, *but how could he know that?* She put the gourd down and opened her mouth to speak, but he held up a hand. "Please, hurry, hurry! Big boss want to see you. This way, come, follow!"

The wiry man led her with a buoyant step toward the wooden door. It opened with a creak before he even touched it. He motioned her in. She hesitated on the threshold. The room inside the door was mostly dark, with no visible window or other outlet. It seemed to be lit by thousands of candles, arranged at different heights and in tiers such that each seemed to hover in its own space. In the center of the room was a rectangular table. Seated before it, cross legged on the floor, was a young girl. She wore a beautiful white robe with a large, silk crimson bow at the back, and a matching bow in her hair. The girl had a commanding demeanor. She motioned T.K. in, gracefully picking up a steaming kettle and beginning to pour a honey-gold liquid into two cups.

"Welcome, Tainken Keilhar," a soft, friendly voice proclaimed. The girl smiled. "Come, sit and enjoy the delight of Monkey-honey tea."

"*Big*-boss?" Tainken whispered to the tall man, who was still standing just outside the door.

He only smiled, motioning her forward. She stepped into the room.

The girl delicately picked up her cup and sipped. "Big, small—these are concepts of space and time. Their usefulness is limited by perspective. To an amoeba, a raindrop is vast indeed." Her every movement spoke of elegance and grace. "The tea, of course, is not made from the monkey, but rather, the sap of the Monkey Tree, mixed with wild honey. It is quite delicious."

T.K. moved slowly into the room. "Am I to understand that I am the amoeba here?"

The girl did not answer, but smiled, seemingly amused. Tainken did not hear the door close, but was suddenly aware that the light spilling in from behind her had vanished, as had the wiry man who called himself *How Loa*. As her eyes adjusted, she peered more carefully around her. What had seemed to be candles had now become stars—a vast array of hundreds, even thousands of points of light in a night sky. She was standing on the edge of a long, rectangular black slab that seemed to be floating free in space. Edging to the side, she looked down, seeing black space, dotted with even more stars below. "Where are we," she mumbled, easing back away from the edge.

"We are neither here, nor there," the girl finally said. "We are in a place where it is safe to speak—a place where none can hear us, or twist our words."

"Twist our words? Why would someone want to twist our words?"

The girl took another sip of tea, motioning once again for Tainken to sit. T.K. hesitated, even though she found the aroma of the Monkey-honey tea intoxicating.

"Existence is plagued by those who find pleasure in folding words like sheets of origami, twisting them to forge meanings of their own design. They would have words mean what they do not say, and say what they do not mean. The Dark Edge like nothing better than to twist words, to give their spin to any truth discovered."

"The *Dark Edge?* Is that term supposed to frighten me? I don't even know what it is."

"Not what, who. The Dark Edge were behind the hijack of the *Aperio Absconditus*. They killed your Captain. I have sensed your feelings there, Tainken. I am sorry for your loss. But we must discuss the Dark Edge. In a round-about way, they were responsible for putting the pieces together that ended with the death of H.S. and his disturbed brother. They actively seek your friends now and will not stop until they have what they want and all who oppose them are dead."

"Why? What is it that they want?"

"What indeed." The girl smiled, giving a slight bow and sipped again at her tea.

"Who are you?" Tainken asked. "I am guessing you are more than the little girl you appear to be."

"And I am guessing you are more than a cabin-girl you professed to be on the *Absconditus*, Tainken Keilhar." The girl said, reminding T.K. once again of the Captain and her time aboard the *Aperio Absconditus*. That is where she had first met Antonio, and Willoughby, and the rest of the Observations, Inc. team. "I say this not to cause you pain. I wish only to point out that we all have the potential to be more than we seem. The sooner we recognize this fact, the greater our ability to act upon our true destiny."

"True *destiny?* What do you know of my destiny?"

"Ah," the girl replied with a smile, "True destiny is a course that opens up to us when we know who we really are, when we no longer have to consult the gilded mirrors of social acceptance that compete for our attentions."

Tainken felt a sudden sense of calm flood through her.

The girl smiled again, giving a soft dip of her head. "Sit. Please, T.K."

Tainken moved closer and lowered to her knees. "How old are you?" she asked.

"How old are you, Tainken?" The girl countered. She paused a moment before continuing. "Age is relative. Did you know that there are stars that lived even before the universe?" She looked out over the night sky. "It is the story of the backside of time. When you begin to see existence as an infinite content, you stop, as a great man once observed, *trying to draw legs on the picture of a snake.*"

T.K. recognized the words. They were from the Japanese film director, Kirasawa. He used the analogy when a film critic tried to get him to post-analyze a scene from his work. It was an obscure reference that few would know. But she did. *How could this being have known she would?* She did not respond, but chose to stay silent. Despite the strangeness of the encounter, she found that she inexplicably trusted this being. She felt nothing but peace and good will from the young girl. She reached hesitantly down, picked up her porcelain cup and sipped at her tea. She was amazed at how delightful it tasted.

The girl looked at her, intensity in her deep, blue eyes. "You have come seeking, and you have found," she said, softly. "We will help you. We will help your friends. There is more that is happening than you know. More than you can know at this time. You are part of an intricate dance, Tainken Keilhar. I am a listener. Sometimes, with the right help, we are able to fine-tune the music."

"We?" Tainken asked. "Why does everything you say have to be so, *cryptic?*"

The girl gave a shy smile. "Space is cryptic. Time is cryptic. Life even more so. It rises on the edge of clashing forces. I am here to help those who seek balance on the blade of the knife." She beckoned at the stars. "It has ever been so." The girl was quiet for a long moment. She finished her tea and tilted her head to one side.

"You seek a way back to the one you love. I can help you. First, you must see why time has brought you here. Time has a logic. You pulse with its purpose. There is always much to know and much to do. The stakes in this game are high, yet you are no stranger to high stakes." She stood, beckoning Tainken up, and then took hold of her hand. "Come. There is a song inside you. It is wanting to be sung."

"I don't hear it," Tainken mumbled. The man, How Loa, had just reminded her of how incredibly un-musical she was, and now this girl was saying she had a song to sing.

The girl smiled, her eyes betraying nothing. Her skin was warm, and delicate, and smooth. She stepped toward the edge of the black slab, let go of T.K.'s hand, then, without even looking down, stepped off into space.

9

Gone Phishing

Willoughby tried to look away from James Arthur, who sat against the edge of the oily wreck of a fishing boat as it lapped gently with the waves. Dr. J was unsuccessfully trying to hide the wide smirk on his face. It was no good. No matter how hard his friend tried to look serious and concerned, a grin kept creeping through.

"Alright," Willoughby sighed. "Out with it."

James Arthur turned away in mock surprise. "I have no idea what you're talking about. In fact, I truly believe you should wear that black eye with pride. I'm sure you worked hard for it, and besides, it gives you that *bad-boy* vibe."

"It hasn't turned completely black—it's more purplish," Willoughby began, but James Arthur cut him off.

"Willoughby, that eye is black." Dr. J seemed to be enjoying himself. "It's black as an abandoned silver mine in Colorado—black as a barrel of crude oil from the heart of Texas."

Willoughby turned away. "Spare me the Wonderful World of Color. I'm not in the mood."

"So, this is a total shot in the dark, but I would guess that Miss Sydney is not very happy about going to London alone with Sam?"

Willoughby ignored the question. James Arthur's smile just broadened.

"Cat got your tongue? Let me guess; you don't want to talk about it. Now, I wonder why that would be? Could it be because someone tried to warn you, and you just said—let me see, what were the exact words? Oh, yeah, I remember, '*I got this.*' Those were the words." Dr. J let out a low hoot. "You said, 'Just leave it, James Arthur, *I got this.*' Then, I see you climbing aboard, and I'll be darned if you didn't get *this.*" He barked a short laugh. "You got this beautiful new eye tattoo!"

Willoughby tried not to let Dr. J see how annoyed he was. "Ha, ha… So, what would you have had me do? Let her hang around until another den of cobras popped up and killed her? Or maybe out here, it would be a sea serpent, or a killer whale."

"Uh, this is India. The water is a little warm for killer whales," James Arthur said good-naturedly. "My point is that there were alternatives. You see, you were the asker, Willoughby, and she was the ask-ee, and you did not properly follow her obvious protocols. Now, if you ever wish to make it to the end of this winding and wonderful road of *relationship* with the most mysterious of all creatures, a woman, you've got to take better care not to violate the highly sacred rules."

"*Highly sacred rules?* We're just—" Willoughby paused. He seemed to have trouble getting his mouth to close. "I, I don't even know what you're talking about."

James Arthur laughed again. "Uh huh. Well, I'll tell you anyway, my friend. You were in direct violation of rule number 5867.13, which explicitly states—"

"5867.13?"

Dr. J blinked. "Yeah."

Willoughby rolled his eyes. "You're trying to tell me there are five thousand, eight hundred, and sixty-seven rules dealing with relationships?"

"Uh, no. There are one hundred and seventy-eight thousand, four hundred and seventy-six rules covering the most mysterious of creatures. They are broken up, you see, into various sub-categories. Some deal with acceptable bathroom behavior, some deal with bodily functions, there is a whole category for humor, and of course, there are tens of thousands of rules dealing with the ins and outs of daily communication."

"Alright," Willoughby broke in. "So, what about rule 5867?"

James Arthur grinned. "Right. Rule 5867.13 says that, *the target male,*" he leaned forward conspiratorially, "that's you. You're the target male."

Willoughby gave him a deadpan stare, devoid of emotion.

Dr. J's grin again broadened. "O-okay then, so, the rule states that *the target male is not, at any time, to disregard the fiery protestations of a head-strong female who may be currently holding a weapon, like a bow.*" He raised his eyes in anticipation and whispered. "Like a bow, or a fist—I'm not entirely sure which did you in." He paused, as if expecting Willoughby to applaud.

Willoughby rolled his one good eye. "Of course she didn't hit me with the bow—that's a Stradivarius! It's expensive. Nope, this piece of work was all about her fist, and trust me, it's more solid than you would imagine!" He made a wild gesture with his own hands. "I save her life—mostly—and then she's hauling off and hitting me! Right in the middle of a casual conversation! I say, we're concerned about your safety, Sydney. We've decided it would be best for you to go with Sam back to London, and she just looks at me, her mouth hanging open, and without a word, knocks me to the ground"

"Yes, I see your problem."

Willoughby seemed a little taken back. "You do?"

"Yeah," Dr. J grinned. "You got whipped by a girl!" He busted into a new round of guffaws.

Willoughby had to fight from grinning himself. James Arthur's laugh was contagious. "Thanks," he managed, averting his eyes.

Dr. J quieted. "Seriously," he said, "timing is your issue. If you brought up London to Sydney on that very day that you saved her, your conversation may have gone in a completely different direction. But you didn't. You had your conversation with her on a *different* day. You see what I'm getting at? That life-saving thing? Over. Water under the bridge. The female mind is not one for respecting past credits. You got to be continually feeding the account."

Willoughby seemed exasperated. "It was today, James Arthur—I spoke to her *today!* I saved her life yesterday!"

"Yeah, but that was *yesterday*. Yesterday is completely different from today." He held out his hands like this was the easiest concept in the world to understand, then leaned back against the side of the boat.

Willoughby stared at him a moment. "Sudoku is a breeze compared to this stuff. Why does it have to be so complicated?"

James Arthur became suddenly somber. He patted Willoughby on the shoulder. "That *is* the question, my friend. The whole male gender feels your pain."

The two were alone in a medium-sized, decrepit-looking fishing boat. They had pushed a mile or so out from shore and then cut the engine. In the distance, they could still make out the jagged coastline of the Gulf of Cambay. Willoughby wrinkled his nose. "Too bad my nose wasn't affected. Then maybe I wouldn't have to smell this amazing vehicle Antonio found for us."

James Arthur laughed again. "Yep, good old Antonio Santanos Eldora Chavez… You can always count on him to strip away luxury. He's the epitome of mean and lean." Dr. J paused, leaning his elbows onto his knees. "He does have a point though. We had phishing attacks on the complex last week, and now this whole thing with Beelzebub and Sydney. It's best we not attract any attention to ourselves out here."

Willoughby looked over. "You think the two were related? Lots of organizations get hit with phishing attacks these days—it's part of this whole security challenge everyone is dealing with. So, you know, to the outside world, the Preserve is a champion of animal rights. I'd say that makes us more of a target."

"Well," James Arthur said, standing up, "be that as it may, we are supposed to be out fishing, and it may be important to our physical security to look the part, so unless you want to be explaining what you're doing out here in some broken Hindu dialect, I suggest you take my lead and start baiting a hook."

Willoughby leaned forward, rubbing at his swollen eye. "Boy," he mumbled, "that girl has a devastating right hook. And speaking of hooks, what *is* this stuff you're putting on them?" He was considering a white barrel full of questionable fish parts. James Arthur had busied himself stringing various bits onto hooks, then throwing the lines into the water and securing the poles.

Dr. J gave a low chuckle. "That, my boy, is bait. To be more precise, you are looking at pure guts—fish guts that is. Honey to the Dactyloptena Orientalisand, or flying Sunfish, among others. But, back to Sydney—you keep skillfully changing the subject—you know, you did tell her you didn't need her."

"*We* don't need her," Willoughby countered. "I told her the truth."

"Yeah, well, rule 2.19 says the truth isn't always the best course of action with a female."

"You wanted me to lie to her?"

James Arthur chose his words carefully. "N-no. I would just be very careful what information you share when."

"Well I did say we needed her more in London with Sam and Hauti."

"Yes, but the problem, bro, is that all she heard was that *you* didn't need her." James Arthur looked over, raising his eyebrows. "Any bells going off yet? She was only concerned about if *you* needed her. Once you stated you did not, the brain was on hold, and the fist was flying."

"Yeah. I got that part."

"Boy, did you get that part."

Willoughby had started to string a squiggly bit of intestine onto a barbed hook. "So, you're saying I could have worded it better?"

Dr. J smiled. "Uh, yeah."

"Okay, then, Mr. Lady's Man, how would you have said it?"

James Arthur thought for a moment, then knelt until he was right in Willoughby's face. His voice clicked into a high falsetto. "I, I don't know how I'll survive it, Sydney, but I'm afraid, just for a few days, we've got to part. Believe me, I'll count the moments until we're together again, but Antonio needs me, and Sam needs you. Promise me you'll call every night—and text every time you're lonely, or you're thinking of me—I'll do the same. I'll only be away a couple of days and then we'll be together again. Until then..." James Arthur moved his face in a little closer.

"Get away you crazy lunatic," Willoughby managed, a look of horror on his face. "And I don't have that high of a voice."

James Arthur laughed, standing back up. He walked over to the side of the boat and peered down into the water. "So, how long did he say to wait before suiting up?"

"Well, he told *you* to wait 30 minutes. He told *me* to stay up here and monitor the equipment because I'm not dive certified."

"Yeah, we've got to fix that. Come stay with me in Malibu and I'll have you surfing and diving in no time."

Willoughby thought about it a moment, and then smiled. "You know, that sounds fun. Much more fun than fighting cobras in the jungle or stringing fish guts onto a barbed hook."

"No kidding," Dr. J looked at his watch. "So, it has been about 28 minutes by my watch. I guess I'll start throwing on my gear." He walked over to a neat stack that included a wet suit, a tank, a dive belt, and flippers. As he sat and started to pull the wet suit on, he looked over at Willoughby. "So, why didn't you want Sydney here? Really. Cobras couldn't attack her out here on this boat, and I don't think you believe sea serpents would attack. Seems to me that you're her best defender against the dark shadow guys and a little alone time on a fishing boat, you know, it's alone time."

Willoughby looked around. "Yeah, fish guts, how romantic. Why didn't I think of that?"

James Arthur gave him a somewhat withering gaze.

Willoughby sighed. "Okay. You want the real story, here it is. Every time she's near me, there are incidents. Who's to say those incidents don't happen because of *me*. I don't want her in danger. I don't want her near that forest, or near a time-hole, or near *me* at all if I can help it. Not until I can figure this thing out."

James Arthur finished putting on the wetsuit, tank and fins. He stood up, pulling on his facemask and adjusting the breathing hose. He then pushed his facemask up and looked at Willoughby.

"Well, just remember one thing. You might have the greatest intentions in the world, but Sydney's life is her life. She has a right to decide if she wants to take the risk to be with you, even though it may be dangerous. All teasing aside, I think the hardest thing for you is to learn to trust her. Trust her instincts, trust her input. She's a smart girl, and she just may end up saving *your* life a few times if you let her." With that, he smiled, pulled down his mask, and started toward the back of the boat. He slung his feet over the side of the boat, balanced himself, and adjusted his gear.

Willoughby hadn't thought of it that way. He mused on the advice for a moment, and then looked over. "It's a good point." He looked around. "So... What am I supposed to do while I sit here, smelling this beautiful aroma? Other than the radio, there's not much equipment to monitor. You guys could have at least left me a laptop and wireless booster so I could run down those phishing attacks or something."

Dr. J looked over. "This is supposed to be a fishing boat—not a phishing boat. While you watch for unwanted guests, maybe you could look like you know a little bit about what you're supposed to be doing. We have sixteen poles out in various holds around the ship. Walk around to them. Check the line. Pull a line in occasionally and check to see if the bait is still good. Who knows, you might even catch something."

"Funny," Willoughby said. "We've been sitting here for almost an hour, and not a single pole has indicated even a nibble."

"That could change. When I jump in, it won't take long for the word to get around—hey, that's the boat James Arthur came from! The entire ocean will be lining up, just hoping to get caught."

"Or, they might see your face and start a mass migration to Jamaica."

James Arthur smiled. "Well, that too, so just in case, I'll keep on my mask." With that, he put his regulator in his mouth, bit down, and slid off into the water. With a wave of his hand and a flurry of bubbles, he was gone.

Willoughby rubbed at his sore eye again. He took a slow tour of the old fishing trawler, absently looking out toward sea. As he came to the last of the poles, all stuck into their ten-inch deep holder notch on the side of the boat, he saw the line suddenly go taught, and the tip of the pole bend until the pole was almost doubled over.

"Very funny James Arthur," he mumbled. But the line seemed to be zigzagging in wild circles, even rocking the boat slightly. "Hello," Willoughby started, but before he could get another word out, a second pole bent over and the line started dancing, and then a third. Willoughby had grabbed the first pole by now and could feel the fish fighting the line below. He grabbed the hand net, hung on the side of the wheelhouse, threw it down at his feet, and then ripped the pole from its mount, starting to reel the fish in. "Hey," he said again, to no one in particular, "this one is either pretty big or a real fighter!"

A fourth pole bowed as the line went taught, and the boat began to pull against its anchor.

10

Knife's Edge

Ten: *Knife's Edge*

Tainken hesitated only a moment before stepping off the slab after the young girl. For some reason, touching the girl's hand had flooded her with a complete sense of calm and trust. With that connection gone, some level doubt had begun to creep in. But she had never lived life on the safe side, so before she lost her nerve, she stepped off.

Immediately, she began to sink—not in an uncontrolled fall, but in a graceful float. She could see the white figure of the girl falling below her, their bodies rotating like two feathers caught in a whirlwind, twirling away toward some unseen floor. Despite the speed of the spin, T.K. did not get dizzy. Nor did she note the passage of time before their feet again touched upon something solid. The slab above them had disappeared. They had stopped spinning. The girl looked up and smiled. She reached out and took Tainken's hand again, leading her forward. With her free hand, she parted a curtain that had seemed to be part of the dark expanse and led T.K. into a cave-like passage. After a time, the passage opened onto a bright, marble porch. The porch was chiseled high into a granite cliff that peered out over a beautiful, blue lagoon.

"Am I dreaming? Or did you put something in that tea?" T.K. heard herself ask. A waterfall fell only feet away, drenching the left side of the porch and sending a fine mist of spray over the thick greenery and vines that covered much of the porch. A polished mahogany rail closed the porch off from the cliff edge. The marble floor was smooth and dark, fading at the edges into the black, volcanic rock of the cliff.

"It is my thinking porch," the girl explained, ignoring T.K.'s question.

The girl walked to the railing and Tainken followed. The two looked out over the deep blue of the ocean. They were about two-thirds of the way up a sheer cliff that must have been a quarter kilometer high. The lagoon far below widened into a horizon of open sea. The white sand beaches were uninhabited and pristine. The edges of the island hinted at jungle green, though a more heavily forested green than any jungle she had witnessed in Africa and South America. *Where were they?*

"Look into the mist. Tell me what you see," the girl said. She let go of Tainken's hand, stepped back from the rail, and sat.

T.K. stared. There had been no chairs visible a few minutes ago when they stepped across the porch to the rail. The chair had built itself from the vines bordering one of the edges of the porch. She had turned soon enough to see that vines had crossed the porch as if in expectation. When the girl turned to sit, an intricate weave of living vine blossomed up in a sudden explosion of growth, forming a unique chair that cushioned and embraced her. A sharp tang of honeysuckle mingled with the fresh scent of the sea breeze. Tainken stared in awe but the girl just smiled. Finally, T.K. turned away. She looked out over the railing.

The only mist was the slight spray from the waterfall. She saw a hint of rainbow in the water, but that was all. *What did the girl want?* She looked back, the question in her eyes.

The girl gestured to a point just to the right. A different vine had grown from the edge and begun to blossom into the base of a seat. The girl motioned for her to sit. Tainken walked to it and complied. The vines grew up, cushioning her arms, neck, and back. All pressure eased from her body. It was the most comfortable, relaxing chair she had ever sat in.

She glanced over at the girl. "How are you doing this? Is it magic?"

"Magic?" the girl said, a mischievous twinkle in her eyes. "I am life. Life is magic. It has always been. You are magic. If I were speaking with Willoughby, there could be a more technical explanation, but this one I give to you is correct as well." She turned to look out over the water, letting the sea breeze catch in her sand-blond hair.

Tainken stayed silent, watching. *Was this real? Was this girl some sort of deity?*

Again, reading her thoughts, the girl spoke. "Your ancestors came from a different planet, did they not, Tainken? They had knowledge others in this world did not. Did that make them deity? How much knowledge must you have to win that distinction? What if you are only from a different country? If you have a different religion, or speak with a different tongue, or follow a different creed? You could still have knowledge that others do not. *Life is life.* I am a being who belongs now to this planet. I am no deity, though I am not human in the same way you are human. You age slowly. I do not age at all. I choose my form now, having lived each life-stage to its conclusion. I am a watcher on the knife's edge. I am your friend. That is all you need know."

Tainken tried to smile. "I, I think I need a friend."

The girl smiled broader. "Yes. More than you know."

T.K. searched the girl's eyes for a long moment. She sensed no threat here, no deceit. "Do you have a name?" she asked. "You know me—you know my people. How is that? You seemed to have been expecting me. Why? How could you have known I would be here? What is it you want? You say you want to help me, but I need more. How can you help me?" She motioned at the arms of her chair. "Can you tell me more about what I'm experiencing? It goes beyond anything I know. Did you put something in that tea? Is this a vision?"

The girl raised an eyebrow. "A vision? Beauty is a vision. Time is a vision. Reality is a vision."

"I mean," Tainken clarified, "is it just in my mind, or is it real?"

"The mind can help us to see, but only the heart can clarify what is real."

"Or what is illusion," Tainken mumbled.

"Ah," the girl's smile broadened. "Illusion. What around us is not illusion? A wall seems solid, yet it is made of molecules, that are made of atoms, that are made of protons and electrons and a nucleus. There is more empty space in your solid wall than there is solid material, and what is solid material anyway? What is a nucleus made of? Each microcosm you conquer opens your understanding to new and smaller worlds of organized motion, does it not? *Illusion?* Yes. When you look only with the mind, your eyes are susceptible to illusion. But that is not how I live."

"You speak in circles—word as riddle."

"And you put too much stock in words. The statesman, Winston Churchill, once said, '*Men occasionally stumble over truth, but most pick themselves up and hurry off as if nothing ever happened.*'" She studied Tainken for a long moment. "You ask questions. I will attempt answers. What does it mean when I say *I am a watcher on a knife's edge?* Life exists in a balance between extremes of chaos and control. I am tasked with guarding the balance in such a way that life continues to flourish."

The girl pulled a long, thin object from a pocket that seemed to just materialize in her white robe. She held the item up for Tainken to see. It was a long, smooth stick. Attached to the top of the stick was a carved head. As the girl held the stick between her palms and began to roll it slowly one way, then the other, T.K. saw that the head's features were only completed on one side. The other side was vague and unfinished. As the stick twisted in her hand, it showed first the right side of the head, fully completed, and then the left, vague and undone. As the girl began to spin it faster and faster, the two segments of the face seemed to merge.

"At your stage, you can possibly grasp matter unorganized, the birth of light, even that there is a process to creation, a blueprint to the multi-verse, but there are things you find it hard to grasp. The timeless void—an infinity of nothingness where existence must find a way to exist. Infinity and nothingness are concepts you think you understand, but you do not."

The girl's hands moved faster and faster. The completed head seemed solid. "The key, Tainken, to taming infinity is motion. A void of nothing is *something*— infinity in motion becomes tangible. It can be defined by its direction, its speed, the depth and breadth of its movement." The head was moving back and forth so quickly now that it seemed to take on its own momentum.

"Motion creates energy. Energy increases speed. Speed creates an illusion of form. Mining energy from the very hollowness of infinity allows finite matter to appear. Building blocks of organized motion are shaped into pattern, combined into element, structured to register force, and begin to exist in a sphere of function."

The girl parted her hands. The stick seemed to fly out of them, coming alive. The long, smooth stem of the stick seemed to become fluid, and then formed itself into body as the head shrunk down to better proportion. Finally, a little man twisted around to glare at them. It quickly scurried away, out of view.

"Enter Chaos and control," the girl said with a twinkle in her eye. She swiftly pulled a thin dagger from her sleeve. It was about the size of a typical letter opener, but had an intricate jade handle, inlaid with topaz, blood-ruby jewels, and highlights of gold. The thin blade had writing on it in a language Tainken didn't recognize, though it appeared oriental in origin. The girl held up the dagger for T.K. to study.

"Control can thwart spontaneity, inhibiting creativity and growth. It slows motion. Chaos thwarts control, allowing potential to run amuck in an unstructured burst. It speeds motion to a point of collapse. Life exists along a thin balance in-between."

While she spoke, the girl pulled a forked vine up from the arm of her chair. She split the vine with the edge of the knife. The left side almost immediately went wild, writhing and curling like a snake while pushing out such a burst of bud and leaf that it eventually imploded upon itself, withering at last to a knot of black char that looked like a mini black hole. On the other side, the vine grew at a steady clip, but unseen sheers seemed to continually nip each new bud, until, at length, the growth of the vine slowed and the vine died altogether, ending up looking much the same as the other. The girl slipped the dagger back into her sleeve and the remaining vine pulled back into her chair. She looked up.

"I find it interesting that your sciences have long noted the dangers of chaos. When Einstein was informed of Georges Lemaitre's work in support of his theory of relativity—math that showed the universe could not be static, but that the fabric of space was either expanding or contracting—he dismissed the work, sure that the universe was eternal and unchanging. He could never accept the existence of black holes either, even though his own equations predicted them. Nature, he felt, would not allow such chaos.

"But it does, Tainken. Chaos wields enormous raw power, enough to attract all manner of beings seeking to increase their level of control. Paradoxical, isn't it? That someone should use chaos to increase control, but they do. So, you see, nothing in our world, nothing in the fabric of our existence, is ever fully at rest. Life exists on a knife's edge, riding a balance that is always being threatened."

Tainken watched the girl long after she stopped speaking. Finally, she gave her head a slight shake. "I'm not sure I get what you're saying. It's interesting philosophy, but what does it have to do with me? This didn't answer my question. How do you know who I am, about my people—how did you know how to find me? What do you want?"

The girl gave a sad smile and then looked ahead, toward the horizon. She stood, gracefully, as if the vines were pushing her up. The vines sank back down as she stepped forward and leaned on the rail. "There are answers, and then, there are *answers*. When a strange answer rings true, perhaps what is needed is to look closer at the question." She turned. "I am a watcher, Tainken. I monitor the balance. If the balance is lost, a great toll is taken, one that reaches beyond your people, your planet, even your system. Elements on both sides of the knife roil and vie. The case for life reaches toward a precarious point. This world that you have become a part of stands very near the tipping point, and you have means to help me still the storm."

"*Me?* How?" Tainken stood, feeling the vines push her gently as she rose. She walked to the rail, not looking back.

The girl followed her every move. "I see only what I must see." She looked out over the water once again. "Willoughby may tell you the world is full of probabilities. For him, calculations and predictions give a sense of clarity. That is not my domain. I operate beyond the logic of the reasoning mind. Only when the full scope of a question is understood can the mind grasp the true answer. Short of truth, one has only optimism. I am fond of a little poem that goes like this: *The optimist fell ten stories, and at each window bar, he shouted to the folks inside, 'Doing all right so far!'*

"Truth is a warmth, Tainken; a comfort. It cannot be discovered in a cold, mirror-maze of logic. It is an infinite spark, a river of fire recognized only in the silent spaces of the soul. One does not need to tell you what you already know. You have been moving toward this moment all your life. What you are destined to do, how you are destined to help, lies inside you already. When you learn to listen, it will speak."

Tainken was riveted. There *had* been times in her life when everything seemed scripted, when she knew what would happen before it happened, and she muddled through like a second-rate actor following the course of a play. She turned away from the girl, looking down at the lagoon.

"Some people," the girl continued in a soft voice, "think that their lives are controlled by what occurs on the outside of their skin, that we, like potter's clay, are molded from the outside in. That is only a small part of the truth. True power—call it magic, call it what you like—works from the inside out. Without this power, form is merely clever automation. The *'you'* the world at large judges is merely a reflection, the amalgamation of deeper, more pertinent truths. The true you cannot be seen fully by the eye. It is only known to the heart. As the inchworm must draw in to stretch out, you, too, must reach within to find the power of what you can become."

The girl grew quiet.

Tainken, too, was silent. Her lips trembled and her limbs felt suddenly weak. Out over the water, a wisp of fog had begun to gather. She thought of the girl's words earlier. *"Look into the mist..."* She stared into it, straining her eyes. In a blink, she thought she saw a shadow, a girl— *was it her?* There it was again. The girl was falling. She often had dreamed this scene, a girl, falling from a cliff, or a high wall. She thought the dream had been about Atlantis, about her being there when it sunk into the sea. But something was different this time. She saw the girl more clearly. The girl had dark hair. There was something in her hands...What was it? She looked closer. *A violin? A bow?* Something told her they had always been there in her dreams. *Why hadn't she noticed them before?*

Sudden realization dawned. *The girl from the Absconditus, the violinist—Sydney!* Why was she falling? Was this the future? Could it be changed? She felt a sudden surge of purpose. She had to get back to Antonio and tell him. He would know what to do. It was time to put H.S.'s horrid death, and the murder of her father, and the loss of her adopted father, and her many years of loneliness and searching—to put those behind her. It was time to grab what normal life she could and live a life of meaning. *But why this image in the mists? What did it mean?* What was she supposed to do? Somehow, this event threatened her, threatened everything. She knew this. She felt a hot flash of anger. *Why was this happening to her— why this sudden connection with Sydney, a girl she frankly loathed?* It didn't make much sense. None of this made sense. So, Sydney was falling—or would fall—but how far, and to what, and why did it matter to her?

"We are all connected," the girl said softly. "What affects one, affects us all."

Tainken turned to speak, but the words froze on her tongue.

"You know," the girl said, a smile breaking across her face. The smile was both spontaneous and genuine. She gave a graceful bow and gestured with purpose back toward the passage leading away from the porch. It seemed suddenly less cold, less forbidding, and less dark.

11

Sea Cave

As James Arthur dove slowly, he found himself having to maneuver through a large school of mackerel. The sleek, silver fish had appeared suddenly out of the dark blue, swirling around him like an undulating cloud. They changed direction in hairpin jerks, engulfing him, and causing him to lose sight of the lighter, bluer water above, which left him feeling somewhat disoriented. Luckily, he had a GPS tracker trained on Antonio. He continued to descend slowly, eventually freeing himself from the living fish cloud as he acclimated to the changing pressure of the lower sea depths. He had tested his ear-bud radio piece, trying to connect with Willoughby, who was busy whooping and hollering about something.

"Whoa! Calm down there, partner! What's the excitement?"

Willoughby sounded like he was wrestling a bear. "There are three—no, five! They're just hitting and hitting, I can't reel 'em in fast enough!"

"Who's hitting? What are you talking about Willoughby?"

"Man, the whole surface of the water is churning—this is epic, *epic*, James Arthur! It's like that, that TV show, uh, what's it called—*Deadliest Catch?*"

"*Deadliest* catch? I'm coming back up there."

"No! No, I can handle it. You see what Antonio needs. I'm telling you, though, when you guys get back, it's going to be like a sight you won't believe. *Ah! Crap...*"

"Carp?"

"No! *Crap!* Listen—can't talk! Bye."

The radio piece went dead. "Willoughby?" James Arthur realized he was shouting into his face mask. A few stray mackerel bulleted away. "Willoughby? Willoughby! Answer me, you, you crazy...*integer!*"

Willoughby's voice came back calm this time. "Did you just call me an integer?"

James Arthur groaned. "Yes! And if you don't tell me what's going on, you'll be even more fractional!"

Willoughby's laughter was short, punctuated by a grunt and then a yell. "Pretty impressive...mathematical...language coming from a surfer—*Wait!* Oh, no, you don't—where do you think you're going?"

"I'm not going anywhere. I'm floating, stock still in the water, waiting for you to tell me what's going on!" James Arthur yelled into his face mask again.

"Ah, shoot! There's another one. Look at that thing flop!" Willoughby gave a short chuckle. "Well, sorry about the boat, but...*Ah!* Really, James Arthur, I've got to let you go. Cheers—"

For a second time, the ear bud went dead. James Arthur hovered, stationary in the water, trying to decide what to do. Finally, he switched his com-link to contact Antonio. Antonio's voice crackled over the static.

"Where are you?"

"On the way down, but I just had a strange conversation with Willoughby. He said something about the water churning and trying to reel in the deadliest catch."

Antonio was silent.

James Arthur continued. "I offered to go back up there, but he said no, he had things under control. Then, he cut me off. What do you think?"

Again, there was a long silence from Antonio. "I think you need to keep coming, my friend. Of all of us, Willoughby is probably most capable of taking care of himself."

James Arthur pivoted in the water and began to descend again. "I'm not so sure about that. After all, he is still a teen."

"Yes," Antonio admitted, "but a very unusual one. You need to see what I must show you. What depth are you? Can you see the ruins yet?"

James Arthur squinted at the darker blue around him. He was beginning to see something below him. At first, it was only swaying beds of kelp and clumps of seaweed. Then, he saw bits of stone and pieces of structure emerging from the deep greenish-blue ahead.

"I think I'm just getting to them. Where are you?" The ruins, for the most part, lay hidden beneath silt, peppered among beds of kelp and seaweed. As James Arthur reached them, a dingy, shadowed world opened to him. Broken bits of stone and towering bits of structure loomed out of the dim waters like ghosts from the night. Dr. J kicked his fins faster. It seemed to him that the ruins went on for hundreds of feet in all directions, though he couldn't tell for sure. The water was too dim and murky. Antonio's voice came through much clearer this time.

"I am waving a flare in front of an almost intact tower. You should be able to see me as you zero in on my GPS. Can you see me yet?"

James Arthur peered at the structures around him, continuing forward, fully leveled out now. "Not yet. Nothing—" he stopped mid-sentence, catching sight of a bright pinpoint of light ahead. "Wait, I think I see you." He swam toward the wavering light. As he got closer, a tall structure came into view, larger than any he had previously seen. "This is incredible!" he sang over the radio. "It's huge, and so well preserved. What is it?"

"I am not sure. Perhaps a prayer tower of some kind. Just wait," Antonio said. "There is much to see."

Making his way to the base of the taller structure, James Arthur could make out steps leading to some sort of entry way. Antonio motioned for him to follow, seeming impatient. He led them around to the back of the tower. Other ghost-like structures emerged from the dim, greenish, blue. Here at the heart of the ruins, many structures were still standing, some several stories in height and narrow, some wider and flat with massive columns. While a handful of columns were still standing, many had collapsed onto the sea floor. Fish and other sea creatures darted among the shadows and skittered across the silt between clumps of seaweed and kelp.

Antonio led them to a narrow alley that began a couple hundred feet from the tower structure. The alley wound through a maze of half buried walls, angled steps, and the remains of low ceiling structures.

James Arthur stopped several times to spin full circle, trying to get a sense of the place. "These are incredible!"

He called out. He pulled his watertight camera from a pouch on his belt and snapped pictures as they trailed deeper into the ruins. He was particularly fascinated by an enormous stone head, severed from its body and lying face up in a courtyard-like opening before a taller wall or building side.

"May I remind you, my friend," Antonio's voice sounded over the radio, "this is not a tourist expedition."

James Arthur nodded that he understood, and put the camera away. He continued to follow as Antonio led them down the length of the high wall, ducking around a corner, and then diving to swim through a wide slit near the bottom of the wall. Dr. J followed into a large, dark chamber. He switched on his underwater torch, keeping Antonio's flippers in his beam.

"So, what do you think this one is? It's huge." he said.

"A temple, I think. What I wish to show you is coming up."

Antonio followed the interior wall to a narrow, almost hidden passage in one corner behind a row of crumbling columns. He trained his light on an area of stone where the thin sheen of sea scum and silt that covered all surfaces down here had been wiped away. Chiseled into the stone was a series of cuneiform-type characters. The characters hadn't seemed to age at all. They seemed to have been reinforced by some sort of silver paint or metal.

"See how well the writing is preserved," Antonio pointed out.

"Yeah," James Arthur mumbled. "What does it say?"

"It says, 'Do Not Enter.'"

James Arthur glanced over, catching the strained look on Antonio's face through his mask. "How do you know?"

Antonio looked directly into his eyes. "These characters…They are Atlantian. T.K. taught me some, or most—I am not sure—of her people's alphabet. She was trying to help me understand the writing on her necklace."

Dr. J whistled into his mask. "You think this is Atlantis?"

"No," Antonio said abruptly. "There would be more evidence of technology. But I do think T.K. was here, and I think she tried to leave us a message. You have not seen the amazing part yet, my friend." He slipped into the passage and motioned James Arthur to follow.

The passage went straight for perhaps fifty feet and then angled sharply right. It passed through what appeared to be a fake wall of some kind, crumbled now around a large crack. They continued through the crack for about thirty feet, and then the passage angled sharply right again through another fake wall, this one completely closed, but with a hole in one corner where the brick work had eroded. The hole was just large enough to swim through. The stone façade of the fake walls was much thinner than the stone of the real ones, though you would never know that from the front.

"It's like we're heading into a labyrinth, a square spiral," James Arthur noted, his breathing becoming heavy, "along a secret passage of some kind. You do know I *hate* cramped spaces, right?"

"Just a little further," Antonio mumbled, his own breathing becoming a little labored.

Dr. J noticed a dull shine coming off the walls of the passage as it turned suddenly up, with metal handholds in the stone. The metal was not corroded, even though it was underwater. He reached his hand out and brushed one wall as he pulled himself up. It was smooth—not like the coarse feel of the other stone in the ruins. "Hey," he started, but just then, the passage abruptly narrowed. He pointed his light beam up, but could no longer see Antonio's flippers. He continued up, starting to call for Antonio just as his head bobbed up out of water. Antonio had pulled himself onto a dry, stone shelf that extended around the narrow entry tunnel in all directions. A strange glow surrounded them. It was not exactly a light source—more like the walls themselves were phosphorescent.

"Wow!" James Arthur marveled. Antonio had already taken his mask off, so he did the same. "The air is breathable?"

"Yes," Antonio said. "It is a small room, so probably no more than thirty or forty minutes for the two of us, but we shall not be here that long, my friend."

Dr. J spun around. "This thing is completely underwater. How in the world could it still be water-tight in here?" The room was maybe fifteen foot by twelve foot with a vaulted ceiling maybe nine feet high at its apex. "You really think we're breathing 8000-year-old air?"

"I don't know," Antonio said. "The air does not seem stale. Maybe there is some technology here to pull air from the sea water."

James Arthur shook his head in wonder. Three of the walls had long, silver sheets of varying sizes in the center of them. The sheets were covered with writing. Some of it looked like the characters Antonio had pointed to outside the passage. Some did not. Small plates adorned the walls to either side of them, and a much larger plate with pictograms on it was directly in front. Behind them, directly across from the wall with the large plate, was a wall with a single word carved and a lever of some kind below it.

"H-h-how is this even possible?" James Arthur began. "How could they have known the city would be submerged and planned for this? Why was this room so important to preserve?"

Antonio was staring at the plates. "I don't know, James Arthur. We both know that the Atlantian people were time travelers."

"Yeah, but we've never uncovered anything like this before. Why only here? Why only this?"

Antonio shook his head. "I asked myself the same questions. Then I began to study the plates and try to interpret the writing. I do not think this was done with the knowledge of the Council of Atlantis. I think this was a private message from one Atlantian who knew how long the message would have to survive to reach its intended audience."

"You think T.K. did this." Dr J took another slow turn to scan the room. He saw nothing else of note. "Could this be a—what does Willoughby call them—a time junction? We should get him down here. See if it's a time hole. See if he sees numbers…"

"No," Antonio said emphatically. "There is good reason why I did not invite Willoughby down here. I used the excuse that he was not dive-certified, but that was not the only reason."

"Okay," James Arthur said, glancing again at the glowing walls and shining plates. "But Willoughby is just as committed to finding T.K. as any of us. Why do you not want him involved?"

"I want very much to involve Willoughby in the search for Tainken. That is why I invited him here in the first place," Antonio said, turning to him. "But you have not read the plates."

James Arthur narrowed his eyes. He turned back and began to study the plates more closely. "Some of the characters look like the ones you showed us back at the Preserve—the ones that were an ancient form of Hindi or something. Others look like the ones you showed me at the entry to the passage. I think you said they were *Atlantian*."

"You are correct," Antonio said. "I believe the attempt was to create a code only I would be able to decipher. Then, if someone else happened upon the room, they would not understand what it said. By combining words from her own language with those, perhaps, of the people who lived in this city, this would just appear to be a strange aberration to archeologists. They may be able to decipher the city text, but that would give them only a limited view of what the plates say. The only readable sentence is the one I shared with the group in our meeting back at the Preserve. If you recall, it was an obvious reference to my cover as a neighborhood barber. You see that sentence here."

Antonio pointed to a sentence located in the dead center of the largest plate. It was artfully set apart from text above it and below it.

"All the other text seems to be a jumbled mix of random words and dots. To the Cult of the mark, or Brotherhood, or whatever they call themselves, the plates appear as nothing but gibberish. But I have been able to find the meaning. It is a brilliant code. The sentence about finding someone to cut hair is really a key to unlock the meaning of the full plates. You may note that the words of that sentence are repeated in different order, with dots beside them, and a word in Atlantian after. The dots indicate the first sentence, the second sentence. The words themselves designate the order in which to assemble the Atlantian words in each of the respective sentences. You do not get the full message unless you unlock the code *and* can read Atlantian, which, it just so happens, I do. As I mentioned, T.K. taught me much of the Atlantian alphabet during our long days in the cave. We had little else to do to pass the time. Now, we are separated, and she knows I will be searching things of antiquity for some clue as to where the time hole took her. It is a perfect clue; would you not agree?"

James Arthur cocked his head, confused. "Well, that means we found her! So, why don't you just share her message and let's go get her?" His tone held a note of irritation. "Why all the cloak and dagger? Why can't Willoughby come down here? What is it those plates say?"

Antonio took a long moment to answer. "They say," he said, moving slowly toward the larger plate; "at least, as near as I can decipher, *'Dark edge rising. The boy of numbers is key. Storm is coming. You will be needed where you are. You must not come. I will find you.'*"

James Arthur considered the words. He pulled himself up out of the water and moved over to the side of Antonio. "What are these?" he said, pointing to three pictograms. "This one looks like a bow and a violin."

"That it does," Antonio agreed. He pointed to the first pictogram, which did, indeed, look like the outline of a violin, and then let his finger drop to neat rows of lined characters beneath the picture. "These symbols below— together, they are a sentence in Atlantian."

"Saying what? This one looks like someone falling off a cliff."

"Yes," Antonio said, his voice was distant. "The first three words here read, *'Music marks in.'*" He paused swallowing hard. "The words then continue," he said, his finger pointing to the characters beneath the second pictogram. "Here, they say, '*mirrored time the,*' and under the third pictogram, a single word: '*fall.*'"

James Arthur shot him a shocked glare.

"*Music marks in mirrored time the fall?* What does that even mean?"

Antonio shook his head. His eyes narrowed as his finger slid toward the last pictogram.

"I am afraid it is nothing good, my friend…"

12

Hyde Park

"Okay," Sydney sucked in a breath of crisp air, "I shouldn't have hit him." She and Sam were walking slowly over a narrow bridge. While she ran a gloved hand along the top of the rail, he stood ram-rod straight, marching stoically, hands clasped behind his back. He chose not to respond to the comment. Sydney sighed and continued.

"It's just, he can be *so* exasperating." She put a hearty emphasis on the word '*so*.' "I didn't mean to hit him in the eye. I was just...knocking on his head, you know? '*Hello? Anyone in there?*' He kept saying that I was *needed* here. Yeah, I feel real needed! Like you *need* to have someone take walks with you."

"Well, I do," Sam threw in, sounding suddenly cheery. Sydney ignored him.

"He said maybe it was better that I wasn't around him for a while—that it might be less dangerous. Doesn't he get that I don't *care* about the danger? It's going to come when it comes, and I, I feel safer *around* him, you know? I *like* being around him. I want to be around him. Somehow, he doesn't get that."

Sydney was wearing a knit, Waterfall cardigan, with a herringbone hem, white blouse, Stella Skinny stretch jeans, and a pair of black Judgment boots. She glanced over at Sam, her bracelets tinkling. Her Linda Farrow sunglasses—a necessity to keep her from being recognized by fans—shaded, but did not hide her dark eyes. A wisp of breeze caught in her hair, bringing with it a brisk chill even though it was early spring. She stopped and confronted Sam.

"What is it with boys? They start out great and then just get...annoying. He treats me like a China doll, like he's afraid I'll break—and after what we've been through together. *Why?*"

Sam merely raised an eyebrow, apparently confident that Sydney would continue whether he spoke or not, which she did within thirty seconds.

"I'll tell you why," she said, leaning in and pointing with her index finger. "He's afraid. All boys are cowards. They're afraid of getting too close, of caring about something or someone. It makes them vulnerable. They won't admit it, but it comes down to they don't want to get hurt. He said the guys don't want me there. They don't want me there because *Willoughby* doesn't want me there. What does he mean, you need my help, Sam? You don't seem to ever need anyone's help. You're, you're like that white-haired guy from the old *Mission Impossible* series. You're always on the fringes, behind the scenes, running the strategy. You're *not* in the line of fire where you need help." She looked over at Sam, whose expression had not changed. "I mean, don't get me wrong, you're a fantastic person, and I enjoy spending time with you. You've been the one that's there for me since H.S. was killed. But, I don't know. Right now, I think I should be with Willoughby." She did not take her gaze off him. "I hope that makes sense. I probably haven't seemed very thankful for all you've done for me, for us. I do appreciate it. You're a true friend. You, you—"

"I won't ever be Willoughby," Sam said with a wry smile. He had started walking again, hands still behind his back.

"Yeah," Sydney said with a sigh. She had come to respect and value Sam's quiet wisdom. She no longer saw him as just a chauffeur or yacht captain. Beyond H.S., she had invited few into her confidence. Sam held onto his smile. He seemed completely calm and undisturbed. *She* felt like a pit of churning lava inside. What was his secret? How did he always seem to be calm and collected and one step ahead of everyone else? *What did he know that she did not?* She gave a short shake of her head, sucked in a deep breath of air, and caught up to him by the end of the bridge.

"Okay, I get it—I'm just being a silly girl. Is that it? Is this funny to you? Why do you just keep walking away? Are you even listening? Are you going to really *speak* with me at all today, or am I just having a conversation with Lord Kensington's ghost?"

"We are in Lord Kensington's garden," Sam said, his smile widening, "not his tomb. You need to stroll. You need to smile. You need to act as if you know this is a beautiful garden and we are having a beautiful day. I have been listening. We are all silly in our own unique ways."

"I'm not having a beautiful day," Sydney said, sulkily. "Why should I pretend to be?"

"Because," Sam said, removing a hand from behind his back so he could pat her gently on the arm, "I believe, Sydney, that we are being followed. No—do not look around. We will stroll leisurely to a bench overlooking the Ferris wheel. Then, we will sit, and if someone is still following, we will take appropriate measures. Maybe Willoughby wasn't so foolish for being concerned."

Sydney furrowed her eyes behind her sunglasses, but visibly, she merely gave a curt nod, linking on to Sam's arm.

They walked, and for the first time, she truly looked at the gardens around her. "I've always loved Kensington Gardens," she said conversationally. She forced her lips into a thin smile. The trees were just breaking into bud and a few early blooming flowers were peppering color across the greens and grays to either side of the wide path. Once they reached the bench, Sydney gave a hurried scan around them. "Do you still see them?" she whispered, leaning in close.

Sam's smile warmed. He patted her hand and motioned toward the bench. "Actually," he said as they sat, "I do not, but I still suggest caution."

Sydney placed her hands in her lap, sitting tentatively beside him, her knees angling sharply toward his long, thin frame.

"Why would someone be following us?"

"We seem to have enemies, Miss Sydney, who do not bat an eye at killing anything or anyone they deem to be in their way. I am not so sure of your assertion that I am not in the line of fire, as you so eloquently put it. I am more inclined to believe that we are all '*in the line of fire*' until we can determine what this group really wants." Sam spoke slowly, his eyes darting back and forth. "As I suggested, perhaps Willoughby was not so far off the mark. While he is not always right, it may be equally true that he is not always wrong, and perhaps, on rare occasions, *you* are the one who is not seeing things clearly."

Sydney looked hard at him for a moment and then slumped into a sigh. "Alright, I guess I deserved that." She pushed back solidly against the cold wood of the bench. "Maybe I'm just too difficult to live with. With my fame, my sharp wit, my—"

"Your humility," Sam added, his eyes twinkling slightly.

"Yeah," Sydney gave a short chuckle, "that too. I do great as an icon, an image, but then I'm supposed to suddenly be a real person. That's when it gets hard. You can't fake that."

"Perhaps that is your problem, Miss Sydney. You try to fake things. I believe you are a fine person as is, Sydney. No person is perfect, though, and you have to come to terms with that."

"I may be a decent person, but I'm not girlfriend material, am I? Not for someone who's the real deal like Willoughby." She looked away, trying to hide her slight sniffle.

"I would not jump to conclusions, Miss Sydney." Sam's voice was warm. "I know for a fact that a certain young man spends a considerable amount of his waking thoughts on what you are thinking, particularly what you think about him. Back in my day, I think they called it a *crush,* though I find the term woefully inadequate in many cases."

"Yeah," Sydney barked a laugh. "They used that word a long time ago, Sam. I think it was back in the 1800s, right?"

Sam tried to hold a stern glance. "Yes, I suppose it was the Stone Ages. I hate to break this to you Miss Sydney, but there will come a day when you, too, join the ranks of *ancient history.*"

"Not me," Sydney said with a tight smile. "I'll never grow old. No matter how many years pass me by, I'm going to stay young, Sam. I've made up my mind." She spoke as if trying to convince herself.

"So let it be written, so let it be done," Sam said. "The lady declares it is to be war on entropy."

Sydney gave a conspiratorial smile. "To the death!"

Sam winked. "What a delicious dichotomy."

They sat for a long moment in silence. Finally, Sydney turned her head slightly, glancing. "Don't take this the wrong way, Sam—you're my friend. I can talk to you. You listen, and I value your thoughts. But somehow, I can't get past this feeling that I need to stay near Willoughby. It's like our stars are hitched together—like we are meant to be together, and I'm terrified that something will happen that, that destroys everything, that makes this impossible. So, I want to be with him now, before, before...I can't. I guess what I'm saying is that I miss him."

Sam seemed to be lost in his own thoughts. "All is not always as it seems," he started. "Some fears never materialize. Some do, but if you see past the moment of the fear, you find the *rest* of the story, and the rest of the story makes that fear inconsequential. Perhaps—" Before he could complete his sentence, a loud crack split the morning air. An unseen force jerked Sam, throwing him against the back of the bench.

"Sam?" Sydney saw pain on the man's face. He was gripping his chest. "Sam!" she screamed, leaning over him. His eyes shot up, his voice pained and barely audible.

"*Sydney, run...!*"

13

Holy Mackerel!

James Arthur stared at the pictograms on the larger plate. He looked over at Antonio. "Are you thinking Sydney?"

"Yes. Who else could it mean?"

Dr. J thought a moment longer. "But, this was carved—what, 8000 years ago, maybe even 9000 years if the carbon-dating can be believed. How could anyone back then know things we don't even know today? T.K. certainly didn't say anything to us before, even after spending all those days in the cave with you. In fact, I got the distinct feeling that she didn't particularly care for Sydney. Why this sudden concern and warning if this is a message from T.K.? I don't care if she is someone from Atlantis, that doesn't mean she suddenly has the ability to tell the future, does it? H.S. was from Atlantis, and he sure couldn't tell the future. If he could, he might still be alive."

Antonio considered the words. "All that is true. T.K. was not fond of our violinist, but think of the context of the whole message. She saw something, or she knows something—never mind how she knows it. The point is, she is trying to warn us. You are right that H.S. could not travel time to the future confidently, only the past, but sometimes, time holes lead to the future, as was the case with the one in the Jurassic Era cave. Maybe T.K. found such a time hole. I do not see how we can just dismiss this message out of hand."

"Why wouldn't she just tell us what we have to do, then? Why go back 9000 years to leave us some cryptic message that we may or may not even get? None of this makes any sense, Antonio."

Antonio gave a shake of his head, sighing. "I am puzzled too, my friend. She was pulled out of danger, but back into the time continuum. Who knows what she saw or how long she was in there. Maybe 9000 years ago is where the time stream spit her out."

"Yeah, but she said not to come after her—that she would find you, right?"

"That is what I understood."

"How? Does she suddenly have an ability to travel the time grid? Even Willoughby, with his talent, is not adept at that yet. It's why you wouldn't let him go back in there. Maybe we should just keep this to ourselves. We have no way of knowing when in the future this is, or even *if* this is the future."

"You are right. There is too much we do not know. Perhaps the future is not set. Perhaps there are good reasons she cannot tell us more. Perhaps we are misreading what we see. I do not know. It is why I told Willoughby we could not leave until you had a chance to see this. I saw this before the incident in the forest. We almost lost Sydney there. I wondered, was that it? Was that the incident we were being warned about? Did Willoughby somehow change what was supposed to happen?"

Dr. J was still staring at the glowing wall. "Speaking of Willoughby, don't you think he has the right to see this?"

Antonio shrugged. "I don't know. Maybe showing him would worry him unnecessarily. He is already so paranoid about anything to do with Sydney. He would want to just lock her away. What if that is exactly what he should *not* do? What if it made her so angry, she turned on us? Maybe her fall is figurative, not literal—we don't know. Would this message distract Willoughby? The message makes it clear that Willoughby is key. It indicates something big is coming, something that could possibly affect more than just us. Perhaps, in trying to warn us, T.K. causes the very problem she is hoping to help us avoid. It is a delicate path we tread here, my friend. There is no clear horizon."

James Arthur studied Antonio for a long moment. "Why do I get the feeling you're not telling me everything that wall is saying?"

Antonio looked down, then back up with a sheepish grin. He sighed. "Because, I'm not telling you everything."

"One of us is supposed to die, right?" His voice was very matter-of-fact.

Antonio gave his head a quick shake. "I don't know. It says, *'my champion, my healer, a long night comes...a sacrifice must be made. Remember me.'*"

James Arthur narrowed his eyes. "*Remember me?* Not *I miss you, I love you,* or *I'll see you soon?*"

Antonio dropped his eyes, giving his head a pained shake.

"Does she sign her name?" James Arthur continued. "The message seems geared to you, and it refers to Willoughby."

"You may also be referenced." Antonio raised an eyebrow. "It says, *my champion, my healer.* The *champion,* of course would be me. The *healer* could be you."

"Or the *champion* could be me. I never healed T.K."

Antonio's eyes flashed with a hint of anger.

"Wait," Dr. J added quickly, "I'm just saying we don't know exactly who she's referring to. But, hey, I get it! You're the knight in shining armor. *Go, Lancelot!*"

Antonio let his eyes drill into Dr. J for a long moment. "I prefer *champion*," he finally said firmly, looking back toward the plates. As he ran a finger over the nearest one, he sucked in a long breath. "There is no signature. I have searched, but can find no mention of Tainken Kielhar, or hidden initials, T.K."

"Listen, Antonio, I know you want this to be a message from her, and there is a lot of circumstantial evidence that leads us to believe it is, but, how can we be sure? Could someone be trying to manipulate us? You would think she might have been more direct—that she would have at least left her name somewhere. There *could* be other people who know the Atlantian alphabet."

"There is one more thing," Antonio said softly. He led to one of the side walls and pointed to a pictogram in the low corner. It was the outline of a fierce plesiosaur; the right eye was open, while the left was closed, with a heavy scratch across it. James Arthur had heard in detail the story of Antonio and T.K. in the Jurassic Era cave, and the plesiosaur T.K. had attacked, scarring its left eye.

It was James Arthur's turn to sigh. "Okay. I suppose you photographed all of this?" Antonio nodded. "Then I say let's think it through for a day or so and get back together in London. We can decide then whether to tell Willoughby."

"I concur," Antonio said. "But there is one more thing I must do. The final words on the wall at the back tell me to destroy this place once the walls have been read.

We have breached the hidden walls that once kept this chamber secret. This room is hidden no more. Great care was taken to encrypt this message, but it is best to keep it from scrutinizing eyes if we can help it. As I showed you, the lever is there. The walls must have been made to be destructible. How quickly that occurs, though, and how much time it will give us to escape, I do not know. I know T.K. would want us to get out, but this is a plan put into action thousands of years ago. It may work. It may not. We could end up below hundreds of tons of stone."

"Never tell me the odds," Dr. J said. "Let's pull it together."

"No, I am more familiar with the winding passages that lead here. You go first, I will give you five minutes on my watch and then catch up. If there is a malfunction, someone must be there to rescue the other, and to return to Willoughby."

James Arthur nodded, then, once again holding his torch in front of him, he put on his mask and submerged into the narrow shaft of dark water. When he reached the bottom of the narrow shaft, he began retracing his steps along the angling passage. He moved with quick precision and had just exited the huge building when he felt a sudden sensation of pressure, followed by a rush of silt and debris that spewed out from the building entrance. The whole stone wall bordering the entrance rocked for a moment, then whole sections of the interior roof collapsed. James Arthur tried to hold his ground as the brownish silt cloud engulfed him, yelling frantically into his radio bud.

"*Antonio!* Antonio, do you read me?"

At first, there was only static, and then a coughing, somewhat croaking voice came back.

"Yes, amigo, I read you well. I am okay. That was most... interesting."

He glimpsed a dark form a few meters behind him dart out from the still churning cloud of debris and dive down and away from the worst of it. It took a few moments for James Arthur to stabilize himself, then he dove down to follow his friend, barely avoiding a fist-sized stone that spewed sideways as a small segment of the outer wall now collapsed. He half rolled, half swam his way to Antonio's side. His friend was bent over, his hands on his knees, behind a low stone ridge a few dozen meters away. Grasping the man's shoulder, he fought to gain footing.

"An explosive? How could an explosive still detonate after thousands of years?"

Antonio shook his head. "No, my friend." He took several long moments fighting for breath. Finally, he croaked in a hoarse whisper. "There was no explosion. Whatever that lever did was purely mechanical, I think— all weights and balances. Still, to work at all after so long..."

The two rested on the bottom a few moments longer, then arm in arm, they began to slowly ascend. They allowed a good twenty minutes for the complete ascension. When they did break the surface, the boat appeared to have moved. They splashed around on the surface, throwing their facemasks up, before finally locating a bobbing white and brown shape far to the left of them. James Arthur glanced over at Antonio.

"Could we have drifted this far? That must be a mile away."

"Willoughby, do you read me? Antonio said, turning the frequency in his ear bud to the frequency Willoughby's receiver was set to. "Willoughby? ...Willoughby, come in?"

Antonio shot a quick glance at James Arthur, raising his eyebrows.

James Arthur squinted, shading his eyes. "I don't see anyone," he mumbled. Then, with a hiss and a low swear, he shook off his air tank and pulled off his mask and wet suit hood. "I'll meet you there," he said over his shoulder as he let go of the gear—letting the mask, tank, and suit sink out of sight. He set off with strong, steady strokes, keeping his eyes trained on the distant bobbing shape.

A strong open water swimmer in decent shape, and an avid surfer, James Arthur still underestimated how winded he would be by the time he reached the boat. Despite a reasonably mild water surface, it still had taken him, according to his fancy dive watch—one of the few items he did keep, another fifteen minutes to catch up with the drifting vessel. He guessed the distance he had covered was a good deal more than a mile. After slowly catching his breath, he pulled himself up using the steel ladder bolted to the side of the boat. Once on board, his eyes began sweeping the deck. There was no sign of Willoughby, and the boat was a complete wreck. Bits of fish guts, overturned tables and barrels, scattered boxes, stray cut fishing lines and mounds of flopping fish bodies greeted him. There was also a strong stench—a sort of oily, organic smell. Soft tapping and flopping seemed to come from everywhere on the deck, overlapping a fair amount of thumping, and punctuated by the occasional thud.

"Willoughby?" he called out.

There was no immediate answer. He scanned the mayhem in front of him. The sounds were being made by not one or two, but literally dozens of fish—fish of all sizes, fish with bits of cut tackle line hanging out of their mouths, fish that were flopping against the side of the deck, hoping to break free. Some fish appeared to have been clubbed and were lifeless, others had been thrown into buckets of water and ice. A few fish flopped in pools of water where buckets had simply been dumped over them. The sixteen trawler poles clamped into tight holds to either side of the boat stood silent, bits of tackle line blowing from them in the slight breeze. A box of hooks had been spilled across the deck. Bait, some freshly cut, was everywhere."

"Willoughby!" James Arthur called a bit louder. A moan came from the right of the cabin. Dr. J hurried over. He found a drenched and disheveled Willoughby. He had blood and fish guts from one end to the other and was stretched out on the deck, a bright trickle of his own blood streaming from one nostril. James Arthur hurried to him.

"What happened?"

Willoughby pushed himself up onto his elbows, wiping at his nose. "Hey, you're in your skivvies!"

"Yeah, well, the boat drifted over a mile. We weren't sure you were okay."

"Ah," Willoughby forced a smile. "I'm touched, James Arthur! You do care. By the way, the boat did not drift. It was pulled."

"Pulled?" Dr. J frowned. "Pulled by what?"

"You wouldn't believe me if I told you," Willoughby grinned, shoving away a fish that had flopped too close.

James Arthur waited for more explanation, and when it didn't come, he frowned. "Willoughby, this isn't a time for jokes! We tried to reach you on the radio, but you didn't answer."

"Sorry, a fish shorted it out," Willoughby said, still grinning.

150

"A fish?" James Arthur said, folding his arms across his chest. "A fish shorted out your radio."

"It was like a tsunami," Willoughby said. "A tsunami of fish. I was pulling in fish and pulling out hooks as fast as I could, and every line was bent over. I threw a particularly large one on the console above the radio to try to keep it still—it was flopping and twisting so much, I finally had to just cut the line, and when I did, it flopped sideways and thumped the radio control with its slimy tail, and I heard something pop. I pushed the fish out of the way and tried to get the control to come back on, but it was dead. I think it may have shorted out a fuse or something."

Dr. J walked over to the radio control and found it was indeed dead. When he came back, Willoughby was sitting up. "So, why are you wet, and why is your nose bleeding?"

Willoughby looked up, obviously somewhat drained. "They just kept coming, James Arthur. They kept coming and coming... One was so big it...it slammed me right over the side...I barely got back up onto the boat. Before it was over, I finally had to just cut the lines. Then, I think I passed out awhile. I guess I hit the railing harder than I imagined." Willoughby looked up. "What time is it? Are you guys done?"

James Arthur was still trying to process the wild tale when a large fish flopped against the back of his leg almost causing him to lose his balance. "Ouch!" he said, kicking it away. He swept the deck again with his eyes. He counted at least two or three dozen flopping fish and another one or two dozen down for the count. *Could Willoughby really have caught all these?*

Willoughby looked again. "Hey, look on the bright side. First, no one at the dock will question our fishing aspirations after seeing this haul. Secondly, I've definitely got dinner covered." He flashed James Arthur his goofy grin.

This time, Dr. J couldn't help shaking his head and breaking into a grin of his own. He went to the wheel house, got a clean rag and a first aid kit, then came back and started cleaning the boy's face. "*Deadliest catch?*" he chided.

"Yeah, Willoughby managed. "This fishing—it's a pretty brutal sport."

Again, James Arthur laughed. About five minutes later, Antonio yelled from the back of the boat. "James Arthur, what has happened here? Is everything alright?" he appeared, still struggling for breath, stumbling around the wheel house with nothing on but his briefs.

"Well, good thing Sydney isn't here to see this! She'd have nightmares for months," Willoughby said, raising a hand and giving Antonio a weak wave.

Antonio looked around at the deck and its flopping occupants.

"Did it rain fish while we were gone?" he began, but James Arthur held up a hand. He pointed to Willoughby.

"This is one tale you'll want to hear from Captain Ahab himself…"

14

Gone

Time slowed even as adrenaline kicked in. Sydney's senses became hyper aware of every sound, every movement. She did not run, but her eyes darted back and forth across the park perimeters. She couldn't find the attacker. People were looking her way. She may have screamed for help—she wasn't sure. She pushed Sam back, helping him to stretch out on the bench. She used his spotless white handkerchief to stem the bleeding from his chest. There were no follow up shots. Sam, it appeared, had been the target.

"Sam! *Sam, can you hear me?* You're hit. I've—I've got to get help!"

She frantically dug in her pocket for her phone as she pressed down on the already blood soaked handkerchief. She pulled out the phone. Glancing up, she saw Sam's eyes go unfocused. His breathing went ragged. Blood trickled from the corner of his mouth.

"*Go-o-o…*" he forced.

"*No!*" She lowered the cell phone just long enough to lean over him. "You're not going to die on me, Sam! I won't let you! *You hear me? I won't* let you die!"

"*So let it...be written,*" Sam managed in a weak whisper, trying to force a smile. His head fell back.

Sydney could barely see the phone in her hand. Her fingers were trying to dial, and she was blinking rapidly, trying to clear her eyes. She made another scan of the area. Still, no sign of a gunman. Sam's hand stopped her from dialing. He motioned her close.

"*Entropy,*" he said, weakly, "*is... the password.*"

"Password?" Sydney heard herself say. "What do you mean, Sam?" Sam pulled her closer.

"*Equation is...*"

"*Equation?* Sam, you need to save your strength." She wiped at her eyes. "Just stay still. We're getting help."

"*Equation...*" he began again, then fell into a coughing fit. Blood came from his nose now.

"*...is...*" he tried again, but his voice failed.

"*Don't talk!*" She ordered. "You're going to be okay..."

The final words came almost as a sigh, formed from his last breath. "*...you...Miss...*" The voice sputtered out. Sam's head fell limp.

"No, no—*stay with me!*" Sydney screamed. "I'm going to get you out of here, Sam! *You're going to be all right!*"

Time shifted. It was no longer neutral—no longer an exhaustive list of sequential activities. Seconds had sudden, dire meaning. Seconds were slipping from her grasp, even as she tried to catch them. She imagined she could see them, bounding away in jerks of staccato motion. There was no way to gather them back. She felt like a spectator, forced to watch as the sad drama unfolded around her. Her hands moved mechanically, dialing. Her voice functioned, but barely, speaking into the phone. It felt as though her mind was trying to push through thick, syrupy liquid. She moved like an automaton. There seemed no cause or effect to movement, no controlling logic, just a sense of drowning, and a growing, uncontrollable panic.

What things come to mind in the spaces between the moments? An image of Virginia Woolf flashed across her mind. The author liked to dissect time. She took the mind to smaller and smaller reference worlds in her short story, *Kew Gardens*. The rose bush is perceived much differently as observed from a raindrop, from a rose petal, through the eight eyes of a spider. Above somewhere, life may carry a sheen of normality, but in the realm of micro-worlds, sound simply hangs in the air, a noise devoid of emotion, unable to hurt, to frighten, to anger, because reference points had changed. Red was simply red—not a growing stain of blood soaking the spotless white silk and oozing across her fingers. The blood flow had become lazy. Perhaps it had stopped. She tried to look away, but it pulled her eyes back again and again.

She sought to escape, to return to her world in a raindrop, where all colors were bright and cheery. She felt her own pulse, throbbing in her ears. It sounded alien. Wisps of other disembodied sounds fell about her like snowflakes. They built a buffer, a blanket, muffling her growing desperation. She had a sudden, parching thirst. Her throat was dry.

Sam gave a last, almost imperceptible shudder. His eyes were already glassing over. His hand went limp. "*Sam!*" she heard her voice sob. There was no response. Sydney suddenly *felt* the wetness on her fingers, a wet, sticky warmth, soaking through the handkerchief. The blood was already turning cold.

"Hey, *Hey!*" a voice shouted.

Sydney tore her eyes away from Sam, from the sticky wetness on her hands. She twisted her head. It was a man with a cell phone. "Geez!" he stopped and even took a step backward. "He's bleeding out! That, that was a gunshot, wasn't it? Who shot him? Is the ambulance on its way? You think he's going to be okay?"

Sydney just stared at him. A sudden, unnatural calm coming over her. She forced her mouth to work. "Are you a doctor?"

"No," he said. "I'm a stock broker, but first aid was part of my basic training in the military. Look, this—this is bad. He's, he's—"

"Dead," she completed. "He's dead."

At that moment, the calm broke. Sobs welled in her like crests of high surf. She looked down, trying to comprehend what she was seeing. Sam's face had gone ashen. It made the blood on her hands even more real. The man came up behind her and gently pushed her away. He placed his own hands over the wound, then looked back and shook his head. Sydney sat. She looked at her now free hands. She wanted to get them clean. She wanted to *wash them*. They felt alien, possessed. She dropped her head down onto her knees. *Why was she so focused on her hands?* He was gone. Gone. *She hadn't said anything important to him!* She hadn't told him what he had meant to her as a friend—how she valued his sparse, timely advice. She shook from sobs, forcing herself to breathe. When her eyes finally cleared, they focused between her knees onto something near the ground.

It was Sam's lifeless hand. It had fallen and lay motionless, inches above the grit and sand of the walkway. Drops of blood dripped from the index finger. The palm was facing up, the digits slightly curled. The fingers seemed frozen. In a slight swirl of breeze, bits of sand blew across the hand. Her mind yelled, "*Close, move!*" But the fingers didn't. They just hung there, frozen sentinels, while one by one, the sands slipped away.

Somewhere far away, sirens were blaring. People were running. Faces buzzed around her like bees. They were speaking to her, asking questions. Someone with her voice answered. But it didn't matter now. Nothing much mattered. She watched them put Sam's body on a rolling stretcher. It was just a body now, a cold, still shell. A word echoed in the surreal blur around her; "*Gone. Gone. Gone...*"

When H.S. had died, there had been pain, there had been emptiness. There had been a void, gnawing at her, pulling her toward its silent blackness, but it had not been like this. The others had been there. She hadn't watched him die. She hadn't felt his blood go cold in her hands. She knew these moments were different than those. These would play over and over in her mind. With H.S., death had been quick, surgical even. H.S. was there, then the cameras went blank, and he was gone. It had been the same on the *Absconditus*. She had not seen the blood, the pain of the incident. She had not been asked to bend over the dying, to stem a hot flow of blood.

While they cleaned her hands, her mind wandered. What had been his last words? She tried to make sense of them. "*...you, Miss...*"

Had he been addressing her, as in, "*Miss Sydney*"? Or had he been trying to say he would "*miss her?*" She followed the stretcher to the ambulance and climbed inside. She sat dutifully where the medical technician directed her to sit. She stared blankly at the body, hidden now under a white sheet.

When they reached the hospital door, she pulled the sheet down one last time. Sam's face seemed so serene, as if he had accepted death as stoically as he had accepted life. She stepped out of the ambulance into a colder, darker evening. A tear dropped and landed on the back of her hand. She looked down at it, but the hand she saw in her mind belonged to another. It hung there, the wrist inches from the ground. It was palm up, with fingers curled slightly. Again, she saw in her mind the little swirl of breeze. Bits of sand blew around and through the still fingers. The hand couldn't hold them anymore. The sands danced on the paling skin, thinning, thinning, and then, ever so silently, a final grain of sand slid down the long fingers, and time, forever, slipped away.

15

Tides

After about an hour of gutting and cleaning fish, Antonio called in reinforcements. The cooking staff from the Preserve may not have been large in numbers, but they knew what they were doing. After the fish had all been gutted, cleaned, and filleted, the staff took their pick, then allowed the team to send some of the fillets, packed in dry ice, home to friends and loved ones. Later, they gathered at the GEPP (Gujarat East Primate Preserve) for a grand fish fry before leaving India on a night-bound flight aboard Observations, Inc.'s private jet.

Once aboard the jet, Willoughby began to pry for information from Antonio and Dr. J. *What about the underwater ruins? Had they found anything that might lead them to T.K.?* Possibly. *Had they found any more evidences of the mark of Beelzebub?* Not really.

All the two seemed to have learned from their last day in the underwater ruins was that the ruins themselves did not seem to hold a doorway or key that would lead them directly to their friend. They had found a pictorial reference, showing a monastery on a cliff that seemed tied to the image of the sea serpents fighting that Antonio had shared with them earlier at the GEPP. James Arthur told him that he had taken the assignment to follow up on this clue while Antonio planned to study the stone box Observations, Inc. had purchased more closely. Antonio asked Willoughby to join forces with Sydney and Sam in sifting through the collected artifacts, computer files, books, and papers they had taken from H.S.'s apartments before reporting him missing.

Missing... The word still sent a stab of pain into Willoughby's gut. He thought of the conversation he'd had with Sam outside the Preserve, staring into the dark tangles of vine from the tree thickets that surrounded the facility.

At that very moment, as if Sam had heard his thoughts, they got the call. Willoughby could scarcely comprehend the words.

"Sydney, slow down...They did what? *Sam?* How is he?... (silence) ...I'm, we're on our way...I'm passing the phone to Antonio."

His hand shaking noticeably, he passed the cell phone to Antonio. His face had gone ashen white. Antonio, too, was unprepared for the news.

James Arthur looked over. "What's wrong? *Sydney?*" Apprehension drained his voice of intensity.

"Sam," Antonio said quietly. "They shot him. He was sitting in the park with... Sydney is a wreck...and Sam, our most excellent friend Sam, is dead."

Everyone sat frozen for a moment. Finally, Antonio finished the phone call with Sydney telling her to meet them at the airport. He closed the phone, put it down, and placed a hand on Willoughby's shoulder. His eyes were focused intently at the ground, his thick eyebrows furrowed with grief.

There were no words for the sense of loss that flooded through each of them. It permeated the room, as thick as a London fog. Willoughby fidgeted. Below the grief, he felt something else. He felt a simmering anger. He felt a decision rising in him that he had been struggling with—a decision that had now been made for him. None of his friends were safe while this insane time traveler, Beelzebub, was pulling the strings. Willoughby could not wait until he was better prepared to defend those he loved. The tide was already turning. He had to somehow take control of this fight. He had to figure out a way to attack this cult, or dark brotherhood. He had to figure out a way to challenge Beelzebub himself.

16

Prayer Sheets

Tainken turned, exasperated. "What do you mean, *jump?*" She was looking over a cliff that fell away at least 230 feet to a rocky patch of frothing sea. How Loa did not blink or flinch. He merely gestured to the empty air with his arm. The cliff was not quite as high as the one she had visited with the girl, but it was not far off either. It was certainly high enough for her to be very dead when she hit the rocks below. The tall man who had led her through a seemingly endless set of passages to get to this cliff, gestured again. "Please, you no be in danger. Just ignore sight of rocks, yes?"

"No!" T.K. said. Was he crazy? The sea below crashed against the rocks of the circular cove. It had a light green tint. T.K. backed away from the edge, trying to comprehend why this man would make such a suggestion. "I can't ignore the rocks! It would be like jumping in front of a freight train and trying to ignore the frantic whistle, or the rumble of the tracks."

"Ah!" How said with a smile. "You make funny joke! This no train. This very big time hole. *You* jump in!" He seemed to feel this was a completely reasonable request.

T.K. scanned the water below again. "I don't see a time hole. I don't even see a disturbance in the air. How do I know there is anything out there except certain death?"

"Same way you know anything worth getting to know," said How, patiently. "Learning best happens from inside out. You close eyes so you come to truly see. You block outside sound so you come to truly hear. Same way baby spider learn to make web. Knowledge best found in here," he pointed at Tainken's head, "and here," he pointed at her heart."

"What are you, some deranged version of Aesop?"

The man raised a questioning eyebrow.

"You know, Aesop's Fables?"

The man furrowed his wild eyebrows.

"Okay, just forget it," T.K. sighed.

The man did not respond to the comment, but moved closer, pursing his lips and narrowing his eyes. He seemed to be studying her head, as if searching for lice. Before she could protest, he tipped her head slightly to one side, running a finger just above and behind her ear and gave a sudden, sharp whack with his knuckle. The pain shot through her head, blurring her vision and causing her to wince. She jerked away, even as the pain quickly receded, and spun on the man. Before she could speak, however, a bright radiance shimmered in the air around her. It seemed to float on pure air. It had a bluish tint, and swirled in a sort of triangular vortex, starting just below the lip of the cliff. It vanished as her eyesight cleared, but there definitely *was* something there, and it was large, about ten feet across.

"Ah! You see, you see!" How cackled, his face beaming.

T.K. stepped carefully to the edge of the cliff to peer over. She rubbed her head. "How did you do that?" she asked, turning back to the man.

"Yes, how did do that," the man smiled. "I flip fine, good switch for good customer! Just for moment—you see, it just as I say. Plenty big hole for to jump in." How bounced slightly on his heels. He waved the crude umbrella he had been carrying. "Now, you pull, I push. You go far. So sad, too bad. Bye, bye." He jabbed Tainken squarely in the midriff with the partially open apparatus. As she stumbled backward, he added; "Oh, and you find I much handsomer than Aesop. He really pretty ugly man!"

She cartwheeled momentarily, then plunged over the edge, stunned. After a moment of panic, she felt the pull of the vortex grab her. Above, she could see the bony figure of How Loa receding from view as he continued to wave.

A sudden pressure built at her shoulder as she was jerked sideways. She felt as if she were being pulled at such an intense speed that her whole body was being first crushed, and then stretched out like a thick spaghetti strand. The bright sky, the man, the cliff all disappeared.

There were a few seconds of sensing more than seeing streaks of bluish light and hints of grid lines around her. Then, as quickly as it began, it ended. There was a jerk—as if all her insides were being pulled through the pores of her skin. Then came a snap and a crack, as if her entire body, bones and all, had been stretched to the limit and were now snapping back into place. This was followed by pain and nausea, and a feel of being submerged in cold liquid. She fought to find purchase, gasping for air, and pushing up from a bottom of mossy pebbles. She struggled to open her eyes, and was just able to clear the water line when she began to choke and retch. She managed to make her way to shallower water, then pulled herself up onto a smooth, stone ledge. She bent over, great rivulets of water draining from her as she looked down, her feet still dangling in the water. Her hands grasped her knees tightly as she heaved and spit into the pool.

It took several seconds for her eyes to clear and her muscles to stop seizing. It had been uncomfortable when she had been zapped to the Prime Hole facility, and slightly worse when she had fallen into the pig trough, but neither experience matched the cold brutality of this fall. She was inside some sort of structure, and seemed to be at the edge of a clear pool, fed by a small stream that cut through a large pyramidal shaped room. She forced her feet over the low stone lip of the pool, and swung around, letting them drop onto a polished stone floor.

She glanced back at the water, seeing that the pool she had pulled herself from was maybe twelve meters across and circular. It had to have been at least eight or ten feet deep in its center, but grew shallow near the edges. The stream that fed it was only a couple of feet wide and the stone lip narrowed around it on either side of the pool. The water had a sweet, earthy smell to it. The pool was bordered by a thin, stone lip, adorned by ornate mosaics. She could see the remains of her heaving floating to one side of the pool, near where the water must have been flowing out of the pool.

"The pool will cleanse itself," a soft voice said in accented English. "The stream of water keeps it from becoming stagnant. The location of the pool directly under such a large time hole gives this space unique qualities."

Tainken looked over, noticing for the first time a perfectly still figure, standing in the shadows a short distance away. The large, stone chamber they were in had a high ceiling, open to a night sky, and small, wooden doors built into the thick walls.

The figure stepped into the light, revealing a small, petite woman with dark hair. Her robe was ornately colored and tied with a deep blue sash. She wore a glittering silver and gold neck piece that held a glowing array of fine jewels. She motioned toward one of the doors, the only one that stood open. "Hurry. We need to get you out of sight before the Temple Priests discover you were here—and they will discover it. They know every inch of their Temple by sight and smell and touch."

Tainken pushed up, staring around at the odd stone room. It was as if they were inside a hollow stone pyramid with the top piece missing. She could see no altars or sacrificial pyres. She saw only bare stone walls, a few scattered wood benches, and the half-dozen or so doors. She wiped water from her eyes and face and squeezed it from her hair. "Who are you? Where am I?" she asked softly.

"You were in this city before—many years ago. You met a man I know, a friend of mine, How Loa. I have been preparing for your arrival now for many months. I have all things ready, but right now, we must hide you. Quick— this way."

The woman was slender and beautiful, with a kind face and delicate hands. She had bright, copper skin, and black silky hair pulled back into a long rope. T.K. caught glimpses of an odd garment beneath her robe. It seemed to be made from strips of greenish cloth, stretched across the arms and legs in horizontal bands. The garment and robe reached almost to the stone floor, but delicate, sandaled feet were also visible. A silver weave seemed to hold the robe taut and in perfect array, connecting a spidery network of thin, silver lines that ran both horizontally and vertically through the brightly colored fabric. She had green laurels tied around her wrists, and a loose laurel wreath upon her head.

T.K. tried not to stare, but she had never seen anything like this. "Who are you?" she asked again.

"My name is Rashrahu. I am second daughter of Ushas, Goddess of the Dawn. Come, please." The woman moved, quiet and graceful, through the door into a tight chamber that seemed to be some sort of prayer sanctuary. She led T.K. to the back of the sanctuary and pressed upon a stone in the stone wall. Her hand print glowed green on the stone, and a heavy panel pushed back to reveal a dry, stone corridor.

As T.K. stepped into the corridor, the woman place her hand on another stone inside the corridor, and the panel slid back into place, sealing off the entry. Almost immediately, a dim green light lit the corridor. T.K. looked up as she followed the woman down the corridor. Thousands of tiny dots of green buzzed and dipped, hovering in a cloud of light against the stone ceiling. It was as if the corridor was lit by electronic fireflies. She could see no wires or forms of power for the tiny dots. In fact, they appeared to be organic.

The corridor seemed to continue in a straight line for roughly twenty meters, then turned at a right angle, continued for about twenty more meters, then turned at a right angle again. As they came to another stone wall, the woman once again placed her hand on a peculiar stone. It glowed green, and the wall moved back to reveal yet another corridor at a right angle. This corridor continued only fifteen or so meters before turning at a right angle. The maze, or labyrinth, or whatever it was continued this way, in a shrinking square spiral, until the two, at last, reached an area where the walls became smooth, with stone rungs built into one side. T.K. followed the woman up the stone rungs through a much smaller stone corridor—maybe four feet square—into a small stone room with a much lower, but still vaulted ceiling. The buzzing green lights seemed to meld right into the walls all around them, causing them to give off a sort of phosphorescent glow. The room had a few blank copper plates against one wall, with a lever on the wall opposite them. Propped up against the other two walls were sheets of blank, silver metal. The woman pointed to them.

"I was told you would help me. I need to know what should appear on these permanent wall scrolls," she said, watching Tainken with a steady smile.

Tainken thought of her meeting with the girl in the white dress. The girl had said she must warn her friends of what she knew. She had seen Sydney's fall, but how would somehow encrypting a message on these walls ever get to Antonio and his team?

"Do you know of my city *Aert Olaneas Tis*, which will come to be known as *Atlantis*?"

"Yes. I know who you are, Princess Tainken Kielhar, and I know of your city."

"Does it still exist?"

"Your city's time is short, as is our time now."

"Can I do anything to save it?"

"Not physically—not from the catastrophe coming. But its legacy, its history? Perhaps. There is much yet to do."

Tainken thought back on the disjointed history that was her past. She had a history that touched multiple millennia. It was almost too disjointed and fantastical for

168

her mind to grasp, like a strange dream, or a crazy fiction—like *Alice in Wonderland*. She struggled to know what to say. A part of her wondered if she had fallen into some sort of madness, if these events were only in her mind, but her senses rejected this explanation. She was here. She could touch, she could feel, she could smell everything she saw around her. This woman, or Goddess, or whatever, seemed anxious to help her, but help her what? What did these copper plates and silver sheets have to do with anything?

The thoughts whirled around in her head, but all she could muster aloud was, "This is your Temple. I don't even know who your deities are. Why would you think I could help you with prayer sheets?"

The woman was silent for a long moment. Then she spoke, as if reading T.K.'s thoughts; "Order and chaos; mortality and immortality; light and darkness; good and evil—there is a border connecting each—a gray area where it is difficult to discern right from wrong, reality from fiction. You stand there now, Tainken. We call it *the edge*. Willoughby may call it a *potentiality*, a place where the equations allow for a variety of different outcomes. Everything here can look differently depending on your point of view. As your perspective changes, so does your world."

Tainken had listened intently to the woman's entire speech, but her mind had stuck on one thought. "You know Willoughby?"

The woman's smile broadened. "Of course I know Willoughby. He does not yet know me, but he will. Guarding the edge, one must look both forward and back. We see Willoughby in both directions."

T.K. cocked her head. "Meaning?"

"Meaning he is one we watch. He may be the key. The dark edge rises. All is at risk."

"But what does that mean?" Tainken was getting frustrated with the riddles.

"It means," the woman said, her face growing deadly serious, "chaos, darkness, evil on an infinite scale. It means a hole in time that cannot be closed—a huge black chasm sucking life and light out of the multiverse. It means the end of all we know, all we love, all we may hope for, unless…"

"Unless what?"

"Unless those of us who guard the edge can stop the rise. Unless we can return the balance."

"You think Willoughby is going to do this? He's just a boy."

"He is who he is. For now, we can only watch. We watch, but not without action. There are ways, perhaps, we can help. There are ways, Tainken, in which you can help. You have spoken with the Young One. When you looked into her mists, what did you see?"

T.K. remembered the girl's words; "You must share what you know. What happens beyond only you and your friends can decide." She looked at the blank silver sheets propped against the stone walls and realized she knew exactly why she had been brought here.

17

A Different Kind of Dying

The sky over London, so often foggy or gray, was crystal blue. There was not a cloud in sight, not one visible indication of the storm Willoughby felt building inside him. As he dressed in the newly purchased black suit and tie he had bought for the funeral, he glared into the mirror at the black silk, which he knotted and re-knotted, dissatisfied with the effect. He did not want to look himself in the eye. He did not want to see the pain and the frustration there. He thought of the last conversation he and Sam had in India along the edge of a patch of jungle.

"Power follows power, Willoughby," Sam had said. "Perhaps he sees more in you than you see yourself. H.S. believed that you could be more than Beelzebub's equal. He believed that you could beat him at his own game. Do not cut yourself short. Ever."

Now, Sam was dead. *Was it his fault?* Could he have—should he have stopped Beelzebub earlier? Did he let his own self-doubts, his own desires for a peaceful outcome, override his duty to face this demon? He didn't even know if the creature was alien, or some altered form of human. He had no idea where the thing would strike next, or what its end game was. He was just beginning to

171

learn to use his abilities and had no idea how to defeat the group who seemed to be doing Beelzebub's bidding. H.S. had called them a cult, or dark brotherhood, but Willoughby had to wonder if some of them were actually the demon lord's army of freaks, like the zombie he had met in Bermuda, or the Desert Witch. He had no desire to kill anyone, or anything. Is that what it was going to take, though, to stop this? *Why him?* Why was he being forced into making these types of choices? He wasn't any kind of a hero. He was just a kid who wanted to be left alone.

He finished knotting the tie, stood motionless at the mirror for a moment, then went to a small couch near the window, sat, and stared out at the vibrant blue sky. There were no answers—only questions that gnawed away at his insides. After a time, the phone rang. He picked it up. The concierge from the lobby told him his car had arrived. He thanked the woman and then hung up. He stared out the window. It was a great view. He was staying in a posh suite near the top of one of the most prestigious hotels at King's Cross near the British Museum in North London. The Great Northern Hotel, built in 1854, was the oldest purpose-built hotel in London, and one of the first examples of the great railway hotels. It had been remodeled in 2013. It was one of Sam's favorites, and the place he insisted Willoughby stay whenever he was in London.

Willoughby thought of the last time he had been here. It was earlier in the year when he came to visit Sam and attend Sydney's latest London Premier. Sydney had been brilliant and he had loved the hotel, though now he thought back on it, he hadn't spent that much time with Sam. That seemed like eons ago now, though it had only been a few months. He turned away from the window, stood, walked to the door, turned the knob, and took the elevator down. *Simple things. Just keep your mind focused on simple things*, he told himself.

As he strode through the lobby toward the side door, he gave a quick, distracted wave to the concierge. The limo had pulled over neatly to the curb. It idled, its engine still running. A smartly dressed man stood beside the open passenger door—a man who was *not* his friend and personal chauffer, Sam—who would never again be Sam. This man gave Willoughby a pleasant nod and offered a cheery greeting, but Willoughby didn't hear it. He had noted a figure already in the vehicle. This man was taller and leaner than the chauffer, with distinctly Asian features. Willoughby recognized him in a moment. It was Sydney's father, Aiyito.

After a short pause, Willoughby ducked into the idling limousine. The driver shut the door.

Aiyito looked over, no expression on his face. "Surprised?"

Willoughby gave a short cough. "Uh, yeah. Sydney didn't tell me you would be riding with us."

"There is no '*us*.' Sydney will meet us at the funeral."

Willoughby said nothing. He just stared at Aiyito.

The man wiped a hand over his smooth, if tired, Asian face. He reached forward and slowly closed the small window that separated the driver from the back of the limousine. Willoughby knew that the glass was specially formulated to be both bullet proof, and completely sound resistant. He turned. "I wanted to have a word with you—alone."

Willoughby held his tongue.

At length, Aiyito continued. "Do you know anything about these killings that you are not telling me,

Willoughby? Did H.S. confide anything to you before your descent to the sea floor with Sydney?"

Willoughby's words were hot and fast. "We've been through this. I don't know where your precious pendant is. T.K. has it, and if I knew where she was, I would also know how to locate the prime hole."

The man watched him carefully. "What are you not telling me?"

Willoughby was in no mood for this type of conversation. He turned, staring out the window.

The man continued to glare at him for a moment, and then looked away. He took a quick drink from a small, green bottle and wiped his lips. "Have you ever wondered, Willoughby, why I see so little of my daughter? Why I see so little of her mother?"

"Not as much as she's wondered it," Willoughby mumbled, still refusing to make eye contact.

Aiyito took the rebuke in stride, pursing his lips before speaking. His words were quiet and deliberate. "I was not always a rich man. Things were not always as they are now. I was a criminal, Willoughby—a schemer, a forger, and somewhat of a thief. I got into trouble. I was on the run. Then, I met a man. He was unlike any man I had ever met before. He exuded power and authority. He made me an offer I was unable to refuse."

"Except for the forger and thief part, you've told me this. You met H.S., he had a major impact on you. He helped you out of your troubles and then you helped him form Observations, Inc. You helped him finance plans to build his secret time travel technology facility. I know all this already, Aiyito."

"You DO NOT know," Aiyito roared, his eyes flashing with anger. "You think you know, but you do not!

I was on the run, Willoughby! Where would I have gotten the money to finance H.S.'s wild plans?"

Willoughby suddenly perked up. This thought had not occurred to him. Aiyito continued.

"The man I met was *not* H.S. The man I met seemed to be able to walk out of the shadows then disappear into thin air. He had odd companions and icy skin. This man always, *always* wore a long coat, inside or out. He would not take it off. I began to wonder if there were horrible scars, or worse."

Willoughby could scarcely breathe as Aiyito continued.

"Have you ever met someone like that, Willoughby? Something tells me you have. This man told me he wanted my help with some financial dealings. He paid my way out of trouble. He set me up in a legitimate business. He had a knack for finding things—very valuable things, and I had a knack for knowing how to sell with a minimum of prying eyes and red tape. In less than a year, I went from being a low-level hustler to a legitimate multibillionaire. Then, he began to call in the chips. He told me of a man who lectured on time and the viability of time travel. He told me to find this man and take an interest in his technology. He guided my early meeting with and subsequent business arrangement with H.S."

Aiyito had now turned his eyes toward the passing shop facades outside the car window. "I was an ambitious man, Willoughby—an ambitious man who was born into poverty and misery. This was the first chance *anyone* had ever given me. Deep inside, I knew I may regret working with this man. Everything about him was…*wrong*. But what choice did I have? My life as a street hustler would likely have gotten me killed. To live as a manual laborer would have driven me mad. So, I took everything I was given, not thinking of the cost. I became good friends with H.S., and though I never had the stomach to travel through one of his devices, the technology *did* fascinate me. I fell in love with a Polynesian dancer and I married her."

Aiyito turned back to Willoughby. "The mysterious man who had given me this chance disappeared. I did not hear from him for several years. I began to imagine that I was free of him. I deluded myself into believing that I could buy protection from him. Then, the man was back. He said it was time to pay up. I tried to distance myself. That was a joke. No amount of money can protect a person from him. He comes and goes as he pleases, and his henchmen are, I don't know how to say it—they don't seem fully human. He wanted information about Observations, Inc. About some pendant."

Willoughby's eyes flared. "*You?* You're the spy? You sold us out on the *Absconditus?* How could you Aiyito? Do you have any idea of the horror you've unleashed; of the people you've killed? I hope your money and power are worth it." He was silent for a moment, fuming. Finally, he sucked in a deep breath. "Does Sydney know? How many more will die because of what you've done?"

"No!" Aiyito shouted. He spun, lunging at Willoughby and pinning him against the far door. "I am not responsible for those deaths—for *any* deaths! I had nothing to do with those events. The man simply asked for information. *Information,* Willoughby! He wanted me to gather everything I could about H.S.'s research. H.S. could never have raised the money to build his machines, his empire without *my* money, without this man's help! So, it seemed fair to me. He wanted timetables, discoveries, agendas, goals... He didn't tell me anything about what would be done with this information. I only knew he was looking for a lost artifact, for the pendant. I assumed it was like any other lost artifact I had helped the man sell. Then I discovered that H.S. kept the pendant on his person—that it was something special to him. Before I could decide what to do, it was stolen from him."

Aiyito let go of Willoughby, moving back over to his side of the car, breathing heavily. "I was misguided, Willoughby, but I am not a monster. I am not a cold-blooded killer. I was played." He looked down and wiped spittle from his lips. "Besides, now the game has changed. It has nothing to do with money or power. I'm trying to protect my family, my wife and Sydney." He looked over again. "When he found that the pendant had been stolen, he went berserk. That is when the first threats came. They were not directed at me. They were focused, at first, on my wife. They were just hints, veiled threats, but they grew into more.

"I thought if I distanced myself from Jaylin—from Sydney's mother—that perhaps she would not be a target. It was a way to protect her, I told myself, but it was easier than I had thought it would be. That is when I realized Jaylin and I had begun to grow apart. She had never wanted a child, but had felt the distance between us growing long before I did. She thought a child might make a difference. I took one look at Sydney when she was born and she melted my heart. I became even more determined to distance my young family from any harm. I encouraged Jaylin to return to her family in Hawaii and her professional dancing career. I offered to bankroll her. She thought I had found someone else, that I was just trying to get rid of her. How could I tell her the truth? She would never have believed me." He sighed. "Anyway, in the end she did move away, and she blamed Sydney for the break up. There were years when Sydney's time was split between us, but I could see she treated Sydney badly, so I got full custody. I tried to keep Observations, Inc., and my darker dealings from affecting her. As for Jaylin, she became bitter and closed her heart to us. Luckily, Sydney had her music, and despite everything, she has grown into a fine woman and a great talent. I know she thinks I don't care about her, but it is not true. I am, and always have been, her most ardent fan."

On some level, Willoughby understood that Aiyito was baring his soul, that he wasn't responsible for all that had happened to him, to Sydney, to H.S., to the *Absconditus* crew, to Sam, but the blaze in his chest refused to go away. "Maybe what Sydney needs is a father, not another ardent fan," he snapped.

The effect of the words was immediate. The man bowed forward. He seemed broken. A part of Willoughby wanted to slug him. *Wasn't he, at least in part, responsible for all those deaths, all the pain and suffering?* But another part knew the truth. *When he met Beelzebub, had he realized how dangerous the man was, and that dealings with this being would have dire consequences?* He thought of how persuasive the being could be in his conversations. Aiyito did not have the benefit of seeing or knowing the being's ability to move freely in and out of the time grid. *If he had been put in the same situation, would he have acted differently?*

He honestly didn't know. His anger did not go away, but it began to turn away from Aiyito. Perhaps the man was a victim—just like H.S., the Captain of the *Absconditus* and his crew, Sam, and all the others. Just another tortured victim. Just another cog in Beelzebub's grand wheel. He looked over at Aiyito, who still held his face in his hands.

"Why have you come to me now? What do you want?"

Aiyito sat up slowly. He wiped a hand across his face. Outside the window, the traffic was slow and the sidewalks were busy, but inside, a pall of silence hung in the air.

"She doesn't know it," Aiyito began, "but I keep close tabs on her, even though I do not physically see her often. I always know where she is, and I get reports... I know of the incident in India. I know about the snakes, and I know he was behind it. They say you had to manipulate time to save her—that there was no other way that you could have reacted fast enough. Is this true?"

Willoughby watched the man for a moment. He gave a slight nod. "You don't know what you're dealing with Aiyito, or what you've done. This man can manipulate time. I have some ability in reading time flows and some knowledge of how to use that information, but I am no match for him. He froze time seconds before three cobras would have bitten Sydney. He wanted to see what I would do maybe—it was all a game to him, I think, and it didn't matter to him what the outcome was. The cobras were coming from different directions. There was no way to save her from at least one bite. There just wasn't time. I reacted on instinct, but it wouldn't have been enough had a monkey Sydney befriended not grabbed one of the striking snakes. He paid for that kindness with his life."

Aiyito bit his lip. "Yes. I am aware of that too. Observations, Inc. is funding a new wing of the GEPP in his name to expand their work to preserve the grey langurs." The man was silent a moment before continuing.

"So, you have no ability to manipulate the time stream?" Aiyito peered at him intently.

Willoughby thought through his answer for a long moment. He wasn't' sure how much he trusted Aiyito. "As I told you, I have...some abilities, yes. I'm still learning what those are. I'm not sure why, but I can see equations in the air that lead to time holes. I have moved physically to cover short distances in the blink of an eye. I can connect time points and stop time, but I am not near as polished as the man you speak of. Whatever he is, he has full mastery of time manipulation."

Aiyito looked away. "I feared as much." He was silent for a long moment, looking out the window. They were fast approaching Bunhill Fields. Sam, it seems, had cut a deal with the City of London years ago. Willoughby wasn't sure how he had pulled it off, but somehow he had gotten permission to be buried in what was now designated by the city as a garden and park. Assurances had been made that no evidence of the burial place would be left after the short ceremony. They had closed and cordoned off the park for the day to allow for the funeral and subsequent replanting to cover the grave site. Willoughby thought of something that Sydney had told him—the grave of John Bunyan, author of "Pilgrim's Progress," lay there. In Bunyan's story, a gatekeeper named Goodwill saves the protagonist from the archers of Beelzebub. It seemed uncannily ironic. Only, he was obviously no Goodwill.

Aiyito looked back. "If he comes for her, can you save her Willoughby?"

Willoughby met his gaze. "I don't know. I do know that she is one of my best friends though, and I would give everything I have trying."

Aiyito watched him for a long moment. "She is lucky to have a friend like you. That is all I can ask." The limousine was now passing the police barrier and being waved into the gates of the cemetery. "You know you have only to say the word and I'll give you anything within my power to give. Anything you need—*anything*—just ask. I would give all that I have to save her." He looked down again, his lip seeming to tremble, then looked back up. "Do you have a plan?"

Willoughby's face showed no emotion. "Yes," he said calmly. "I think it's time to take the fight to him."

18

Funeral for a Friend

Willoughby hadn't been to many funerals. He had an aunt who died when he was very young. His *Grans*—that's what he called his grandmother on his mother's side—had passed away when he was ten. He could still remember her lying there, peacefully, in her coffin. He remembered thinking at first that she was just sleeping, but there was something about the body—about its stillness. Something was missing, and that something had made him ache inside.

It was a while after H.S. died before they were able to hold a funeral for him. They had held a small gathering after the dust had settled. Only the team had been there— the team, and Sam. Willoughby realized now that he had begun to think of Sam as a part of the team, although the man didn't contribute more than logistical support. He was never actually part of projects. He was always sort of just *there*, somewhere in the background. Willoughby had long counted the tall, quiet man among his friends—first as his chauffer, then Captain of H.S.'s yacht, and lately, with Antonio more preoccupied with finding T.K., Sam had become a trusted confidant.

The coffin came into view. It was long and narrow, black in color, and tastefully adorned with polished silver trimmings. True to form, Sam had left detailed instructions for his funeral and burial rites. Willoughby had thought that only the team would be there—much like the farewell ceremony for H.S., but there were at least two dozen dignitaries standing in the shaded section of the park. Willoughby had not recognized any of them, but Sydney had come to stand beside him and had leaned over to whisper in his ear at least a dozen times. "That's the liaison for the Ministry of the Interior... That's Lord MacDonald of Berkshire..."

The list of dignitaries went on. There were a few wealthy business moguls, and several attractive women, dressed in various tones of mourning. Sydney had no idea who most of the women were, though she was quite sure one was a semi-celebrity on a local cable channel.

Antonio, Dr. J, and Hauti arrived only moments before the ceremony was set to begin. They greeted Willoughby warmly, but when he drifted toward Sydney, they gave him space. Sydney had latched onto him from the moment she saw him, giving only a cursory greeting to her father. She hadn't said anything about the last time they were together, or about his still recovering bruised eye, but as soon as they had escaped the scrutiny of her father, she had thrown herself on him, hugging him like she would never let him go.

"It was awful," she had said, simply.

"I know," Willoughby had responded. "I'm so sorry, Sydney." That was all he could think of to say. She finally let him go, but never let go of his hand.

The short service started when a man with a heavy Scottish brogue stepped forward and said a few words over the grave. A team of five Scottish pipers played a mournful tune called "Going Home" as the coffin was lowered into the grave. There had been no viewing or extended farewell at a local church. Sam had wanted a simple, if elegant, goodbye.

Antonio, James Arthur, and Hauti were some of the first to walk by the grave to pay their respects. They were meeting with Aiyito for lunch to discuss what they found in India. They invited Willoughby and Sydney, but both declined. After their friends left, the two moved to take their place near the end of the line paying last respects. In a matter of only minutes, the coffin would be buried, the grounds would be returned to their unblemished beauty, and the garden would be reopened to the public. Willoughby knew that Sydney must have been disappointed that she had not been asked to play at the event, but there was no hint of disappointment or frustration as she stood over the grave.

"You were always good to me," she said, trickles of soil falling between her fingers. A single tear glided down her cheek. "You were a true friend, never afraid to tell me what needed to be said …We can't lose what imprints on the walls of our heart. That is where I hold you, Sam. That is where I remember you. I'll, I'll miss you."

Willoughby's own words did not seem as eloquent. "I wish I'd had a chance to say goodbye. Who do I talk to now about all the crazy things that seem so important at the moment? You were always a great listener. That made you a special kind of friend. You told me you would never abandon me, and I know you wouldn't. So, I'll just keep imagining you're with me. I'll picture you, sitting quietly up there somewhere, listening…and I'll, I'll just keep talking."

As Willoughby threw down his handful of dirt and walked away from the grave, a plump, bespectacled man put a hand on his shoulder.

"Mr. Willoughby VonBrahmer?"

Willoughby had turned to follow Sydney, but stopped, looking at the plump man more closely. The man was immaculately dressed.

"Mr. Willoughby VonBrahmer?" The man repeated.

"Yes?" Willoughby had initially felt apprehensive, but seeing that the man had a kindly, earnest face, he relaxed. The man tried for a soft smile.

"I'm so sorry for your loss. My name is Grierson, John Grierson of Grierson and Sons. We managed Sam's estate, and have been retained to execute his legal will. He names you as a recipient in that will, and he instructed us to read to you the following. He also requested that we deliver this envelope at the close of his funeral."

As the man fished in a coat pocket with his left hand for whatever he was supposed to read, Willoughby noted the large, brown envelope he held in his right hand.

"Ah, here it is," he said, pulling out a crumpled note on yellow paper. The man cleared his throat somewhat theatrically.

"Willoughby VonBrahmer, as you well know, I am not one to stand on ceremony. I have instructed Grierson and Sons to make this simple. I own a set of three corner apartments in Covent Garden. The third floor apartment is mine. All three apartments, and everything in them, is yours. This *Last Will and Testament* is fully executed when you are given the envelope with the deeds and keys to the apartments. No further contact will be necessary from Grierson and Sons. All legal transfer fees and taxes have been prepaid. I wish you to proceed to the apartments post haste and take full ownership. Had I been fortunate enough to have a son of my own, I only wish he would have been half the young man I have found you to be. You are the one I trust to best manage the properties and all that is inside them."

The man cleared his throat again and handed the crumpled paper and the envelope to Willoughby. "Congratulations," he said, his smile treading thin. He leaned down adding, "I could help you should you ever decide to sell those apartments. They should draw upwards of three million pounds, British sterling on the open market, and there is likely a million more pounds in art and furnishing between the three apartments if not considerably more. Sam comes from old money, though he was not one to flaunt it. Here is my card." He presented Willoughby a black card with white lettering that said, "Grierson and Sons, Legal and Financial Services" across the top.

Willoughby stared at the crumpled note for a long moment, rereading it. Then, he wiped at his eyes, carefully folded the note, and placed it and the card into his pocket and shook the stout man's hand. "Thank you," he said, turning to leave.

Sydney had stopped dabbing at her eyes with a tissue and turned to catch the tail end of

Willoughby's conversation with the man from Grierson and Sons. She had seen the man hand the note and the envelope over. She approached, pushing her tissue into a sweater pocket.

"What was that all about?"

Willoughby gave a quick glance around. A few final people were filing past the grave. The pipers had left, replaced by a group of men in neat coveralls, a large "O" emblazoned on the front pocket. The man from Griersons was already gone from sight.

Willoughby took Sydney's hand. "Where are Antonio, Dr. J, and Hauti?" he asked, skirting her original question.

Sydney looked around, as if surprised to find the others had really gone. "I don't know. Antonio said something about things he had to do at the London office before meeting with my father for lunch. Dr. J said something about getting in a few reps at the gym before lunch. They did mention possibly meeting up for dinner. I think they realized you and I need some time alone." She looked over at him. "We do, don't we?"

This time, there was an earnestness in her glance. No mischievous glint sparked in her eyes. Willoughby smiled, giving her hand a slight squeeze. "Yeah, I guess we do." They watched the men in neat coveralls for a moment.

"Who scheduled the Observations, Inc. team to be here?"

"I don't know," Sydney said. "Probably my father."

Willoughby hadn't seen Aiyito since the early moments of the funeral. His eyes searched the entire area around the grave site. The man was nowhere in sight.

"He doesn't stay around long, does he?"

Sydney gave her reddened eyes a slight roll. "Really? You're just figuring that out? Heaven forbid he should have to give me more than a casual hug and a peck on the cheek. I mean, I'm only his daughter."

Willoughby thought back to his discussion with Aiyito before the funeral. *Should he say something to her about it?* He pursed his lips. Now did not seem like the time.

"So, you never answered my question. What's with the envelope and the note that man passed to you? Who was he?" she asked.

Willoughby leaned in close. "It appears that Sam left me some things in his will. That man was from a company called Grierson and Sons. He was…executing the will."

"His will?" Sydney said, turning toward him. "Here, at the funeral?"

The way she said it made the idea sound ridiculous, and in a way, it was. Willoughby shrugged. "He said that's what Sam asked him to do. The note was from Sam. He said I was like the son he never had—well, in so many words. And he tells me that he has three corner apartments in Covent Garden, and he's leaving those to me and everything inside them."

Sydney's eyes flew open wide. "He left you corner apartments in Covent Garden?"

"Yeah."

"Do you have any idea how valuable real estate there is?"

"The guy from Grierson mentioned something about three million pounds, British sterling."

Sydney barked a short laugh. "Increase that by about half. How was Sam able to afford apartments in Covent Garden?"

Willoughby shrugged again. "I thought you were staying in them? Antonio said you were going to his apartments in London."

"The apartments I went to, and I do believe Sam set them up, though I thought Observations Inc. owned them, were about half a mile from Kensington Gardens. Don't get me wrong, they were nice, but they weren't in the million pound range."

"The note said he wants me to go there like, post haste, to take ownership, or something like that. The Grierson guy also said that the art and furnishing in the apartments was worth another million pounds or so. He said Sam came from '*old money*,' though he didn't flaunt it."

Sydney's eyes narrowed. "Yeah, he would have had to come from money. I'm sure he didn't make that much working for Observations, Inc. I mean, don't get me wrong, they pay well, but not *that* well." She seemed to come to a decision. "Okay. Let's go."

"Right now?"

"Yeah. Why not? I don't have anything pressing this morning. Maybe it could help us get our minds off of…of all this," she said, motioning toward the grave.

Willoughby thought for a moment. It was Sam's apartments. A part of him felt like it would just leave him feeling more depressed and despondent. But he was also curious, and if truth be told, he was glad to have Sydney with him as he looked at the apartments for the first time. He didn't want to have to face the apartments alone. He gave a short smile. "Okay," he said. "I guess it's off to Covent Garden."

19

Covent Garden

On the outside, the apartment complex was about what Willoughby would expect, having some idea of Sam's tastes. It had a stately elegance, impeccably maintained, with only slight hints of modernization. Deep red brick offset the impeccably lush landscaping. The corner apartments were slightly larger and rounded such that there was no corner edge, only an expansive balcony with a beamed roof and hanging plants as well as potted greenery. Polished oak highlighted the French doors that led onto the patio, and a built-in grill, a smattering of oak furniture, and a decorative railing completed the space. It was the same on each floor with only slight variances in color. From the outside, Willoughby had to say he liked the look of the three suites that anchored the three story complex.

Sydney looked over at him. "Why three apartments?"

He shrugged. "I don't know. Maybe he liked the different views. Maybe it was a security thing. Maybe he had a thing about neighbors. Maybe he just got a deal on buying all three apartments together and thought it was a good investment."

"Maybe he had a couple of mistresses," Sydney offered.

Willoughby barked a short laugh. "Different mistresses that close together? That would be lively."

"Well," Sydney grinned, but never took her eyes off him. "Your ideas don't hold up so well either. If it was neighbors, then why not four apartments? You would want one so there's no one below you, another so that no one is above you, and one to each side. He has the above and below covered, but what about the neighbors to either side? I don't know if I buy the security thing either, and it seems like if he bought them for investment reasons, he would have tenants in them."

Willoughby studied the building again. "It looks like the corner apartments are substantially larger than the other ones. Maybe he really liked this view and had plans to eventually unify all three apartments into a single dwelling."

Sydney did not seem convinced, but gave a tentative nod. They worked their way around to a beautifully manicured hedge, leading through a small grotto of trees to a heavy wrought iron gate. The gate was locked, but hidden under a wave of ivy hanging from iron gateposts was a small guard station. The security officer on duty waved them through the opening gate after viewing their credentials at a small window.

As the gate swung closed, they moved further inside what turned out to be a deceptively expansive courtyard, anchored in the center by a polished wood pavilion and an immaculately landscaped pool. Water cascaded down a small rock island to one side of the pool. Trees and greenery made the formation look almost natural, with a Jacuzzi seemingly fashioned out of pure rock. The open end of the pool was tiled. Italian marble steps led down into the water. A stone deck to the far side of the pool housed a dozen or so shaded tables and a smattering of wood and fabric lounge chairs. The entire central complex was ringed by mature trees and shrubs, with roses and other flowers planted throughout with abandon.

Beyond the ring of trees were more shrubs, and the doors to the apartments. It became immediately apparent why Sam may have wanted to own a full vertical row of apartments. Each series of three vertical apartments had a single glass door entry. The door was opened by way of a thumb print scanner, and led into a lush corridor that gave entry to the first floor apartment on the one side, and to a small gold and mahogany elevator on the other.

Willoughby and Sydney lost no time in locating the door that accessed the series of vertical apartments Willoughby had inherited.

"So how do we get in?" Sydney asked. "Wouldn't the scanner have been set to Sam's thumb print?"

Willoughby raised his thumb toward the small reader. "I'm not sure," he said, "but Sam was pretty thorough. Maybe he planned for this possibility."

He pressed his thumb against the pad for a long moment, but nothing happened. Just as he pulled it away, however, the words, "Welcome Willoughby" flashed across the small LED screen and the elevator door slid open.

Sydney's eyes widened as they stepped in. "Where did he get your thumbprint?"

Willoughby took a moment to answer as he watched the heavy glass door glide shut. Opening the accordion door to the elevator, he found three buttons, one for floor two and floor three respectively, and one for the roof. Next to the buttons was a retina scanner. "Yeah," he mumbled, "and how did he imprint my retina for the retina scan?" He leaned down and pressed the third-floor button, allowing a brief beam of light to scan his eye. "This is pretty high-tech security for an apartment."

Sydney nodded. "True, but you said there are millions of dollars' worth of art and antiques in these apartments. It seems justified to me."

Willoughby shrugged as Sydney stepped in, they closed the elevator door, and the small cabin began to rise. He studied Sydney. "You're not your talkative self today. I mean, I don't blame you. I know it had to have been awful to have to go through all that alone. I thought you would be safer."

Sydney looked away for a long moment. The elevator had completely stopped before she turned back to him and made an embarrassed attempt to swipe at her eyes. "Okay, I accept your apology. And, I shouldn't have hit you. So, we're square, right?" She fought the hint of a yawn. "I haven't gotten much sleep over the last couple of days. When I did finally doze last night, I had this weird nightmare that I was trying to get a baby grand piano up a flight of stairs. I was completely by myself, so I had to keep propping one wheeled leg up on the next step at a time, and then pushing the piano a little bit, and then lifting the next leg, and the stairs kept getting steeper and steeper until I was holding the whole weight of the piano, and it was pushing backward. I knew if I let it push me over the edge of the step, I'd lose my balance, and the whole piano would come crashing down on me and crush me…"

Willoughby pushed back the elevator door. "Sounds intense," he said, stepping out of the elevator and motioning for her to follow. "Let's make sure and steer clear of baby grands for a while."

"Yeah, no kidding," Sydney said, looking down and not moving. "I awoke in a cold sweat. It was awful. The apartment was dark, and silent, and I was all alone. I don't like being alone in the dark at the best of times, and after watching Sam…" Her eyes were tearing up again, showing a sudden vulnerability.

Willoughby stepped back into the elevator and put an arm around her. "I think you should stay in a hotel tonight. I'll get an adjoining room." He started to ask why Aiyito didn't stay with her, but then he thought of their conversation and realized why he wouldn't."

"Thanks. I'm just being stupid," Sydney said, letting Willoughby lead her out onto a small, paneled entryway.

"I don't think so," Willoughby insisted. "I would have probably been just as uncomfortable. In fact, I would have probably had every light in the apartment blazing and some sixties sitcom blaring on the TV."

Sydney smiled. "So, you have nostalgic feelings for *Giligan's Island?*"

"Hey," Willoughby grinned back. "Don't knock it—my mom would usually let me watch it after I got home from school in the afternoon. It was pretty fun, and there were no man-eating grand pianos." He turned to her. "You do realize that most people have nightmares about vampires, and monsters, and people chasing them with knives, not killer pianos, right?"

A recessed skylight illuminated the cozy corridor to the apartment. A full set of armor stood to one side of the ornate oak door, and a glass case, with an embroidered antique Kimono and a collection of Samurai swords, was displayed to the other side of the door. As Willoughby took out what appeared to be an electronic key, the door clicked open and all lights winked on, as if in welcome.

Sydney wiped her eyes and let her smile widen. "Yeah, well I've had weirder dreams."

"Like what?" Willoughby said, stepping through the doorway into a wide central room that seemed to be part living room, part den, part ranch-style great room. Sydney had wandered over toward a beautifully preserved and intricately carved antique organ against one wall.

"Oh, like one time I dreamed I was stranded on a deserted island, and I was trying to make the best use of everything I had with me, and I had started to string my bra up between two trees to catch rain water, but then I thought, *if it doesn't rain every couple of hours, I'll die of thirst…*" Her voice was nonchalant and her eyes had not moved from the organ, which she was still inspecting with a calculated thoroughness.

Willoughby started to think through that revelation, then gave his head a slight shake. "That's," he paused, "I'll, uh, I'll plead no comment on that one." He walked over to the organ. "I didn't know Sam played an instrument."

"He doesn't," Sydney said; "at least, not this organ." She had lifted the lid and was inspecting the yellowed keys. "Nobody has played this organ for years. It's clean and immaculately kept, but you can tell when an instrument hasn't been used."

Willoughby narrowed his eyes. He thought of asking what an organ that never got played was doing here, but when he glanced up, he noted the picture that hung there.

"If I'm not mistaken, that's an original Monet." The painting was of a woman standing on a grassy hill in a white dress, holding an umbrella, with a small boy looking on, just visible over the crest of the hill. Sydney raised an eyebrow, then began to wander the rest of the room.

"So, who is Girrard?" She asked, looking at another painting that appeared to belong to the French Impressionist movement. The picture was of a walkway bordering a wide river. Once again, a woman in a white dress was walking along a wrought iron railing, this time with a young girl in tow.

"Girrard?" Willoughby said. "I don't know. Let me look it up." He pulled out his cell phone. In moments, he looked up. "Not as valuable. Thomas Kinkade did some impressionistic work under the name of Robert Girrard early in his career."

"It's a beautiful painting," Sydney said, "but why hang it across from a Monet?"

Willoughby shrugged. "Sam didn't put much stock in what other people thought. He liked what he liked, and that was good enough for him. I would guess it may have something to do with the woman in the white dress."

The two continued to stroll, finding an eclectic blend of priceless and somehow sentimental artifacts. It was as if a story were being laid out here, but you had no idea of who the key characters were and where it started and where it ended. Willoughby couldn't help but feel that the scheme of the apartment was odd. It struck him more as a museum than as a real residence. The central great room was almost octagonal in shape. The longest flat wall contained the front doorway. Directly opposite, on the other side of a center arboretum, was the wall that opened to the covered balcony they had seen from outside.

On the right side of the octagonal room, three equal lengths of paneled wall bumped out to create the shape of an octagon. Each segment of mahogany paneling offered a door. The closest door opened into the largest of the rooms, obviously a master bedroom with a large master bath and walk-in closet toward the back. The second door opened into a large, utilitarian closet. The third opened into an expansive study and library. All rooms were impeccably clean, tastefully, if eclectically decorated with a preference given to English Manor décor and French Impressionism, with some Renaissance flavor, and hints of the amateur scientist or naturalist sprinkled in for good measure.

On the left side of the octagonal room were three more paneled walls and three more doors. One opened to an immaculate, well stocked kitchen with attached pantry; one opened to a combination sauna and guest bathroom, complete with claw tub and a walk-in shower; and the last door opened to a generous guest bedroom.

Willoughby stood in the center of the room studying its layout. The more he looked, the more he saw that the room was not just octagonal, but that there were other mathematical angles at play here. He found every angle in the room seemed to lead his eye back to the arboretum at the center of the apartment. It, too, was octagonal in shape, with what appeared to be clear glass walls. The centerpiece of the arboretum appeared to be a carefully constructed rock, tree, shrub, and flower display. As Willoughby walked slowly around it, however, he noted that each octagonal glass pane was blocked such that the only things visible beyond the natural centerpiece were bits of solid colored paneling or nondescript sky. Upon closer inspection, he noted that the skylight opening above, letting light spill down into the arboretum, did match the Covent Garden sky outside almost exactly, but something still bothered him. He took one more slow walk around the central octagon just to be sure, then turned to Sydney. She had stopped investigating the décor and was watching him curiously.

"This arboretum is a fake," he said softly.

"What do you mean?"

Sydney had been walking slowly around the expansive room, continuing to study the wealth of art on the walls, and the glass cases of eclectic collectibles, commenting on a case of large African Scarab Beetles, a collection of 16th century Mardis Gras masks, an impeccably detailed model of the H.M.S. Victory, the invulnerable flagship of Lord Nelson, and a collection of all the Bentley Touring models from post-war to present day. She stood open-mouthed now, next to a case of beautiful but flawed diamonds that shimmered in the bright light of the display case.

"I mean, it's not an arboretum," Willoughby continued. "Those are solid walls, not glass. The nature scene we think we see is a hologram."

Sydney made her way to the center octagon, studying it as she went. "How do you know?"

Willoughby paced slowly around the structure, staring first up at the ceiling, and then down at the floor. "It's very well done, so nothing major. Just a lot of little things which combine to create a conclusion…Ah!" he said, bending down. He put his thumb over what appeared to be an ordinary knot hole in the hardwood floor, only inches from the edge of the octagon. His thumb appeared to slide into the floor, then there was a moving bar of light, as if his thumb had been scanned, and a clicking noise. Both Willoughby and Sydney looked up.

A slice of dark appeared on the supposed glass panel in front of them. Willoughby cautiously waved a hand into the dark. Lights flickered on, illuminating an octagonal room. He stepped in, followed closely by Sydney.

The hidden room was small, but buzzed with activity. Immediately to their right was a one person, standing elevator. Willoughby let his eyes trace the rest of the room. The walls were capable of projecting multiple feeds of video and data, much like the black wall Willoughby had interacted with on H.S.'s yacht. At near waist level, a marble counter protruded from each of the octagonal wall segments. Its impeccably polished black surface seemed to be a projector bed for various three dimensional displays. As he studied them, Willoughby made out five distinct stations along the smooth counter top. Each was continually crowded with crawling number displays, varying grids, and camera footage, often reflected from different angles on the wall above. Approaching one of the counter displays, Willoughby swiped his hand over it. The crawling bank of numbers vanished and two words appeared, hovering in midair: "Team Locator."

"It's like H.S.'s control room on the *Pesci Pecolli*," Willoughby said, "only more extensive." He walked around the small room, swiping a hand over each counter segment. "Look at these digital labels;" he said, reading them aloud. "Team Locator, Company Personnel, Time Grid Anomalies, Financial Assets, Physical Assets, and Security." Sydney pointed back to the first counter.

"What are the dots with coordinates? One says, JA, who is near HQ, and over here is AV, and here together, in green, are SS and WV." She looked up. "Sydney Senoya and Willoughby VonBrahmer...They're tracking us. We're green, probably, because we're here."

"Yeah," Willoughby said. "They told us they were tracking us, remember? I guess it's just easy to forget." His voice fell almost to a whisper as he studied the 3D displays over the various counters. His eyes stopped on the one labeled *Company Personnel*. A display of names scrolled up. The list stopped scrolling and one name blinked—*Aiyito Senoya*. Willoughby clicked the blinking name. A three-dimensional hologram in a light cube showed Aiyito in his office. Aiyito was seated at a heavy desk, drinking back a small cup of clear liquid. He looked up and spoke:

"What do you want?"

A pale-skinned man stepped into frame. "*What do I want?* Oh, there are lots of things I want, Aiyito."

Willoughby felt the hairs on his neck prickle. He knew this pale-skinned man. He reached up quickly and stopped the playback by wiping his hand through the image. His mind was racing. Aiyito had confessed to meeting Beelzebub—to helping him try to find the pendant. Here was proof, but Sam knew about that? And was that the full story? What had Aiyito *not* told him?

He shook his head, turning around. He didn't want to think about it—not here, not in front of Sydney. Despite her tangled feelings toward her dad, Aiyito *was* her dad, and he knew that still meant something to her. The news that he had played a role in the hijacking of the *Absconditus,* naively or not, would paralyze her. They couldn't afford that right now. All of them needed to be alert and on top of their game.

Still, this one video segment inspired so many questions. *If Sam had known about Aiyito's betrayal, had H.S.?* Why hadn't this information been shared? He walked to the one-man elevator—a raised silver circle surrounded by a cage made from thin, gold rods. He ran his finger over a small control panel about shoulder high in the cage. This was not the time to deal with revelations about Aiyito. He checked over his shoulder to see that the security footage was gone and the readout of Aiyito's name was, once again, blinking.

"Hey," Sydney said. "That was my dad. That was Aiyito."

"Yeah," Willoughby said, blocking her from getting to the console. "It was some kind of stock security footage. Listen, Sydney, we've got to see what's on the other floors—or wherever this elevator leads. None of this is making sense. I could understand if we found such a place in H.S.'s rooms, but we found nothing—only books, mountains of notebooks, and old computer gear. Why would Sam have access to such high tech?"

Sydney thought about it. "Yeah," she said. "It's weird. Sam was the logistics guy. You might expect him to have access to sailing charts, and possibly a quick path to underground parking, but not highly sophisticated tech gear." Sydney moved silently up behind him. Willoughby at last found the cage catch, sprung it, and stepped inside.

"Let me go down first," he volunteered. "If it's safe, I'll send the standing platform back for you."

Sydney gave a curt nod. "Just don't take all day."

On the second level, the mystery deepened. The second level held only a single mahogany table. It was odd looking, like someone had taken an executive boardroom table and cut it cleanly so that only a quarter of the table remained—the point of the cut melding seamlessly into one of the octagonal wall segments, which seemed to be made of opaque glass. Three high-backed chairs surrounded the end and sides of the piece of table. As Willoughby stepped from the elevator platform and sent it back up for Sydney, the light slightly dimmed in the room and the walls around him came alive. The effect was breathtaking. He was looking out now at a full, expansive boardroom, with a beautifully intact table surrounded by twelve high-backed chairs. The table was neatly arrayed with built in keyboards at each chair and black, shiny, three-dimensional displays just beyond the keyboards. The room appeared to be high above London, with floor to ceiling glass walls all the way around.

The elevator hissed to a stop behind him and he heard Sydney exclaim, "Wow!"

"It's not real," Willoughby said. "Only a small piece of that table, and the three end chairs, are really in this room."

"I surmised that," Sydney said. "This is a view from the other side of London."

Willoughby marveled. "I've never seen the illusion of a room look so real," Willoughby added. "There are no seams or flaws. You feel like you could walk right over and look out at Big Ben and the Thames."

"I've seen this room once before," Sydney added, stepping out of the elevator cage. "It's the Observations, Inc. boardroom. Why has Sam recreated it?"

Willoughby's thoughts were in a whirl. "When you were there, was the board in session?"

Sydney thought for a moment. "Yes. They brought me in to report on the staff and chain we had found in Oban, Scotland—the chain H.S. showed you in Bermuda."

"Where did H.S. sit?" Willoughby asked.

Sydney again paused, then pointed. "There, at the far end."

"Who sat here, opposite him?"

Sydney's eyes widened. "I don't know. They referred to him as the Director, but his features kept changing, and each time they did, all the other images would glitch. It was odd. H.S. had warned me about it. He said many of the board members were anonymous, even to the rest of the board, and so used digital projections of themselves that they could modulate. Only their voices were real."

Willoughby stopped his slow pacing and blurted out the question that was burning in his mind, peering hard at Sydney. "Could the height and width of the image you saw in the Director's seat possibly be consistent with the height and width of our friend, Sam?"

"You're not thinking…" Sydney slowly pulled out one of the chairs and sat. "Yes," she said at length. "Yes, it could."

Willoughby began to pace again. He kept shaking his head. Finally, he stepped over to the elevator cage. "It has to be on the third level," he said. "The answer has to be there." He climbed in the cage and pushed the button to take him down to the final, or ground level floor. Sydney, too, seemed lost in thought, unwilling to speak.

As the elevator cleared the second floor and glided down to a stop, Willoughby found himself immersed in what appeared to be an austere country manor. The scent of flowers and freshly cut hay hung in the air. Sheep bleated somewhere in the distance. He was in a drawing room of sorts. British landscape pictures hung on two of the walls. The illusion of space was as complete as the boardroom above. A small fireplace was housing a small, wood fire just to his right. He stepped out of the cage and sent the elevator back up. He could feel the fire's warmth, but as with the floor above, the back half of the room was obviously behind the glass walls. Willoughby reached out, starting toward where he thought the glass wall would begin. His hand was stopped short. The real dimensions of this room seemed considerably smaller than the one above, and less octagonal, as if someone had cut off one whole corner of the octagon. Only then did he notice that the corner was filled with an easy chair. A motionless figure was seated in the chair, it's eyes watching him silently. The figure was dressed in a dark suit, tan shirt, and long, dark tie. He was tall and lean.

"Hello, Master Willoughby," a familiar voice said. Willoughby's eyebrows shot up. "S-s-Sam!" he stuttered.

The figure gave a slight bow. Its face beamed at him. Before he could move, the elevator descended behind him. Sydney let out a gasp.

20

Blood Moon

Tainken spent almost three months preparing the silver sheets under Rashrahu's careful instruction. The plates were made from a form of metal unknown to the modern world. The Goddess appeared mysteriously and sporadically, instructing her on how to use steam to make the metal malleable and easy to imprint. Each night as she finished her work in the secret room, Rashrahu would lead her back to the pool in the temple. She had been introduced to one of the acolytes at the temple, a girl barely out of her teens by the name of Eashea. The girl lived not far from the temple and gave her a place to stay in the daytime. She fed her two sparse meals a day. Tainken mostly slept when she was at the girl's home, but occasionally, she would walk to the markets with Eashea. She learned some of the local language. The city around the temple was not large in area—probably less than a single mile in circumference—but it was complex and densely populated. Eashea let her borrow one of her simple tunics and helped her hide her blonde hair beneath a bright headdress. She used a cocoa based cream to darken her skin and no one seemed to pay her much mind.

When dusk came, Eashea set off for the temple where she worked the night shift, cleaning and refreshing the temple grounds. She would leave T.K. at the temple pool. Rashrahu would come for her shortly after, and they would work through the slowly warming nights. In the morning, Eashea would be there to take her back to the little room where she slept. Eashea never asked T.K. what she did at the temple. Tainken assumed Rashrahu had spoken to her, but this was never confirmed. It was as if Eashea questioned nothing to do with the temple or with Rashrahu.

As for Rashrahu, she spoke little beyond the words needed to teach Tainken how to prepare the silver sheets. T.K. asked her why she called them prayer sheets when they were hidden from view in a secret chamber far in the depths of the temple. The woman said simply that they came in answer to her prayer to help stop the slow rise of the *Dark Edge*. Tainken asked who the *Dark Edge* was. Rashrahu said they were many. "They hide their hearts in the gray of the edge. It is difficult to know them in the daylight, but in the dark, they draw their own kind."

When asked why the *Dark Edge* planned to destroy the world and create in its place a sucking blackness, The Goddess answered, "Our very existence is based upon a balance of light and dark. It is governed by exacting rules. If those rules are disrupted, the balance is lost and chaos ensues. The *Dark Edge* is ascendant in chaos for their very mantra is control. In chaos, many become confused and frightened and are drawn to any voice that offers control. The *Dark Edge*, of course, gives their offering at a price. Many of their followers actually believe they serve a just cause—they believe they are saving a world on the edge of collapse. But as the light of spontaneity ebbs and creativity is lost from the world, society becomes enslaved by their own fears. The path to enlightenment is lost. Social structure begins to implode as more and more buy into a narrowing, restrictive world view. Turning the tide can be done, but only at great cost and effort. We of the light cannot, of ourselves, change the choices of you in the flow of time. We can only be vigilant. We can only encourage the good. Nurture the brave and fearless. You have a gift to be able to bridge between our realm and theirs. You must use this to help check and defeat the *Dark Edge*."

That was all she would say about it. But she was masterful with her hands, showing Tainken how to carve wood blocks into small pictures and then stamp them into the soft metal, then how to cool and polish the metal. It was back-breaking work, but T.K. felt pride in the first finished sheet. She was instructed to put her vision only on one sheet, the largest sheet which hung directly opposite a large lever. Rashrahu warned her never to touch the lever. "It will bring down this whole temple," she said when further questioned.

"One lever?" T.K. asked.

"Yes. A single person can pull it. It is the technology of your people—as are the glowing walls. They hid much of their technology in this city. It was set up as a sort of observation post where they could learn more about the curious people of earth."

"You are not Atlantian. What are you?" Tainken asked.

"I am something similar. I was here before your city. I visited Atlantis. It was a beautiful city. I met your father." Once again, this was all she would say.

The two smaller sheets of metal to either side of the larger one were completely dictated by Rashrahu. She said they were messages for Willoughby—he alone would know how to read and decipher them. She made sure T.K. understood that, once the metal cooled, no force around it could dent or scar it. "Even if the temple collapses on these plates, they can be found unmarred by the rock and rubble that buries them."

The final thing that Rashrahu instructed Tainken to do was take a small scroll she held out to her. "The blood moon is coming," she said. "It will soon be the start of your long night. When the night is over, you will be asked to make a sacrifice."

"A sacrifice? Here in the temple?"

"No. Far away, in the time of your friends. Here…" T.K. took the ornately rolled scroll. She at once recognized it. It bore the seal of Atlantis. "Open it," Rashrahu encouraged. The seal seemed to open on its own accord. T.K. unrolled the scroll and read.

"But this—these are instructions to—"

Rashrahu looked up. The earth trembled and rocked slightly. She looked to T.K., her eyes fierce. "It has begun. Outside, it is the night of the blood moon. We must get you away, quickly."

She was on her feet in seconds, leading the way out of the chamber. Tainken had no choice but to hastily roll up the scroll in her hands and follow. The earth shook again, more violently this time. Walls cracked and dust and steam hissed into the corridors.

"What's happening?" Tainken screamed.

"The time has come more quickly than I imagined. Your long night," Rashrahu yelled back, "has begun."

21

Ghost in the Machine

"Who are you?" Sydney shouted, fire in her eyes and venom in her voice. "If this is some kind of joke, it's not funny."

The figure in the chair did not get up. It did not immediately speak. It stared at Sydney for a long moment, and then said softly, "Hello, Sydney. I know this must be a shock. I know Sam was with you when he was shot. I'm sorry that I could not prepare you better."

Willoughby looked from Sydney to the calm, seated figure. "You're not Sam?"

The figure smiled. "I am *a* Sam, but not *the* Sam."

"What's that supposed to mean?"

"H.S. began to worry a few years ago that someone may be able to breach our security and infiltrate our organization. As a caution, he provided Sam with a very sophisticated computer program that had the ability to observe, learn, and strategize. This ingenious program immediately began to learn from many things. First, from the Observations, Inc. data banks and computer systems. Then it studied the actions of the Observations, Inc. teams over time and tracked each of the key Observations, Inc. personnel. After the break-in at the St. Petersburgh facility occurred, the constructions of this core of master computer complex was accelerated and this soon became the hub of all Observations, Inc. activity. Here, I observed most closely the man you knew as Sam. I created a sort of alternate imprint of his mental thoughts, his physical appearance, and his daily mannerisms.

"When the flesh-and-bone Sam, who I refer to as *the* Sam, discovered this shadow function in the program, he did not delete it. In fact, he improved it, creating a boardroom persona who could stand in as his double at uninteresting board meetings, etc. This shadow persona began to anticipate what the flesh-and-bone Sam would do, or what he would say, often even before *the* Sam acted. The flesh-and-bone Sam knew that his physical self could not live forever, and he wanted to make sure that someone was around who knew his goals and desires and would be able to finish what needed to be done. I am that someone. I do not expect you to call me Sam, but I do hope you will consider my input as you would have his. In respect for the man who I consider my maker, I call myself *Sian.*"

Sydney cocked an eyebrow. "Shawn?"

The face of the entity showed little emotion. "It may sound that way, but it is spelled differently. The name was given to me by *the* Sam. It is based in part on *Sam I am* from the Dr. Seuss book *"Green Eggs and Ham."* The flesh-and-bone Sam also added the word *now*, which gives us the full acronym, *S-I-A-N for 'Sam I Am Now.'* *The* Sam wanted it to be a name. I am not sure of my feelings, but James Arthur, were he here, would likely say, '*I like it, I do, Sam I am.*'"

The image made a slight grimace. Willoughby recognized the facial expression, with a start, as a very Sam-like attempt at a grin. It took a minute, but as he further analyzed the image's words, he realized that this computerized *entity* was trying to make a joke. He did not let his mind dwell on the attempt at humor, however. He was struggling to come to terms with a computerized intelligence so effectively mimicking the appearance and mannerisms of a friend.

"So," he mumbled, "you're a robot."

The statement seemed somewhere between a question and an accusation. Willoughby felt confused. On the one hand, he wasn't aware of anyone who had been this successful at imbuing a robot with so realistic and casual a demeanor—even an ability to attempt humor. On the other hand, this machine had stolen the voice, the look, even the mannerisms of his good friend.

The Sam persona did not take offense. "I'm not a robot per se," it began. "I consider myself to be more an *artificial intelligence*. I am currently using the same technology that H.S. demonstrated to you aboard the *Absconditus,* namely a three-dimensional, holographic projection using pigmented magnetic dust to create a very natural, very lifelike persona."

"That's a projection?" Sydney asked, both eyebrows raised this time.

Willoughby continued to study the image. He walked slowly forward until he was stopped by the wall of glass protecting the image. He narrowed his eyes. "When H.S. used the technology on the *Absconditus*, it was impressive, but I knew within moments that it was only a projection. There were slight glitches, tiny nuances in sound that gave it away. I sense none of those with you."

"Yes, I have continued to study and improve upon his original technology. Regrettably, my physical persona is tied to only a few holographic chambers set up to accommodate me, but my mind, my voice can be accessed anywhere on the Observations, Inc. network."

"Your mind? Your voice?" Sydney, who remained standing at the entrance to the elevator cage with her arms crossed and eyes narrowed, replied. "You talk as if you think you're human! You're a computer projection..." She glanced around the octagonal-shaped room. "What is this place?" Her lips pulled into a frown. "Why does a chauffeur and part-time yacht captain have a hidden, state of the art control center *in his residence?*" She was obviously irritated. "There's something we haven't been told here. What was Sam's *real* role in the organization?"

Willoughby found himself nodding. He wanted to know the same thing. This was not at all what he had expected from the man *he* knew as Sam. He turned toward the incredibly realistic persona, who was looking up thoughtfully, entwining his fingers just as Sam would have done. The figure tilted its head back and spoke.

"I'm afraid the man you knew as Sam was a carefully created ruse. The persona you knew was no more real than I."

"What do you mean?" Willoughby said, beginning to feel irritated himself.

The figure did not answer, but merely reached a hand forward and tapped an area near the end of the easy chair. The lights dimmed, as did the sounds from outside. The cozy country cottage vanished, leaving only a dark void. A three-dimensional face appeared in front of them. It hovered in the air, fully four feet in height and possibly three feet wide. Willoughby could just make out the man's neck and a bit of his bony shoulders. The face, and the shoulders, appeared to be those of Sam. The face gave a crooked smile and spoke.

"Hi Willoughby. I knew you would find my hidden command post and my computer simulation. The fact you are watching this means I am now dead. I know you are confused about several things, beginning with why I left you this inheritance, and how I could afford such lavishly furnished luxury apartments in so exclusive a part of town on the salary of chauffer and yacht captain. They are valid questions, and the answers are simple. I left this mystery to you because I feel you are the key player in what is to come. The truth about the Sam you interacted with and thought you knew is simple—he was a carefully crafted fiction meant to keep you from suspecting the truth. It was never my intention to mislead you, but in this high stakes game that you and I have been sucked into, I remain convinced that my initial anonymity will give you in the long run a greater chance for success. Before I get to my reasoning, I want you to understand that my comments and discussions with you have always been completely real. It is just that the person they came from is not the person you thought you knew.

"My full name is Samuel Allen Wasser—and yes, that is *the* Samuel A. Wasser of Wasser Worldwide Investments."

Willoughby's mouth dropped open. Wasser Worldwide Investments was one of the biggest, and by far, richest investment firms in the world. To imagine *his* Sam—the Sam he knew as his personal chauffer—as a worldwide mogul on this scale stretched conceivability. The voice of Sam continued.

"In my younger years, there were few who did not know my name, and fewer still who did not recognize my face. I was constantly hounded by reporters and photographers. I had inherited a sizeable fortune and was at the helm of an enormous conglomerate. I turned my inheritance into a global empire—and all of this occurred before I reached the age of thirty-five. I was rich, famous, and very, very lonely. I grew tired of all the pressure and pretense. Everyone believed they knew what I wanted, what I needed, and they had agendas of their own they tried to push forward. It grew tiring. It was constant stress. I was the most eligible bachelor in the world, and yet I had no one I wanted to call to ask out on a date. As Sydney will attest, fame has its price. And yes, I do know a thing or two about being young, brilliant, and...completely misunderstood.

"So, I decided something had to change. I did not like being watched. I was not particularly fond of the social scene, nor did I wish to spend my days hanging out at the high halls of commerce. The flash and glamour of money had lost its pull on me. I felt there had to be more to life, more to me. My family's roots go all the way back to William the Conqueror, you know. I come through the William de Warenne line. I am proud of my ancestry. Would my addition to that legacy be nothing more than the safeguarding of fortune and privilege? Do not fortune and privilege give one a chance to make a difference, to, at least in some small way, change the world?

"At first, I thought my restlessness and self-doubt might go away after I slipped from the limelight. I poured myself into my work. I built my sizeable fortune until I was one of the richest men in the world. But I found this was not enough. The more money I made, the more I felt weighed down, even trapped by the fortune I had accumulated. I found that retiring from the social limelight did not release me from social obligation. I began to long to be anonymous, to simply disappear. I wanted to know what it would be like to live a simpler and less structured life.

"When I confided in an uncle just before he passed away, he actually forced a chuckle. 'I know what you mean,' he said. Then he added, 'There are times that the weight of having too much can seem as heavy as the challenge of having not enough. I have thought to myself that it would be nice to just slip away. To disappear into a time where no one knew me, where I could keep my name, my money a hidden secret, and see what life looked like when you lived a quieter life.'

"Suddenly, he sat up. A twinkle came into his eye. 'Why not?' he said. 'What is the use of having money if you don't use it for something crazy and wonderful occasionally?' He asked for a scrap of paper and jotted down a name and a number. 'He's an odd fellow,' the uncle said, his eyes even brighter. 'I made his acquaintance a while back—a strange man who never seems to age. He teaches a lecture series at Harvard, or Cambridge, or one of those… A lecture series on the coming feasibility of time travel.'

"I took the scrap of paper. *Time travel*. It sounded ridiculous. Everyone knows that time travel is impossible. But the idea continued to nag at me. '*What is the use of having money if you do not use it occasionally for something crazy, and wonderful…?*' I pulled out the scrap of paper my uncle had given me and I looked the man up. He was a visiting professor with Cambridge University. His time travel series was offered twice a year. On a lark, I decided to sign up. I soon became, as my uncle before me, fascinated with the man and with his theories. The more closely acquainted I became with Hathaway Simon (people with money, of course, have no problem getting acquainted with whomever they like), the more I became convinced that there was something to the man's assertions. I also began to believe that there was a lot he was holding back—a lot he was hiding. I confronted him with my observation. 'Well, well,' he said, 'it took you a while, but you do know how to observe.' That is when he invited me to form with him Observations, Inc. He looked me square in the eye and said, 'I will teach you to observe a world you did not know existed. I will introduce you to a technology that is real, that works. You can travel in time, Samuel Allen Wasser. I know. I have been there and back.'"

"I did not ask where '*there*' was. I did not consider him a dreamer, or a lunatic. I simply sat back. I observed and I listened. I bankrolled what some would have considered to be a completely harebrained scheme, and I learned he spoke the absolute truth.

"You may be wondering why I stayed in this time once I learned it really was possible to, as my uncle put it, 'disappear into time.' The answer is two-fold. First, H.S. was adamant in teaching me of the danger of going back and somehow affecting what was meant to be. Most of his travel in time was for observation only. There was little or no interaction with the timelines he visited. Secondly, as I became immersed in helping H.S. build Observations, Inc. into the secretive organization it has become, I found I enjoyed it. I was having fun. True, I became somewhat of a social hermit. I was sought after less and less for social functions I never chose to attend, and then, thankfully, I was all but forgotten. There were movie stars, sports heroes, politicians, musicians, and more visible corporate movers and shakers to accost, so the press finally began to leave me alone. A silent partner billionaire who allows his more newsworthy companies to be spun off, and seldom shows up to board meetings, was simply not strong headline material. I learned that I did not *have* to go to a different time to disappear. I found I liked working with my hands and I could couple that with my affinity for fine automobiles and beautiful ships. That is when H.S. and I came to a deal of sorts. I created the personas of Sam the Chauffer, and Sam the yacht Captain. I grew comfortable with the arrangement.

"So, there you have it." The image of Sam leaned back, spreading his arms wide before folding them again. "I have run the board for Observations, Inc. for well over twenty years now, though none of the board members, outside of H.S., have any idea what I look like. They know me only as the fearsome Mr. W. I attend meetings as a virtual image, one with a slightly liquefied face. Yes, I must confess that much of the board may believe my face looks almost inhuman, like a watercolor left too long in the rain. I scramble my voice and only communicate in writing electronically. I find it most rejuvenating to live incognito.

"Which brings us to my personal lair," the figure gestured around him. "You have found my hidden command center—my mad-scientist laboratory, my base of operations. I knew you would find it. You have also met Sian. Please forgive the Dr. Suess pun—the name based on *Sam I Am,* with the addition of the word, *now.* Perhaps a silly pun, but with an element of truth. I poured myself into the virtual intelligence. H.S. had always been concerned that enemies with advanced technology could think and move as fast as we, perhaps even faster. This became an even stronger concern after the St. Petersburg break in. So, as was his way, he felt technology could provide an answer. He set out to create a virtual agent to watch over Observations, Inc. that would be the most advanced on the planet, perhaps one of the most advanced virtual minds ever created. He charged this mind with monitoring and improving our technology footprint and working to safeguard the biological assets of the organization. At first, I found the idea of a learning virtual entity a bit jarring, but I soon became absorbed in the project. H.S. thought it a joke when I first suggested that the entity have a visual component that allowed it to pass for my twin. I considered it a safeguard, a way to preserve what I hoped to achieve. I wanted it to understand how I think, what I feel. Sian not only looks like me, but if we were successful, you will find he speaks, he thinks, and he problem solves like me, only infinitely faster. I will let you be the judge.

"I hope you enjoy the comfort of the apartments, and in the absence of H.S. and myself, that you take seriously the heavy responsibility of continuing the mission of Observations, Inc. I leave you not only my fortune, which Sian can help you access at any time, but I leave you a bit of myself—perhaps the best parts of myself—to help you navigate the way.

"I know the words may sound cliché, Willoughby, but marriage was never really in the cards for me. I never had a child, or an heir, but when I met you, I began to see what I had missed. Your step father seems like a fine man, but I must confess, I sometimes wished he was not. I sometimes wished you could have considered me as a father figure. I would have been proud to consider you a son. I guess my leaving all this to you is my attempt to solidify the feelings I could never openly express. Perhaps I am fooling myself, but I sensed, more than once, that you also felt a connection with me. I have always believed that you, Sydney, Antonio, and Dr. J can effectively lead this organization, safeguarding its secrets, even improving our various technologies. But we have powerful enemies— enemies who may feel they have succeeded in cutting off the head of the organization by eliminating H.S. and myself. You will need the combined strength of the team to survive. But, survive you will. I know it."

The man gave a sad smile. "Sian will bring you up to speed on what we know. There is much more for you to uncover here in my nerve center. I am sorry I could not be here in person to have this conversation with you. I planned to tell you everything as soon as I was convinced it was safe to do so. I feared that telling you too much too soon would only make you more of a target than you already were. There have been many attempts on my life that I did not share with you. There were attempts on H.S.'s life that were not shared with the team as well. We both knew that odds were not in our favor and sooner or later, one of those attempts would succeed. If you are listening to this, that most likely means that one has. It also means that you, Willoughby, and your team will now become the primary targets. I have tried to leave you everything you will need to defeat this dark brotherhood, whatever they are. My best wishes Willoughby, and to all the team. God speed."

The image evaporated and the room went dark for a moment. Then, the view of the quiet cottage gradually reappeared, lights sparkling in its chandeliers. Sian was still in the armchair staring silently out at us. Willoughby turned to Sydney.

"What do you make of this?"

Sydney stood stock still, as if stunned. Her eyes seemed glassed over and her mind a million miles away.

Finally, she turned slowly. "It's...incredible. I remember hearing my father mention board meetings with the intimidating *Mr. W,* yet, my mind can't seem to place Sam in that role. He was playful, gentle, kind when he was around me."

She glanced over at the computer projection. "Up until a couple of months ago, I considered H.S. to be the primary force behind the organization. In fact, to me, H.S. *was* Observations, Inc. The board was just my father, and some other businessmen who rubber stamped everything. I mean, Sam and others on the board did needed legwork from time to time, but it's...it's hard to take this all in. Sam was, well, you know, *Sam.* He was always around—at least, when H.S. was there. The two were almost inseparable. Now I realize why." She turned and gave Willoughby a slight smile. "One thing he didn't mention, though, was that he hated the physical process of time travel. It made him, well, ill. H.S. swore that Sam became a paler shade of green every time he went through the time stream. We would joke that it was somewhat like an earthquake around him after he got back from a time jump. His hands would be shaking for days. H.S. would constantly be talking about some era or other, and would turn to Sam, telling him he really should go, and Sam would promptly look sick and leave the room." The smile faded from her face.

"Now, come to find out he was at the center of everything... It's like being told that the boy next door is the king, that he was hidden away for a while for safe keeping, but, now he's back. I mean, I liked Sam—I loved Sam. He was pleasant, and comfortable with his old-school manners, and prim sort of ways. He was a good organizer, a good driver, handy with an automobile, a great yacht captain, and now, but, but, uh, I didn't see financial genius, brilliant strategist, corporate mogul, the wind behind H.S.'s machines. It's a lot to come to terms with."

"Yeah," Willoughby said, stepping over to a high-backed chair near one side of the room, "I agree, on all of those counts."

Sounds of sheep bleating came again from somewhere outside, and Willoughby could swear he felt a slight breeze on his cheeks. He looked up to see curtains trailing out from an open window—the illusion was flawless. Sian locked eyes with him, staring intently.

Willoughby sighed. "Sorry," he said. "It's a lot to deal with."

"Take your time," the image said. "I am sorry it had to be this way. We could wait until later to continue our conversation—until you have had a better chance to digest things."

Willoughby stared at the still figure in the chair with both anger and wonder. The fact that this *computer program* did not use contractions, a common distinction of Sam's speech, made him seem even more like his lost friend. It made the hurt of knowing his real friend was gone even more acute. He was tired of learning the truth about things only after the fact—when it was too late to do something to stop whatever catastrophe had come. But what was, was. He couldn't change that. But maybe, just maybe, this Sian could make things different moving forward. This was no ordinary artificial intelligence. Nor would this be a common electronic surveillance center. If their enemies had been after H.S. and Sam for some time now, that would mean Sam was right, they would start zeroing in on the remaining team. He had to know what assets he and the team had. He had to know what Sam and

H.S. knew. There would be time to mourn and reminisce later. Now—he felt it in his very bones—*now* was the time to act.

"We will continue *now!*" he said forcefully, surprised by the vehemence in his voice. He tried to lower his tone. "We're fighting an enemy I don't even understand. I need to know why you're here. What do you do? What do you know? What does this place do? How can it help us?" He pointed at the projection. "Before you answer, there's one more thing. I don't like that you're such a perfect likeness of my friend Sam. I want you to find a way to distinguish yourself physically—maybe not this instance, but at least by next time we meet. Are you good with that?"

The projection thought for a moment, then gave a slight nod and smiled.

"Sam would have approved, I believe. It helps you separate the man from his creation. Now, to business. You are a mind I can work with." He nodded toward two padded chairs. "Please, sit." After Willoughby and Sydney both moved to the chairs and made themselves comfortable, he continued. "What do I do? I monitor every news station, every Interpol sight, the surveillance at Langley, communications from the Kremlin, the activities of several criminal organizations and keep an eye on a number of terrorist cells... In short, I offer you an interface to the largest intelligence gathering network the world has ever seen. I look for trends, anomalies, I analyze strategies, and I deliver reports. With *the* Sam gone, I also manage Observations, Inc. I manage all his private and secret holdings. I track the locations of each member of the team and attempt to anticipate threats and eliminate them. Why am I here? Because the flesh-and-bone Sam did not want this work to end with his death. He felt it had infinite worth to this world. What does this place do? It responds to my will, and now, to your commands.

"At my core, Willoughby, I am a molecular computer. I reside in an electronic fortress the likes of which has never been seen on this planet before. From here, I can communicate with every electronic device in the world. My communication protocols are scrambled, encrypted, and shielded with massive algorithms, taken from the Riemann Hypothesis solution you developed, in fact—a solution never officially released to the mathematical community.

"Oh, by the way, I was impressed. There are few biological entities who could have cracked this hypothesis. At least, few currently alive. That was some clever work."

Willoughby brushed aside the idea that the computer had given him a compliment. He focused his gaze. "So, what have you learned from all this information gathering? What have you found that's of interest to us? With all this monitoring, and analyzing, and reporting, what can you tell me?"

The image paused, again cocking its head. "I have learned much from my information gathering. You are a flawed people—brilliant in some aspects, foolish in many others."

"I don't want to know what you have learned about mankind," Willoughby interrupted. "I want to know what you have learned about Beelzebub, about the brotherhood that is after us. What can you tell me that can help the team?"

Sian gave a tick of a second to deliberate. "I found much on the history of the secret brotherhood referred to anciently as the 'Dark Brotherhood,' or 'Dark Edge.' I have tracked them all the way back to Egyptian times, to the mythical *Council of Nine*. There seems to be an intersection point in a cathedral in France. Sam believed there was evidence of an active cell of the Brotherhood there, and we have record of visits to the Cathedral by both the man called Belzarac and the one called Reese. As you know, both were involved in the hijacking of the *Absconditus*. Sam was preparing to hire a private security team to infiltrate the cathedral, but he was not able to complete the preparations. I have learned little about Beelzebub. He has gone by many names and he spans almost the known history of man. His propensity for time travel makes it difficult to pin down when or where he originated."

It occurred to Willoughby that this entity had not answered the questions in sequential order as a computer program would. It seemed to have a level of consciousness and could make decisions on the fly based upon fluid situations. Despite his irritation at having to look at the speaking image of his friend and know this image was a lie, he was fascinated by the achievement in artificial intelligence.

"Okay. That's something. What else?"

"I am following every traceable lead that could uncover the whereabouts of what H.S. called the Prime Hole Facility, and T.K. I believe there is substantial merit to H.S.'s opinion that Atlantis was buried first by earth, then by water, and finally by ice. The latest edition of the Times Comprehensive Atlas of the World shows a previously unseen world of canyons, lakes, trenches and mountains beneath the ice in Antarctica. There are stress fractures, indicative of volcanic and earthquake activity."

"The Einstein-Hapgood papers…" Sydney said, her voice trailing off.

"Yes," the image said, glancing her way. "Data from British Antarctic Surveys show physical features that include mountains the size of the Alps and deep sub glacial trenches. The map was compiled from recent Bedmap2 compilations. A large, multi-national group of scientists contributed to the project. It took over 50 years, but the map includes previously unknown details, including unusual magnetic lines on the edge of the landmass nearest the tip of South America."

"South America?"

"Yes."

"Can you show me the data?"

"Of course, but it is extensive. Do you wish me to go through it all now? It may take several hours, possibly even days."

Willoughby looked down at his watch. "Uh...no. Not now. Anything else?"

The image paused a long moment.

"Yes. I have been tracking all Observations, Inc. personnel, retroactive to the moment H.S. entered this timeline. I have been asked to scour all security log entries and all personnel files. I am attempting to isolate a common thread and thus track the security breach."

"Do you have any suspects?"

"I do. Sam and I began to find small common threads centered around one person. The threat could be serious. I do not wish to go into it here. The information is sensitive. I was told to share it only with the Director. You, Willoughby, are now the Director."

Willoughby narrowed his eyes. "I trust Sydney implicitly," he said, but his mind was racing. *What if it was Aiyito? What if the image was trying to protect her, just like he was? Or had the intelligence read his mind?*

The image hesitated.

"So, tell us," Sydney piped up. "We need to know."

The image stared back at her, long and hard, and then spoke. "We are beginning to suspect your father."

There it was.

"My father?" Sydney intoned. She looked over at Willoughby, confused. He didn't know what to say. She looked back at the projection.

"Why? What proof do you have?"

"A considerable amount, actually." The image was silent for a long moment. Finally, he continued. "None of it is conclusive, but I advise we assemble the team and go over the data together. *The* Sam believed we could only succeed as a team. As I began to explain earlier, this facility is designed as a safe-house, an electronic nerve center, a lab facility, a mission center, and a transportation hub. It is equipped with a time door and a vast subterranean store of various supplies. I can facilitate outfitting each of you for whatever missions you feel it prudent to undertake. I agree with you Willoughby—the time to act is *now*. With your permission, I would like to text the team, asking them to converge here at 1800 hours. I will sign your name to the text, of course."

Once again, Willoughby had the feeling that this electronic entity could read his mind. "Well, then say six o'clock, because I don't speak in military time, and neither does the team."

Sian smiled. "Very well. I have also taken the liberty of ordering a fine gourmet meal, starting with a baby gem salad with pancetta and anchovies, then followed with beetroot ravioli, and a Boba Jams milky matcha green tea."

Sydney was still staring at the entity. "I want to see all the data you're basing your accusations on—all of it," she said, an edge to her voice.

"Of course," the image said. "Is the menu acceptable, Miss Sydney?"

Sydney didn't answer. She stared for a moment at the image, then motioned to Willoughby with her chin and climbed back into the one-person elevator. Before pressing the button to take her back up, she paused and stated a single word; "Entropy..."

For the briefest of seconds, the image seemed to glitch. It cocked its head up toward Sydney.

"Is that a question?"

"Maybe," Sydney said, her brow furrowed in concentration. "Tell me about the equation."

Again, the image cocked its head. "The second law of thermodynamics states that energy and heat dissipate over time. The equation is stated as—" The image paused, holding up a single hand and the equation appeared, hovering as glowing blue numbers in midair:

$$dS \geq 0$$

The image again looked to Sydney. "Willoughby could have easily told you this and explained the concept of entropy to you in some detail. I will repeat my question; why did you state this word? Why did you ask me to repeat the question? Were you testing me, Sydney? Did I pass the test?"

Sydney did not answer. She merely reached to push the button on the elevator. Before she could, the voice stopped her.

"There is an instruction from Sam for you, Miss Sydney. In the corner of the guest bedroom, you will find the original Martin Company D-45 China Dragon guitar, built to commemorate the milestone of 700,000 guitars sold worldwide. Sam purchased it at great expense. It was to be a gift. Please allow me to offer a detailed description. The guitar was crafted completely by hand. The image in the central and lower area of the peghead is a 'bi' or 'pi' disc, often found in tombs of Han Dynasty emperors. The image on the fingerboard is based on a painting from about 1st Century B.C. The dragon on the pickguard was inspired by an inlay on a tray from the 14th Century. The two inlays on the tailpin strip are Buddhist vajra, symbols of deep awareness and mental clarity. The calligraphy on the heel cap translates to 'harmony.' Sam asked me to give it to you upon your first visit to the command center. You are welcome to take it with you today."

Sydney showed no emotion as she stared at the image, her finger still hovering over the elevator button. Finally, without a word, her finger descended and the elevator slid out of sight. Sian watched her, then turned to Willoughby, lifting its head slightly.

"Sam thought she would be pleased. It was a considerable victory to convince the firm to sell that guitar. We had to commission an exact replica to hang in its stead at their corporate headquarters to keep the purchase secret."

Willoughby had been watching Sydney, gauging her reaction. He turned back to the image, thought for a moment, and then shrugged. "She's Sydney," he said simply, "and let's skip dinner."

Sian considered this, then raised an eyebrow and gave a nod. Neither spoke, letting the soft sound of the sheep, and the breeze, and a sound of laughter, as if children were coming home from school along some not too distant country lane, wash over them. At length, the elevator came down, empty. Willoughby breathed in sharply, and then turned toward it. The gold door slid open. Willoughby stepped in. As he turned back, his mind was in a whirl. *Why had Sam bought Sydney such an expensive guitar? Why had Sian chosen this moment to give it to her?* As he pressed the button and the small, one-person cage began to slide up, he looked one more time at the composed, blank-faced image in the chair. The image was following him with its ghostly real-looking eyes.

"Willoughby," it said, "I need you. Sam was my friend as well. I want to go after those who did this. Their time will soon be over."

There was barely a moment before the elevator cleared the room, just enough time for Willoughby to cock his head in thought.

22

Unto the Breach

Sydney had already found her way out of the secret rooms. Willoughby exited the command center as well, spinning to watch the atrium doorway close behind him. Once again, it created the sense of a seamless, glassed arboretum with a carefully constructed rock, tree, shrub, and flower display. He couldn't help but marvel at the meticulous detail of the illusion, but Sydney gave him no time to admire it. She had been bent over the open case of a beautifully detailed guitar, just as Sian had described it. When Willoughby approached, she quickly closed and latched the case, and then led him directly to the door without a sound. When he started to speak to ask about the guitar, she held a hand to his lips. She led him down to the grounds and then back through the entrance gate and onto the sidewalk bordering the front of the apartments. She turned right and walked a full three blocks before finally stopping and turning, pulling him into a sheltered alcove.

"That thing is creepy!" she burst out. "I don't trust it. And what is this?" She nodded toward the guitar, holding it up slightly. "Why would Sam buy me this? We were good friends, but this is about a million-dollar guitar! And why did he give it to me now, right after telling me he suspects my father of being the traitor who sold us all out? There's—this is, this is *crazy!*"

Willoughby considered his words carefully.

"Yeah, it's…" he started, then conceded the points. "This *is* crazy, and Sian *is* creepy. He's a level of artificial intelligence we've never seen before. The answers he gave to our questions had an element of random. Did you notice? He didn't always answer questions in sequential order. He made jokes. He didn't just randomly throw out some canned one, but pulled off spontaneous humor, and he gave me a compliment. He answered our questions in a stream-of-conscious fashion. He appeared to be thinking ahead, analyzing our reactions, adjusting on the fly. He used the pronoun 'I' consistently. He spoke with the same tone and accent of Sam, down to the smallest detail, never using contractions, and he seemed concerned about our emotional states. I'd love to get in and have a look at the software algorithms behind him."

"Fat chance of that. Even its—and I say '*its,*' not '*his*'—image is protected by thick glass. My guess is that it's the same kind of bulletproof glass used on the Observation Deck that looked out over the Jurassic Era Sea. That was impenetrable even to a 20-ton plesiosaur."

Willoughby cocked up an eyebrow. "Huh." He hadn't thought much about the glass, but Sydney was right, it had been thick. He pursed his lips.

"Hey, what was all that about '*entropy*'?"

"I'm not sure," Sydney sighed. "It was something Sam said just before he died. He said '*entropy*' was the password, and then he started saying something about an equation, but he, uh, he never…. finished."

She looked away.

Willoughby gave her a moment. "Can you remember any more? What exactly did he say?"

Sydney sighed, wiping at a tear. "He just said, '*Entropy is the password. The equation is...*' That's it—oh, except his last words sounded something like, '*is you miss.*'"

"Is you miss?"

"Yeah. It didn't make much sense to me either, but this, this intelligence, or whatever, seems to feel it's Sam's alter ego, so I thought it would be able to shed some light on the password and the rest of it."

"Huh," Willoughby said for a second time. His mind was trying to make some sort of sense out of Sam's last words. Finally, he shook his head. "I don't get it—the password, the equation, the cozy cottage? None of it makes much sense. What artificial intelligence has ever cared about aesthetics or atmosphere?"

Sydney picked up the thread. "Yeah, and why the attention to detail? Was that for our benefit? I could hear sheep bleating. I could even smell a hint of honeysuckle and mowed grass on the air. Why the charade? In fact, how do we know that this projection is what it says it is? How do we know that any of what it said is true? I'm calling the others." She pulled out her cell phone, but Willoughby stopped her.

"Not on your iPhone. Remember, he said he's monitoring all Observations, Inc. personnel. He'll have your number. He'll be tracking it and monitoring everything you say. We need to find a red phone box."

It took them almost twenty minutes to locate the classic red of a London phone booth. They crammed in together and rang up the gym where Dr. J had told Sydney he would be. They had to wait another ten minutes before

James Arthur was finally located and picked up the receiver.

"Why are you calling me here? Why didn't you call my cell? Is something wrong?"

Willoughby gave Dr. J an abbreviated version of finding out about the inheritance, visiting the apartments with Sydney, what they had learned about Sam from the video they had viewed, and about the artificial intelligence that seemed to believe it was Sam's alter ego. Dr. J was silent for a long moment.

"If you hadn't just come from a funeral, I'd swear you were leading me on. That's a lot to take in."

"Tell me about it," Willoughby said.

"So, if this Sam number two, or whatever you want to call it, is tracking us, won't it see us get together and wonder what's up?"

"Not if we converge at a coffee shop on the other side of the park and then walk through the park together, coffees in hand."

James Arthur grunted approval. "Could work. I'll bring Antonio up to speed on the way over. By the way, we got your text about the meeting at the apartment about ten minutes before you called. I wondered what the address was. I wasn't aware we had apartments at Covent Garden."

"Yeah, our lives seem to change by the moment these days."

"Roger that. Don't waste money on the parking meter, right?"

James Arthur hung up. Willoughby looked at his watch. It was almost three o'clock, and he realized for the first time that he was starving. He and Sydney walked through the park and found a coffee shop that also sold sandwiches. Sydney put her guitar down, holding it between her knees. Despite her confusion about the gift, it was obviously something she immediately cherished. He didn't know much about guitars, but he could tell just from his limited glance that this one was a beauty.

"So, I didn't know you played guitar."

The waitress stepped over and he ordered a cucumber and goat cheese sandwich (might as well win a few points for eating healthy, he reasoned) and Sydney ordered a walnut and cranberry salad plate. He texted both Dr. J and Antonio the name and address of the coffee shop, being careful not to mention anything about the previous phone conversation, but rather, inviting them to come early so they could chat for a while over coffee and then walk through the park together as it was a nice day.

Sydney finally answered him. "I wasn't aware that anyone knew I play guitar," she said. "I've kept it a carefully guarded secret. I have an acoustic guitar in my apartment—nothing like this, but a nice one. I never take it anywhere, though. How did he know? Was he spying on me?" She looked around as if trying to determine if it was safe to say more. She leaned forward slightly. "I started teaching myself guitar and piano around the same time, before I started seriously studying violin. I told my father and H.S. that I could hold my own on the piano, but I've never told anyone that I can play guitar. It's a sort of therapy for me. I use my guitar to…to write more personal things. Songs and such. I don't know how Sam could have known."

"Maybe he didn't," Willoughby suggested. "Maybe he just thought it was a beautiful musical instrument and something you would appreciate as a musician.

He glanced down at his phone. Antonio had just texted back that he was on his way. James Arthur responded moments later. The fact that the invite was texted would make the meeting look less suspicious.

The waitress finally brought their food, and he tore into the sandwich. It was delicious. After a few bites, he noticed that Sydney had become strangely quiet. She picked daintily at her salad, then stared aimlessly out the coffee shop window.

"I'm sorry," he finally said. She turned.

"Sorry for what?"

Willoughby took a minute to collect his thoughts. "This was different than when we lost the others," he said softly. "You were right there. You heard his last words. You, you watched him die." It was his turn to stare out the window a moment. "It must have been really hard."

Sydney reached up and wiped a tear away. "I had his blood all over me, all over my hands."

"Do you think it was Beelzebub or the Dark Brotherhood?"

"I don't know. Who else could it have been?"

"You didn't see anyone unusual at the park?"

"No. Sam did. He knew we were being followed. I was..." Her voice trailed off. She bit her lip, then continued. "I was caught up in me, in my problems, and he was being vigilant, like we all should be. He thought they were after *me*."

"What do you think?"

Sydney looked at him. "I think that bullet went right where it was supposed to go. I think that bullet was meant for Sam, which means someone knew who he was. That means the leak, or spy, or whatever is feeding information to the brotherhood, knows more about Observations, Inc. than you and I."

Willoughby took a bite of his sandwich and chewed. "The police didn't find anything. They know the shell that killed him came from a long-range sniper rifle, so the shot could have come from almost anywhere. Now we have the ghost Sam left behind begging us to help him track down the killers."

Sydney raised an eyebrow.

Willoughby looked up.

"Yeah. After you were gone, it told me it was my friend, and that it wanted to help us track down the ones who did this to Sam. It said their time was over."

"Do you believe that?" Sydney asked.

Willoughby pondered the question for a moment. "Maybe," he said. "We don't yet know the extent of Sian's capabilities. I also think we don't have many options. The team is getting picked off one by one. Maybe we've got to take the risk."

Sydney looked at him, but said nothing. They finished their sandwiches and coffee in silence. Antonio was the one to break the spell.

"Buenos dias, my friends!" he said as he bustled into the little shop. He purchased a hot chocolate at the counter and walked over, taking note of the guitar Sydney was clinging to but not saying anything. On the surface, he seemed his smiling, jovial self. But Willoughby could tell that underneath, he was concerned.

"So, do you mind if I pull up a chair?"

"Of course not. Good of you to come, Antonio. It has been a bit of a rough day." Willoughby said, seeing James Arthur step through the door with Hauti.

"Am I okay parking in the back? I brought my car," Dr. J called out as he approached the table. Willoughby was going to let the comment go, but Antonio took the bait.

"I forgot—and what is your car today, James Arthur? Wouldn't be an Austin Martin, would it? Perhaps you think that you have become the new James Bond, since we are in London?"

Dr. J grinned. "While it would be an improvement over the long British tradition, I only rented a car so that Hauti and I could get up to Edinburgh later in the week. I've got a book signing there."

"You may need to cancel it," Willoughby said flatly. He bent forward lowering his voice so no one beyond the table could hear. "We can't just keep pretending we can ignore these people. We need some answers before someone else gets targeted."

Antonio nodded. "I am afraid it may be too late for that. We are all targets."

Dr. J was the first to respond.

"Well, thank you for that cheery assessment, Mr. Valdez."

Before Antonio could respond, Willoughby rose to his feet. "Guys, we should get going. We can take the rest of this outside."

"But I haven't gotten my coffee yet," James Arthur complained.

"No, you don't drink coffee," a voice behind him said. "You certainly don't need the caffeine. I got you a Seltzer Water, and I got *me* a cup of coffee." It was Hauti.

James Arthur stared at her in mock surprise. "*I don't drink coffee?*" he mouthed. "Seltzer Water? What is '*Seltzer Water*'?"

Hauti handed James Arthur a clear bottle which he held with two fingers as if it were liable to explode. The group slowly filed out of the coffee shop. Once outside, Willoughby turned to them.

"Good performance. Now—a leisurely walk through the gardens while I fill you in. Please stay close so I don't have to speak loud." The group huddled closer, James Arthur complaining softly to Hauti about the Seltzer.

Antonio gave him a warning glance.

"What?" Dr. J said. "You heard the man. He called it a '*good performance*.'" As they passed a trash bin at the park entry, James Arthur dropped the bottle of Seltzer Water into it. "Oops!" he said to Hauti. "It slipped—really."

Hauti gave him a look that could have made wet coals burst into spontaneous flame. James Arthur, still smiling, shrugged. Willoughby tried to ignore the entire exchange. He was focused on filling the team in. He told them of the man at the funeral, the odd set of three corner apartments, the hidden rooms, and the revelation about who Sam was, and about the artificial intelligence who called himself *Sian*, and that the intelligence now wanted to speak with them. By the time they were halfway through the park, he had finished. Sydney, who had been silent through Willoughby's entire briefing, was the first to speak up.

"Let me add that I don't trust this, this *intelligence*—and not just because he has, he... I just don't trust him, or '*it*.' The thing is...slippery. It gave me this very expensive Martin Company special issue guitar because it said Sam wanted me to have it. It said my father is suspected of being the traitor who sold us out. It doesn't behave like a machine. I'm not convinced it's even on our side. As Willoughby suggests, it has a great deal of resources at its holographic fingertips. That means it wields power. We just don't know enough yet. For all we know, it could have had some kind of control over Sam."

Dr. J barked a short laugh. The group turned to him.

"Am I the only one who finds this whole thing ridiculous? I mean, look at it. If it weren't for the fact that Sam was our friend, and one we will miss, I would say it was comical. Here we are, '*Observations, Inc.,*' a company comprised of those who look beyond the obvious and see what others don't, and you're telling us, in essence, *the butler did it?*"

Willoughby narrowed his eyes. "Chauffer—not butler."

"Whatever," James Arthur continued. "The point is, either the man deserved an Academy nomination for his acting skills, or maybe we are not as bright as we thought we were. Why didn't any of us catch this? Why didn't any of us even suspect?"

Willoughby dropped his head. "I'm most to blame here. He drove me to school for almost two years, and I never thought of him as more than just a nice guy and my driver. It's funny how you can look at people with your preconceptions and they seem to dutifully fill the role. I should have stepped back. I should have looked deeper. I saw what I chose to see, not what was there—what was convenient, not what was reality. It was only with the hijacking, with the visits from Mr. B, that I began to dig beneath Sam's austere demeanor. Now, he's gone."

They were nearing the other side of the park. "Whether we should or should not have suspected is immaterial now, my friends," Antonio said, staring straight ahead. "We must look at what this information means to us now. If what Willoughby heard is true, then Sam was certainly not involved with Atlantis, or with any of the issues that seemed to spark the hijacking and subsequent death of our esteemed H.S. So, the question I ask you is, why was he targeted?"

The group walked in silence a moment, pondering the question. "Because he was protecting Willoughby?" Sydney offered.

Dr. J glanced over. "We're all protecting Willoughby. He's the one this Beelzebub thing has latched on to."

It was Hauti that gave the most plausible answer. "Perhaps it's because he was getting too close. Someone felt he needed to be silenced."

No one spoke as each mulled over the possibility. Antonio finally nodded slowly. "Yes... I believe our friend Hauti has hit upon something. I think we should speak with this *artificial man* and try to determine what it was that got Sam targeted." He looked around the group. Hauti gave a short nod. James Arthur nodded as well. Willoughby looked over to Sydney, and seeing a slight bob of the head, he agreed as well.

"It is settled then. Let us go see what this ghost in the machine has to say.'

As they crossed the street and hopped onto the sidewalk bordering the Covent Garden Apartments, Hauti looked up at the three-story facade. Willoughby couldn't tell if she was impressed, or apprehensive. As they made their way past the manicured hedge, however, and through the small grotto of trees to the heavy wrought iron gate, he heard her whispering low, almost to herself.

"Once more unto the breach, dear friends, once more..."

23

The Long Night

The blood-red hue of the moon threw a sinister pallor over the village as ash filled the air. "It's the mountain—a massive eruption!" Tainken screamed over the chaos. Several streams of molten fire dripped down the pointed peaks in the distance.

"More than that," Rashrahu corrected. She was heavily cloaked, with her face hidden. She led T.K. steadily, calmly, toward the city wall despite the chaos all around them. As they moved away from the screams and crying of the terrified people flocking the temple, Rashrahu explained more. "The blood moon is the night of destruction. This city will sink into the sea." She reached the wall and led T.K. expertly to a small niche. A narrow slit opened into a dark, musty passage. The cloaked woman took a torch from the wall sconce and struck it against the black rock wall, lighting it on the third try. She pushed away a low curtain of cobwebs and started down the passage. "Careful," she said casually. "The spiders in the higher webs of the tunnel are harmless, but the ground is riddled with burrows of what you may call the *Black Wishbone* spider. They can be very aggressive when

241

disturbed and are highly poisonous. We must assume the earthquakes have disturbed them."

T.K.'s eyes dropped immediately to the ground, which seemed to be crawling in the flickering torch light. "*Great!* You're just full of good news," she mumbled, trying to dodge spiders, duck under cobwebs, and retain her footing as the shaking of the earth grew. A sudden jolt threw her against the passage wall where she felt something drop onto her hand. She screamed, slinging it off, just in time to feel a spider climb onto her bare ankle. Screaming again, she slammed her foot against the black cavern wall, smashing the creature before it could bite her. Gritting her teeth, she lunged forward to catch up with Rashrahu, whose torch light was far ahead. She felt her feet crunch down on crawling things twice and slapped one spider as large as her hand off the back of her leg just as it dug in, preparing to bite. Stumbling out an equally narrow slit on the outside of the wall, she ran toward Rashrahu at the edge of the jungle, still screaming and slapping at her legs and robe. Only a meter or two away from the Goddess, she tripped on a jutting root and fell hard, banging her head onto the harsh bark of one of the gnarled trees. Blood trickled down her face as the ground continued to roll and heave beneath her.

Rashrahu approached quickly and bent down. "Are you okay?" She examined the cut on Tainken's forehead, then offered her a hand, pulling her to her feet with barely an effort. She checked T.K.'s robes and hair for spiders. When she was convinced that none were clinging to her, she led them forward into the jungle. "Come," she said. "We still have a fair distance to travel and the going will be difficult with the quakes."

Tainken gave a nod. She was still trying to catch her breath and slow her heartbeat. "You got one thing right," she mumbled. "The night has already been long."

She tripped and fell at least a dozen more times, bruising her shins and scratching her arms and legs before they reached a sort of clearing. Rashrahu never stumbled and she had not seemed the least concerned about the spiders. Curious, T.K. thought, as she watched the Goddess seem to glide effortlessly, winding through the jungle terrain as if it were a well-worn path. T.K. could see no path at all. "What are you?" she finally asked when they made a rare stop, allowing her to catch her breath. She sank heavily to the tall jungle grass. "A tigress? Even with the ground shaking, you navigate the jungle like you know it."

Rashrahu did not answer at first. Her focus was directed at a low rock wall, covered with thick vines and foliage. She walked toward it and began yanking at vines. "Help me," she said, looking over.

Tainken groaned and pushed to her feet. "Sure. Are you going to tell me what this is all about? Please don't say this is the cave of some sort of sacred cobra."

Rashrahu flashed her a brief smile. "No sacred cobra. I navigate the jungle because I can speak with it—I can sense it. It tells me where to walk, where to go."

"Well, then maybe you could have let me carry the torch."

Again, Rashrahu smiled. "It would have slowed you down. You need to be gone before the earth sinks."

"Earth *sinks?* Shaking and exploding isn't enough?"

"This entire valley, including the city, will sink into the ocean this very night. Thousands of lives will be lost."

Tainken tilted her head up. "Then we've got to go back. We need to help those people."

"I can return to them when you are gone. I can try to ease their pain. I cannot stop what will be, Tainken. I am a watcher from a distant people—much like you, though more skilled in my knowledge, my understanding. I do not control nature or time, nor do I have power over life and death. I can only observe and act, hoping to limit any damage to the balance that must continue to exist. You are to play a part in what is to come. That is why you must go."

"I'm sick of riddles, Rashrahu. Speak plainly. Are you going to tell me what I'm supposed to do?"

Rashrahu raised an eyebrow. "You have finished your message. It is time for you to return."

"Return where?"

"To your friends."

A pang of hope sprang up from within her. "How? How do you plan to get me back to my friends?"

Rashrahu did not answer, but tore frantically at the vines. T.K. could see now that they covered a sparkling, smooth surface. She pushed up from the ground and began to help the woman tear away the remaining vines and foliage. She noted in the dim light that parts of the rock wall were covered in writing, carved into the stone around a rectangular, glass-like surface with a large, sun face symbol carved into its center.

Tainken stared at the writing in neat rows that followed the contour of the rectangle. She realized with a start that she recognized the symbols. *They were Atlantian.*

Rashrahu looked over. She could see the comprehension on Tainken's face. "You know this writing, don't you? You can read the words."

Tainken nodded.

Rashrahu continued. "The jungle brought me here many years ago, to first meet your people. They would travel in and out from the rock face. They called it a '*door*.'"

"A time door," Tainken mumbled. She cocked her head. "I haven't read my native language for a long time."

Rashrahu stood beside her, breathing heavily for once. The torch light flickering in her eyes. The ground, which had been relatively quiet for several minutes, lurched. Tainken fell backward. There was a loud rumbling. The trees around them swayed and the earth below her rippled like a wave. Rashrahu did not fall. In fact, she seemed to barely notice.

"You are running out of time, Tainken Keilhar. You have the crystal computer around your neck. You always carry it. You must run at the image of the huge sun—*now!* I have seen your people do it."

T.K. struggled to stand. "But the door will just take me back to the prime core. I'll be right back where I started from."

"No," Rashrahu shouted above the chaos of the earthquake. "Before, you did not find the entry into what is left of your frozen city. Before, you did not realize that you were in the same time as your friends. Before, you did not have the map to the control panel for the core mechanism. You did not have the instructions on how to destroy it."

T.K. had started toward the rock face, but stopped, staring over at Rashrahu. She fingered the small scroll in her pocket, remembering the instructions on how to engage the self-destruct mechanism of the prime core. Her chin shot up defiantly as she raised her voice to be heard over the thunderous rumbles. "I can't destroy the prime core mechanism! My people for generations poured their soul into building it. If there *is* anything left of my city—if there are others of my people who somehow escaped the calamity and have survived—to destroy the mechanism will destroy *any* link I may have with them! It will bury my city forever in rubble and ruin!"

"Yes," Rashrahu shouted, her eyes equally fierce, "but if you fail to destroy the mechanism the darkness will consume it. The Dark Edge will rise and *all* could be lost—you, your friends, your people, even this entire world. This is your choice, Tainken. It is your destiny. You either make the sacrifice, or you do not. Understand that we, the watchers, see no other way. Go! *Hurry!* Time is short!"

Tainken hurt everywhere, but most of all, inside. Everything came at her, too fast, too disjointed. She had tried to use the quiet weeks at the village to bring some clarity to her mind. For so long, she had focused on one thing—survive long enough to find the one who murdered her father and destroyed her world. Now, that man was dead. Now, there was Antonio, and Willoughby, and Observations, Inc. Could she leave her past behind? That past still pulled at her. She forced herself to move forward. The ground rolled mercilessly. Rashrahu held her torch high, its jittery light illuminating the carved image of the sun on what appeared to be a polished glass. T.K. ran at it, dodging and weaving while the ground rolled. The glass wall began to glow. Reaching up a hand subconsciously, she grabbed hold of the crystal computer and her necklace, both bobbing against bare skin beneath her tunic.

The crystal was warm to the touch. A few strides away from the glass surface, the crystal computer and necklace burst into sudden illumination. Shards of blinding light leaked out from her tunic, highlighting her set eyes and taut features. A new boom sounded and the ground jolted violently, ripping open behind her. She leaped at the glass wall, clamping her eyes shut. They had blurred anyway, tears streaking down both cheeks. She slammed into something at once hard and cold. It gave way, yanking her in a sharp tug, one that she knew would take her back to the cold tomb of the prime core. Would she be able to do what this Goddess had asked of her? Would she be able to sever ties with a past that was perhaps as much fantasy as memory now?

24

Assignments

Willoughby led the little group through the front entry and directly to the center atrium. As he bent to scan his thumb, he heard comments of both amusement and wonder at the décor of the rooms. Then, the small dark slit of a doorway opened, dispelling the illusion of the central atrium. Hauti let out a sharp gasp and Antonino gave a low whistle. Sydney darted ahead of all of them, moving confidently toward the brass, one man elevator, guitar in hand. She held the instrument like a girl holding a stuffed bear some cute boy had won for her at a County Fair. The group filed into the small control room, aghast at its contents and curious of its purpose. Sydney stepped into the brass elevator cage.

"I'm going to by-pass the boardroom and go straight to the third floor," she said. She pressed a button, and the cage descended. Willoughby glanced down the elevator track, waiting for the cage to return. Then he, too, stepped in and descended. He heard Sydney call up to him.

"Wait until you get a load of this!"

Willoughby tried to look over the golden rail as he passed the second floor. "What?"

"Just wait," Sydney called up.

A few moments later, the elevator finally returned to the top floor. James Arthur motioned for Hauti to climb in, he heard a sound like a screeching gull wafting up from below. "He has birds down there?" he asked.

Antonio could do nothing but shrug. As the elevator eventually returned and descended with James Arthur, he caught the whiff of a familiar scent—*it was the briny smell of the sea.*

Willoughby was pacing when Antonio finally ascended into the room. He watched his friend's expression carefully as the cage slid to a stop. What he and Sydney had earlier found to be a cozy country cottage had been transformed into a conference room, and not just any conference room. It was the conference room from the Pesci Pecolli.

The Pecolli was H.S.'s personal yacht. One window on the outer wall was open, letting in the sounds and smells of the sea. As Antonio stepped from the elevator, Willoughby noted for the first time that the floor even seemed to move, enforcing the illusion that they really were on the yacht.

Everyone was quiet for the first few minutes, taking time to appreciate and marvel at the illusion. Willoughby was, once again, awed by the detail of the illusion. If he didn't know better, he would swear they were underway, somewhere in the mid-Atlantic Ocean, on the Pesci Pecolli. Willoughby's head shot up as he searched the room. The projected image of Sian, the artificial intelligence who mimicked the look and mannerisms of Sam, seemed nowhere in sight.

"Sian?" Willoughby called out. There was no answer—just the sound of the breeze, and the gulls, and the water gently slapping the sides of the yacht as it bobbed in the waves.

"So," Dr. J started, "how do we get the mystery man to appear? Strike up a chorus of 'Domo Arigato, Mr. Roboto?'"

Antonio was tapping on an invisible barrier that closed off the far end of the conference room. Suddenly, without warning, the main door to the boardroom, the one on the other side of the glass, burst open. The tall, lanky shape of Sam strolled in, carrying a cleaning rag and a bottle of wood oil. He was wearing the crisp uniform of a private yacht captain.

"Ah," the image proclaimed with a slight smile. "Back so soon? I see you brought the team. Good. Please, be seated." The image gestured toward the chairs around the board room table. The team exchanged glances. Willoughby was the first to sit. He was trying to contain a smile. Sian had chosen a yellow bow-tie for his uniform. Willoughby knew from his time with Sam as his Chauffer that the man detested both bow ties and the color yellow. Obviously, this was Sian attempt to comply with his earlier request that the image somehow distinguish itself from the real image of Sam—at least, for Willoughby.

Sydney decided to follow Willoughby's lead, and sat just to his right. Antonio then sat, followed by Hauti. James Arthur was the last standing, but the first to speak up. "Hey, before we move on to this cozy *business as usual* façade, how about you tell us who you are and what's really going on here. We buried our friend Sam early this morning. That makes you an imposter."

The image was not looking at James Arthur. His eyes had locked onto Sydney. She had placed the guitar case down beside her.

"I see you found the instrument," he said, still smiling. Sydney did not respond. "Good," Sian continued. The image then looked at Dr. J. "Yes...James Arthur Washington. I have looked forward to meeting you. Your book on life mapping was illuminating from a standpoint of programming human life simulations."

"*Programming human life simulations?*" James Arthur mouthed, looking over at Hauti.

"Yes. I must confess it is a hobby of mine. I have created and run over four billion human life simulations so that I could better anticipate human reactions and better influence human interaction chains. Your book talks about finding the right life program for the individual. I, too, seek this goal. I trust Willoughby and Sydney filled you in on my genesis and purpose. So, you know I am not a Sam imposter, I am Sian, and I am here to assist and help protect you. What, particularly, do you wish to know about me?"

Dr. J seemed to be struggling to keep up with the intelligence. It took him a moment to answer. "Well, first, do you have to look that much like Sam? It's creepy. You're a machine, not our friend. Second, you want us to call you Sian? Third, if you are such an advanced computer, with almost unlimited access to worldwide information, why couldn't you predict some of what's happened? Why couldn't you stop the killing—why couldn't you save Sam, and maybe some of our friends from the *Absconditus?*"

The others seemed content to let James Arthur take point on the questioning, Antonio perhaps most obviously analyzing the image and its responses. The image raised an eyebrow.

"All excellent questions Dr. J., I cannot change my form—it is what it is. Your limited contact with Sam makes it difficult for me to visually distinguish myself to you, but I shall try, at least, within the extent that my programming allows. My programming is adaptive, but just like your book, there is a path most comfortable for me, and the decisions I make are final."

"Meaning?" Antonio had finally spoken. The image looked at him.

"Meaning, Mr. Antonio Santanos Eldoro Chavez, that I, and only I, control my programming. It cannot be tampered with by outside forces. All who had access to my programming interface are...no longer active."

"*Dead*," Sydney interjected.

Sian narrowed his eyes. "Yes, deceased. So, I have sealed the access bridge."

"*Sealed the access bridge?* What do you mean? You're a computer intelligence. What if you malfunction? Don't you need software updates, hardware maintenance, user input?" James Arthur was visibly perturbed. "What if we need to get in there and see what is going on with you? Why would you completely close yourself off?"

"I am a self-contained system, capable of managing my own maintenance and evolution as an intelligence, much like you James Arthur. In short, I was built to not need outward assistance. I was built to be impervious to outside forces. Your best access to learn what is going on inside me is trust, just as it is between two biological beings on this planet." The image looked straight at Willoughby. "I will not explain everything just yet, but there are reasons for the programming that maintains my looks, and these will eventually become apparent. For now, just know that while I am not Sam, he poured his knowledge, his hopes, and his dreams into my Ethernet. I am not the Sam you knew, but then, you did not know Sam as he really was. Perhaps it is most accurate to say I am the Sam that you never knew."

The image let the words sink in for a long moment before continuing.

"As to your second question, yes, I would ask you to call me Sian. It is an acronym for '*Sam I am, now,*' and it was given to me by the Sam you did, and did not, know. It is a name to distinguish me, and is adequate for my tastes. I hope it suits your needs." The image placed the rag and wood oil down and reached a thin hand forward, bringing up a holographic control tablet from what appeared to be a seamless surface near the curved end of the board table. "As for your third question, this is partly why I asked Willoughby and Sydney to invite you here." He manipulated a few buttons. Shades slid down over the outside windows. The lights dimmed and a series of active graphs and charts began to populate the air around Willoughby and the team. "There are more than ten billion events per day that intersect and affect the unfolding of a single team member's timeline over each twenty-four-hour period. I am monitoring multiple team members. Defining an event, one that could prove significant to a catastrophic, such as the Absconditus hijacking, is much easier in hindsight analysis than in real time. I do wish to point out, however, that I did recommend against the voyage on the Aperio Absconditus."

"Why?" James Arthur said, trying to make sense of the numerous evolving graphs around him.

"I had noted anomalies. After a full analysis of the St. Petersburgh break-in—and I was not fully online until after the break-in, I determined that the thieves were not after technology, but rather information about our Antarctic initiative. We knew from your report, Antonio, that they found your recruiting front *The Corner Barber*, and were monitoring you and Willoughby. There were also several crew members who became ill shortly before the voyage and had to be replaced. Whomever set up the Absconditus hijacking had access to time travel, or had started planning the hijacking long before the St. Petersburg break-in. The replacement crew members had exemplary work histories and spotless records dating back to several years before the St. Petersburgh incident."

Dr. J turned his attention back to the image.

"What about Sam? I can understand, based on who I know we're up against, why the hijacking could have happened. But we should have had more warning that Sam was a target."

Sian gave a tight-lipped frown. "Sam was very careful. Only a handful of close associates ever had any idea who he really was, and none are currently alive. Even at present, I have no idea why he was targeted."

Willoughby spoke up this time. "Do you think that Sydney was really the target? Maybe Sam just got in the way."

Sian slowly shook his head. "I have carefully analyzed all the police forensics, the timeline, and every shred of pertinent data. There was plenty of time for the gunman to take a second shot. Sydney did not opt for cover. Her concern was for Sam. She was a true friend to him to the very end, for which I am grateful. The placement of the bullet was too expert for an errant or accidental hit."

"Do you have anything on the gunman?" Antonio asked.

"The shot came from an MK 12 Special Purpose Rifle. The weapon is a favorite with the U.S. Navy Seals, Rangers, and other Special Forces teams. There is no video of anyone within a 35-mile radius carrying anything that resembles such a weapon, or a case for such a weapon. Footprints were inconclusive. They seem to begin right at the edge of a camera blind spot, and then disappear on the other side of a thicket of brush. It was as if the gunman just appeared and disappeared. One interesting thing—bits of seaweed were found in the brush, along with traces of seawater. Odd, isn't it?"

Willoughby gave a quick glance at Sydney. "No. Not really. Sydney and I have had dealings with a zombie henchman who Beelzebub—I assume you've heard about our dealings with him?"

Sian nodded, encouraging Willoughby to continue. Willoughby was again struck by how perfectly this artificial intelligence had the mannerism of Sam down.

"Anyway, Beelzebub keeps a bunch of zombie-like things in stasis, stored in a trench where the *Absconditus* sank. He claims to have many of these. It could have been one of them. If it is, that means that Beelzebub is pulling the strings. He must have found a time hole in one of your camera network's blind spots."

The image of Sam looked up, his face completely motionless for a long moment, seeming to process the information. "You are correct. Satellite scans detect a small magnetic anomaly in a space just beyond where the footprints disappear. The space is completely outside our camera views. The anomaly is below what we consider to be our concern threshold, however. The power needed to use it for movement through the time-space continuum would be enormous. Where does this being, this *Beelzebub*, access his power from? There are no structures nearby with time door signatures."

Willoughby sighed. "I don't know. We've been trying to figure that out. We don't even know what he is—if he's even human. We know he can take over human forms. He seems to have a predilection toward particularly ruthless and violent people. For example, he's currently cohabiting the body of *Aribert Heim*, the famous Nazi war criminal."

Again, there was a pause from Sian. "H.S.'s files on Beelzebub are extensive. His information, however, seems somewhat incomplete. You never discussed this with Sam?"

"No," Willoughby said. "Why would I? I thought he was just a chauffeur and a yacht captain. I know Sam was aware of Beelzebub, because he was there when the man, or beast, or whatever he is, visited me with one of his zombie henchmen—a guy we were introduced to on the *Absconditus* as Gates. He's a real piece of work..." Willoughby gave a slight shudder, as if trying to pull his mind away from highly unpleasant thoughts. "Anyway, I only really discussed Beelzebub with Sam after the incident at the Gujarat East Primate Preserve, and we pretty much just talked about what happened there."

The image stared at Willoughby for a long moment. "I wonder why Sam did not record this discussion."

"I don't know." Willoughby said.

Antonio jumped in. "You told Willoughby that you have information for us. I believe it had something to do with H.S.'s search for the prime hole."

Sian was still staring at Willoughby. After an uncomfortable pause, it turned. "Yes. That, and other Observations, Inc. priorities. The information I have follows three tracks. First, the Antarctica track: I can give you a full accounting of H.S.'s research into a large, magnetic anomaly found on the northern edge of a submerged lake, Lake Vostok. The Support Office for Aero-physical Research (SOAR) reported recently an increase there of 10,000 nanoteslas, which, of course, as some of you may know, is one billionth of a tesla, a measure of magnetic strength. This increase is beyond the already abnormally high 60,000 nanoteslas characterized by the Vostok Station. Vostok Station is a Russian research station located on the ice above the lake.

"H.S., as you know, wanted to find the Crystal Computer in hopes of activating the facility, which was designed to withstand any catastrophe, even hundreds of feet of ice.

"In addition to the mysterious concentration of nanoteslas noted by Vostok Station, H.S.'s own satellite research found large pockets of trapped oxygen between 70 and 130 meters below the Vostok Station. He believed this is why the Russians built the station where it is—that they know about the air pockets, and have been secretly burrowing toward them."

"Why would this so interest H.S.?" Antonio asked, his eyebrows knitted together with a look of intense concentration. "Scientists the world over have studied air pockets trapped in the ice flow for years. It is a common way to track climate change."

"Yes," Sian said, "but scientist typically study *tiny* air pockets, or bubbles, by way of coring. The air bubbles located under the Vostok Station are enormous. They range from several hundred feet to almost a quarter mile in circumference. Perhaps even more startling, they follow a roughly uniform shape, that of a slanted dome. The slant follows the same angle of rock core samples from rock outcroppings in the same general area, as if a whole island slid down beneath what eventually became an ice sheet."

There was a stunned silence. Antonio was the first to break this. "It is, indeed, interesting, my friend."

Sian ignored the comment. "The second track became a priority after the St. Petersburg break in. We had been aware for some time of a group who call themselves the *Dark Brotherhood* or *Dark Edge*. They have been well documented over the centuries, primarily by monks in remote monasteries, such as Verlam and Great Meteoron in Greece, Sumela in Turkey, and Mont Saint Michel in France. Their shadowy activities, however, did not interest us until, as you know, video footage from the break-in revealed their distinctive tattoo.

"Since that time, Observations, Inc. has been working tirelessly to compile all information known about this group. The library at Mont Saint Michel is particularly rich in details. None of the information, however, has been deemed worthy of release to the public. There is little from the monasteries available online. We have hired scholars to visit and document the library's contents, but their efforts have been blocked. Our agent was told, for example, that yes, there was much more to see, but only for one deemed *worthy* by the Senior Abbot. We need someone to infiltrate the order at Mont Saint Michel and gain access to its library. Here are some pictures of the monastery. Have you seen it before?"

Sian looked from James Arthur to Antonio. Neither spoke at first, both studying the series of 3D pictures hovering above the boardroom table. Finally, Antonio spoke up. "Some of the…carvings found from the submerged site in the Gulf of Khumbhat bear a strange resemblance to Mont Saint Michel. Don't you agree James Arthur?"

Dr. J didn't answer. He just stared at the projected image.

After a time, Sian continued. "The final track regards information uncovered implicating a member of the board for Observations Inc. who may have been involved in the St. Petersburg break-in."

"Involved? Who?" James Arthur jumped in.

Sian did not answer him immediately. "Due to the sensitive nature of this information, I was instructed to assign this track to Sydney and Willoughby. It is their choice what they choose to share with you."

Willoughby felt the stares of Antonio, Hauti, and James Arthur all turn his way. He kept his eyes forward, on Sian, only glancing once at Sydney, who also didn't say anything. Finally, Antonio turned back to Sian.

"Do you have a suggested plan of action?"

"I do."

Antonio waited, but the projected image did not continue. "Well?" he finally said.

"Are you with me, Antonio Chavez?"

"What do you mean?"

"Do you trust me?" Sian said, seeming completely sincere.

"No," Antonio said. "You are a machine, my friend. I cannot be sure of your programming. I *will* listen to you, though. I shall listen to your plan and choose for myself if it is a plan that I can follow."

Sian broke into a grin. "You are no fool, Antonio. That is good enough for me." The lights in the room dimmed. A large hologram lit up in the center of the room. It showed a white landscape with a row of freight cars, connected to each other in such a way as to form a long mobile home. Beside the home stood a large, spherical structure that looked almost like a water tower.

"Your assignment, Antonio, would be Antarctica, for that is where we believe we will find clues as to the whereabouts of T.K. We requested some time ago that you be allowed to visit and document the Volstok Station. Your interest is in the structural integrity of the facility and how it has helped the outpost stand up to the rigors of the Antarctica winter. We have planned your trip to coincide with a changing of the guard there. You will arrive a day ahead of schedule. There will only be two guards to greet you. They have received well-timed bribes to insure you get whatever access you need and no one follows up on your work. We have arranged to have the new team of Russian scientists delayed for a day in arriving. This will give you two days with minimum scrutiny to explore the facility, find the Russians' secret tunnel, and explore what they have learned about the domed air pockets and stray nanoteslas. I have already scheduled a flight for you that leaves around midnight tomorrow. I have purchased all the artic clothing and gear you will need, had it boxed, and am having it transferred to your London hotel. All the papers you will need are in your personal inbox, as well as a primer for useful Russian phrases. You will have a satellite phone that is far more advanced than any of your fellow scientists, and will be able to reach me at any time. Please use your phone sparingly. Are there any questions?"

When Antonio gave a curt nod, still processing the information Sian had just given him, the image turned to face James Arthur and Hauti. He waved his hand over the dark table, and the hologram above it abruptly changed. It now showed a much more detailed image of a small, round island rising to a pointed peak. Almost every visible inch of the mountain was covered by the solid montage of buildings that made up the Mont Saint Michel Monastery. Stone cathedral walls, roads, and pathways all led to the pointed spires of a church that formed the peak of the small mountain. "James Arthur, you and Hauti have been granted an audience with the Abbot of Mont Saint Michel. Most likely, he will deny you access to the catacombs where the monastery's secret libraries are located. This time, however, we have connections inside. A man will seek you out, one who will give you the codename, '*fifth friend.*' He will help you get the information we need."

"'*Fifth friend?*'" Willoughby asked, a bit of alarm on his face.

"Yes. Is there something the matter Willoughby?"

Willoughby remembered the brief conversation with his father. Hadn't he referred to someone who called himself *the fifth friend?* He looked up, shaking his head as if to clear out the memory. "No," he said. "It's just, that's a strange name."

"What does that even mean?" Hauti asked.

"We don't know. It is an old contact of H.S. The friend sent word that he can help get us into Mont Saint Michel. That's all I can tell you. I have downloaded his precise instructions to your inbox, Dr. J. I have also sent you a detailed report of the layout of the Monastery and an overview of key personnel, security details, and a suggested list of supplies. You will note I am sending you with sophisticated protection gear. They allow no weapons of any kind on the island, but we have suspicions that the Dark Brotherhood may have infiltrated this facility at some level, so you will need to be careful.

"The two of you are booked on a flight that leaves late tonight. A limo is waiting outside at this moment to take you to gather your supplies and create preparations."

"Uh, thanks—wait, what do we call you? SW?"

"Sian." The image seemed somewhat amused by James Arthur.

"Yeah, well, whatever, look, I know we're all chummy now, but if you don't mind, I'm perfectly capable of driving myself. I brought my own transport."

"If you are referring to the yellow Lamborghini you drove here, I'm afraid it will be of little help to you now. The London Police towed your vehicle away five minutes ago. It seems you parked illegally, ran over a three-hundred-year-old concrete planter, and mowed down two hedge bushes. The cost for damages should run you between eight and ten thousand, and the ticket from the British impound authorities will be close to a thousand. I have instructed one of our financial agents to pick up the tab and buy the car so you do not continue to rack up rental charges. We will sell the car to you to recoup what we can. At any rate, we feel you are better off hiring a limousine and a driver for the remainder of your stay in Britain."

"*What?*" James Arthur gasped with exasperation. He looked over at Hauti, then back to the others. "That planter was right in the middle of the road! I tried to swerve, which is why I took out the bushes. I was going to glue it all back together or something after we were done here."

Hauti shook her head. "I told you, that wasn't a road, it was a sidewalk, James dear. I also told you to slow down, to look at a map before we came. I said, 'Where you're leaving that car is *not* a parking space.' Did you listen? Did you listen to *anything* I said? Like that the authorities wouldn't take kindly to your hitting an heirloom planter and mowing down manicured bushes. Frankly, I think Sian has a point."

"Hey, I didn't *mow* down anything. I swerved, *relocating* a few bushes a few meters and clipping an old planter. When I was done fixing it, they wouldn't have even noticed. There was no reason to tow my car."

"The report mentions that the planter, which had survived precisely three hundred and twenty-six years before its encounter with you, now lies in roughly 18 pieces," Sian added.

"It was *that* old?" Dr. J looked to the others. "Hey, the thing was ugly. The neighbors will probably thank me." He shook his head. "Wow, accused of a mow and taken for a tow." He looked up at Sian. "So, if they've already towed my car and thank you, by the way, for picking up the damages, why don't I just stick around until we're done here and the team and I can leave together?"

"Believe me when I say, James Arthur, that you *are* finished here."

"Oh, so you're saying you want me to leave?"

"I believe that is what I said," the image continued, no emotion on its face. "Your limousine is waiting. You have a tight schedule."

James Arthur looked to Antonio. "So, you guys okay with this? Mr. Roboto here telling us what to do."

"He has information we lack, my friend. I would suggest we give this...*projection* the benefit of the doubt for now."

James Arthur stared at him for a moment, and then shrugged. He turned to Willoughby and Sydney.

"I guess I've got to leave this grand assembly." He smiled. "It seems my limo awaits." He turned toward the door, but Antonio stopped him. He had picked up a pen from a nearby counter and was jotting something onto a small slip of paper.

"Here," Antonio said, slipping the paper into James Arthur's hand. "This is a friend of mine. He has a body shop and can get what I understand is soon to be *your* Lamborghini fixed up in no time."

James Arthur looked down at the paper, read it with a raised eyebrow, and then stuffed it into the pocket of his jacket. He grinned at Antonio. "Don't freeze off anything important up there in Antarctica." He clapped Antonio on the shoulder, motioning for Hauti to follow.

She started after him, rolling her eyes as she gave Antonio a hug. "I'll try to keep him out of trouble. She walked over to Willoughby and Sydney. "So, what are you guys   doing?"
Willoughby smiled. "Oh, probably computer work—you know, spreadsheets, statistics, and data mining."

James Arthur had stepped into the one-man elevator. He made a face. "Well, that sounds like a thrill a minute, Sydney. You sure you don't want to come with us?"

Sydney shook her head with a sad smile. James Arthur looked to Willoughby. "Hey, whatever you guys end up doing—or wherever you go—you be careful. I'm still not happy with your surfing skills. When this is over, I want to see you back on my beach. Understood? I may even teach you how to drive a Lamborghini." He smiled and pointed at Willoughby.

"From what I hear, you might want to learn to drive one first." Willoughby smiled back. "Seriously, take care of yourself Dr. J."

"Will do. You take care of the music princess, you hear?"

Sydney, who had just finished whispered goodbyes with Hauti looked over. Dr. J had just started his ascent. "Princess? I'm stunned. I think that's the nicest thing you've ever said to me, James Arthur. Why the sudden compliment?"

"Well," James Arthur said as the elevator slid toward the ceiling, "You picked a good boyfriend." The elevator disappeared.

Hauti sighed, then walked over to Willoughby and gave him a long hug—actually, a bit *too long* of a hug for his liking. He saw Sydney raise an eyebrow, but she didn't say anything. The elevator slid back down, empty now. Hauti moved gracefully to it and stepped inside. As it began its assent, she smiled, pointing to the center of her forehead and then back at Willoughby, using her forefinger as the barrel of a gun. She winked and made a sound as if firing. Then she, too, disappeared into the ceiling.

Willoughby stared up after her for a moment, his eyes furrowed.

Sydney was watching him. "You want to explain that?"

"The winking? Uh, no. Everybody winks at me all the time. I don't get it." Willoughby seemed to be having a hard time taking his eyes off that section of ceiling. The empty elevator once again appeared.

"Yeah, well what about the impassioned hug?"

Willoughby gave a shrug. "It was Hauti. You want to try to explain her?"

Antonio barked a short laugh. He had started toward the tiny, golden elevator. "Well, I suppose I should get a move on as well." He looked at Willoughby directly, his eyes squinting slightly. "Before I head back to the coffee shop, though, I think I'll check out this wounded planter. This should be a sight worth seeing, don't you think Willoughby?" He gave a sly smile. "Moral of the story—what you drive may not be as important as *how* you drive."

He stepped into the elevator and punched the button. Willoughby and Sydney were soon alone in the room with the intelligence they called Sian.

"I thought you might appreciate discretion, Master Willoughby," the image said as soon as the elevator had returned empty.

"Yeah, thanks," Willoughby said. "What's your plan?"

"I really am your friend, you know," Sian said, seeming to ignore his question. Willoughby cocked his head. This was the second time that the computer responded in a manner that made it appear as if it were capable of independent thought.

"Okay," Willoughby said. He threw a quick glance at Sydney, who was staring directly forward at the image. "That's a bit weird—you've mentioned that twice now—but, okay. So, I ask you again, what do you have planned for Sydney and me?"

Sian swirled a finger and a holographic image of a large complex of old buildings appeared floating in the center of the room. It looked like some sort of medical facility or school complex. The hologram revolved slowly.

"I plan for you to go to Port Arthur, a historic prison in Tasmania. Flight records show that Aiyito took a flight into Hobart International Airport on October 10th, 2014. That was two days before the St. Petersburgh break-in. He hired a cab at the airport that drove him the 94.6

kilometers to this location, dropped him off for three hours, and then returned to pick him up."

"So?" Sydney broke in. "It was a long cab ride, I'll give you that, but it doesn't prove anything. He may have been just taking a break. Maybe Australian history is a hobby of his. There could be any number of reasons why he would take such a trip. There's nothing in what you've told us that links this to the break-in except that it was around the same general time frame. Have you looked at what everyone connected with Observations, Inc. did for those two days?"

"Yes, I have. There were anomalies with this trip that flagged me to dig deeper. Aiyito did not log the trip in his company calendar, which is unusual for him. He made no mention of it in any of his itineraries or personal logs— again, *unusual*. The tickets were purchased by his friend and fencing partner, Edo San. Edo told us that Aiyito gave him cash, plus a small bonus, to purchase the tickets. The result is that the transaction never shows up in Aiyito's personal financial records. What's more, the cab driver specified in his manifest that Aiyito requested he be dropped off at the prison well after dark. This old prison is now a tourist attraction on the island, but closes to the public at 7:00 PM. Aiyito requested to be dropped off at 10:00 PM. He instructed the driver to pick him up at the same spot at 4:00 AM the next morning, five hours before the prison opens to the public. In questioning the driver, he claimed that Aiyito did not tell him much. In fact, he said that Aiyito did not speak much at all. He was polite and tipped well. The driver said he did not ask many questions. There are lodgings nearby, and he thought this might be some sort of clandestine meeting with a lover. Upon more persuasive questioning, the driver did admit to taking an additional two hundred Australian dollars to keep his mouth shut and never speak to anyone about this trip to the prison."

Sydney was silent for a long moment. "Okay, so maybe he did have some secret he was trying to protect, but this doesn't necessarily relate to the break-in at St. Petersburg," she said, her voice less confident than before. "Maybe he *was* meeting a woman there or something."

"One more thing. The facility does have surveillance cameras in almost every corridor and on several of the outbuildings. I hacked into their security database. I found two sections of surveillance video missing from that evening—one from the entry gate to the facility, the other from one of the corridors in the Y wing. I surmise he paid someone handsomely to erase these segments. I can prove he has been grafting money from the accounts for quite some time. H.S. and Sam were both aware of it, but it was never at a level that caused them to terminate his position. Whatever else, Aiyito has always been good at managing the board members and keeping certain parts of Observations, Inc. activities hidden. He was able to give the company a needed legitimacy if prying eyes came snooping, and the fact that he was a little shady as a character added to his worth. Anyway, a very small, high tech camera with a long focal length was found by one of our satellite sweeps of the area. We believe it was recently installed, and is located high in a tree at the far end of the prison parking lot. The camera is unknown to the guards who work at the prison. The feed is not recorded in prison storage or monitored by prison staff. As near as we can tell, it goes directly into an intelligence gathering net, possibly because the lot has been used for various transfers of sensitive information. I hacked into the security net and was able to obtain the following footage. Watch the clip."

A grainy video clip played on the glass surface that separated them from Sian. It showed the parking lot from where it bordered the water at one end to the crumbling walls of one of the prison structures at the other. There were two street lamps illuminating the end of the parking lot nearest the crumbling walls. An older, lighter colored car with the taxi sign clearly visible pulled into the lot and stopped under one of the lights. A man got out. The taxi pulled away. The man walked to one of the street lamps and stood there. The video froze. Sian spoke from behind the image.

"This is precisely 9:52 PM on the night of October tenth. We isolated and enhanced the image. Here is a close-up of this man's face." The close-up was obviously Aiyito. "At 9:59, a motorcycle pulls up." The video resumed. In only a few minutes, as Sian predicted, the motorcycle pulls cautiously into the lot. The driver rides up to Aiyito, dismounts the bike, and pulls his helmet off. The video again freezes. An enhanced close-up of this man's face shows in the top left corner of the frozen image.

Sydney gasped.

"Do you recognize the man?" Sian said flatly from behind the image.

"Yes," Willoughby said, his eyes narrowing.

"It's Reese," Sydney said, almost in a whisper.

"Correct," Sian said as the video image disappeared and he became once again visible in front of them. "It is the man called Reese, who, as I understand it, was a key figure in the hijacking of the *Absconditus* and the death of H.S."

Willoughby turned to Sydney. She was no longer looking at Sian. She was just looking away. He turned to the intelligence.

"Why did you cut off the video? What happens after Aiyito meets with Reese?"

Sian seemed to be watching Sydney. He turned his hollow eyes toward Willoughby. "Aiyito spoke to Reese for approximately thirteen minutes. Reese handed him a folded parchment of some kind. We believe it may have been a map. When Aiyito unfolded the map, Reese pointed at it several times. The conversation seemed to get heated. Then, Reese put his helmet back on, climbed on his bike, and left. Aiyito watched him go, stared at the map for a few minutes, and then headed off in the direction of the entry gate to the prison. He was not picked up by any of the surveillance cameras inside the prison complex. That leads us to believe that the map may have noted the location of all surveillance cameras and that Reese was pointing out a route that would allow him to go mostly undetected.

"As I stated, there are two gaps in video footage—one at the front gate at precisely 10:14 PM, the other a feed from one of the outlying buildings close to a segment of fence that was being repaired at 3:13 AM. Again, from the security net, we picked up Aiyito stepping into the parking lot lights at precisely 3:37 AM. We surmise he exited the prison where the fence was in disarray, walked around the full perimeter of the prison, and re-entered the parking lot from the northeast. That is consistent with both the time the recorded video shows as well as his direction. At 3:52 AM, the taxi reappears. Aiyito climbs in, and the car pulls away."

Sian stopped speaking. Willoughby glanced at Sydney. Her face was ashen. "We don't know what that conversation was," he stated, turning back to Sian. "What happened inside the prison? Why did Aiyito go in alone, and what did he do for five hours? We still don't know that this was related to the hijacking."

Sian stared at him blankly. When he spoke, his voice was devoid of emotion. "We believe, Willoughby, that Aiyito was after something that exists in one of the halls or corridors of the prison. We believe it may be the same item the hijackers were searching for on the *Absconditus*. We have scoured every corridor of the prison and found little of use to us. We felt that you, with your special abilities, might be able to uncover something we could not. We also feel you should visit the prison at the same time of night in case the hour of the day holds significance."

Willoughby raised an eyebrow. "You want us to go to Tasmania and visit a spooky, old prison in the middle of the night?"

"Yes, that is it precisely," Sian confirmed with a wry grin. "Your tickets are waiting for you at the Quantus ticket counter at Heathrow. Your flight leaves at 6:00 PM tonight. I hope your trip can unlock the mystery of Aiyito's involvement. It may clear him. It may condemn him. We only want to uncover the truth. Is this a suitable risk, Miss Sydney?"

The image looked over at Sydney, who did not answer. Instead, she turned, walked to the small elevator, holding her guitar case loosely, and left the room without a word.

Willoughby watched her go, then turned back to Sian. "She'll be okay," he said. "Why do you keep saying

271

'we.' You said, '*We* want to uncover the truth.' Who is we?"

Sian pushed back with a sigh. "Sam and I, of course. You have lost a physical continuation of Sam, but not the memory of who he was, how he lived, how he affected your lives. Don't you feel him still with you? I do. I live with his thoughts, with his impressions, with his obsessions. For me, Sam feels ever present. In this issue, I was speaking for both of us." He paused momentarily, then bore down on Willoughby with a piercing stare. "Watch her closely, Willoughby. I fear for her. I fear for you."

There was something strange in the soft, familiar voice. Willoughby cocked his head slightly, staring back at the image for a long moment as he slowly back-pedaled to the golden elevator cage that had slid silently to a stop behind him. He finally turned away, stepped into the elevator cage, and pressed the button to ascend. He glanced back toward the image sitting at the head of the boardroom table. Sian was not watching him or even looking his way. His eyes were turned toward the open window, looking out to sea, his thoughts lost somewhere beyond the realistic façade of his own sophisticated control center, as if control were more than a mere technology, and comprehension was waiting out there, somewhere just beyond his grasp.

25

Heart of Ice

Total darkness was not what T.K. had expected. The tomb-like prime hole facility was cold, but not this cold, and while it had been sterile and clinical, she had at least been able to boost the lighting to full strength. The darkness around her was so pitch black as to be oppressive. *Where was she?* She pushed her hands out and felt around her. She had landed on all fours and was now kneeling on a surface that felt like crusted snow or frosted ice. A shiver ran through her. She had to find shelter. She had to find warmth—*and fast!* She was already beginning to feel the effects of the bitter cold. Her movements became faster, fingers flying over the frost crystals and ice as she propelled herself forward, searching for—for *what?* What did she hope to find? She wasn't sure, but her mind, her soul told her to search.

Her hand brushed against something smooth and metallic. It was frozen to the floor of this dark space— whatever it turned out to be. The item was about a foot in length and roughly two inches in diameter as near as she could tell. It was lying at an angle, which suggested it was not a part of the floor, but something that had become entrapped in the floor ice. She pulled and beat on the item with her fist, but it would not break free. Spinning her feet around, she kicked at the object with all her might. On the third kick, the ice cracked, freeing the item. She felt around until she found it again and picked it up. Working feverishly, she used her partially frozen fingers to break off the remaining bits of ice. It was a long, cylindrical tube of some kind. There were markings on one end of the tube, and a mushroom-shaped bulge at the end. A memory tickled her thoughts.

"Light stick," she mumbled, her hands quivering.

This was Atlantian technology to be sure. The symbols were Atlantian. The shape was of an item her people had called "light sticks." They were more reliable, more elegant, forms of portable light. They keyed only to Atlantian DNA, and were powered by self-perpetuating power sources. She slid her fingers and palm up and down the smooth rod, trying to trigger the "on" mechanism, but had no success. She was shivering now, shaking so that it was hard to work her hands. Running them a little further along the floor, she came to a frosted segment of wall that seemed to be divided into shelves. On a shelf about two feet from the floor, she found several other light sticks, some frozen solid to the shelf, but others able to be pried loose and seemingly intact. Her hands probed the pile, finding and trying half a dozen of the devices before one finally burst into bright, white light.

The light blinded her for a moment. She pushed to her feet, crouched and shivering. As her eyes cleared, she found herself in a small room at the edge of a circle dais. The room pricked a memory. *She had been in this room before—with her father!* She tried to ignore the cold and the shivering and forced her mind to think. It had been so long ago. She was just a girl. The memory crystallized in her mind. Her father was standing near here while men appeared on the dais. They each grabbed a light stick and a, a... She looked around. A clatter of pole-like implements lay frozen in a heap on the ground. They had the same markings as the light stick, with one end curved into a thin blade, while the other end had a mushroom bulge at the end, similar to the glowing bulge at the end of the light stick.

T.K. looked away from the poles. Weapons would not help her right now. She was going to freeze if she could not find some way to get warm. She quickly scanned the room. A doorway near the end of the oblong room was frozen half open. Lining a wall near the back she noted a series of tall niches carved into the stone wall. The image of her father flashed back. He was watching the men appear, drop off a light stick and pole, then file past to one of the wall niches. There, they pulled off their thick parkas and gloves, a padded helmet, and some sort of colorful tunic. As they dressed back into normal Atlantis attire, they lined up in ranks and passed through an outer doorway into the city. A sudden realization hit her. It had been a drill! She had been observing some sort of disaster drill, meant to test city defenses.

She stumbled toward the wall niches, shaking uncontrollably now, with her mind racing. *Why the parkas, the gloves?* Her city had been on a temperate island. Had they known something was coming?

The first four niches were empty. The fifth had a protective skin. She studied the skin. It had no knob or latch to open it. She swung around, looking for something to throw at it. She was shaking convulsively now, whimpering to herself. Upon finding nothing substantial, she stumbled to the small pile of poles, most of them broken, and freed up one that was intact. Ramming the knife blade into the sides and edges of the skin, she tried to pry it off with no success. She spun the pole around, sobbing with frustration, barely able to hold onto it because of the violent shaking of her shoulders. The blunt end of the pole had no better success. She stepped back and swung the pole with all her might, slamming it into the niche. The skin did not budge. She hit it repeatedly, each blow building in intensity as she vented her frustration. Amazingly, the pole did not break, but then again, neither did the niche skin.

Finally, breathing heavily and sobbing with cold and exhaustion, she dropped the pole and sank to her knees. She was feeling very tired suddenly. She just wanted to lie down, and close her eyes. She knew it was hypothermia setting in, but what was she to do? A part of her didn't seem to care. Then the words of the girl came back to her: "*The warmth of truth cannot be discovered in the mirror-maze of cold logic. It is an infinite spark, a river of fire known only to the heart. One does not need to tell you what you already know. You have been moving toward this moment all your life...*"

She screamed in a deafening groan, pushing herself to her feet. She felt herself sway and reached out a hand to steady herself. The second her full hand was flat against the niche skin, it moved, whisking away into the side of the niche. Stale air wafted out, making T.K. choke. She almost fell into the open space behind the skin, but caught herself. The parka hanging there looked perfectly preserved. There were gloves on a top shelf, and a face mask of sorts. They had all been perfectly protected from the elements. She fought for enough muscle control to throw on the parka and then the face mask.

Once she had pulled the parka tight around her, she sunk against the wall again, curling tight against her knees, trying to stop her body from trembling as new warmth began to spread through her. When she could finally control the shivers somewhat, she sat back, and then slowly pushed to her feet. She turned back to the wall niche and pulled out the gloves, sliding them onto her hands. She found the helmet and pulled it down over her head.

Everything was a few sizes too big, but once she snapped the helmet to the sides of the parka, a soft hum ensued. The inside of the helmet shifted to shape to the contours of her skull. A thin, pliable material slid down the back of her neck and under her chin, connecting the helmet to the face mask. T.K stared down with amazement as the parka seemed to suddenly activate as well. It tightened around her, fitting her form. Thin, gold spiders of material slid down her legs and encased her soft-skinned boots. She felt pulses of warmth begin to spread throughout her body now, but it was still several long minutes before the shaking of her body finally had fully subsided. As her muscles stilled, exhaustion began to overtake her. There were no sleeping quarters here, and she did not feel she had the strength to go exploring, so she turned, pushing her body back into the still open niche, the only place in the room not encased in ice. She leaned her head against the side of the niche wall and allowed her body to relax and enjoy the warmth.

As she sat there, drifting toward sleep, her mind turned again to what had just happened. *Atlantis was supposed to have been destroyed. How was she here now in one of its security stations? Why did her memories contain this place with parkas and gloves? Why had her father brought her here?* She mused over possibilities. *Could he have glimpsed some of the coming tragedy that would befall her family, her city? Could he have been trying to prepare her for a time when Atlantis would sink below a sea of ice?*

She wrapped her arms around herself. One last thought tickled at the back of her consciousness. *If they had known about the coming disaster, had they prepared for the catastrophe? Could they have survived it? Could they be living somehow in this underground world of frost and ice?*

As she faded to unconsciousness, a brief sound, very far away, logged itself into her brain for analysis. It could have just been the ice crackling. Or, it could have been something else...something moving and very much alive.

26

Mirrored Time

Willoughby sat quietly in the seat next to Sydney. Luckily, the plane was not full and the end seat near the aisle was not taken. Sydney stared out the window as the plane taxied slowly into position on the runway. She hadn't said much to him when they arrived at the airport. They had grabbed a sandwich and boarded their flight. That was it. They had said maybe fifty words between them. He didn't blame her for not being her chatty self. It had been an unusual day and an unsettling week and he didn't feel much like talking either.

He pulled his windbreaker tighter around him, his hands slipping into the pockets. His right hand touched upon the smooth jade of the small box with the golden clasp, the box that How Loa had given him back in Bermuda. He hadn't really thought of the box for a while, but as he was packing for this trip, it suddenly came to mind. On a whim, he had decided to bring it. He still had no idea what it was, or why the strange oriental shopkeeper had insisted it was for him. He was also somewhat confused as to why How had put it in his left pocket when he was in the time stream, trying to find his way back from his encounter with the Desert Witch. Somehow, the box had seemed to guide him back to Sydney and the others. *Why?*

He ran a finger over it, seeing in his mind the intricate figures carved into the jade—small dragons with tails entwining. He had yet to find a way to open the little box, but How had indicated that it came from his birth father, Gustav. He briefly thought of the final meeting with his father. It seemed a lifetime ago. His father had told him that "*all that is worth knowing wants to be known.*" He had spoken of the inchworm, saying that Willoughby needed to pull his thoughts in before he tried to reach out.

Willoughby sat back, resting his head against the thin cushion in his chair. What his father *hadn't* told him was anything about the box. He tried to pull his thoughts in. *What wanted to be known right now?* When he was in the open time grid, How Loa had indicated that the box could somehow guide him back to safety—back to Sydney, Antonio, and Hauti. That meant it had to somehow be connected to one of them. He supposed it could have had some connection to the Jurassic Era facility itself, but he doubted that. Maybe the contents of the box didn't want to be known. But it *needed* to be known. He thought back to his first experience with the raw time grid. Hadn't he been wearing this same windbreaker? *Had the box been in this same pocket at that time?* He couldn't remember. He had traveled back to a concert hall in St. Petersburg, Russian, where Sydney was performing, after hearing echoes of Sydney's music in the grid.

Suddenly, it seemed very likely to him that the contents of the box were somehow tied to Sydney, to her music. The time grid didn't lie.

He sank back into the head cushion with an inaudible sigh. So many questions were swirling around in his head—what was this box? What was in it and why could he not open it? Why had Sam been shot? Why had Aiyito come to a prison in Tasmania in the middle of the night? Why did the artificial intelligence Sian fear for Sydney and for him? What did all this have to do with Beelzebub and the Dark Edge? He tried to focus his mind, to truly listen, but he heard nothing.

He thought back on the few hours since their meeting with the team at Sam's old apartments. As soon as he and Sydney had left Sian, Willoughby started looking for Antonio. His friend had been waiting for them out at the front of the apartment complex.

"Ah, so you understood my invitation," he beamed.

"Invitation?" Sydney had been clueless of Antonio's intentions.

Antonio simply smiled. "I thought you might want to go check out the scene of the great planter disaster with me," he winked. "Then, we could walk back to the coffee shop. Does that sound agreeable?"

Sydney gave a slight shrug and the three began walking. Willoughby knew that the real purpose of the excursion was that Antonio wanted to talk. He was looking for an open area without any surveillance and walking back through the park to the busted planter and then to the coffee shop on the other side would provide them time to compare notes. When they were well into the park, Antonio turned to them.

"What do you think?"

"About Sian?"

Antonio nodded.

Willoughby took a moment, as if trying to find the right words. "I don't know. He doesn't behave like a machine."

"My thoughts exactly. He seemed to be thinking of not betraying confidences, of not hurting feelings. I have never seen this sort of abstract thinking in a programmed being. It could be that H.S. applied technology well beyond anything we have known. Or—"

"Or there could be someone, or something else pulling the hologram's strings," Willoughby completed.

"Exactly. He has a lot of information about us. If he really is that advanced, he may be able to monitor our movements, our every telephone conversation or text message. Here..." Antonio handed Willoughby a cell phone. "This is my cousin's phone. Sian does not know you have it. I will get another cell phone from one of my other family members and that way, we know we can speak without being monitored. I will get one to James Arthur as well."

"You really think all this is necessary?" Sydney asked. "Somebody just shot that thing's creator. Wouldn't that put it on our side?"

"Unless Sian had something to do with Sam getting shot," Willoughby mumbled, airing a concern that had begun to weigh on him. "I'm not saying I believe that," he added hastily, "just that...well, we don't know enough yet. We don't really know what we're dealing with. I can't say I feel comfortable around that...uh, intelligence."

"Well," Antonio said, "actually, I hope you are right Sydney. It would certainly be nice to have someone on our side with the kind of resources that thing has. But, to Willoughby's most excellent point, I think we have been through enough to know that there is no way we can see the road ahead of us clearly. We find ourselves in the middle of a game that we do not even fully understand. All we can do is skillfully play the hand we are dealt. Whether we like it or not, caution is necessary."

Sydney looked at Antonio, and after a pause, gave a quick nod. "Agreed. I also believe we have to be absolutely open with each other. So, I think it's only fair that you know…Sian suspects my father, Aiyito, of being a traitor to the organization. He shared with us some evidence that Sam had collected. It could indicate that Aiyito was feeding information to the Dark Brotherhood cult. We're on our way to Tasmania to check out some suspicious activity that Aiyito was involved in there."

"Aiyito?" Antonio's brow furrowed with concern. "That, that is…unexpected. It seems a bit outlandish to me. What do you think, Sydney?" He watched Sydney closely, only glancing briefly at Willoughby. Sydney dropped her head, apparently unable to answer at first. Then she looked up, her words curt and matter-of-fact.

"I think it's a load of hogwash," she said. "At least, suspicion of him being a spy. It's possible, though, that someone is using him."

Willoughby welcomed this chance to direct the conversation without betraying his commitment to Aiyito. "That's exactly my opinion. Our trip to Tasmania is more to try to determine who might be trying to use him and how." He felt a flush of red spread over his cheeks. *He already knew who was trying to use Aiyito. Should he tell them?* Aiyito *was* an unwilling accomplice to the *Absconditus* tragedy, though. Wouldn't that stir a lot of resentment and emotion that they couldn't afford right now? How would it affect Sydney? Would she even believe him? *It was Aiyito who needed to tell Sydney, to explain everything to her.* He had gone over and over it in his mind. This was not his information to share. He had made a promise to Aiyito, and he needed to stick with it. Still, he felt a pang of guilt at remaining silent.

They had slowed in their walking pace. They were close to the area where a clean-up crew was busy at work removing the remains of a large, busted planter. Antonio waved them clear of the crew, pointing them toward the coffee shop. "If Aiyito is involved, sending the two of you that far away to trace his steps does not seem like a good idea to me. Whether he is knowingly involved or being manipulated, either way, such a trip could spell danger."

"I don't know that we have a choice," Willoughby said. "We sent Sydney and Sam here to London, worried about their safety, and you see how that turned out. Is it any safer for us to go with you to the Arctic? Is it safer to go with Dr. J to the lair of the Brotherhood? I think our 'safe' options have dwindled. Now, it's more about finding answers. Otherwise, we'll never find a way to eliminate the threats that stalk us."

Sydney had never taken her eyes from Antonio. "He's my father, Antonio. This is something I must do. I need to prove that my father would have nothing to do with the slaughter of innocent people, at least, not knowingly. Otherwise, how can I live with myself? How can I ever face him again?"

Antonio was silent for a moment. "I understand," he finally mumbled, not sounding like he understood at all, "but have you thought that this may be playing right into the Brotherhood's hands?" Antonio looked over at Willoughby.

"So, what do you suggest?" Willoughby said. "They just killed our friend. They may be manipulating Sydney's father. Leaving them alone and doing nothing obviously isn't working. Taking the fight to them is the only option I see."

Antonio sighed. "You are right, my friend. But there is one other thing I must tell you." They had stopped walking now, just out of earshot of the coffee shop. "I found something in the ruins. I think it was a warning for you and Sydney. I showed James Arthur to see if he agreed, which he did. We were thinking how to bring the topic up to you when Sam's death derailed our plans. I think you need to know. When I was exploring an almost intact temple in those submerged ruins in the Gulf of Khumbhat, I came upon a secret room. The walls were filled with pictograms and text. I recognized some of the text from the Atlantian that T.K. taught me when we were in the cave together. It was hidden among words and characters that seem more a distant form of Hindi."

"Why didn't you tell me about it?"

"The Atlantian text referred to a '*boy of numbers*' who it claimed must be protected. It showed a girl with a violin falling. There were the words, '*Music marks in mirrored time a fall.*' We worried what impact such messages would have upon the two of you, especially after the snake episode in the jungle."

Willoughby didn't seem to want to talk about the snake episode. "I thought you said those submerged ruins were like 9000 years old. How could they have anything to do with Sydney and I? Are you saying someone from Atlantis travelled to the future, then back to the past, where they carved a warning onto a hidden temple wall—one they expected you to find 9000 years later? That's a lot of conjecture. I suppose you think it was T.K.?"

Antonio thought for a moment. "Perhaps. I am almost certain the message is not just Atlantian, but that it comes from someone who at least knew T.K. There are clues that refer directly to T.K."

"If you think T.K. was there, then you found her, right? We've got to get back to that city, the one 9000 years in the past, the one we started exploring off the coast of India. Why in the world are you going to Antarctica?" Willoughby seemed exasperated.

"Because," Antonio began, "the message told us not to come to that city in the past to find her. It indicated that I would be needed *here*."

"Needed here?"

Antonio shook his head slightly. "It was a strange message, part prophecy. It may be that it is critical I follow the course I am on—that we all do. It mentioned a storm and stated that the Dark Edge would be rising. It spoke of a sacrifice. It mentioned a champion and a healer and a long night. It said, 'You will be needed where you are...I will find you.'"

Willoughby thought for a moment. "*Dark* is certainly the operative word these days. We're constantly pushed into making decisions with sketchy and inconclusive information."

Sydney jumped in. "Okay, so you have a clue you think is from T.K. that shows a girl with a violin, and she's falling—not with a knife in her back, or a sword running her through, she's just falling. Did you ever think that maybe T.K. is just mad at her predicament and expressing her frustration that it wasn't me falling through the time grid instead of her? She never seemed to like me—she barely tolerated me on the *Absconditus*. Why would she suddenly be trying to save me from some terrible, falling fate? I think you're reading too much into this."

Antonio frowned. "Sydney, my friend, I know T.K., and despite your experience, I know she would try to help if she knew you were in danger. The message seems to be an attempt to warn you, to warn *us*, of something."

"Of what? Antonio, T.K. knows we're all in danger. It's probably more likely that she blames me for everything, and she's threatening to push me off a cliff if I ever get in her way again."

Antonio seemed taken back. "I think you are missing the point—"

"Oh, no, I got the point," Sydney said with a sarcastic smile. She turned to Willoughby.

"Do we have to listen to this? I've got a lot to do to get ready, and I don't see how this is helping anything."

She turned and set off, heading away from them toward the street.

Willoughby sighed, touching Antonio's arm gently. "You've got to admit," he said, "it feels like a stretch. Even if that is a message from T.K., Sydney's right—how do we know it was a warning for Sydney? The two did not exactly hit it off. Are you sure it was a violin the girl had, it couldn't have been something else? Did any of the prophecy call Sydney out by name?"

Antonio shook his head, looking down. Willoughby put a hand on his shoulder.

"That may have been someone else falling, or some kind of symbolic message." He glanced after Sydney, and then looked back. "Also, it's kind of poor timing for this conversation."

Antonio huffed. "*I know.* I know, my friend—but you needed to be told. We should have told you earlier."

Willoughby sighed. "Yeah. You should have. But you didn't, and that's water under the bridge now. Listen, I'll think over what you've said, and we'll be careful. How about you? Do you really think that it's best for you to go to Antarctica?"

Antonio shrugged. "It is where I would have been going anyway. I get the sense that T.K. was saying we should not do things differently. Maybe she's just warning us to keep our eyes open."

Willoughby forced a smile. "Always a good idea. You take care of yourself, Antonio."

"And you," Antonio said.

Willoughby turned and was about ten meters away when Antonio called out his name. He looked back. "What?"

"Sydney," Antonio said. "Stay close to her." Willoughby nodded.

That had been it. That had been the whole conversation with Antonio, yet his friend's words had continued to haunt him as he caught up with Sydney, and they called in a ride from Uber. Partly, it was his own words about the fall possibly being symbolic. He had not wanted to share this with Antonio at the time, but the idea of Sydney being the first to fall to the Dark Edge made some sense with her father being wrapped up with Beelzebub. *How will she react when she discovers the truth?*

Willoughby tried to push the thoughts away, to pull his mind back to the here and now. He looked over at Sydney, her head now resting against the curve of her headrest, her eyes still staring out the window. The plane jolted a bit, causing the '*Fasten Seat Belts*' sign to blink on. It forced Sydney to pull her eyes back from the window and begin to fasten her own belt.

"Penny for your thoughts," Willoughby said softly as he clicked his own belt into place. She looked over at him.

"I'm just thinking of my dad—of Aiyito." She turned away, glancing back toward the window. "We may not have always seen eye to eye, but I don't think he's a bad man."

"Neither do I," Willoughby added.

She gave him a short-lived grin. Turning back to the window, her voice became somewhat distant. "When I was young, he and my mom were fighting all the time. Mom didn't like the secretive nature of his job, and she didn't want to be pinned down with a child and a home to manage. I used to hide from the noise in my father's study. He had a large collection of classical music CDs. They took up almost one whole wall. He taught me how to us the CD player when I was barely three. I guess he thought it would keep me from hearing the fighting. It changed my life. I found I could escape into the music. The notes, the melodies, the harmonies, they became the landscape of my dreams, and then, they became a soundtrack for my life. My emotions, my pain, my elation—a musical score defines everything. I began to write music as other girls write diaries."

Willoughby listened, fascinated. This was a Sydney he had rarely seen before. This was a Sydney with her guard down. She turned to him with an almost conspiratorial smile.

"I started writing music on the piano. I took piano lessons for two years and had already moved to a fifth-year competency when I switched to the violin."

"Why did you switch?"

"Tonal quality," Sydney said without hesitation. "Tonal quality is very important to me for some reason, and my dad couldn't keep our piano in perfect tune long enough to satisfy me. With the violin, I had more control of the tuning, and thus, the tonal quality."

"That's why you also play guitar?"

Sydney shrugged. "We've talked about music before. You know a bit about my music tastes. It's hard to write a Norah Jones or Regina Spektor tune on a violin. So, my musical needs sort of spilled over to the guitar—especially for song writing."

"You write songs? With lyrics? I've only heard your classical and semi-classical compositions."

"Yeah," Sydney's voice seemed far away and distracted. "My guitar songs are more personal. I don't use them often in my performances, and never with the lyrics." The voice trailed off, then Sydney turned, her eyes boring into him. "Willoughby, I think I know why Aiyito was at Port Arthur. I think I told you when we first met that my dad took great pride in my musical accomplishments, despite how little he seemed to care about being my father."

Willoughby thought again of his conversation with Aiyito. How could he tell her that her father really did care? There had to be a way, but perhaps now was not the time. He bit his words back and forced himself to just listen.

"One of the things my father constantly did was to find me obscure music pieces from all over the globe. Few people know this fact, but I have one of the largest, most varied collections of original sheet music in the world. I checked the dates. The day after that video was taken of Aiyito at the Port Arthur facility parking lot, I got a special delivery package from my dad with an old piece of original sheet music." She reached into an inside pocket of the designer bag she had carried on to the plane and pulled out an old piece of parchment paper in a thick, protective sleeve. It was wrinkled and worn and had splattered ink and a scrawl of musical score on it. The bottom of the page was missing. It looked like it had been burned away. The entire bit of paper was encased in a plastic cover.

"Aiyito said he purchased it from an old prison in Tasmania. The bottom of the sheet of music was burned away, as if someone had started to destroy the piece but was stopped. Only this bit was saved, and I think it's only missing a few stanzas, but, *wow!* The music written was so brilliant and fresh, it inspired me to write an entire piece around it. There was no composer's name on the sheet, only initials: D.K. My father said the score had been found by one of the prison caretakers hidden inside a wall that was receiving maintenance. I found the music so compelling that I included it in my St. Petersburg show. I gave credit in the program to *a mysterious donor who wrote brilliant music.*"

Mention of the St. Petersburg show piqued Willoughby's attention. "Have you played it since?"

Sydney tipped her head thinking. "No," she said, almost surprised. "I was so angry that Aiyito did not attend the performance as he promised that I buried the musical score of that entire show at the back of my collection."

Willoughby didn't say anything. He had a sense this meant something, but he wasn't sure what. It was like there was a definite connection, but it was obscured in his mind. Sydney continued speaking, almost to herself.

"But why would Aiyito be going to the prison at night? And why would Reese have been involved?"

Willoughby shook his head. "I don't know. Maybe this purchase wasn't exactly legal. Maybe this was the best way for the transaction to happen where it would not create any suspicion. No one appeared to be there at the time so there was no one to see the transaction. Maybe some of Reese's shady activities had nothing to do with the hijacking."

They were both quiet for a moment and then Willoughby sighed. "Not to change the subject, but you don't really believe T.K. would carve a message on a 9000-year-old wall just to make a dig at you, do you?"

Sydney grinned. "No. I was just mad that Antonio never told us."

"So, what do you think the whole falling thing could mean?"

Sydney thought for a moment. "I don't know. It could have been figurative—a lot of pictograms from early antiquity were. Also, I know Antonio wants to *think* it was a message from T.K., but do you really think it was? And do you really think it was about me? I mean, what really ties it to me? The fact that the prophecy, or whatever, mentions music? That the figure falling is holding something they think is a violin? From what I can tell, Antonio and T.K. got pretty tight living in that cave together for so long. Then, as soon as they find a way out, they're separated. You really think the first thing on her mind is to send out some cryptic message to warn a girl she frankly didn't care for a whole lot?"

Willoughby thought for a moment. "So, why didn't you and T.K. get along?"

Sydney let out a huge sigh. She blinked several times, her eyes watery. "I didn't feel like I had any real friends then. I mean, I had H.S., but he was more of a father figure, and there were the others on the team, but I mostly just sparred with them. When I found that T.K. and I were to share a room together, I thought, here's a chance. Being a world-famous musician, you don't get many of those. But then I met her. She was polite, but obviously felt I was eccentric and spoiled, which I probably am, and she made it very clear that *friendship* was not on her agenda. She focused on her tasks and had little time outside of that for social interaction. Now that I know she was once a princess, and I understand her objectives on the Absconditus, it all makes sense, but at that time, I just felt hurt, and I must say, I struck out at her pretty hard. I was awful to her."

"Well, she's a big girl, and I didn't get the sense that she harbored any real ill-will toward you. You just weren't on her agenda. The most frustrating thing to me about these pictograms that Antonio believes she left is that they didn't let us see them. I texted Antonio to see if they took photographs of the pictograms, but he says they didn't have time. A self-destruct mechanism was rigged into the room so that the temple destroyed itself as soon as they exited. If we had been able to look at them, maybe we wouldn't have seen a person falling with a violin. It could have been an angel flying with some sort of instrument, or a lot of different things. Any ideas about the words, '*Music marks in mirrored time a fall.*'?"

Sydney pursed her lips. "No clue. We don't know the context."

The '*Fasten Seat Belts*' sign clicked off and Sydney unbuckled hers. "Listen, sorry to climb over you, but I need to make it to the powder room before they bring the drink cart back and block the aisle." She squeezed past him. He sat quietly for a long moment. A quick image flashed in his mind of the portion of Sydney's performance he had seen at the Miriinsky Theater in St. Petersburg. An entire stage of full length mirrors shattered at the climax of a number. *Music marks in mirrored time a fall?* Could it be that easy? What was the importance of St. Petersburg and the concert there? What was the music he had heard in the time stream?

His mind wandered as he stared out the window at the already darkening sky.

27

Port Arthur's Ghosts

The flight from London to Hobart seemed eternal. Even though the plane had left Heathrow Airport at precisely 6:10 PM, they had endured roughly 18 hours in the air and two quick stops before they finally touched down in Hobart, Tasmania. Due to crossing numerous time zones, they arrived a full day later than they left at just after 9:00 PM local time. Sydney was tired and crabby, and Willoughby didn't blame her. He felt jet-lagged, cramped, stale, and hungry himself.

For the first ten hours or so, they had tried to keep conversation up, talking about lighter subjects such as movies, the merits of new bands, upcoming concerts on Sydney's schedule, and even conversations about the unique items for sale in the airline magazines stowed in the pockets in front of them. They tried to watch a lame in-flight movie about international espionage, and then took a stab at trying to sleep. In Willoughby's case, it was hopeless. No matter how he tried, he couldn't get comfortable.

When Sydney pushed upright from her own dozing, requesting coffee, and wiping her eyes, their conversation resumed. It turned back to Aiyito's involvement with the brotherhood and the challenges their friends faced. Willoughby suggested possibilities of how Aiyito could have wound up having dealings with Reese, trying to solidify the idea of Aiyito being used by them. He got as close as he felt he could to telling Sydney about her father's meeting with Beelzebub, pretending to speculate while stating things he knew to be true. She narrowed her eyes at him a few times, but did not question his speculations.

In quieter moments, he further considered what Antonio had told him about the pictogram in the ruins. *Who could try to throw Sydney from a cliff?* Beelzebub? That made no sense. He could easily hide her somewhere in a time junction and use her as leverage, or experimentation, or who knows what else, as long as he needed. But if it wasn't Beelzebub, then who? The *Dark Brotherhood?* What would they have against Sydney, and why would Reese be involved? After all, Reese had been with Belzarac, not the rank and file of the Brotherhood. What could be his connection with an old musical score hidden in a wall at Port Arthur Prison? Had Reese just been the closest goon to the prison? He seemed to remember that the man was from Australia.

They finally disembarked from their plane and were cleared through customs. As they stood just outside Hobart International Airport and called over a taxi, Sydney turned to him.

"I need food, sleep, and time to freshen up, and not necessarily in that order. I think I'll just have something sent up to the hotel room. Meet you in the lobby in the morning at seven o'clock?"

"Seven o'clock?"

"Yeah, sorry—the ferry for Port Arthur leaves at eight-fifteen. This allows us to have breakfast together."

Willoughby just nodded. He wasn't up to arguing about anything. He just needed a bed, and he needed it *soon*. Fortunately, it was a short taxi ride to their hotel, barely ten minutes due to the late hour. The Salamanca Inn was nestled in the heart of the quaint city. Sydney had pointed out with delight that the accommodations were only a few miles away from the Cadbury Chocolate factory when she first looked up the hotel online. Right now, though, neither of them were thinking chocolate. They unloaded their bags, tipped the driver, and suffered through a very cheerful desk clerk who wanted to ask them 101 questions—especially Sydney. Luckily, he did not recognize her as the world-famous violinist she was or they may have been there all night. Finally, they were signing off at their adjoining doors.

Sydney looked over with a wry smile. "I don't suppose you want to try for the kiss of a lifetime before we part?"

Willoughby grinned. "You don't think we'll fall asleep leaning against the wall? It could end up such a deep kiss that they call the morgue."

"Yeah," Sydney winked, "but what a way to go." She slipped into her room.

Willoughby stumbled over to his door, mumbling to himself as he dragged his rolling suitcase in. "*Why does everyone always wink at me...?*"

The sound of the phone's shrill ring woke him out of a deep sleep. It took a few moments for him to get his bearings. He answered, hearing an equally cheerful desk clerk wish him a pleasant morning. He stared at the clock. It was, indeed, 7:00 AM. He looked down at his crumpled clothes. He had not called for room service to deliver a late snack. He had not showered. He had not even undressed and pulled down the covers. He barely remembered requesting the wake-up call before he flopped onto the bed and fell into a deep sleep. He did remember a strange dream, though. He had been walking down the street the hotel was on and all these woman and girls were winking at him, and when he didn't do something, they all got mad and were chasing him.

What a nightmare, he thought. Then, he remembered some of the girls hadn't looked half bad, and concluded there were far worse nightmares to be had.

After a quick shower and a change of clothes, he still felt groggy, but at least a bit more alive than the previous night. Sydney was her immaculate, chipper self in the lobby.

"I already called an order down, so they should be ready to serve us breakfast about the time we get seated."

She led him into the restaurant, and true to her prediction, the waiter served them within minutes. The gourmet breakfast was superb and Willoughby began to feel as if the day were definitely looking up.

"Where to now?" he asked, wiping his mouth with a linen napkin.

"We need to get to the ferry—remember? I told you last night."

"I don't remember a lot about last night," Willoughby confided.

"Ah," Sydney smiled. "You don't remember forcing your way into my hotel room in the throes of a passionate kiss? Then—"

"Okay," Willoughby interrupted, "I think that must have been the online novel you were reading on the plane, because that would be something I would definitely remember, and if it was somebody else, that's definitely something I don't want to know about."

Sydney paused, cocking her head. "You know, it may have been somebody else. Maybe that nice young man at the desk last night."

Willoughby laughed. "You kidding? That guy would have talked you to death long before the kissing started."

The two exited the hotel and caught a taxi. Willoughby had wanted to call an Uber or Lyft driver—more anonymous—but the taxis were already waiting in a queue along the curb. Within minutes, they were at the pier and on the morning ferry to Port Arthur. The ferry was relatively empty, only a handful of sightseers venturing out this early on a brisk day that was far from the height of tourist season. They picked a spot along the rail where they could be alone, looking back toward the town as the ferry chugged away from the dock. Sydney had her guitar with her, and now took it out and began to tune it. Willoughby hadn't even remembered her checking it in at the airport, but he wasn't surprised. She had barely let the instrument out of her sight since Sian had given it to her.

"So, when are you going to let me hear one of those songs?" he asked, sheepishly.

She looked over. "You really want to?"

He nodded. The air was crisp and the salty wind played with Sydney's hair. A bird cried from overhead. Sydney pursed her lips. "I don't share my songs with just anybody, so you have to promise no thunderous applause or waving cell phone lights at the end, okay?"

Luckily, Willoughby had been to a few concerts—some of them Sydney's—and knew that fans often waved cell phones with the flashlight activated at the end to try to get the band to play one more tune. He nodded. Sydney turned back to the guitar and began to strum a few chords and pick out a tune. When she seemed ready, she looked back up at him.

"I wrote this song about a year before I met you. It kind of explains what I was going through, and what I was talking about when you asked why I didn't hit it off with T.K." She looked away, staring over the railing into the wind, and began to play. Her voice was pure and beautiful. She sang with as much passion as she showed when she played, maybe more.

"The world is so lonely at night
Alone in the cold shadow light
Crying my daydreams like ribbons on air

"Friends made of Papier-mâché
Reach for their hands but they just blow away
Nothing is real when there's no one to care

"And I ask myself
Where could he be?
Isn't there in all the world someone to be there for me?
And sometimes my life feels like a dream
An empty ship lost out to sea
But I've got to see it through
I've got to hold on 'til I find you
"Because you know how hard it is to be
Just another lonely kid like me

"So, I hide the truth in the hurt of my song
I prove to the world I am tough, I am strong
Convinced I can shoulder the weight of the lies

"But baggage can break even stone
And carry the cold to the heart of each bone
Leaving the truth to bleed out from my eyes

"And I ask myself
Where could he be?
Isn't there in all the world someone to be there for me?
And sometimes my life feels like a dream
An empty ship lost out to sea
But I've got to see it through
I've got to hold on 'til I find you

"Because you know how hard it is to be
Just another lonely kid like me...

The guitar chords faded. Sydney was silent. Willoughby saw her wipe at her eyes and realized why she didn't share her songs in her concerts, she felt every word so intensely. He almost felt embarrassed, like he had been caught reading someone's private diary. Yet, the song had been so haunting and rang so true. He moved his mouth to speak, but no words came.

Finally, when Sydney had composed herself, she turned to him, a huge smile across her face. "Well? You're the first to ever hear it."

"It was, it was beautiful. I mean, wow—I don't have the words. It, it haunts me."

"Hmm," Sydney said, putting the guitar away. "There's a few other things I would rather do, but I guess I'm okay with haunting you."

"It was really good, Sydney."

The two were silent for a while. He thought of earlier boat trips they had been on together, first on the *Aperio Absconditus*, then on H.S.'s yacht, the *Pesci Pecolli*. This trip, though, felt different. There was certainly as much at stake, but they were different. He felt comfortable in Sydney's presence, more like he could just be himself and that was okay.

"Hey, I'm impressed," he said, looking over at Sydney. She had stood and was staring over the railing toward the far bank.

"At what?"

"Well," Willoughby grinned, "you didn't even seem to notice all the great shopping around the hotel. In Bermuda, your shopping spree threatened to sink the whole boat."

Sydney grinned. "Slight exaggeration."

"Not much," Willoughby said, grinning back. He remembered the five taxis filled to the brim and Sydney's battles to fit everything in her cabin. He followed her gaze to the receding shoreline. "You know, I miss those Englishmen," he said, referring to H.S. and Sam. "Only, one wasn't really English, I guess."

Sydney studied him. Then, she gave a short nod and looked away again. After a time, she said, "Let's not think on dark topics today, okay? I need to hold it together." She fell silent again for a moment, then straightened briskly. "I think we'll be able to get on the one o'clock tour at the prison. Do you have the course Sian mapped out that bypassed all the cameras, and the location of the building where he thinks Aiyito went?"

Willoughby nodded, taking his cue. He took out his Surface Pro, booted it up, and opened the file in question. Sydney was looking over his shoulder. She pointed at the screen.

"We'll have to figure out which tour gets us into that building. What do you know about Port Arthur?"

"Not much. It was named after the Lieutenant Governor, George Arthur, and it was set up as a punishment-oriented timber station. Later, it became a famous prison, and then, it became a tourist site. I seem to remember from my reading that it was a pretty nasty place at one point, then became a model of new prison reforms later."

"Yeah," Sydney said. "Except, you left out the ghost part."

"Ghost part?"

"Uh huh. It's one of the hottest sites for ghost hunters in the world—a haven for paranormal investigators and the like."

"Which means…?"

Sydney gave him a sarcastic smirk. "Which means it's a really popular spot for seeing ghosts."

"You think we'll see a ghost?" Willoughby perked up.

"No," Sydney said, "I happen to believe the whole thing is a lot of nonsense, but it does mean that the place is probably creepy at night."

"Hmm," Willoughby said. "Really creepy and we *want* to be there at night?"

Sydney rolled her eyes. "Says the boy who faced zombies, witches, and a cobra den?"

"Well," Willoughby countered, "ghosts have never really been my thing."

"And cobras are?"

Willoughby smiled. "You got me there."

"Just think positive. Maybe it will be positive and we can call it Casper. Besides, some boys would die to have a cute girl on their arm when the going gets spooky."

Willoughby looked at her. "Yeah, it's the dying part that doesn't quite fit on my list of dream dates."

"Well, mine either. But, you take what you can get." Sydney flashed another forced smile. Her voice fell to a whisper. "And you hope that what you get is something worth having." She looked over, her voice deadly serious now. "Am I something worth having?"

Willoughby wasn't sure how to respond to the question. "Uh, sure. What do you mean?"

"I'm good with music, but outside of that, who am I really? Every time I start to get close to someone, every time I think I'm starting to know where I am, who I am, life spins me around and I'm just a confused soul searching for answers again."

"Well," Willoughby mused, "I think it's that way for most of us. It's *life*."

Sydney thought for a moment and seemed to come to agreement. She turned to face him more directly. "When I found music, it opened a door for me. I could escape into it—away from the bickering of my parents, away from the feelings of inadequacy, feelings that it was all somehow my fault—why my parents didn't get along. There was a structure in music, and if you did it right, the structure was bright, and clean, and beautiful. When my father bought me my first violin, I had already started composing on the piano. I could see the music in my head. I could see where it needed to bend, where it needed to go. No teacher ever had to ride me to practice. I worked and worked until the sound from my fingers could match the visions in my mind. I wanted that harmony between hand and mind more than anything. More than food. More than play. Sometimes, more than air. I look back and think about those days, and I'm surprised I survived."

Sydney stopped speaking for a while, looking back over the water. Strands of her shiny black hair blew across her face, and Willoughby noticed that she was wearing multiple bracelets and long, dangling earrings. They were signature Sydney attire, but she hadn't worn any bracelets or anklets since the funeral. *Maybe this was her way of trying to mend, to move on?* The bracelets made a clinking sound as she raised a hand to push a strand of hair back behind her ear. He was reminded, just for a moment, of that first day when he had seen her on the deck of the *Aperio Absconditus*. With her penetrating eyes, her shiny black hair, and the slight ping of musicality about her, she was the most wildly beautiful thing he had ever seen. He fell in love with her on the spot. She stared back at him.

"Now, I'm afraid all over again. I'm afraid of losing it all—of losing my music, of losing the bit of a father who gave it to me, of losing you. I had a friend die in my arms. That's not the kind of thing you just walk away from." She took a long pause. "Am I just being stupid?"

"No," Willoughby said. "You're just being human." He thought for a moment, then he turned to her. "It's like you told me on the plane—your world is your music. You need to get back to it as soon as possible. You need to put everything you're feeling out there in musical form. Then, you can see it. You can organize it and polish it, and bleed and cry through it. I think it's the only way you'll find your way back to peace. You need to put it in a song, like the one you just sang."

Sydney smiled at him as her eyes grew suddenly moist. "How'd you get to be such a sage? Where's my mathematician?"

Willoughby shrugged. "Where's my hyper active, sing-song dancer who made music just by breathing?"

Sydney wiped at her eyes. "Maybe she's still making music. The tune has just gotten a little harder to hear."

"Maybe the mathematician is still calculating—it's just that the equations have gotten longer and the solutions more elusive—and by the way, you said 'no dark topics,' so dry those eyes."

Sydney wiped at her cheek, then reached over and grabbed his hand. They were comfortable in their silence for the rest of the ferry ride. By the time they reached Port Arthur, she seemed to have rejuvenated. She led the way, pulling Willoughby in her wake like a teacher pulling a school boy.

"We need to get on as many tours as possible. See if they have any nightly ghost tours—they're conducted by lantern after hours," she said. "We'll do all we can today and compare notes. We can pick up any tours we missed tomorrow, and scout out the path Sian thinks Aiyito took to miss all the cameras. Then, tomorrow night, we'll wait until after everyone leaves—after the evening lantern tours are concluded—and sneak over here. Sound good?"

They were soon standing in the Visitors Center near the main gate, in a building that held a café, a gift shop, stroller and wheel chair rentals, a booth for booking tours, and racks of brochures about the prison and about things to do in Tasmania. Sydney grabbed one of the Port Arthur

Visitor Guides and handed a Ghost Tours brochure to Willoughby.

"Ah, too bad—no Ghost Tours tonight, and I was SO looking forward to it!'" Willoughby didn't even try to hide his smile. Sydney sighed.

"Yeah, looks like it." She hadn't let go of his hand since the ferry. "So, we'll do the Asylum and the Separate Prison tour first. Just let me stash the guitar in one of the day lockers."

Willoughby leaned in, lowering his voice. "You're storing a million-dollar guitar in a public locker?"

"Yeah," Sydney said. "Who would suspect that?"

Willoughby shook his head, thinking this was not a good idea, but not wanting to fight with Sydney. It was her property after all. He turned his thought toward the tours.

"Separate Prison?'

"Yeah," Sydney said. "They call it that because they tried a new form of punishment there where they kept inmates alone all day in tiny single cells. They were only allowed out for an hour a day to exercise. Creepy, huh?"

"Creepy doesn't even begin to describe this place," Willoughby said. Sydney had found the day lockers, fed some coins into the slot and slid the guitar in. She made sure to spin the combination lock and try the latch. The locker was secure. Willoughby stared out the open doorway toward the ruins. "You sure you want to be here *alone* at night?"

"Quit being such a wimp," she mumbled as she navigated him up to the ticket window and bought a ticket for every tour offered. The ticket girl seemed delighted.

"You blokes will have a righteous time," she smiled.

Willoughby winked at her. He had no idea what a *bloke* or a *righteous time* was, but this was his way of getting back at all those girls who winked at him. As they moved off, he leaned over and whispered to Sydney conspiratorially.

"It seems we have become '*blokes*,' whatever that is, and we are to have a '*righteous time*,' though I do not believe that is a religious reference."

"'*Blokes*' just means like, '*guys*,' as in '*You guys are going to have loads of fun.*' The *righteous time* bit, though— that was weird, like something out of the sixties."

"Well, maybe *she's* from the sixties. Maybe she's just a ghost," Willoughby whispered back, making a "*Bu-wah-ha-ha!*" sound.

Sydney rolled her eyes.

By 4:00 PM, they had gone on two walking tours and a twenty-minute tour of the harbor by boat. Willoughby had heard interesting tales about an inmate named William Riley, about the prison officers caste system, more than he ever wanted to know about Smith O'Brien, an Irish Protestant Parliamentarian, and he had learned that the Point Puer Boy's Prison had been the first juvenile reformatory in the British Empire. Most of the boys had ranged from fourteen to seventeen, but they were as young as nine. He tried to envision what a nine-year-old could do to be sent to a place like this and simply could not.

They both sank into the wicker chairs at the Visitor Center's Café with gusto. While they had grabbed a quick coffee and snack in the Asylum Museum Coffee Shop, the amount of walking had helped them build up a healthy appetite. Willoughby took no time in ordering a burger, and Sydney ordered the chopped salad. The food was served after a relatively short wait, and none too soon. Willoughby took an enormous first bite.

"Mmm..." He chewed, smacking his lips. "This food is so good, it's almost criminal."

Sydney cracked a smile. "Believe me, you wouldn't look good in stripes."

"Hey, it would be better than the poor souls who had to strip to the waist and wade into freezing water up to their necks to repair the good Empire's ships."

"Well, just remember," Sydney warned," that those poor souls may have murdered your great-great-great grandmother."

"Ah, but from the photos I've seen of my great-great-great grandmother..." He winked at her. He was getting good at this winking thing.

She opened her mouth to respond, but before she could, a wiry, ragged man sat down at their table, smiling brightly with a partially toothless grin.

"Aye, mates—don't let me stop the flow of conversation. You were saying lass?"

Sydney looked over at the man, then to Willoughby.

Willoughby shrugged. "Uh, could we help you, sir?"

The man grinned again, then barked a short laugh. "Yeah, that'd be a sight all right—the bloody blind leadin' the blind. It's more likely that I can help you. Yeah... I reckon."

Willoughby and Sydney waited, but the man just sat there, grinning at them.

"Well?" Willoughby finally said.

The man bent forward, leaning as far as possible over the table. "You won't never find what you're looking for on the tours you're taking. You need a special tour."

"A special tour?" Sydney asked. "What do you mean?"

"Well, lass, the tours you're on are informational for sure, but you need a different kind of tour because you're looking for a different kind of, shall we say, *fun?* You see, your ordinary ectoplasmic demon doesn't have the, let's see, how shall I put it—doesn't have the musical quality you're really in search of."

"Ectoplasmic demon? You have no idea what we're in search of," Willoughby countered.

"Oh, but I do, you see." The man grinned. "It's all part of my business."

"Really? And what is your business?" Sydney asked.

The man turned to her. "All right—a fair question. I guess you could say I'm in the import and export business. I mostly trade in information from, shall we say, rather exotic sources. Usually, it's more export, but today, I'd say it's a little of both."

"What do you mean?"

"Well, I believe you two might know one of my associates. He's a man who's a legend in the information trade if you know the right circles. He's a queer sort. He goes by the name How—"

"Loa," Willoughby completed. Sydney threw him a quizzical look.

"That's right," the grinning man, still hunched over their table, said. "As he, himself, might say; '*How—* "

"*Low can you go…*'" Willoughby completed, his voice trailing off.

28

Cold Welcome

T.K. was not sure how long she had been sleeping. She only knew she was warm and rejuvenated and felt ready now to face what lay beyond the ice and cold of this closed chamber. The light stick was still burning at her side. She lifted it, stood, and stretched. Nothing had changed in the frozen locker room, or the outer chamber with the platform. She recalled the noise she had heard as she was drifting off. She paused, listening, but could hear nothing. The air was unnaturally still and the frozen world within her sight was silent as a tomb. She moved quietly toward the open door on the opposite side of the platform. At the frozen gap that had once been a doorway, she paused, and looked down to see one of the pole weapons she had tried to use earlier to pry open the last protected locker. It still had its curved blade intact. On instinct, she leaned down and picked it up.

As she cleared the doorway, stepping out from the cold chamber, the glow from her light stick was swallowed in the vastness of the dark, cold landscape that awaited her. Her eyes adjusted slowly to far flung shadows and an eerie, glittering cold that was draped across the silent structures around her. Slowly, she began to place some of the buildings. This had been a government sector of the city. Parts of a council building still stood, ghost-like in the distance, its columns visible, though encrusted with several inches of ice. Parts of the ceiling were smooth and dome-shaped. These sections of ceiling correlated with areas below where buildings were intact, though covered in ice. Other sections of the ceiling seemed torn by long rips. Here, heavy flows of ice had spilled through, in some places completely engulfing the structures below. The ice flows crushed anything below, forming a terrain of icy cliffs.

T.K. moved to the doorway of a palace atop an icy incline. Most of the structure was in ruins, shattered between tons of jagged ice, but one full wall, a few doors, and a small corner, which had been the cook's quarters, had survived.

"They must have tried to create a dome shield to protect the city," she mumbled aloud. She couldn't bear the total silence. "It may have worked for a time, but eventually, the ice got too heavy. They couldn't survive down here in the cold."

Of course, no one answered her. She stood in the doorway for a moment, and then made her way back down the incline and continued through the portions of the city that still stood. Memories sparked in her mind. For the first time in years, she saw the faces of people who had once lived in this city—who had smiled and waved at her—who had stood in lines along the street as she walked by with her father. She heard the ghost voices of children calling her name. Some parts of the city were so destroyed that it was difficult to find a route through, but she kept going.

As she neared what had once been the sea wall, the city all but disappeared beneath cliffs and mounds of ice. Over one of the largest of these, T.K. peered down into a deep crevice. The crevice cut off what had been the lower half of the city. It was easily thirty to thirty-five meters across, and possibly sixty to eighty meters deep.

She strained, looking down into the crevice. A crude path had been chipped into the steep cliff side, and far off to the left, T.K. was sure she could see a hint of light. She doused her own light, pushing the light stick into her parka pocket.

The dark was immediate and almost complete.

Almost.

But far away to the left, there seemed to be a pinprick hint, a barely discernible glow. It could have been her imagination, but it was enough to send her mind spinning once again.

What if some of her people had escaped? That would have been thousands of years ago, though. Surely, with global warming and shifting ice shelves, any escape they had found would be long gone.

Yet there it was—the hint of a dim glow. Her mind came back to what any survivors would have done had they escaped out onto the ice. Could they have made it to civilization? Could they have hidden themselves somewhere, or perhaps, as H.S. had done, could they have integrated themselves somehow into various cultures of the world? Could there be some hint of her people in the annals of history, or hidden away in some other forbidding corner of the world?

A sudden thought gripped her. Antonio had told her that Willoughby had an ability to see time hole equations in the very air around him. Some of her own people had exhibited that skill. *Could Willoughby somehow possess Atlantian blood?*

A sound interrupted her thoughts. It was much closer this time—possibly just over the ice ridge she had just climbed down. She froze, listening. No other sound came. "Probably just the ice," she mumbled to herself. But the sound had spooked her and focused her in on her most immediate tasks—she needed to find the prime hole. It would have been toward the north of the city. She had to find a way in, then use her necklace and pendant to somehow shut down or disable the facility. For the first time in many days, her hand went toward her throat where the pendant and the necklace both hung. She couldn't touch them through the suit coating her, but she could feel them. One hung just at the base of her neck, the other, low between her breasts. She knew Rashrahu wanted her to also destroy the pendant and necklace, but she wasn't sure she could do that. It was her only link to her past, to her people. "*It is our people, our world,*" her father had told her when he gave her the necklace. How could she let a thing like that become lost forever?

A sound came again, this time from the top of the ridge behind her. T.K. spun, sliding the light stick out of her parka pocket. It flared. In the light, she saw something moving across the top of the ridge. It was a being of some sort—a snow beast. As it started down from the ridge, ambling toward her, she realized with horror that it was a huge man, white because his features were covered with frost and ice. The pupils of his eyes had been bleached white. His mouth seemed frozen open, making his attempt at speech hard to discern. This was no man. This was some sort of talking corpse.

"T...K...We ...hind ...you..." The hiss was followed by a rasp that may have been an attempt at a laugh.

T.K. backed up. "What are you?" She screamed. "How do you know my name?"

The being did not slow or stop. It kept ambling forward. It did not answer.

T.K. noted that it did not blink its eyes, nor could she see any hint of breath.

"Stop!" she cried, holding up her weapon.

The figure was small and seemed somehow familiar despite the lifeless eyes and the ice crusted hair and features. With a chill, she noted something else. The moving figure had a uniform on. Even with the ice, she could tell it was similar to the porter uniforms worn by those on the *Aperio Absconditus*, the ship where she had served as Cabin Girl, the ship where her adopted father had been Captain, where he had been murdered, along with his crew. She recognized this figure now. It had been one of the mutineers.

"Y-you," she shouted, pointing the curved blade at the form. "You were onboard the *Absconditus*. Antonio told me that ship would be sunk."

The figure stopped now. "...esss," it hissed.

Another sound rang out from T.K.'s left. This sound shattered the silence of the frozen world.

"Yesss! You be not so stupid girl! We be sunk. We be dead. But no matter. You join us."

The words were followed with a booming laugh.

T.K. located the source of the sound—a huge, black-skinned figure whose face, hair, and tattered clothes were also covered with ice. The figure's eyes were bleached white as well and its hand held a long knife. The figure spread his thick, muscled arms.

"Princess...*you be home!*"

The air filled with hisses and grunts of laughter as four other stumbling figures appeared atop the icy ridge.

29

The Keeper

"Almost a week, and we have nothing," James Arthur mumbled, leaning back in his chair and glancing up at the rays of low sunlight hitting the walls of the abbey. The outdoor café at the La Vieille Auberge Hotel was practically empty, as were the streets in the quaint French city of Mont Saint Michel.

"Don't exaggerate," Hauti sighed, looking over a steaming cup of latte. She took a sip and then put the mug down. "This is only our fourth day here and we do have something. We know a lot of the history of Mont Saint Michel."

"Yeah," James Arthur agreed. "We learned that the abbey was built on a rock and it changed ownership numerous times, mostly between Brittany and Normandy, and that the abbey population has vacillated from a peak of almost 1200 people to a current population of, what was it? Oh, yeah, fifty!" He looked over at Hauti with a wry smile on his lips. "Why in the world, my dear, do you think that is? I mean, it's such a *happening* place."

"I think it's beautiful," Hauti said. "It's quaint, it's quiet, and it's romantic. It also gets three million visitors a year. We just happen to be here at a lull time."

"Yeah, the story of my like. I always seem to hit the lull times—and by the way, I would call this a *lull you to sleep* time." Dr. J looked over. "You really think it's romantic?"

"Absolutely," Hauti said, sipping more of her latte. "We've also mapped out the whole abbey."

"That we have," James Arthur said, raising a finger for emphasis. "We know every corner of that place, and we've found—drum roll please—*nothing!* Remind me, my good woman, what, precisely, was it that our friend, the ghost-in-machine-clothing, thought we would find here? Unless I'm mistaken, the HQ of a sinister brotherhood should *not* be quiet, nor particularly romantic."

"You are correct, good sir." Hauti humored him. "Our bastion of artificial intelligence claimed we would most likely be denied access to the catacombs by the Abbot, which has, thus far, been accurate. We are now waiting to be contacted by one calling himself '*the fifth friend.*' Should this person materialize, they are supposed to help us learn where the monastery's secret libraries are located, and how we are to get in."

"Yes, and remind me my good lady, how we're supposed to find this '*friend*'?" Dr. J glanced behind him with mock surprise. "Was it not here, yet, we seem to be quite alone. So, how do you propose we find this guy, or, excuse me, this woman? We seem to have failed at letting the '*friend*' find us, even in a crowded place like this. Why, look, there are precisely *two* other people in this whole restaurant—one is a monk, and the other, a waiter. Perhaps our Digital Director is not as good a friend with this guy as he thinks. What do you suppose we would find in this library anyway?"

"If I understood correctly," Hauti said, finishing her latte and pushing the cup and saucer to the center of the table, "I believe we were to locate the information recorded by the monks on the Dark Brotherhood."

"Did our Holographic Host not also indicate that the Brotherhood could have infiltrated this place? What if the Abbot himself is in league with them? What if the Brotherhood has somehow infiltrated the whole order and put their own people in place? With only a handful of other merchants in the town and tourists, it would be easy to use this island as a base. Then, keeping the place quiet would be part of their strategy. If this is the case, they may have destroyed any damning information in the library archives long ago. Any progress on getting those sonar pings? It may be interesting to track activity below us, in the catacombs of rock. We also requested outgoing communication logs."

"Well, the pings would be inconclusive, for one thing," Hauti said. "They would also alert anyone who may have something going on down there to the fact that we're snooping around. Also, you only requested the communication logs this morning. I relayed the request to Sian, but as interested in our endeavors as I'm sure he is, I doubt we are priority one to him. I suggest we give it a few days."

"And do what in the meantime?" James Arthur groaned, exasperated. "We've walked the full length of the island a half dozen times. We've explored every street."

A waiter dropped the check off in a black cardboard sleeve. Hauti reached down to grab her purse, then fished around for her stack of euros. "How about shopping," she said. "There were some fun-looking shops on the road up to the hotel."

James Arthur did not answer. He merely rolled his eyes, as if torture would be more fun.

Hauti gave a short laugh and opened the cardboard sleeve. She froze, then spun around. "The waiter—where did he go? Did you see where he went?"

Dr. J scanned the open café. "No. Why? Is there a problem?"

Hauti opened the black sleeve and showed it to him. On the back of the customer's copy of the receipt, something had been written in French by someone with superb penmanship.

"What does it say?" James Arthur mumbled, trying to discern the words. "I don't read French—I work hard enough just to speak it."

Hauti turned the card back around, her eyes never leaving his. "James, you *don't* speak it," she said. "You throw sing-song syllables on the air which the French, with their keen intellects, are usually able to divine. It's not the same thing."

James Arthur shrugged, unperturbed. "Okay, so we've established I'm not exactly ready for the *Champs-Elysees*, so tell me what it says."

Hauti lowered her voice to a whisper. "It says, *'You are right to suspect the Abbot. Libraries would be too dangerous and probably fruitless. Plan B—meet me tonight after final prayers in the Crypt of the Massive Pillars. The Keeper.'*"

"*Keeper?* That sounds a bit ominous. I thought we were supposed to meet someone called *the friend*," James Arthur whispered back. He scanned the small plaza again. It was empty. He looked back to Hauti. "At least it's something. It appears our top-secret mission isn't a bust after all. It would also appear that it's not so top-secret—

or, at least, that there are those who know we are here. I just hope they're the *friendly* type, no pun intended. How do you propose we get into the abbey for final prayers? They close it to the public at seven PM."

Hauti looked around as if thinking. Then her face broke into a quick smile. "Well, I guess we go shopping."

30

The Ice Dome

Antonio spent much of the first day at Volstok Station doing exactly what the guards thought he was there to do—investigating the sparse camp and the half-dozen structures that formed it. At the same time, he pumped the guards for information about the domed air pockets and what the scientists had learned.

The guards were genial enough, though they had a limited command of English. It wasn't until later that first night, as he pretended to share a bottle of vodka with the two, that he began to feel like he was finally getting somewhere. He only pretended to drink, discreetly depositing his liquid into a nearby coffee mug. He volunteered to do the dishes so that he could pour the almost full mug down the drain. The guards were overjoyed. Some of the dishes appeared to have been sitting in the sink for at least a week. He topped off the night by playing a few hands of Durak, a popular Russian card game he had researched on the plane over. He gave his brand-new pack of cards to the smaller of the two guards, a man called Jude, in exchange for a promise to drive him to the tunnel site in the morning.

As far as information, Antonio learned that both guards knew that the scientists had found a series of crevices and had created rope ladders and makeshift bridges to descend into them. They hoped that the crevices would lead to one of the open-air pockets, but as yet, they had only found various ice tunnels and caves with thick ice ceilings. Neither guard, though, knew about the nanoteslas or the massive air pockets H.S. had been so interested in.

When morning dawned (dawn being more of a concept than a reality this far north as the sun was up all day for much of the year), he went into the main quarter for a cup of the thick, brown liquid the guards liked to call *coffee*. Jude sat at the small table, a bit bleary-eyed and obviously hungover. He pushed a mug and the coffee pot in Antonio's direction. Antonio poured himself a half cup of the liquid. It tasted horrible, but at least it was hot and the smell masked the odor in the quarters. Odor had been a big problem when he first arrived at the station. The smell had almost knocked him over. It had been all he could do not to wrinkle his nose and retch. Since doing the dishes and emptying the garbage, though, the smell had become tolerable. Antonio asked where the larger of the two guards, a man called Kensky, was. Jude explained that he had gone out to the "shed" to work on his snowmobile. Jude sipped at his coffee.

"You hold your liquor well."

Antonio remembered that he was supposed to be hungover and grimaced. "Only on the outside," he said. He took the mug and the pot of steaming liquid.

"Did you remember, my friend, that you promised to drop me off at the ice tunnels this morning?"

"What?" Jude said sarcastically. "No American breakfast—no greasy eggs?"

Antonio feigned feeling sick, which made Jude chuckle.

"We get you to the tunnels. Just relax."

Antonio gave him a forced grin and sat back in his chair, sipping at his coffee. Truth was, he could only bear to be in these tight, smelly quarters with the guards for short periods of time. While he could tolerate it better today, he did not feel he would ever grow accustomed to the station's world of no showers, little social interaction, and few baths. The two guards had joked that they only bathed at three-month intervals. While the new group of scientists coming meant a bath was soon needed, neither of the guards seemed anxious to jump at the chance. Who could blame them? The temperature was such that warming water fast enough to fill a bath was probably impossible.

Antonio finished his coffee and ate a few stale hunks of rye bread while waiting for Jude to finally stand and groggily stumble toward the door. Antonio pushed to his feet, careful not to appear too anxious. He threw on his parka, face mask, gloves, and boots, and then slung his backpack onto his shoulder. Jude thought the pack held only food, water, and some standard ice climbing tools. His companion, Kensky, had routinely checked it the day Antonio arrived. Hidden below a false bottom in the pack, however, was a secret compartment that housed other tools—a machete, a powerful SAT phone, specialized Observations, Inc. weather gear that could protect two individuals in sub-freezing weather for some time, and other trinkets.

Jude stepped outside and Antonio followed. They went to one of the larger sheltered pods where a huge door had been thrown open. There were four snowmobiles and a larger snow cat. Jude stopped in front of the snow cat. He called over to the larger guard and spoke to him in Russian. Kensky grunted back, stood, and fished a key ring from his pocket. He tossed it over to Jude, who turned to Antonio smiling and jangled the keys. He jumped up onto the cat, opened the driver's side door, and climbed in. The cat sputtered to life after only two tries, and rumbled out of the makeshift shed, stopping a few feet away for Antonio to climb in.

Once they were buckled in, Jude hit the gas. The cat moved with surprising speed over the snow-covered terrain. The engine was so loud that neither spoke much for the next eight to ten minutes. They pulled up to a row of low ice spikes, jutting up from the ground at the foot of a range of larger ice-covered hills and mountains. Jude spun the snow cat around to a full stop, leaving the engine rumbling.

Yelling over the sound, he spoke in slightly slurred English. "Here are you, Professor. I advise maybe you don't go too deep in crevice. I advise you stay safer at top. I be back for to pick you up in, how you say, in late of day. I give two blasts on horn. We don't want for to come to look for you. Kensky can get very angry."

Antonio nodded, also yelling over the engine. "Yes, we would not want Kensky to get angry! Thank you, my friend."

Once Antonio jumped down from the cab, the snow cat plodded away.

Turning back to the narrow slit in the ice with a sigh and a bit of a shiver, Antonio shouldered his gear. "I must get moving or I shall freeze to death," he mumbled to himself. Then, mimicking Jude's thick accent, he added, "for we would not want for to have Kensky get angry." His soft chuckle echoed off the ice walls, becoming lost in the bitter arctic wind.

Within minutes, he was below the surface, following a jutting path down into the ice. The path meandered about six to ten meters below the surface for a while. Light broke through at various points, usually in small cracks that led up to the hostile surface terrain. In some places, however, soft light filtered through a mottled ceiling of several tons of transparent ice.

As he followed a few rope ladders down to ever-deeper pockets of crevice, the light became increasingly rare, forcing him to pull out his heavy-duty flashlight. He crossed a few makeshift bridges and skirted several bits of the crevice floor that had been roped off with yellow caution tape. Drawing close to the tape, he could see that the floor had fallen away into even deeper crevices. He shined his industrial strength beam into several of these but could only make out more jutting ice, in some cases, far, far, below.

The ice popped and cracked, unnerving him. He thought about pulling out his iPod and drowning out the noise with music, but he needed to be alert to all sounds so that he didn't miss something that might be more than just shifting or popping ice. He continued, treading softly, his ears tuned for any sound that could be more than shifts in the ice.

When his watch read just over two hours in the ice tunnels, he glanced around, taking stock of his position. He decided he would turn back as soon as he rounded the next bend. Barely a foot away from the bend, however, he heard a loud crack and the floor dropped from under him.

Grabbing at a small ax at his belt, he flung it wildly, slamming it against the cave wall, hoping to find purchase.

The ax scraped a line in the ice, but he had spun into an awkward angle and had hit the floor below before he could do more than slow his fall a little. Luckily, the wall tapered in a bit, and that somewhat broke his fall. The drop was only about ten or so meters. He landed in a heap on the crushed ice and crusted snow.

Groaning, he slowly pushed up. He was bruised but did not seem seriously injured. The area directly around him was dark. He sat, breathing heavily for a moment, then took stock of himself to assure that he had not damaged anything.

He reached for his spare flashlight, his main light having been lost somewhere under the fallen ice. Clicking it on, he swept it across the new space. It took him only a few seconds to realize how lucky he was. He had not fallen into another ice tunnel, but onto a sheer ice ledge. He crept on all fours the half-dozen meters to the edge and peered over.

The ledge sunk into a crevice at least a hundred meters deep. He could make out in the flashlight beam that the ledge he had fallen onto sloped down and eventually reached the crevice floor. He cautiously rose and began making his way down, hugging the crevice wall. There was something odd about this new crevice. For one thing, it was within the general area where Sian had suggested he search. For another thing, the bottom of the crevice was narrow, but incredibly smooth, as if hundreds of feet had packed the trail down. He moved cautiously, his ax at the ready, as the ice continued to pop and crack. In a few places, the ledge had collapsed and he had to improvise a way around.

Once he reached the bottom of the trench, he noted a dim glow ahead and to his left. The worn path seemed to go in the same direction. After a few hundred meters, the path veered into a narrower crevice. A small, round hole of light penetrated the ceiling, reflecting off a long, twisted stalactite. About thirty meters further down the crevice, another hole of light reflected off another twisted stalactite, and thirty meters beyond that, another. In fact, the entire length of the crevice was lit by uniform round holes that allowed light into twisted stalactite formations. The consistent spacing of the lights and the uniform positioning of the holes left no doubt. This was definitely *not* a natural phenomenon.

The crevice continued for maybe two hundred meters. At the end, it opened into a cavern of sorts where a cave-in had opened a much larger hole in the jagged roof above. The hole was not completely open to the arctic sky, but a soft glow penetrated it, giving a degree of dim illumination. Antonio carefully scanned the space. The cavern was about sixty meters wide and about twenty meters deep. A curved ice dome walled off the entire back side. Approaching the dome carefully, he knelt and felt the sheet of ice. Though thick, it was also smooth and geometrically uniform—once again, too much so to be a natural phenomenon.

He took out his small ax and began chipping at the barrier. When he had penetrated to about three inches deep, the ax hit something hard. He carefully cleared away ice, creating a spot about ten inches in diameter.

Some sort of wire-mesh webbing seemed to form the outer shell of the ice dome. He couldn't tell how thick the ice was on the other side of the mesh as his hatchet seemed unable to penetrate the white-gold surface.

Antonio followed the smooth curve to where it intersected with the side of the cavern. A small gap existed between the dome and the edge of the cavern. Antonio decided to explore it to see if there might be a breach or a break in the dome wall. He took the backpack off his shoulders, and with pack in one hand, and flashlight in the other, he eased himself into the gap. He slid farther and farther around the dome, the light dimming and then disappearing as he went. Once or twice, he thought he heard something, but upon listening closer, he determined it to be only shifting ice.

He pushed into the gap for perhaps twenty minutes before it became too narrow to continue. He stopped, panting, and triggered the glow-dial on his watch. He had spent close to an hour now exploring the crevices and the ice dome. He needed to get back or his Russian friends would come looking. He pulled out a water bottle to get a drink and wolfed down an energy bar and handful of granola. Just as he was lifting his backpack and was turning to begin sliding back out of the stifling gap, he froze. He had heard something again, but this time, it was not shifting ice. It sounded more like a clash of swords. Then, muffled and very far away, he was sure he heard someone scream.

31

Frankie

"Do you ever think of death?" Sydney asked, staring out at a cloudless sky with more stars than she had ever imagined.

Willoughby was busy seeing if he could locate any of the constellations he knew here in the Southern Hemisphere. "What?"

They were sitting on a bench near the waterfront in an out of the way corner of the prison. The stranger, who had approached them claiming to be a friend of *How Loa*, had instructed them to wait for him on this bench after the last tour was completed. He had assured them that the guards never checked this corner of the prison, though he didn't say why.

Sydney turned to him. "Do you ever think of death?"

Willoughby found the question a bit uncomfortable. "Well, uh, I spend most of my time trying not to—especially when we're sitting in a semi-dark, creepy corner of a haunted prison."

Sydney smiled. "Right. Well, I do. I think about it all the time. Let me see that locked box the Chinese guy gave you again."

"His name is How Loa," Willoughby offered as he pulled the small, ornate box out of his pocket. They had

330

been here for a little over half an hour. Willoughby had brought her up to speed on his first meeting with How Loa, and his strange dealings with the Oriental man since.

"So why did you bring this tonight?" Sydney asked.

Willoughby shrugged. "How told me I should keep it with me."

In truth, he wasn't entirely sure why he had brought it. He knew it was supposed to be important to him somewhere, somehow, but that was all. Except, he had begun to suspect that it had something to do with Sydney recently, though she seemed as baffled about it as he was. She studied it for a moment, then looked back out over the dark waters.

"Something about being near the ocean at night brings a feeling of overwhelming loneliness. It makes me think of death."

"Really? Why?"

Sydney looked over with a grin. "I honestly don't know. My mom used to say that water would always have a pull on me because I was born under the sign of water. I remember when I was little, I used to have this dream sometimes. I would wake up in a city that was on this vast shore. The city was completely empty. There were no sounds, no movement, just stillness and silence. I went running from house to house, from street to street, but there were no people, no moving things. Panicked, I turned toward the only sound I could make out—the hiss and crash of the sea. I felt myself being drawn toward that shore, where wave after wave thundered against the rocks. For some reason, the sound drew me but also terrified me." She went silent for a long moment, and then continued. "I woke up screaming. My mom was the one who came to comfort me. She would sit at the edge of my bed, and hold me, saying, 'There, there… Just a nasty old dream. Haumea sent her to you."

"Haumea?" Willoughby was partly asking the question because he was curious, and partly to mask a stab of fear that had suddenly struck at him. He had once had a similar dream about Sydney on the beach, being drawn toward the water. Only, in his dream, Beelzebub had been there. He looked up to find Sydney was staring at him.

"*Hello!*" Sydney said, her eyes wide.

Willoughby realized he had zoned out for a moment. "Oh, uh, sorry."

Sydney hesitated for a moment, then continued. "I was telling you about Haumea, the mother of Pele, and mother of Ha'aika, patron Goddess of dancing, specifically Hula. Haumea was sometimes considered a trickster." She paused, making sure he was still listening, and then turned back toward the water and resumed her story.

"Anyway, she would say Haumea sent that dream to me because she wanted a song from us. 'Come,' she would say; 'we must sing that dream away, you and I.' Then we would sing, a simple, Polynesian tune. It was one I came to know by heart."

Sydney began to sing, soft and low, a beautiful, simple melody.

Wai Ola, water of life,
From the sea, rising high,
Clouds of joy, in the sky, water of life…"

Willoughby said nothing. He just watched her.

As the song finished, she was silent. The notes of the song seemed to hang in the still, dark air. She looked over, her face slightly flushed.

"That song came from a favorite video my mother would play for me when I was a toddler—I still remember it, '*Leon and Malia Sing the Songs of Hawaii.*' I loved that video."

Sydney looked away, studying dark ripples on the water of the small harbor. Her voice had turned somber now. "At that time, I also loved my mom." She looked back across the bench, her eyes lightly glistening. "How does it happen, Willoughby? How do we let ourselves lose the things we love?" She handed him back the small, gold box. He slipped it back into his pocket. It was his turn to look away. He pondered the question, thinking of his own father and the final moments they had shared.

"Sometimes," he finally offered, "we may think we don't have a choice. We may come to believe that the world is a big place that knows more about losing than about finding." He turned to her. "But that's a lie. We can't let it take hold of us. The truth is that we hold what we really love forever. We can never lose what touches us inside, what warms us from the inside out. That kind of touch only comes when someone is already a part of us."

Sydney watched him, studying him, peering deep into his eyes.

Willoughby wasn't sure what was happening. He only knew that Sydney's eyes, at that moment, seemed brighter than all the stars put together.

She leaned forward, and to his surprise, he felt himself leaning to meet her. They kissed, long and hard, lips brushing, then reaching, then finding, curling in upon each other. There was a vulnerability in this kiss, an opening that invited soul to entwine with soul until identity was confused and the two could never again feel that they were truly alone.

Willoughby wasn't sure how long the kiss lasted. It could have been a moment. It could have been a lifetime.

As Sydney pulled away, she smiled. "You're getting better at this."

He smiled back. "Well," he looked down, suddenly a little embarrassed, trying to think of something else to say. She put her hand in his. "Well," he repeated, liking the sound of the word, "I had to."

Sydney had already turned and was looking out over the waterfront again. "My mother... It's been ages since I thought of my mother."

"Yeah," Willoughby agreed. "You hardly ever speak about her. Do you visit her?"

"No. Worse yet, she never visits me. I haven't seen her in almost three years. She stays away from my concerts. She never writes—not even a Christmas card. I tried to call once. She hung up. When I worked up the courage to try again the next day, the number had become suddenly 'unpublished.' I am dead to her."

"Why? What happened?"

Sydney stared at him. "Happened?" She spoke as if coming out of a trance. "I don't really know. She was there, she was my Mom, then, she was gone, and she was not. There was no big fight. I must have done something to hurt her and she stopped loving me. That's all there is. She just stopped loving me."

Willoughby stared, trying to comprehend the words. *Mothers don't just stop loving you*, he thought, but what could he say to her? He was certainly no expert on motherhood. Did Sydney's mom somehow find out why Aiyito had distanced himself? Did she hold that against Sydney for some reason? Did she, like Aiyito, have some misguided idea that she would endanger Sydney, or would hold her back if she showed love? He tried to imagine what could have happened to cause the rift that had obviously developed between mother and daughter. Before he could settle on a good response, though, his thoughts were cut short. The well-accented voice of their self-appointed guide rang out in a low growl.

"Alright… You ready to meet the beastie?"

"*Beastie?*"

The man chuckled. "Oh yes, he's a real trip, he is. Some call him *the Banshee*. Don't be surprised when he makes a lot of racket. He doesn't get many guests these days."

Willoughby looked over. The tall, grizzled man stood with a slight stoop. His hair was greased and stringy. His nose was hawkish and pointed, his eyes were narrow and piggish, but it was his hands that drew the most attention. They were disproportionately huge, a fact made even more creepy by the bony man's name—*Frankie.*

32

There be Dragons

James Arthur scratched at the rough garment that hung loosely from his shoulders for about the tenth time in as many minutes.

"So, how many monks did that guy say wore this thing before me?"

Hauti simply ignored him. They were moving slowly through a large room with cold stone floors and dozens of thick, stone pillars in neat, geometric lines. Each pillar was about three feet in circumference and rose to a decorative sconce about twelve feet up. From there, the pillars fanned out like the cone of an antique gramophone, to meld into the sand-colored ceiling. She and James Arthur both had bowed heads. They moved in synchronized strides, with the hoods of their newly purchased monk's robes pulled up and obscuring their faces. Hauti was deep in concentration, aptly playing the role of the humble monk. James Arthur was visibly jittery, scratching and pulling at the rough cloth of the robe.

"Would you *settle down?*" Hauti hissed discreetly after checking to make sure they were alone. "You're like a feral dog with a flea infestation."

"Apt analogy," Dr. J whispered back. "I wouldn't be surprised to learn that a dog with a flea infestation *was* the previous owner of this robe! How much did we pay for these things?"

"They're authentic," Hauti countered.

"Uh-huh, so is a corpse's corset, but that doesn't mean I want to put it on!"

"Keep your voice down!" Hauti whispered intently. "We are supposed to be in meditative prayer!"

"Tell the fleas that!" James Arthur whispered back. "What are we even doing here?"

"Waiting to meet the keeper."

"The keeper of what? If he wears a robe like this, it could be *fleas.*"

They walked in silence to the far end of the hall where the smooth, patchwork stones of the abbey curved in, framing a massive, narrow window. The window was divided into four sections, two of which were smaller and in the shape of thin, parallel rectangles. The upper sections were taller rectangles, fully rounded at the tops where the stonework inlay of the window curved to a pointed peak. Moonlight streamed in through the glass, casting eerie shadows on the stone floor. The moon's glow seemed brighter than the dim lighting which highlighted each decorative sconce along the row of pillars. The light was still cold, though. James Arthur gave an almost imperceptible shiver.

"How long is this guy going to make us wait? It's almost ten o'clock. Someone will be in to shoo us to bed soon."

At that very moment, the abbey bells began to chime ten. Hauti and James Arthur had turned, making their way slowly back toward the far end of the hall when Hauti suddenly stopped.

"Did you hear that?" she whispered.

"What?" Dr. J searched the total silence.

"The chimes stopped at nine. There should have been ten. Listen—sounds from the hotel, the wind, the far-off sounds of the sea—there's nothing."

James Arthur inclined his ear. Hauti was right. Everything had gone deathly still and quiet. He felt an involuntary shiver work again up his spine. Then, there was a sound, a sort of clicking sound, like mice scurrying over stone. He looked to Hauti.

"Mice?"

Before she could answer, there was a swift blur circling the nearest pillar to their right, spiraling up toward the light of the decorative sconce. A second skittering sounded from the pillar just opposite it to the left. The blurs were long and mostly thin—maybe twelve to thirteen inches at the thickest, and less than two inches thick at the tip. As the blurs slowed, James Arthur could make out a long, alligator-like head with stubby, clawed arms and maybe fourteen inches back, a set of clawed feet. From snout to tip of tail, each beast was roughly one to one-and-a-half meters in length and covered in black scales. Only when they stopped was Hauti able to get a good look at them. The one on the right coughed, sending a brief shower of spark down the length of the stone pillar. It's yellow, slit eyes peered down at her as it cocked a narrow snout. It seemed perplexed.

"That's a really big, really odd mouse," Hauti whispered, being careful not to move.

"They won't harm you," a deep, gentle voice said, echoing from the shadows. "Meet my good friends and companions, Mac and Beth."

An imposing figure in a dark brown robe stepped around a pillar and into the dim light. He was medium height, with broad shoulders and a peaked hood pulled high over his head. Only parts of his face were visible—a hawkish nose, strong cheek bones, a tuft of sandy colored hair. Heavy leather patches covered the shoulders of the robe almost like armor, and he wore thick leather gloves, the kind a handler of birds-of-prey might use. He made no effort to remove his hood or step closer.

James Arthur and Hauti stood motionless for a moment, taking in the sight. "So," Dr. J said, finally recovering his voice, "that's, uh, that's clever. Mac and Beth—like the play. I take it you're a fan of Shakespeare. I also take it that you expect us to believe this isn't a trick and there really are such things as dragons."

"There once was," the man said wistfully. He walked to the right column and raised a gloved hand, touching it to the side of the column. The strange beast wrapped tightly around the stone began to move again. It skittered in a spiral motion, leveling, and then angling its body down, crisscrossing its own tracks to move back down the column to the gloved hand. It moved quickly across the hand onto one of the thick leather patches across the left shoulder of the man's dark robe. Its tail continued to wrap around the man's arm until it was almost completely covered. It had a snout almost the shape of a weasel's, but stunted at the end, and Dr. J could now see wings folded across its back. Judging from how far back the wings extended, they were quite large. He guessed the beasts had a full wingspan of perhaps three to possibly four meters. A hint of smoke seeped from large nostril holes onto the stranger's shoulder. He didn't seem to notice. Hauti finally found her voice, though she still spoke in almost a whisper.

"That doesn't hurt?"

"Not at all," the man said, easily responding to her words. "Looks are sometimes deceiving. These creatures are closer to the bird family than the lizard. They are surprisingly light and very bright. These two are well trained."

The stranger glanced over, watching the beast settle into a relaxed rumble that almost seemed to be a purr. The Dragon—Hauti and James Arthur weren't sure if this was Mac or Beth—raised its scaly head and snorted, leaving a slow, lazy wreath of smoke drifting around the stranger's cloaked head. Behind the back legs, the long, thin tail wrapped tighter around the hooded stranger's arm, across his shoulders, and down onto his chest.

"So, is this one Mac or Beth?" Hauti seemed to have gotten over her shock. She took a tentative step forward. The little dragon had been watching her with shiny, intelligent eyes. They were almost entirely black with only a hint of fire yellow around the edges and in a slit across the middle. When she began to take another step, the beast moved on the arm, suddenly excited. It blew a warning puff of flame.

"Do not suppose they are pets," the man said, not making any sudden moves.

Hauti stopped and let her arms drop, though she never broke eye contact.

"Fortunately for you, this is Beth. Mac may well have taken to the air by now."

Mac, on the adjacent column, was keeping vigil on James Arthur, watching his every move.

The man gave a low, raspy chuckle. "Draco Volans," he continued softly. "Once there were thousands of them, living in a range of habitats that stretched from central Africa all the way to the British coast. Now, there are but these two in their weight and category, though I believe we may have more soon."

"Beth is pregnant?" Hauti's eyes widened.

"She has laid five eggs. This has happened before and none hatched. This time, however, I have seen them tip and heard faint scratching from inside them."

James Arthur tried to discern the face shadowed beneath the cloak's hood. He could make out little beyond the chin, mouth, prominent nose and eyes, and tuft of blonde hair.

"I'm supposed to believe you raise dragons in your backyard?"

The man smiled shyly. "You have never seen my backyard. The species which history has called the dragon originated roughly 130,000 years ago. It flourished, with dozens of variations, until fairly recently. It is an intelligent animal—a descendant of the Raptor, though more clever and better able to adapt. It proved the bane of human existence and development for thousands of years. Perhaps that is why humanity has never been able to let the memory of their great foe die.

"As a species, however, dragons began dying off about 8000 BC. Their demise was fueled primarily by changes in the climate. The swamplands and rich sulfur deposits of earlier ages began to disappear. Predators, including man, adapted, and evolved, and became more effective at guarding their lands and food stores. By 5000 BC, the dragon population shrunk to only a few hundred. The beasts have exorbitantly long lifespans, so a few actually survived into the Middle-Ages, hiding in rocks and clefts in sparsely populated northern islands, like the Hebrides off the coast of Scotland. I rescued these two from a den not far from Petra, James Arthur. I believe that's an area you know rather well." The man looked at Dr. J, his expression inscrutable. James Arthur remembered his none-too-pleasant visit to Petra where he was forced to square off against a desert witch. *How did this man know about that?* He was obviously some sort of time traveler, but was he really on their side?

After a moment, the man continued. "My dragons, however, are not the reason I am here. Nor are they the reason you sought me out on this cold night."

"Well," James Arthur said, "why are you here?"

The man studied Dr. J. "I need your help. And you need mine," he said quietly. "Follow me. We are in a junction, but it is already collapsing. We will be exposed here."

The man walked to the opposite column and repeated the exercise of touching it with his gloved hand. Mac, the other dragon, curled around it, a little rougher than the first. Dr. J saw for the first time that the man's robe was made of something more than fine cloth. It did not wrinkle or give under the steely black claws of the dragons. He looked over at Hauti who gave him a silent shrug.

Once the second dragon was in place, the hooded man led them silently to the hallway. Behind an aging statue of the Blessed Mary, they followed him down a set of stone steps to a wooden door, opened a crack. He stuck his foot into the crack and carefully opened the door wide. He ushered them in.

They stepped into a narrow stone passage where more stone steps led down. The hooded man gave one arm a

342

swing and the dragon on that arm hopped up onto the man's broad shoulder. This freed the man to quietly close the door, leaving them in pitch dark. Suddenly, a light flared. The hooded man held up a long stick, tipped with a bluish flame. He ushered them on.

"A—light instrument. Not a wand," he explained with the hint of a smile. "The dragons are not disturbed by its bluish light. These steps lead into the dungeons. Most of the dungeon cells are charted, and many are accessed on tours, but the current occupants of the abbey do not know *all* of their secrets. Some dungeon rooms were hidden. Politically dangerous prisoners were sometimes held for years. Many of these prisoners died here, never even knowing where they were. I will lead you to one such cell. We can talk more freely there."

He had been leading them down the stone steps as he spoke. They went down at least ten or twelve flights of stairs, then along a short corridor, and into a small room with only a tiny window carved high into the rock. A single rough table, a chair, a crusted bucket, and the molding remains of a wooden cot completed the furnishings of the room. The man walked to a crack running down the rock opposite the moldy bed frame. He worked his hand into the crack up to his wrists, and then he gave a swift pull. A segment of the stone wall swung back revealing a dark hole. The man motioned them to follow. More stone steps led down, these much deeper, winding, and narrow.

Once both Hauti and James Arthur were in the cramped spiral stairs, he instructed Dr. J to close the hidden stone door by pulling a small chain on the inside of the door. Once the stone was closed to their guide's satisfaction, he turned and started down the stairway. The spiral steps led down two full turns, then opened out onto a much larger room with smoother walls, polished floor, and less meager décor. Remnants of religious paintings still clung to the walls. There was a heavy wood table with two wooden chairs and a full bed with spider webs cocooning the posts. A dresser, a wash bowl and bucket, and a caved-in trunk rounded out the furnishings. The dragons seemed at home here, and slithered off the man's arms to glide to the floor and then disappear under the bed. The man motioned for them to sit on the chairs, which were free of cobwebs. He walked over to lean against one of the heavy bed posts.

"As I indicated in my note to you, this abbey has come under the influence of the brotherhood who call themselves the *Dark Edge*. Their money has been funding its restoration for years. Many of the monks here are genuine and not aware of this influence. Some, however, are strategic plants. The abbey is vast and has many unused corridors, making it a perfect place to conduct business for the Edge. We believe it is an unofficial European headquarters for them."

"Who is *we*?" Hauti asked.

The man did not hesitate. "We are the edge on the side of light. We are charged with keeping faith with the world, of protecting hope."

"Protecting hope?" James Arthur said after seating himself. "That's a tall order."

"Yes, it is indeed."

"How, exactly, do you do it?"

"First," the man said, "we try to make sure that there is a world to keep faith with."

"Meaning?" Hauti said, also taking a seat.

"Meaning the Dark Edge are about power. They would bleed the world for the power it can provide. They would tip the balance, causing time to collapse on itself, sucking all that was your earth into a nothingness so great that the weight at its core defies measurement."

"Why?"

The man cocked his head. "I do not understand your question."

James Arthur leaned forward. "Why would they want to destroy themselves? They destroy the earth, they destroy us, and they destroy themselves. This whole war thing with the *Dark Edge* makes no sense to me."

The man sighed, looking down at his gloved hand. "That is because you are not familiar with who you are dealing with. Do the rank and file understand the ultimate objectives? Rarely. They understand an increase in power and privilege available to their rank. They do not look at what is to come. They only care about pleasure in their present and power enough to pursue it. The one who leads this group is a master manipulator. He is not one of you."

Hauti's voice was quick and direct. "Are you one of us?"

The man looked at her a long moment. "Yes, and no. If we had the time, I believe you would come to see me as a kindred spirit. Was I born on your world? No."

"What do you know about this Beelzebub, or whatever he calls himself—the one who leads this brotherhood, or *Dark Edge*, or whatever they call themselves?" James Arthur had narrowed his eyes, folding his arms across his chest. The hooded man seemed to consider the question.

"He is known to us. He is not one of us, and he is only one of many who lead the Dark Brotherhood."

"So, let me guess; you and these—these time traveler demons," James Arthur continued, "have some sort of ancient grudge, right? Now, you bring it to our world, catching us in the crossfire. What if we don't care about your struggle? What if we don't want to align with either of you? What if we just want you to leave our world and let us alone?"

The *keeper* seemed to narrow his eyes. His head tilted quizzically. "Do you watch many, what do they call them, sci-fi movies? That sounds like a movie."

"Well, yes," Dr. J confessed. Hauti jumped in.

"Actually, there are several movies with that basic plot."

The man's face broke into a sad smile. For the first time, the man's eyebrows were visible. They were blond, offsetting the deepest blue eyes that James Arthur had ever seen, eyes that seemed to glow.

"Unfortunately, this is no movie. This is very real. *Life* is my struggle—and yours. This is a *we*, not an *us* or a *you* scenario. *We* fight or *we* die. There is a cold logic in the cosmos. Yours is one of the rare worlds where life can find purchase. Do you realize what a gift that is? I think not. The loss of your world, of the life on your world, hurts not only you, but every inhabited world in the universe. All life is connected. All life fights together for the right to exist. Only by consummate struggle is the shining crown passed from generation to generation."

James Arthur glanced to Hauti and then gave a twist of his head. "Wow. I didn't expect a 'Save the Whales' speech."

"No. Yet, that may be the speech you need to hear. The option for you is not whether you align or don't align with sides of a war. Your choice is how you choose to fight a war you have always been a part of. Your enemies, on the slide toward chaos, are what you call parasites—the ultimate consumers, feeding on power. They see power as a means of control, and control as a conduit to unchecked pleasure and self-satisfaction. They feed off the *process* of life, but are unwilling to contribute to its sustainability. They upset balance. They believe they are in control, even as time tips into a spiraling collapse, feeding on itself as it leaves devastation behind.

"Only the constant fight to reach—to rise, to touch radiance—can counter the deadly lure of oblivion. Life's architects, its producers, its spinners of dreams, its tellers of tales, bind order with hope. We encounter times when we are called upon to wield fist and sword, but at the end of the day, hope is our strongest weapon, James Arthur. We must win our small battles, leaving trails of hope wherever we go. I am here as your friend, as a fellow warrior. I am here to give hope. I am not your recruiter. I do not seek alliance to address some other-worldly feud. The *Friend* sent me because you seemed in need of hope."

James Arthur seemed unaffected by the man's impassioned speech. "Why don't you tell me exactly what you want from us, then we'll discuss this whole *fellow warrior* thing."

The man finally pulled his hood back.

Hauti gasped.

James Arthur pushed back in his chair.

The man's face started vacillating, changing rapidly in a succession of different skulls. The chin, mouth, and nose were mostly stable, thought the eyes flickered in and out. At first glance, the man appeared young, with sandy brown hair and golden skin, but the eyes on this young face were black voids. Then the head changed, shimmering to

347

become bald and pale, the skull visible through a paper-thin sheen of skin. As the skull changed, the face lightened and the eyes became suddenly vibrant and visible—the bluest of blues, like James Arthur had seen earlier.

"I have become a creature between times," the man said in explanation. "My appearance is stable when I am in my home, but fluctuates when I am outside it."

As the two recovered from their shock, James Arthur spoke. "Your home is—is it what Willoughby calls a, a junction?"

"Willoughby?" the man said, cocking his head. "Yes, your friend, the mathematician. Yes, I do live in a time junction. Quite a large one. That is very perceptive. Now, to business. You can call me the '*keeper*.' So, what do we want of you—what do *I* want of you? I want you to stop your friend, Sydney, before it is too late."

Hauti now recovered her voice. "Stop her from what?"

The *keeper* looked at her. "She is soon entering what we call an *anomaly*. It is a schism where time turns in on itself, like a snake devouring its tail. It is a powerful disruption. In the wrong hands, it could start a chain reaction, ripping away time, ripping away all we know, ripping a hole into the fabric of what is."

"Does this, this anomaly thing have to do with her falling?" Dr. J asked.

"Yes," the man's face was in flux again, "it does."

"How do we—how do we stop it?"

"You don't stop it," the man replied. "It will happen despite all of our efforts. Only the mathematician has a chance to contain the breach, and there is very little we can do to help him. But we must try."

"Do you know why we're here?" Hauti asked. "Do you know what we came looking for?"

"You came to get into the libraries. You thought that would help you learn to defeat the Brotherhood. As I told you, those libraries have been compromised. You would find little of use to you in them."

"Yes, but there's something more," James Arthur said. "There was a carving. Another of my friends (his name is Antonio) found it while excavating an ancient city off the coast of India. He thinks it was a message to us from a friend who became lost to us in the pages of time. He thinks it was warning of something happening to Sydney. There was a high wall. It looked in the carving as if Sydney were falling from the wall."

"Yes. That is the riddle. One of great talent must fall from high upon a rocky wall—*soon*, if my reading of the signs is correct. We must travel to a monastery high in the mountains of Trabzon, Turkey. It is called in the local language, *Sumela*. The monastery has been dedicated to the Virgin Mary. It is now over run, or controlled by the *Dark Edge*. That is where they have taken your friend."

"Wait a minute," Hauti jumped in. "We've been scoping this place out for days, and you expect us to just drop everything and follow you to a high mountain. Why would we do that? We hardly know you."

"Because you want to help your friend, and if we delay, you will not be able to," the Friend said.

A loud growl sounded from beneath the ancient bed. All eyes turned in that direction. The growl was followed by an immediate sound of scuffling, and more growls. Then, there was a sound like choking, or coughing, a pop, and a whoosh, followed by another. After a pause came a third whoosh. A smell of sulfur filled the air, mixed with an even more distasteful smell.

"I must apologize," the Keeper said with a somewhat sheepish grin. "It appears that Mac and Beth have found a snack. Perhaps a small rat."

Hauti wrinkled her nose. James Arthur recognized the smell as burning fur or flesh. He tried to breathe in through his mouth.

"You said the Brotherhood have completely overrun this monastery—Sumeya, or whatever."

"Sumela," the man offered, pushing away from the bed post and carefully pulling the dark hood up over his head. "You are correct. By our last count there are more than thirty of them there. But not to worry. We are sufficient in number, and I can transfer us through a time hole to a cave only a few miles walk from the monastery path."

"Sufficient in number? We are three, and we don't even have weapons."

"Ah," the *keeper* said, "but, we have dragons…"

33

Cry of the Banshee

Willoughby had never been a great fan of creeping around in dark places at night. A thin bank of fog had appeared faintly at the far edge of the moonlight shortly after their local '*guide*,' Frankie, had approached them. The fog had moved quickly, rolling inland as the man motioned them up a slight incline. He held a flickering lantern, but it did little to light the way. He led them along a winding path toward an isolated set of buildings. Fog began to thicken in patches. Willoughby and Sydney found it increasingly challenging to keep up, but Frankie didn't seem to care. He had a complete mastery of the terrain, and no patience for those who were not as fortunate. Turning to face them, he held the lantern up to his face. "Hurry up you two. We haven't got all night." He sneered as Sydney stumbled and Willoughby reached to catch her. It seemed a joke to him that the path was hopelessly uneven and the ground full of holes. He held the lantern over toward a looming wall.

"This here is the Separate or Model prison complex." He swung around again. "If ya ask, they'll tell you that only parts are open to the public because of restorations in progress. But that's only partly true." He turned away and started off into the fog again, his voice echoing over his shoulder. "My old man used to tell me stories of the beastie that haunted one of the cells. It drove more than one inmate mad before they closed the place off. Dad was Irish, you see. He believed he had found a true banshee." Frankie stopped and turned around, holding the lantern close again. "You lot know what a banshee is, right?" The fog swirled around his bony face, hiding parts of it in shadow.

"It's an Irish mythical creature," Sydney mumbled, trying to keep from tripping on the uneven ground. "I believe they are usually purported to be female. The locals will tell you to avoid combs left lying on the ground as they are traps to lure unsuspecting souls to the banshee. They wear gray or black cloaks, have long, white hair, and are known for their high-pitched screams, which many attribute to the screech owl."

Frankie leaned, making sure he was close. He gave a wry smile. "Oh, this is no owl, missy! Nor is it a myth. I've seen it. Whether it's female or no, I can't say. I know it was a man what died in there just before the specter started to haunt. I'll tell you another thing—I don't want to see it again. Just so you know, I don't plan to."

"You're not going in with us?" Willoughby asked, stepping up beside Sydney.

Frankie shook his head. "Absolutely *not!* I agreed to take you to the building, then give you directions to the cell. I will leave ya the lantern, though."

Sydney glanced around. "How will you find your way out of here without the lantern?"

The man had turned and started walking again. He broke into a laugh. "I know these ruins by heart, missy. Walked them with my dad, and then alone. When the banshee came at me, I threw the lantern at it, to no effect.

I then ran through thicker fog than this, making it out the gate in under five minutes. You don't need to worry about me."

The three of them fell silent, still picking their way along the path. The fog curled into shapes around the swaying lantern. Within minutes, the bony man slowed and held the lantern high again. This time, its light fell upon a gray, stone building, which loomed up out of the fog like an abandoned fortress. Frankie turned back to them, but before he could speak, Sydney stepped forward and snatched the lantern.

"You said it was a man who died in the cell just before this, this apparition started appearing. Do you know his name?"

"No," Frankie said, smarting a little at having the lantern snatched away. "I heard he was a sort of *political* prisoner. He'd been high and mighty some said—a music man of some sort. Composed a symphony in Russian they said. Lots of controversy surrounded his death. Some say it was a fire. Others claim the body was never found. The guard on duty that night was let go and never heard from again. Whatever happened in that cell, it weren't a good thing, missy."

Willoughby had looked away from the man. He studied the building front, or at least as much as he could make out of it in the dim light. Blackened window cavities seemed to suck in fog, then breathe it out in swirling curls. *Just a trick of the light*, Willoughby assured himself.

Frankie led them to a large, heavy wooden door, inlaid with bands of black iron. He pulled a key from his jacket pocket and unlocked the door, seeming suddenly in a hurry.

"The cell is on the second floor. You'll find a flight of stairs midway down the main hall. Go up the stairs and turn left. The cell door you're looking for has construction tape closing off the doorway. Don't remove the tape. You can duck under it easily enough. The show generally starts around one o'clock to one fifteen. You have maybe fifteen to twenty minutes, maybe less. Good luck."

Frankie gave them a quick nod, then drifted off into the fog. They watched him go. Willoughby gave a sigh.

"Remind me why we are doing this?"

Sydney held the lantern high, studying the stone frame and the door. She pushed the door. It creaked open, causing tendrils of fog to swirl around them like arms trying to pull them in. She stepped inside onto a dusty wood floor.

"We need to search that cell room. There must be something in that room that my father needed. Perhaps it's the reason for the ruse about the banshee."

"And if it's not a ruse?" Willoughby asked quietly.

"Then we have another fine horror to add to our growing list," Sydney answered, pushing away cobwebs as they made their way down the main hall. Willoughby followed, shaking his head.

"Who would have known dating could be such fun?" he mumbled back.

Sydney shook her head, but neither laughed. They had reached the stairs now—a rickety affair with well-worn wooden steps that seemed to creak even before you stepped on them. The stairs led up to a narrow, worn landing, then switched back, leading the rest of the way to the second floor. Sydney waited for him at the top of the stairs.

The fog was not as thick inside the building, even though most of the windows were opened or shattered. By the time they reached the second floor, it had thinned to only a soft haze. "I don't think we're in Kansas anymore," Willoughby mumbled, noting what appeared to be slash or burn marks on the walls and ceiling. The door barred with construction tape was already visible three doors down on the right. They approached it cautiously.

The door to the cell was the same iron-banded heavy wood as the front door. It was slightly ajar. Willoughby carefully pushed. It was heavier than he had imagined, and stuck from lack of use. He pushed hard, throwing his weight behind it this time, and it slowly groaned open just enough to let them squeeze through.

He let Sydney push through with the lantern first, then he followed. The room was small, about ten feet deep and eight feet wide. It was mostly empty, with bits of rubble strewn across the uneven stone floor and a warped old case in one corner. Sydney pulled out the sheet of music her father had given her and studied it. Willoughby took the time to study the room.

The walls were blackened. He ran a finger across them, but the black did not appear to be from soot. It appeared as if the stone had been fused with something, or partially melted. He had just leaned forward to inspect the discoloration closer, wondering what kind of fire could have done this, when Sydney gasped. He spun. She was staring directly at him. He glanced over his shoulder, but saw only the blackened wall.

"What?" he said, looking back at her. Sydney's eyes grew wide. "*Numbers*," she said pointing. *"I see numbers!"* He looked to where she was pointing. Sure enough, tiny streams of numeric equation were spilling out of the corner of his pocket.

"You can see those?"

Sydney nodded. He looked back to the pocket, slid his hand in, and pulled out the small, locked box. The number strings were brighter now, spilling down all around the box, just as he had seen them do when he had first been given the box by How Loa. On that occasion, however, he had been looking at the box with the aid of the brass spy glass that the mysterious shopkeeper, Mr. Loa, had given him. Why was he able to see the number strings now, unaided? *Why was Sydney able to see them?*

"It's your box," Sydney said.

Willoughby nodded.

"Why is it doing that?"

Willoughby gave a shrug. "I have no idea." He reached carefully forward and placed the box onto the floor in front of them, moving over to stand beside Sydney. Before he could say anything more to her, the air directly above the box exploded. The initial flash of light was so bright that it blinded him. It hurt.

Sydney gasped, then a high-pitched, oscillating whine filled the air. As his eyes began to clear, he saw a glowing form, fuzzy and indistinct, floating in the air. Tiny, tangled lines of moving equations spilled down what appeared to be its head like writhing strands of hair. The whine came again. He wanted to clap his hands over his ears. He looked across to Sydney. Her face had changed and she was listening intently.

"What is it?" he yelled above the din.

This seemed to snap her out of some sort of trance. She glanced at him, then back at the flowing image. "Don't you see it—and hear it? There's structure and rhythm. Watch the movement of the light—that section near where the left shoulder would be. See? It pulls back, slowly, as the pitch of the whine rises, and pushes as it recedes. I *know* that movement. That's a violinist playing. I get bits of the tune, but," she cocked her ear as the sound came again, "but it's really distorted."

Willoughby cocked his head. The bright image floating in front of them seemed to be pulsing, almost coming together to form a discernible body, then distorting again. He noted the movement Sydney was referring to from the blob of light. There did seem to be a definite coordination between sound and movement. He wasn't sure if it was power of suggestion, or if there really was purpose in the motion, but he felt he could envision a violinist. Bits of number strings snaked down the writhing form, twisting at its feet into steady streams that flowed toward the box.

"Close your eyes," Willoughby shouted. "Just focus on the sound. I'll try to focus on the numbers and whatever this thing is." He felt instinctively that this image was not there to harm them, but why was it there? And what was it? Could it be another experiment of Beelzebub? Another creature isolated outside of time?

Looking to the side of the flowing equations, his eyes again fell on the old case propped in the corner. It seemed newer suddenly—not warped and corroded as his first impression of it had been. Its improved condition also allowed him to better note its shape. *Was it a violin case?* The hard shell of the case was pitch black, the same color as the blackened stone, so was it possible that he hadn't seen it clearly? *But why was it here?* Surely, these rooms were routinely searched and cleaned. He walked over to the case. It seemed antique in design, but barely worn and it was definitely a violin case. He looked back. Sydney still had her eyes closed, listening intently. Willoughby grabbed the case, undoing the clasps, and opened it. A polished, beautifully preserved Stradivarius and its Pernambuco bow were tucked neatly inside. He placed hands over his ears. The whine was getting to him. He could feel his heartbeat quickening, his head throbbing to the rising and receding. He had to stop it. He grabbed the instrument and stood. Maybe Sydney could drown it out. Maybe it would stop to listen to her. If even for a moment it would be a relief. He could barely think from the racket. He could barely breathe.

"Sydney!" he screamed, holding out the violin and bow. Her eyes flew open. It was like she didn't even see him. She only saw the violin. Grabbing it, she placed it to her chin, raised the bow, and began to play. The whine became more distinct and softer. It melded with and molded around Sydney's notes. Slowly, the two sounds merged, like two artists reaching some sort of harmony, some sort of symmetry. No longer screeching and wild, the tune was brilliant and beautiful and made the heart want to sing.

The fuzzy light solidified into a defined being. It was a man—tall, with a thin, haggard face. His long, black hair was pulled back in a tail that hung halfway down his back. He wore a puffy white shirt and torn breeches. His feet were bare. He had been beaten and battered—that was obvious, *but his violin was immaculate.*

Willoughby looked to Sydney. Her eyes were closed again. She was lost to the music, playing with a passion he had rarely seen in her. The piece was unbelievable. It had divine rifts, overlaying a soft, melodic underbelly. He found that he, too, was getting swept up, lost in the flowing cadence of the sounds bathing the room. It was transporting him somewhere vaguely familiar. He tried to place the feeling. The tune reminded him of what he had heard Sydney play with her Polynesian chorus on the *Absconditus*, only this time he was not under the influence of Kava. The flow of the music did not move in the direction of Sydney's dance on the *Absconditus*, however. It carried him past that, to, to…

For a brief moment, he caught a glimpse of a theater full to bursting, and of Sydney on the stage, and of mirrors crashing down around her. It was a glimpse of the performance he had seen in St. Petersburg when he had first ventured untethered into the time stream. Only now, there was the hypnotic beauty of the music swirling around them. It built, soared, and spun his mind in a whirl of deep imagery. Then, abruptly, it stopped.

Willoughby opened his eyes. The image of the man was gone. Sydney held the violin to her side, panting—her eyes wide. He noted a shimmer and looked down. The small box at their feet had opened. Inside was a glistening crystal shape. At its heart, a single black line moved back and forth in a patterned wave. "It's oscillating," he said, looking up. "Whatever is trapped in that crystal is a sound and it's oscillating. *A musical note?*"

"Yes," a voice rang out—a voice he knew all too well.

It took Willoughby a moment to pull his mind back from the beautiful music and focus on the dread that suddenly stabbed at him. He spun, finding Beelzebub standing perfectly still behind Sydney. The self-proclaimed lord of demons leaned against the burnt wall. He took only fleeting notice of Willoughby. His focus and concentration was on Sydney.

"Finally, you come full circle," the gaunt creature said softly. "You know, don't you? Bravo. You found the final piece to the puzzle, and you got there on your own. I am impressed. But it is time to drop pretenses, Sydney. It is time for you to complete your grand performance. This is the moment you have tried to run away from. You know that. You cannot run anymore. You must play, as sad as the tune may be. It is the purpose you were built for. You try and try, but you cannot escape your destiny. This time, you will complete the composition. You will play all of it. History, *time* requires that of you. You have slowly approached this realization. Why make it harder than it needs to be?"

Sydney turned and stared at the demon, her face unreadable. *Was she surprised, shocked by his sudden appearance? Did she know who he was? Did she have any clue what he was talking about?*

There was no shock, no question in her face. If anything, there was only realization and then something new; resolve. Willoughby watched, completely confused.

Beelzebub stepped forward. "Take back the note! *Complete the composition!*"

Sydney said nothing.

The tall, bony man, his black trench coat buttoned to the neck, smiled. "So be it. You will comply. You know that. I am only here to save wasted effort if I can, and I will be here every time you are brought back until you fulfill what you must." The being pushed away from the wall. "I wondered how Willoughby would read the challenge at the cobra pit. I had no fear, though, that you would come out of the den unhurt. I almost wish Willoughby had been unsuccessful. I would have liked to see what happened if a snake reached you. I had a feeling you were the key. It was you all along, wasn't it? Your pathetic father could not help you. Your clueless boyfriend still thinks he is *protecting* you. Your mother knew, though. She came to me. Did you know that? Oh, she did not know who I was. She did not know what I did. But she knew you were no ordinary child…You have nowhere to run, Sydney. H.S. is gone. Sam is gone. Time will wipe you from its pages if you choose to continue to resist—you already feel that. You will be less than the Desert Witch if you do not comply. You will *never have existed*."

Willoughby tried to follow the conversation, but he felt like he had walked in on the tail end of a long and vicious argument and he couldn't make sense of it.

"Do you have any clue what he is talking about?" he mumbled to Sydney. "Does any of this make sense to you? Or is this more nonsense thrown out just to confuse us, to try to manipulate us somehow?"

Sydney didn't answer. Her eyes were still fixed on the intense, black stare of Beelzebub.

Beelzebub held the stare a long moment, and then looked over at Willoughby. "Poor Willoughby," he snorted. "You see, I am not the one who has been doing the manipulating. Your friend here has known for some time that something was amiss. Life was not the same for her as it was for others. She can see things—oh, yes, she did not tell you until today, did she? She can hear things. She can make others experience the meld of moments in her mind. She knew she somehow controlled those moments and learned to weave that into her music. For her, becoming a superstar was all about manipulation, pure and simple. People hear her music and feel something more than just notes. Now, time has caught up with her. Now payment has come due for gifts given. Moments are slipping no matter how hard she tries to hold on to them—slipping away like grains of sand through the still fingers of a bloodied hand."

He turned back to Sydney. "Those were your thoughts were they not, Sydney?" He glanced back at Willoughby. "Did you know your girlfriend here is ultimately responsible for the death of Sam? She is responsible for the death of H.S. She doomed those poor souls on the *Absconditus*. Think about it Willoughby. She is the only one of your group who was there every time things went wrong. She let you believe, the whole time, that things were happening because of you. That is why she punched you when you sent her with Sam to London. You forced her to be there when the inevitable happened. You forced her to have to witness it first hand, to come away with blood on her hands. You see, boy, you have been in the presence of a monster all along, one trying to run, trying to use you as a shield from time itself, and you never knew it. In fact, fool that you are, you fell in love with her."

Sydney said nothing. Willoughby felt confusion at first, and then a sudden rage bubbled up inside him. This demon did not know Sydney—*not his Sydney!* The things he said—they, *they were impossible!* He burst forward, fists raised. He was done with this creature's misdirection and manipulation. As his arms closed on the bony figure, he drove the gaunt creature back. The being's skin felt like crumpled paper. The odor of swamp-rot filled the mist around his buttoned trench coat. As the creature approached the wall, however, it abruptly stopped moving. The body became as hard and cold as stone. Time equations erupted into the air, sending a flurry of movement at Willoughby. Moments swirled around him in nanosecond progressions—brutal moments in this very cell, aimed at someone who stood at the very spot where he stood. For the merest blink of an eye, he was the occupant in the cell during each punch, or slash, or slam of gut-wrenching pain. He was standing just in the right place to take a punch, feel a whip, take the crack of a rod across his chest. The butt of a gun slammed into the side of his head. He staggered sideways, and fell, crumpled, and stunned, against the far wall. He felt blood running down his cheek. Dazed, he was barely able to take in the scene that unfolded in front of him.

In staccato bits, he watched Sydney step forward, bend quickly to pick up the shimmering shard from the box and drop the violin and bow back into the case, and race at the wall behind where Beelzebub had been. Willoughby glanced around wildly, looking for the gaunt figure. Beelzebub was bent over, closer to the corner. Willoughby's attack seemed to have affected him. Sensing movement, he looked up and lunged at Sydney, but he missed, and Sydney disappeared. Looking closer, Willoughby could now see the faint number strings emanating from what had to be a time hole. Moments too late, Beelzebub gave an angry howl as his fists slammed into the small box, the number strings tightening around the open box, seeming to protect it. Beelzebub slammed his head back against the wall.

"*You fool!*" he spit toward Willoughby. "*I can control her! I fix her mistakes! Time will rip us apart, and it will be on you! If I cannot stop her, you have doomed us all!*" He spun, and dove at the wall after Sydney.

Willoughby's head felt like it was splitting open. The room spun around him. Sweat mixed with the blood streaming down the side of his face. He tried to yell, to call out, but it came out only as a breathless hiss.

"*Sydney...*"

He felt nauseous. Leaning to the side, he scarcely had time to vomit and push away before he spiraled down into a deep, unconscious abyss.

34

Frozen Fear

T.K. sensed a movement to the left and spun to face the first stumbling corpse as it crested a ridge and lunged at her. She whirled easily away, dropping her light stick, but driving a swift kick into the partially-frozen flesh of the figure's abdomen. While this gang of zombie nightmares had her outnumbered and were bigger, she had the definite edge in speed and agility. The walking corpse she kicked doubled over, allowing her to drive an elbow down hard onto its neck. As the wiry body sprawled onto the ice and did not move, she backed up so that she could bring her weapon around, firm in both hands.

"I can take you apart!" she said. "All of you!" She threw a glance around. She could see at least four distinct shapes now, including the man still flat on the ice. The muscled leader of the band seemed strangely amused by her words. He motioned the other stumbling forms forward, seeming content to stand on the ice crest and watch. The corpse at her feet stirred, and slowly pushed up to regain its footing. It held its head as if she had damaged the neck. Its skin was ghostly pale, with a faint hint of tattoos beneath a thin covering of frost. The body was lean, though its arms and chest were firm and muscled.

Tainken pulled two more light sticks out of her pocket and threw them to the ice. They created an arena of light about ten meters across that enclosed the moving corpse on the ice. Two of the other animated bodies stumbled into the glow of the light sticks as well. T.K. backed up against a bit of jutting ice to protect her back. She held her pole weapon in front of her, testing it for balance, and pointing it at one and then the other of the creatures as they stumbled forward.

"We got us a fighter boys." The huge figure on the crest bellowed out. His voice carried the hint of a Caribbean accent. "She think she not ready to die. She think she kill what already be dead." His voice was labored, as if he were having to force air into his lungs to be able to speak. He grinned, letting white teeth catch a glint from the light sticks.

T.K. ignored the heckling. She gauged the speed of the two approaching forms while focusing on the corpse that had pushed back up to its feet. They would all reach her at relatively the same time, and she did not like the odds of three, possibly four against one.

In a swift spin, she flew at the wiry one who had just regained his footing. She attacked from the side and behind, swinging her weapon in a low, powerful blow that brought the cold blade in a level slice just below the left ear. The weapon had been designed to keep its edge in any weather, and though lighter weight than iron or steel, the weapons of her people were balanced and strong. The blade severed the corpse's head cleanly, flinging it back, where it rolled down a short slope and disappeared over the edge of the ice crevice. The headless remains fell to its knees and toppled. To her astonishment, there was little blood. What did ooze from the remains was thick and black and not even enough to stain the ice.

Stunned by the spectacle of one of their own falling, the taller, bony corpse to the left froze in its tracks. The shorter, stockier one to her right, though, used the moment of distraction to attack. He had crept closer than she'd realized and dove forward, slamming his bulk against her from the side. He drove a short, stubby knife at her mid-section. She screamed. The knife was unable to penetrate her suit, but the blow still knocked her to the ice where a sharp, protruding shard of icy stone did penetrate the suit slightly, leaving a tiny rip and a gouge in her side just below the right arm. Acting on instinct, she rolled away from the jagged outcrop just as the stout shell of a man rose and lunged a second time.

Holding tightly to her weapon, she came up from her roll, slicing with the blade. It caught the walking corpse on the arm from the underside, sinking in and ripping the muscle above the bone. The arm fell limp as the thing shrieked and its hand dropped the knife. The taller figure stumbled forward again.

She crouched, angling her weight to one side as the injured form recovered, spun around, and grabbed the knife with its good hand. It lunged again. Tainken waited a half second, then sprang, her left boot swinging out with all the force she could muster. She kicked at the corpse's remaining good hand, aiming for just below the wrist. The face of the corpse was hideous and contorted. Its jawbone was apparently broken so that the whole lower chin was now frozen at a strange angle and the mouth was permanently ajar. As her boot connected, there was a crack, and the knife flew free. The thing howled. She looked but could not see where the knife landed.

The corpse bent over its wounded hand also looking for the knife. T.K. took advantage of the moment, planting her other booted foot into its abdomen and shoving it back. She spun, pulling her weapon around.

The tall corpse had reached her now, closing the gap so that her weapon was useless.

She rushed at it, lowering her injured shoulder, and slamming into its side.

It groaned, tripping over a frozen bit of broken rock and falling over a small ice bank.

T.K. spun again, just as she heard the stocky corpse rush at her, this time, from behind. She brought the blade across in a swift cut that cleanly severed the thing's good arm just above the elbow. The corpse howled, planting the stump into the snow to freeze it as its face distorted even further. It slowly turned back toward her, moving with grim determination as it stumbled in a halting arc to stop a few meters to her left. She saw out of the corner of her eye that the taller corpse had climbed back over the small ice bank, closing in on her right side.

"What are you?" T.K. barked in frustration at the corpses closing in on her. She tried to calm herself, to catch her breath.

"We be the nightmare you don't want to see," the raspy hiss came from somewhere above and behind her.

She glanced back. The muscled form that seemed to be orchestrating this attack had moved from his perch on the ice crest and was making his way down an ice embankment ten meters behind her. The ones on her sides began closing in. Using her advantage in speed and agility, she ducked under the tall one's lunge and rolled forward, hopping back to her feet, and swinging her weapon in a wide arc to keep the stocky one at bay. She backed slowly toward the edge of the ice crevice.

"You be trapped!" the large corpse rasped, smiling again. He continued approaching slowly, deliberately. The tall corpse had recovered from his lunge and approached again from the right.

T.K. continued to swing her weapon, backing clear to the edge of the deep crevice. The stocky corpse stepped into the swing and the blade sunk into his hip, grating against the bone. Tainken jerked to free the blade and was barely able to bring it around in time to rake the tall corpse's belly, slicing a meter-long gash. The corpse grabbed itself, falling backward to the ice. It looked up just as Tainken swung the blade high, twisting to gain momentum and brought it down hard, severing its head just above the collar bone. By now, the stocky corpse had reached her. It grabbed her in a vise-like grip with the stump of its arm, using its forward momentum to careen her toward the edge of the ice cliff. T.K. managed to curl and kick the demon off her. It tottered for a moment, waving its stump to try to gain balance, and then fell, soundlessly, over the side of the cliff.

Tainken pulled her legs back from the cliff and rolled over to rise when the last of the corpses, the leader, slammed into her, pushing her over the edge. As she began her fall, she steeled herself to not panic. She slammed the blade of her weapon at the ice wall, trying to stop her descent. The blade only skimmed the ice. Tainken twisted frantically in the air. Her eye caught sight of a slight outcrop in the wall positioned about two feet from another jutting bit of ice. She threw her arms out to position the pole between the two bulges, the blade down. The pole wedged between the outcrops, the blade biting into the ice as T.K. threw herself forward with all her might. The jerk was almost too much for her arms, and her body slammed into the ice wall, but she somehow managed to hold on. She gritted her teeth, setting her chin as she tried to pull herself up onto the pole, scrambling with her booted toes to find some sort of foot hold. She hadn't the strength to pull herself up, but she did manage to dig the toe of one boot into the ice far enough to give some relief to her arms. They still burned, as did the gouge in her side, but held fast. As moments ticked by, though, she began to feel shooting pains through her body and blood trickling down her side. She couldn't hold on forever. She glanced down. The corpse she had pushed over the edge had landed about twenty meters below, a sharp bit of stone debris piercing through its chest. Most of the floor of the crevice was lined with stone debris and bits of rock, encased in a heavy sheen of ice. If she dropped straight down, she would land on a fairly level bit of ice, but if she fell just a few feet further out from the crevice wall, she would likely end up impaled.

She began to slide her hands, arms shaking now uncontrollably, toward the non-blade side of the weapon pole. Perhaps if she could work the end free, she could swing down, pulling the blade free, but buying herself at least a few feet, and then she could drag the blade, slowing herself so that she could survive the drop. Before she could implement her plan, however, there was a grating sound and ice showered down on her head. She barely had time to look up before huge dark boots slammed into the pole, snapping it cleanly in two.

She fell, only glimpsing the muscled leader of the group sliding down on top of her, holding two long knives against the cliff wall to slow his descent. One knife caught on the same jutting rock that had stopped her, but it did not bite into the ice as her weapon had done. Instead, it ripped free of the muscled hand that held it, grazing his face. She saw no blood, but then, she was fighting frantically to angle her own body and push against the ice wall for what drag she could muster.

When she slammed against the first piece of jutting ice, the pain was unbearable, but it slowed her enough so that, hitting a second jutting piece of debris with her opposite arm did not rip the arm off. She did hear the bone clearly break. She screamed again, just as she hit the bottom. Her helmet banged hard against a slight rise in the ice. The face screen shattered, and the biting cold rushed in. The world was spinning. She felt herself roll. She bent, trying to protect her broken arm. She couldn't breathe. Her eyesight swam and then went dark.

The next thing she knew, she was on her knees, panting and throwing up blood onto the white ice. She was shaking uncontrollably from the cold and the fall, acting purely on adrenaline. Her eyes focused. She saw the leader of the corpses. He had a mangled hand and was trying to force one leg to straighten. It was obviously broken. She glanced frantically around, and spotted the blade end of the broken pole. Dizzy and still retching, she crawled to it and snatched it up. Pain from multiple points in her body hit her in a wave so immense that it caused her to fall to the ice, again spitting up mouthfuls of blood. The corpse was not bleeding at all, and had managed to push up onto his good leg, stumbling awkwardly, using the broken splint of a pole to hobble. T.K. used her last ounces of strength to force herself back onto her feet. She swayed, pointing the pole blade toward the demon corpse. It was hobbling back toward the far, smooth ice wall. Something about the wall seemed strange, but Tainken could not get her brain to focus. She could only think of one thing—she had to kill this thing, whatever it was.

She saw the form stop and a huge, muscled arm reached down, retrieving one of the long knives it had used to slide down the ice wall. It turned to face her.

"Now," it croaked, seeming only to breathe in order to speak. "We finish this."

T.K. attacked, throwing everything she had into one wild push. He slammed backward against the smooth ice as she drove the pole blade hard into his side. Spent, she fell back to the ice onto her good shoulder. She pushed backward, but couldn't seem to get her legs to work. She inched away, trying to ride the excruciating pain while keeping her eyes on the huge form towering over her. It forced a smile as it slowly pulled itself off the blade that had lodged at least six inches into its side before imbedding itself into the ice wall. Once completely separated from the blade, the hulking form took one hobbling step forward.

"*Now, you die!*" the moving form hissed, forcing breath out. It brought its long knife up, holding it tightly in its good hand.

T.K. tried to shove back further, but her eyes were watering from the pain and she wasn't sure if she was moving or not. Then, the ice all around shattered, and shards were flying everywhere. She feebly raised her good arm to shield her face, when a dark shadow came into view. It was the huge corpse falling. It seemed to be coming at her in slow motion, the bleached white eyes shining. T.K. had a fleeting thought. *It was light here!* How was she able to see? The light was behind the ice wall. The black figure came closer and she expected to see the long knife, falling toward her now unprotected neck. *But there was no knife!* Something else was strange. Something was protruding from the jaw of the corpse—*the point of a pick.*

Tainken was barely able to slide her broken arm out of the form's path as it slammed onto her legs. The wave of pain made her shriek, and once again, she couldn't breathe. Then, someone was pushing the heavy weight off her. She tried to focus. Someone was calling her name.

"Tainken! Tainken, my friend, are you okay? Where are you hurt?"

Her eyes swimming, the world spinning, she actually thought she saw Antonio bending over her. She saw his face coming closer. She wanted to touch that face one last time, to say goodbye. She felt someone frantically pulling at the shattered remains of her helmet, putting something under her head, something over her. It was a nice dream, to see Antonio one last time.

"Say something--speak to me!" the voice ordered. Her mumbled words were barely audible. "You...sure...took your...time."

Her head lolled to the side. She could no longer hold the dream. The pain was too great. She slid away, into the dark.

35

The Russian Connection

Willoughby felt an intense throbbing at the side of his head as he drifted back to consciousness. He was lying head down in a small pool of blood. He tasted and smelled vomit and realized he had narrowly avoided falling face first into it when he blanked out. He pushed slowly to a sitting position, having to lean against the wall once he was fully upright. The sky outside the window was light gray. He had to get out of here. The place would be opening soon, and he would have a hard time explaining his state. After several attempts, he was finally able to push himself to a standing position.

He leaned into the wall, struggling to stay upright, and breathing heavily. He lifted a hand to the side of his head, feeling for the wound. The bleeding had slowed, but the wound still oozed. He felt nauseous and weak. He closed his eyes and tried to think over what had happened. *Why hadn't Sydney helped him? Why had she run and taken the item from the box?* It had seemed like some sort of portable time junction from the math equations he saw pouring out of it—a time junction centered on a tangible sound, or note, trapped in a tomb of crystal. How had she seen the numbers in the air around the box? How had she seen the numbers telling her that a time hole existed in this room? She hadn't seen the numbers in H.S.'s cabin on the ship. *Or had she?* Could something of what Beelzebub said be true? *Could she have known more than she let on all along?*

He thought back over his time with her. He refused to believe it. His feelings for her were based on a connection that went deeper than surface suspicion. He cared for her in a way that took her into his inner world. He believed she cared for him in the same way. There was an unspoken trust between them, which meant there had be something he wasn't seeing, an explanation that Beelzebub either didn't understand, or was trying to hide from him. He thought of his promise to Aiyito to try to protect her. He thought of Antonio's warning, of the etching in the ruins in the Bay of Cambay that showed a girl with long hair and a violin, and how it depicted her falling. Now, Beelzebub was chasing after Sydney. He seemed to believe she was trying to run away from something—he had said it was *time*. He had wanted her to complete a musical score. *Why?* Was a part of it somehow contained in the crystal? Was Sydney somehow the one who could release it? Sydney's playing had opened the box, the one he had been given with no key. The crystal inside was some sort of junction, it had to be. Could you build a junction around a piece of music? *How did all this fit together?*

"Think, *think!*" he sagged against the wall, trying to come up with some kind of solution, some kind of plan. But nothing came. As the dizziness and nausea eased, he opened his eyes again and scanned the room. Maybe Sydney had left him some message or clue. He could see nothing on the walls. He noted the violin case open on the floor. Sydney had dropped the violin and bow back into it, but haphazardly. He stumbled forward and opened the case completely. Only then did he notice that something was protruding from the violin strings. The paper was old and fragile. It had been placed in a protective sleeve. As he carefully pulled the aged paper out from the strings, he recognized the paper and the writing. It was a scrap of the score Sydney had shown him—torn from the bottom of a larger sheet. The jagged bit of paper appeared to hold the bottom two stanzas to a larger page of music. It was as if someone had purposely removed the last stanza of the composition. *Could this be the bottom to the sheet Sydney had?* Yet, the bottom of hers had been burned off, hadn't it? He had not seen this bit of parchment when he had handed Sydney the violin and bow. *Had it been there all along?*

He studied the violin. There were initials, very small, but carved into the wood grain of the violin: D.K. On the inside of the case, he found a scrap of newspaper. He could not read it, but recognized the language—it was Russian. He thought of St. Petersburg, of Aiyito sending the music to Sydney just before her St. Petersburg concert, of the fact that he had been drawn to St. Petersburg on his first venture into the time grid untethered, when H.S. had been training him how to navigate with the aid of a crystal computer. Somehow, St. Petersburg seemed to be central to what was going on. He walked to where the empty box still lay on the floor, the box that until a few hours ago, had no key. He carefully put the scrap of parchment into it. Moments ago, when Sydney's music had opened it, the box had housed a pulsing shard, one which Sydney had taken with her. He closed the lid of the box and slipped it into his pocket. He then replaced the violin and bow properly, and closed the violin case, latching it, and then picking it up by the handle. He looked to the wall. He could still see the number strings outlining where the time hole had been, though they were much fainter. Holding the case to his chest, he ran at the wall and jumped.

36

St. Petersburg

The sharp tug of the time stream made his stomach further lurch. All around him, glowing streams of equations flowed past, carrying him in their wake as if he were floating on a river. It was a sensation now familiar to him, but he still found it fascinating. He searched the barrage of numbers for some hint of Sydney. He saw none. There were no numbers that seemed to glow brighter for him, no hint of Sydney's music to guide him as had happened when he went back in time to observe bits of Sydney's performance in St. Petersburg. The numbers swirled around him so fast that he was barely able to catch more than a snatch of equation here, a hint of one there. *Why had he heard Sydney's music in the stream before?* Why had he seen a glowing equation he knew was right? Where was that equation now?

There was so much about travel in the raw time stream that he did not know, that H.S. had never had time to teach him. He thought that, at some point, maybe Sam would be able to at least give him access to H.S.'s notes or files so he could learn more. But that never happened. Antonio had been determined that Willoughby spend time away from time travel and from Observations, Inc. He felt that Willoughby needed the chance to know what it was like to be an ordinary, if brilliant, teenage boy. It hadn't worked, though, because Willoughby knew Beelzebub was out there, somewhere. He had met his father back in the time stream. He had freed a witch, saved lives, and seen lives lost. There was really no way of going back to "*normal*" after experiences like that.

He spun slightly in the stream, searching frantically. *Could he get trapped in here?* Trapped forever outside of time? What about Sydney? Even if she could suddenly see the equations around the holes, she wasn't a mathematician like he was, and she had less experience. She wouldn't know what to do in a time stream. *How would she know how to get out of it?*

A ribbon of equation curled into him. It wrapped around his head, flowed down his arm to the violin case, and then wound itself about the thinner portion of the case where the neck of the violin rested. It glowed brighter than the other equations. He studied its number strings. He recognized faint bits—he reached out and grabbed hold of the string. Immediately, he was jerked from the time stream. After a short, familiar sensation of being shredded and pulled through a sieve, he slammed back together, sensing himself in open free fall. He tumbled down onto something soft and cold. He pushed for solid ground, fighting to get his head up and his feet under him. The cold wet stuck to him. It was dark. As his eyes adjusted, though, he could see it was not pitch black. There were a few fluttering lights here and there. He finally managed to stand, and discovered he had fallen into a field of heavy snow. There were no stars in the sky, but it was obviously night. The cold was mostly quiet. He brushed as much of the snow off as he could, prodded around in it until he found the violin case, and made for the nearest of the fluttering lights.

As he waded through what must have been at least twenty inches of light powder, he came to a higher bank of hard-packed snow. He made his way up and over the icy embankment. *Why was it that these time holes always seemed to take him to snow, and dark, and cold?* Why couldn't he come out on a beach in Hawaii at least some of the time? He sighed. Luckily, he did have a jacket on, but the air here felt like ice compared to the damp cool of Port Arthur.

On the other side of the embankment, he saw a familiar building—the Miriinsky Theater. *St. Petersburg*, he thought to himself. What was it about Sydney and St. Petersburg? There was something here he had to find, to uncover. *Otherwise, why was he being brought here again and again?* This time, the building looked much newer. Lamps still burned along its exterior, even though the building and surrounding streets seemed empty. In the flicker of the lamps, he could see that a soft snow was still falling. The lamps were an antique style with oil and wick, not the electric street lights he had seen the last time he was here. *Must be earlier in time*, he thought. *Possibly early 1900's?*

He glanced up and down the street in front of the theater. It was completely devoid of cars. Only the occasional wagon, or horse-drawn carriage dotted the sides of what appeared to be a cobblestone road. Willoughby tried to make his way across, dodging the steep ice ruts left by cart and carriage wheels. A skiff of new powder blanketed the road, making the hard-packed ice underneath even more slippery and difficult to navigate. He hurried across toward the wide boulevard to the theater, brushing snow from his trousers, from his hair, and stamping his feet to keep them warm. As he climbed the steps at the front of the building, he could see that the doors were chained shut. He turned and looked out at the quiet street.

He had obviously gone back a considerable distance into the past, but how far? Surely, Sydney was not here. He had seen no other footprints where he had landed across the boulevard. He pushed under the theater eaves to escape the falling snow. What could he do? Stand around shivering and stomping his feet until morning and hope he didn't freeze to death? His thoughts were interrupted by the sound of shouts and the clopping of horses. A shot was fired somewhere far away and there were muffled sounds of a brawl and screaming. Then, the air went quiet again. Moments later, he heard the distinct clip-clop of horses.

Glancing around, he found a dim alcove to hide in, but the horses continued toward him. He peered out from the shadows and could make out two large, white horses coming, each bearing a burly man. Were they palace guards, or law enforcement? What did they call the soldiers working to enforce the Czar's will? *Cossacks?* They had the black, shiny boots and white ballooned trousers, thick coats and gloves, and fur caps. Willoughby pushed further into the shadows. On the one hand, the men might get him out of the cold. On the other, he didn't speak Russian. They might throw him into jail and shoot him as a spy. One of the horses drew up. A man shouted words in thick Russian, pointing to the footprints he had made in the snow.

"*Кто есть показать себя!*"

Willoughby had no idea what the words meant, but the man had seemed to follow the footsteps with his eyes and was staring right into the shadow now. Willoughby did not move. The shout came again. The other rider had also turned his horse to face the shallow eaves of the theater. The husky voice shouted something else. The second Cossack started to dismount from his horse, brandishing a rifle with a long bayonet on it. The man began to move cautiously toward the theater.

Willoughby glanced down at his clothes, thinking fast. Surely the theater was not so old that the Russians would not know what an American was. Perhaps they could find someone who spoke English. At least he wouldn't freeze to death.

But how would he explain his clothes? Why he was here? The gash on the side of his face? Would they steal the violin? Most likely, they would at least confiscate it. He didn't know enough about where he was or who these men were to trust them. The man on foot shook his rifle and spoke to the other man in Russian. Willoughby took advantage of the moment to bend and pick up a stick lying near his feet. He threw it toward the horse the man had just dismounted. The men, embroiled in argument, did not see the movement. The stick hit the horse on the back leg. It jumped and whinnied, whirling around toward the snow embankment on the other side of the street. Both men spun to see what had spooked the horse. Willoughby darted out from the shadows. He tried to move as quietly as possible, staying toward the softer snow near the building, but this slowed him down enough for the man still on horseback to glimpse him clearing the corner and heading into a wide alley. He shouted to the other man, who quickly mounted his horse, and the two were in pursuit.

Willoughby made no effort at stealth now. He ran flat out, trying to stick to the shadows as much as possible, but keeping his emphasis on speed. He heard the horses start down the alley at a full gallop, the men shouting. They would catch him in moments. *He had to find somewhere to hide, but where?*

Darting around a corner, Willoughby crossed a street, and ducked down a different alley. Wagons and freight were lined up in bunches to either side. He heard shouts from the excited men. Their horses were thundering toward the alley.

How did they know? Had they seen him? Could they make out his footprints in the snow?

He searched frantically as he ran, looking for a place to hide. He saw a wagon covered by an old tarp of some kind. He stopped, grabbed a corner of the tarp, and jumped up onto the wagon, planning to climb under the tarp, but a hand grabbed his upper arm and yanked him from the wagon. He tried to fight, but another hand slapped over his mouth. Strong arms jerked him down, twisting him behind one of the wagon's huge back wheels. The hand remained over his mouth as the man holding him went completely rigid. Willoughby could hear the horses just entering the alley. They had slowed to a trot. The men were conversing in Russian. Willoughby tried to still his breathing. The horses appeared to split up, one to each side of the wider alley. They trotted slowly from one pile of crates and barrels to the next. The horse closest came to the wagon they hid behind. It stopped. From his perch on the horse, Willoughby heard the supposed Cossack twist in his saddle. He ripped back the tarp that covered the wagon and inspected the contents for a moment, then yelled something to his counterpart. His voice sounded suddenly surprised and happy. The other Cossack came over. There was a clinking of glass as something was pulled from the wagon, and then a short bark of a laugh. One of the Cossacks slapped the other on the back, then they turned their horses and headed at a trot out of the alley. Willoughby felt the man holding him relax. The hand came off his mouth. The man helped him stand, whispering quickly in Russian. Willoughby sucked in deep gulps of air, bending over.

"Thanks," he said, "but I don't speak Russian."

There was a brief pause, and then his rescuer whispered in heavily accented words.

"You don't speak proper English either," The man chuckled softly, "which can only mean one thing—you must be American, no?"

Willoughby eyed the man. He was tall and thin, with wide shoulders and a burly coat with no hood. He had graying hair, a prominent nose, and narrow, intelligent eyes. He guessed the man to be older, perhaps in his mid-fifties, but with a vigor about him.

"You—you can speak English!" Willoughby said excitedly.

"Yes," the man said with a slight chuckle. "I speak many languages, but keep your voice down. We must get off this street, *now!* The vodka bottle I planted under the tarp was only half full. Those goons will drink it in no time and be back." He motioned Willoughby toward a set of icy steps that led down to a basement door. "Follow, quickly!"

Willoughby followed the man into a dark room that smelled of coal and damp mold. His rescuer closed and locked the door quietly behind them. He grabbed Willoughby by the shoulder and led him through the pitch black into a narrow passage. Once they were about ten meters down the passage, he stopped. Willoughby heard him fumble with something, and then a match was struck. They were standing next to a low table. He lit an oil lamp. This seemed to be some sort of abandoned hallway. A full length, ornate mirror was next to the table. The man stood in front of it and with his free hand, slid his fingers over a hidden latch. The mirror swung open, and the man motioned. Willoughby followed him through the hidden doorway into an even narrower passage that was dug out of the frozen ground and lined on both sides with warped, weathered gray boards. Willoughby stepped in and the man swung the mirror shut.

"It is safe to talk now," he said, turning to Willoughby. "Did the Cheka do that?" He pointed to the wound on Willoughby's head.

"The *Cheka?*"

"Ah, you are right—they are no longer Lenin's secret police. Under Stalin now, they are called the NKVD. I am certain they were the ones following you."

"No, they didn't do this."

"Who did?"

"It's…a, it's a long story."

The man looked down at the violin case which Willoughby still held tightly. "Did you steal that?"

Willoughby looked down, seemingly surprised that the case was still in his hand. "Uh, no, I didn't steal it."

"You are a musician then?" The man motioned and continued to lead Willoughby through a catacomb of roughhewn tunnels, glancing back to let Willoughby know he was waiting for an answer.

Willoughby shook his head. "I'm a mathematician. My name is Willoughby. The violin…I don't know how to explain the violin. It's, a, it's part of the long story."

"A mathematician?" The man stopped, peering curiously back. "But you are merely a boy. Where are you from?"

"Uh, not sure you would believe me. Let's just stick to my name for now. As I mentioned, it's Willoughby."

"You speak like an American, Willoughby, but you seem educated. This is sounding increasingly like a long story I should hear."

Willoughby was starting to feel claustrophobic. "Could we get out of these tunnels first? Where are you leading us?"

The man shrugged and gave a shrewd smile. "If you wish. I am leading you to my current work studio." He turned and began walking again. "We are almost there—only two more turns."

Willoughby followed him around the first turn. "Who are you?" he asked. "Why are you helping me?"

The man stopped and turned again. "You don't know me?" He held the oil lamp up so it fully illuminated his face. "Look closer."

Willoughby studied the man's face. It did look faintly familiar, but he couldn't place a name with the face. "I, uh, you look somewhat familiar, but I'm at a loss. What year is this?"

The man's eyes raised in a gesture of surprise. "What year is this? 1933. Were you hit very hard on the head?"

"Hard enough," Willoughby said, "but that isn't why I asked the year—"

"Let me guess," the man interrupted. "It's a long story."

Willoughby nodded. The man gave a curt smile, then turned and continued around the last corner. He came to what looked like a dead end, but with a few quick hand movements, he clicked another latch, and the supposed dead end swung open. They entered a large studio of some kind. There were half a dozen mirrors lining each wall, including the one they had just stepped through. Willoughby watched the man close the mirror back carefully. He turned and approached, his gloved hand extended.

"My name is Meyerhold, Vsevelod Meyerhold. I happened to be on my way back from meeting a friend. It is why the bottle of vodka was only half full. I heard the NKVD shouting and heavy gallops coming my way. Then, you appear—a boy, running with a violin case... I thought, *'He is an artist who has been caught outside after curfew.'* I even believed it may explain your clothes. Artists, you know, can be eccentric, but in these times, we must stick together. That is why I helped you." He walked over to a small coal stove, stocked it from a bucket with bits of dry wood first and then coal, and lit it. When it finally glowed and heat started to take an edge off the icy cold, he turned his attention back to Willoughby. He waited a while longer before taking his coat off, and motioned for Willoughby to sit. "So, it seems you are not an artist. Your clothes and shoes are, let us say, unique, and you are bloody and almost frozen. Whether the NKVD got you or not, if you had not found me, I think it doubtful you would have made it to sunrise." He pointed toward a high-back wood chair. "Pull that closer and I will tend to your wound. Then, perhaps, you tell me the long story."

Willoughby had edged closer to the stove and was unwilling to move away from his position. The man chuckled and pulled a rough-hewn wooden chair over. Willoughby sat, allowing the man, who insisted on being called Vsevelod, to wash the cut on his forehead. His new friend poured liquid from a brown bottle onto a clean cloth and pressed it to the cut. The searing pain caused Willoughby to jerk. More gently this time, Vsevelod cupped his hand around the back of Willoughby's head to hold him fast and reapplied the cloth.

"This is alcohol. I know it burns, but it will kill infection."

As the pain eased, Willoughby began in halting sentences.

"I, I do know who you are—at least I've read some about you. It was from a girl who was an admirer of yours."

Vsevelod smiled. "Ah! Now you speak my language! Who might this girl be?"

"You don't know her. She's a friend of mine."

"Try me. I might. As they say, I do get around."

Willoughby winced again as the man applied a fresh coat of the liquid to a gauze pad and held it in place. He began to wrap a long strip of cloth around the full breadth of the head to act as a makeshift bandage. Willoughby leaned back once the man finally released him. He gave a shallow sigh.

"No. You've never been where she is. You can't go there, and I don't think you've met her here. You would have found her clothes even stranger than mine, and I'm sure you would have mentioned that. No, I don't think the two of you have ever met. The girl is a violinist, a very famous one."

"Then surely, I will have heard of her. You say she is an admirer. Where is this place I cannot go? Does this famous violinist have a name?"

Willoughby leaned forward, staring into his hands, and wondering how much to tell Vsevelod. Finally, he decided to go for broke.

"Her name is Sydney, Sydney Senoya. She's from the year 2016, as am I." He looked up, watching the tall man's face.

Vsevelod raised his eyebrows again and pushed back in his chair. He was quiet for a long moment, and then leaned an arm over onto the small table. He stared at Willoughby, studying him for a long moment. "You are certainly fascinating—I will give you that. Perhaps, I think, you may believe what you say. Your dress is certainly outlandish enough. Do you hope to impress me with your acting skill?"

"No. I'm no actor. I told you—I'm a mathematician. I solved the Riemann Hypothesis when I was eleven years old. I was recruited by a secret organization that has a technology that allows one to move back and forth in time. I see flux numbers, floating in air, which allow me to find time holes, and I have…some skill in navigating them."

Vsevelod barked a short laugh. "Some skill, but not a lot," he broke in. "That's why you came to Russian in the dead of winter, at night, with such…clothing. You see, my friend, there are holes to your story."

"Well," Willoughby seemed a bit taken back. "Yeah. I guess. Sydney, the violinist—"

"That's her violin I'm to assume?" Vsevelod broke in again, this time pointing to the violin that Willoughby had dropped to the floor a few feet away.

"Uh," Willoughby winced again—this time from frustration, not pain. "No. The violin is part of the long story. See, Sydney jumped into a hole we found in Port Arthur, Tasmania."

"Port Arthur?"

"Yeah."

"The penal colony? I think it is now a prison."

"Well, yeah. I guess it's a prison now, but in my day, it's just a museum. Anyway, I didn't even know she could identify time holes—she'd kept that from me—and I don't know if she has any skill in navigating them."

"You mean there could be another like you, a female violinist, roaming around out there in the cold?"

"Well, maybe, but I don't think so. I mean, I think it was the violin that brought me here. I'm not sure where she went."

"The violin that is not yours, and not hers, *brought* you here? I thought you said some sort of mathematical hole brought you here?"

Willoughby groaned. "Ahh—see, I told you. It's complicated. When you're untethered in the hole—"

"Untethered?"

Willoughby closed his eyes for a moment, forcing himself to take a deep breath. When he spoke again, it was with forced restraint. "When we use the organization's technology, there is a doorway on both ends of the time hole—kind of like bookends. A sort of narrow path is created and you know where you'll end up. If you just jump into a time hole without those *bookends*, you're just free-floating through time. You can be guided, though, by an object you wear or hold, especially if it is from some previous time or different space because *things* try to find their way back to their own time, especially if they were taken from that time unnaturally. At least, this is what I think. I had this violin, which I think belongs to someone in your time, and it's tied to my *long story* somehow, but I'm not sure how yet, though I'm convinced it was taken unnaturally from its place in time. Sydney jumped into the time hole because a, a... I don't know how to describe him—a demon—was chasing her."

Vsevelod burst out into a hearty laugh. "So now we are jumping into mathematical time holes, led by a magic violin, and chased by a demon! You are a creative soul, I will give you that!"

"I didn't say the violin was magic, and I'm telling the truth." Willoughby stared Vsevelod down, never batting an eye.

"Okay," Vsevelod said, finally settling down. "Let us just say this is quite a tale. Can you show me any proof— any proof at all—that you are a boy from the future? Tell me something that is going to happen. Tell me something only a boy from the future would know."

Willoughby thought for a moment. "I can't tell you things. That would change outcomes." His eyes widened. "I can tell you this though—you disappear for a while, and little is known about you, except personal accounts of your work. It's only when they find your play notes, and papers, hidden in the walls of some famous Russian film director's home, that you really start to be studied again." Willoughby stopped speaking, worried that time may swoop down and yank him from the room, or that the roof would cave in. Vsevelod grew very quiet. His face became serious. He stared at Willoughby for a long moment.

"Why would Sergei put you up to this?" he finally asked.

"Sergei who?" Willoughby said, exasperated. "I don't know a Sergei. I only know this story because Sydney told me about it."

Vsevelod studied him closely. He spoke slowly. "You've never met Sergei Eisenstein?"

Willoughby shook his head. Vsevelod continued to speak.

"No one knows that I have entrusted many of my papers and notes to Sergei, who is far from famous as a film director, but does dabble in the new art form. No one could know of our plan to hide my notes and journals away in the walls of his home should Stalin's purge continue. No one knew but myself, Sergei, and Zinaida. The information is too dangerous to trust to anyone else."

Willoughby looked up. "Zinaida?"

"She is my wife," Vsevelod corrected. "She is back at our apartment. I was… I was restless tonight." The man was silent for a long while, still studying Willoughby.

Willoughby's mind raced. *Zinaida*…Why did that name seem somehow familiar to him? Sydney had told him something about Meyerhold's wife. *Had she mentioned the wife's name, Zinaida?* What, exactly, had she said?

Words came back to him in a flood of sound and image. He was on the crescent slab of beach in Bermuda. Sydney was talking and he was fixed on her sparkling eyes as strands of shiny, black hair blew in front of them, teasing in the breeze. "*His wife was brutally murdered—a woman he loved more than life itself—and then he was arrested and accused of being a spy. He was shot by a firing squad…*"

What about Meyerhold's story, about Sergei Eisenstein, and St. Petersburgh, and Sydney's concert at the Miriinsky Theater, could have anything to do with a violin found in an abandoned cell in Port Arthur, Tasmania? Everything had to be connected somehow, but how? It was like he had pieces of a puzzle that he knew had to fit together somehow, yet no matter how he turned them, and flipped, and tried to tie them together, he could not come to a picture that was clear.

"Okay," Vsevelod finally said, jolting Willoughby back to the present. "For interest's sake, let us say that I believe you. There are still many questions that must be answered. Why are you here? What is that violin? Why is a demon chasing your girlfriend?"

Willoughby knew he had to be very careful. He could only tell Vsevelod about the pieces of the puzzle that did not involve he, or Zinaida, or Eisenstein, or St. Petersburg. In short breaths, he began to unfold his story to the older man. He started with the disappearance of his father, Gustav, and then about his solving of the Riemann Hypothesis. He told of his recruitment by H.S., of his encounters with the being who called himself Beelzebub, of the sinking of the Absconditus, meeting Gustav in the past, his defeat of the Desert Witch, and the journey that had led him through Port Arthur to be here, now. When he completed his story, the wick in the lamp Vsevelod had lit was burning low and dim slits of sunlight were streaming in from two high, narrow windows in the far wall. Vsevelod had not interrupted the tale. He had risen a few times to grab a small hunk of cheese and hard bread, and some weak wine, which Willoughby had nibbled at and sipped as he spoke. Now, however, the man rose and excused himself. He ducked through a narrow door explaining he had to relieve himself. As soon as he left, Willoughby realized he, too, needed to make use of the cramped water closet. When both had visited the washroom, the two settled back into their chairs, studying each other for a long moment.

"So," Vsevelod began, cautiously opening the violin case at Willoughby's feet. "The mystery you weave seems to revolve around this violin. There are initials on it. Do you see?"

Willoughby glanced down "Yes…D.K."

The man considered for a long moment, rubbing at his eyes. "Well, I do know a man with those initials—a violinist named Dimitri Korsakov. His father was a naval hero and renowned composer. He, however, never became more than a musical nomad, a gypsy of sorts. He roamed the countryside collecting and revising local folk music, and spent time in Britain, where there was a scandal of sorts. He escaped the authorities there and returned to Russian, only to be promptly arrested by Lenin for crimes unknown. To my knowledge, he is still in Kresty Prison. I have friends who have contacts there. I can ask around."

Willoughby felt sluggish. Exhaustion, the brutal beating he had suffered (albeit short), and the drain of trying to understand what was really going on, all took their toll on him. Still, he experienced a glimmer of hope. He nodded but did not say anything. He had talked so much over the past hours that he had run out of words to say. His adrenaline had also faded and he could barely sit up straight in the chair. Vsevelod walked to an old wardrobe, pulling out a full change of clothes, a heavy coat, and a fur hat.

"First thing, though, I need to get you back to the apartment. You are exhausted. You need some sleep, as do I. Zinaida can cook us a fine meal when we are rested."

Willoughby did not argue. He simply nodded again and began to slip into the musty-smelling clothes.

"This Sydney," Vsevlod said; "You care for her, don't you?" His eyes were penetrating and his gaze direct. Willoughby met the gaze. He felt as if a dead weight were on his chest.

"Yes. I—it's my job to watch out for her. I, I'm responsible…"

Vsevelod's eyes did not move from him at first. Then he stepped forward and patted Willoughby on the shoulder, a note of tenderness in his voice. "Of course you are, Willoughby. We are all responsible for each other." He walked over to a point below one of the window slits and peered up. Brighter sunlight spilled on his face.

"I think, Mr. Willoughby, the time traveler, that you were sent to Vsevelod for a reason. I am not saying I fully believe you, but as you get to know me—*if* you get to know me—you will find I am a bit of a romantic. We must work together, you and I. We must unravel this, this mystery that time has handed to us…" His voice trailed off for a moment. He placed a hand out, leaning against the wall, still peering up. "Time," he continued, "I have long considered this hazy river we swim in. I am most interested in its patterns. Rhythms spill out of all life, weaving and mixing, creating meaning in a flow, and we call it time. My school of Biomechanics—my work in the theater— revolves around capturing and strengthening the faint and meaningful arcs and lines in these patterns. It is how I make my patrons think, how I force them to deeply feel. Funny you should appear just as all the patterns I have begun to make sense of in my life have begun to unravel. It is as if time has heard my pain, and you, my friend, come in answer to my call."

He became silent, his gaze a million miles away. Willoughby finished pulling on the musty clothes Vsevelod had provided. He placed his hands in the rough pockets of the heavy wool coat his friend had supplied. He took a step forward.

"Where to now?"

Vsevelod jerked himself back into the present.

"Ah," he said, "and now you look much more like a fine Russian!" He gave Willoughby a weak smile. "Follow. Stay close. It is, perhaps, a twenty-minute journey." He spun, checked to make sure the hidden entry to the tunnel maze was properly shut, then led Willoughby to a larger door. They moved quietly up a short staircase to the upper floor. It appeared to be a boarding house, or an artist community of some kind. Willoughby caught glimpses of a painting studio, and a man at a potter's wheel. Vsevelod led them to an ornate front door. He called greetings to a bearded man who they passed in the hall. Willoughby said nothing. He just followed close behind.

Outside, the cold was biting, and the morning sun glinted so bright on the snow that it hurt his eyes. But the city of St. Petersburg was a remarkable sight. Curls of black smoke wafted up above many of the old mansions. The street was crowded with horses and wagons and the occasional Model-T car, which seemed the height of technology for this time period. Vsevelod stopped, looking back. Perhaps he noted the look of wonder in Willoughby's eyes as he looked around, trying to take everything in at once.

"Come," Vsevelod said gently, motioning forward, his face splitting into a low grin. "To most of us, this is not a new world."

Willoughby closed his mouth, realizing how he must appear. He gulped, smiling sheepishly, and hurried to catch up, fighting to keep the slightly too-big boots he wore from being pulled off his feet by the ankle-deep snow.

37

Life Flight

Strange thoughts surfaced in the confusion of T.K.'s mind. There were moments when she felt she was floating. She could look down and see a tall man carefully dragging a body on a sled made from what looked like parts of a nylon tent and a thermal blanket. Then, she felt bumps and pain, and someone was moaning. Then she was looking down again at the strange scene.

It was the person being pulled who was moaning.

A girl with a strange suit on.

Her!

Then there was darkness again, fading into light. A man was yelling into some sort of hand-held device. She heard strange names, Jude and Kensky. She heard a sound like helicopter blades, and someone was lifting her. The pain spiked and then there was only darkness again.

The next thing she was aware of was the sound of Antonio's voice. He was speaking to someone with his back to her. She heard static and crackles and then a voice on the other end with a British accent. She blinked, trying to focus, and noted a tube running down from a silver pole and into her arm. The other end of the tube was connected to a drip bag, hanging from the pole. This was not a hospital. It was cramped and she could hear the drone of rotors. *They were still in the helicopter. How much time had passed?* There was no way for her to know. *How did she get here?* She was barely conscious of her body, still seeming to float outside of herself. There was no sensation of pain. *What did that mean?* Was she alive? She tried to move, but couldn't seem to connect with her own muscles. Maybe she was in that state of hovering, somewhere between life and death. Maybe this was all an elaborate dream. But Antonio seemed so real. Maybe he had found her. Maybe he was trying to save her, and the tube was applying some sort of drug to try to warm her, or to stabilize her, or something. It was all so confusing. Maybe this all was a trick of the mind and she lay dying at the edge of her ancient city, covered by thousands of tons of ice.

She glanced again at Antonio. No, he was real. He had to be. He was *really* there, beside her. She knew it inside. Her heart felt his presence. She tried to focus her thoughts, to listen, to comprehend the words being spoken. *She felt so cold!*

"...stabilized now...resting," the voice said. "Yes...amazing—a whole city under the ice...I do not know what the Russians will do if they find it. I tried, to cave in the way, to make it hard to discover. It should take them a while. ...No, I did not tell them where I found her. I only said it was an off-shoot of one of the caves—that it looked like she had fallen in a crevice and could not get up. I hid the suit and dressed her in the spare clothes in the kit." There was a long pause here, then Antonio's voice continued. "Sumela? That's a mountain monastery, isn't it? I don't know. Where is it? Greece? ...ah, Turkey. Why are you going there? ...*Dragons?* You are serious! ...Oh, I am sure, James Arthur ... No, *you* listen! I won't be able to leave for a while, but it will help no one for you or Hauti to get yourselves killed! …Dragons indeed! Who knows what kind of wild animals they really are. Okay, but promise… James Arthur, you are not listening. We are flying her to McMurdo General, a three-room hospital located here in Antarctica. Once I know she is out of danger, I will take her by ship to a bigger facility in New Zealand… Yes, yes, I will tell her when she is awake, but you are changing the subject. James Arthur, no, James—"

Antonio slammed a fist against the side of the helicopter, swearing under his breath. T.K.'s mind was reeling. *Russians?* What were Russians doing near Atlantis? *Dragons?* Why would James Arthur be at a mountain monastery? What time were they in? They had helicopters…A thought seized her suddenly—if the Russians found the buried city, they may also find the prime hole. She had not been able to destroy it. A blinding sense of purpose surged through her. She had to get up! She had to go back, to destroy the cavern, to bury, for the last time, the beautiful ancient city of her birth. Where were the pendant, the locket… *Were they still around her neck?* She tried to move her lips, to speak, to force her arms or her legs to work, but nothing happened. She tried again. This time, her arm moved slightly, bumping into Antonio's back. He spun.

"You are awake! How are you feeling? Can you speak yet?"

"Back," she managed to croak in a barely audible whisper.

"Back?" Antonio said. "Yes, you are back. We will get you to a doctor."

T.K. shook her head. She tried to lean up, determined. "Back!" she repeated, then added; "Go back...destroy...Russians..."

Antonio looked down for a long moment. "I can't go back, T.K. The Russians will not let me back on their base—they believe I am probably a spy. I did cave in the tunnel that led to the crevice and the city. I only had a quick moment to view the ruins from the crevice where I found you. What I saw was magnificent, but finding you again, my friend—that, *that* was the most magnificent moment of my life! Once you are safe and recovered, we can think what to do. We will try to ensure that no one ever finds an intact Atlantis."

"P-pendant," T.K. managed.

Again, Antonio took several long moments trying to determine what T.K. was trying to say. Finally, he shook his head. "I am sorry, Tainken. I found no pendant."

"In," T.K. began, "ci...ty. Prime hole facili..." her voice failed.

"I did not see the prime hole facility. I saw only ruins. Surely the technology is not functioning after all these years."

"Fully," T.K. managed after some time. "Fully," she repeated.

A sudden look of concern clouded Antonio's face. After another long moment, he leaned back with a sigh. "That is not good."

"Sydney," Tainken whispered, "will fall."

"Yes," Antonio said softly. "We found your engraving in the ruins off the coast of India. Willoughby is aware of the concern. He is watching over her. They are heading to Tasmania. Dr. J and Hauti are in France now, but heading to a monastery in the northern mountains of Turkey. I am not exactly sure why."

"Su...Sumela," Tainken said, her voice seeming far away.

"Yes. You heard?"

"Monastery..." T.K. managed, "...wall..." Her voice faded.

"*That* wall?" Antonio thought for a moment. T.K. seemed out again. He grabbed his SAT phone and dialed hurriedly. When Dr. J's voicemail clicked on, he slammed a fist against the side of the copter.

"James Arthur—it's, Antonio. T.K. was awake a few moments. She seems to believe that Sydney's fall may occur in Sumela. Watch any monastery walls! Call me when you get this." He tried another number and got a "Your call cannot be completed at this time," message. He tried Sydney's number with the same result. "Willoughby's not answering his phone, Sydney's not answering hers. James Arthur and Hauti may be walking into a trap, and I am in the Antarctic," he mumbled, concern in his eyes. He thought quietly for another moment. The helicopter bumped through a bit of turbulence, causing T.K to moan in pain. Antonio turned and gently placed his hands on her shoulders, pinning her tightly to the cot. When the turbulence faded, he again picked up his satellite phone and dialed. After only a few seconds, he spoke. "Sian? Yes, this is Antonio. I am afraid we may have a problem..."

When Antonio completed his phone conversation with the artificial intelligence, he tucked the phone back into his pack. He pushed closer to T.K. and began to stroke her hair. "What a life we lead," he whispered, mostly to himself.

To his surprise, T.K. responded. "H.S..." she moaned, as if in her sleep. Antonio saw a tear slip down the side of her cheek. He remembered in that moment that T.K. had been pulled from the attack of the plesiosaurs at the Jurassic Sea facility before she knew about the fate of H.S. He realized she must be wondering if H.S. survived. He could only imagine what she had been through over the months they had been apart. Just seeing the frozen ruins of her beautiful city of Atlantis, and then the battle with... whatever that was under the ice. He watched another tear slide down her cheek and reached to take her hand.

"There was nothing we could do. It happened very fast." His voice went quiet for a moment and then he added, "But, you are back with me, and I am not letting you go... I will *not* lose you again."

Tainken did not stir or say anything, but Antonio did sense a slight twitch of her fingers, as if she were trying to squeeze his hand back. Then, the hand went limp.

38

The Anatomy of Movement

"So, you have come to study with Vsevolod, to learn more about his theories of Biomechanics for the Theater?"

The woman's accent was noticeable, but she spoke fluent English. She was not particularly tall, but had a regal stance with her head held high, and that, coupled with her thin frame, gave her a sense of height. She was lean-boned, with a pleasant face, and she dressed in a style that bespoke both sophistication and elegance. It was easy to see that movement itself was an art form to this woman. With every small change in posture, with every reach of her hand, or expression from her face, there was a hint of meaning, a whisper of purposed intelligence. She was a woman who controlled her circumstances—not one to be trifled with. Willoughby barely remembered having arrived at the apartment that Vsevolod and Zinaida shared. It had been quite early in the morning. He had been shown to a comfortable parlor couch, had leaned back into the cushions and the world had faded to oblivion. He awoke to the smell of baked bread and bacon. Zinaida had placed a plate of steaming buttered bread, bacon, and scrambled eggs onto a small, ornate table in a narrow nook at one side of the parlor. Zinaida was sitting there, staring somewhat blankly at a wall of framed pictures. The photos, depicting different moments in her and Vsevelod's careers, were lit by the flickering glow of a hurricane lamp which acted as a centerpiece for the table. When she noted his attempt to sit up, rubbing his eyes, she invited him to the table. After a few tries, he finally made it to his feet. Once he had seated himself at the table, she commanded him to eat, and then watched him like a curious cat, waiting to see how he would respond.

"Uh, sure," he finally said, hurriedly swallowing. He vaguely remembered being introduced to Zinaida, but he had no idea what Vsevelod had told her about who he was and why he was here. He knew next to nothing about his new friend's theory of Biomechanics, but did remember several references to it in his research on the Mariinsky Theater. Meyerhold had first directed there in 1908 or 1909 he seemed to recall. It was a famous staging of the opera *Tristan and Isolde.*

Willoughby had been led to the theater once before— by the sound of Sydney's playing. His first venture into an untethered time hole had taken him to a concert at the Mariinsky in late October, 2015. He sensed then that this was not an arbitrary occurrence. Sydney had told him once that Vsevelod's theories had revolutionized stagecraft. She was a passionate fan of his. He assumed that's why she had chosen one of his favorite theaters for her concert. He thought back, trying to remember what he had read about the man's specific techniques.

Biomechanics of the Theater, one notation had stated, drew heavily upon concepts of human motion, using pace, rhythm, and a focus on specific movements to help extend a text's emotional impact. The idea was that movement could be used to communicate at a subliminal level, one that emotionally enhanced the theme of the spoken words and music. Sydney had used this concept in the choreography of her unique theatrical performances. *What was her connection to this time, these people?*

Zinaida raised an eyebrow, waiting for him to continue.

"Well, I think it's a concept that could revolutionize theater. It sort of brings a fourth dimension into three-dimensional space... I want to know more."

This seemed to appease the probing eyes leveled on him. Zinaida lifted a cup of steaming liquid and took a sip. "Our world is built on movement—movements that seem random and unfocused. But observe closer and you find underlying themes that are hidden to the casual observer. All movement has its roots and causes, often unseen, but still felt at some level by the unconscious. By mining these rifts and veins, by unraveling the anatomy of movement around us, Vsevelod is appealing to a level that is hidden below conscious thought. It allows him to use the stage to convey hidden meaning—to unleash barely conscious emotions. The theatrical experience then gives the viewer a chance to see beyond the context of a piece and understand simple, raw truths that lay at its core. Do you understand what I am saying?"

Willoughby almost let his mouth drop open. *Did all people in this time speak in such intellectually charged sentences?* He thought through what she had said, and then pursed his lips. "It's a fascinating concept. It could help one bypass censorship."

Zinaida smiled. "You are very bright for one so young." She took another sip from her steaming mug.

Willoughby took a bite of the still-warm buttered bread. It was a little heavy, but he was hungry enough that anything tasted good. "Where is Vsevelod?

"He went to the prison to discuss something with a man we know there. He said it had something to do with the violin you carry. Do you play?"

"No," Willoughby admitted, "but a good friend of mine does. I'm looking for her."

"Ah! I sense a romantic connection. Did she come with you to Russian? You are brave to come into Russian at such a time as this. How did you come? By train? By ship?"

"Well," Willoughby thought, "I met this girl on a ship..."

"The best way!" Zinaida smiled, looking down into the steam of her coffee. "Oh, to be young again, and full of the energy for adventure! Is she a violinist?"

"Yes," Willoughby said, not sure what else to say.

"How is she related to Dimitri?"

"Dimitri?"

"*Dimitri Korsakov*—the man Vsevelod went to see in Kresky prison." Zinaida seemed at once suspicious and annoyed.

"Oh, Dimitri," Willoughby said. He tried to come up with some tale that would make sense, but Zinaida's eyes were shrewd and intelligent. He knew she would see through any lie. He sighed. "Truth is, I don't know Dimitri. I just found a very nice violin that had initials carved into it, and Vsevelod thought Dimitri might know who it belonged to. The girl I'm looking for—her name is Sydney—had been playing the violin just before she, she disappeared. I'm hoping it will eventually lead us to her."

Zinaida studied him for a long moment. "You seem very young to be on your own."

"I'm seventeen," Willoughby said. "I could draw a man's wage." He thought this was correct for this time period and area of the world. *Why hadn't he listened better in World History and Geography?*

Zinaida smiled, despite herself. "So you are," she said thoughtfully. "You are not a runaway, are you? Where are your parents? Did they come with you to Russian?"

"No. They're back in America. They think I'm in India at a jungle preserve."

Zinaida's eyebrows again raised when the back door to the kitchen burst open and a frosted and half-frozen Vsevelod bustled in, slamming the door behind him. He pulled his wool hat off, slapping it against his thigh, and then strode straight to Zinaida, angling his body to kiss her gently, yet not let a single snowflake fall onto her dress or skin. He spoke to her in Russian and she answered, flashing a shy smile toward Willoughby.

Willoughby caught Vsevelod's eye. "What did she say?"

"She wants to know if I think you are an American spy."

"What did you tell her?"

Vsevelod gave a hearty laugh. "While I am sure you are dangerous in your own way, you are not quite secret agent material."

Zinaida joined in with a soft chuckle, placing a hand over her mouth to hide her amusement. Willoughby wasn't sure, but he had the feeling he had been slightly insulted. The merriment of his hosts was contagious, however, and he found himself smiling as well. He decided to play along.

"So, you don't think my violin case hides a pop-out sabre?"

Vsevelod barked a short laugh. "I'm sure it does! And those clothes you were wearing, the ones that made you so inconspicuous—they are most certainly OSS issue, right?" Vsevelod winked. "I think Zinaida wants to keep them for our costume chest."

Willoughby had no idea what the OSS was (possibly a predecessor to the CIA?), but he continued to smile, realizing for the first time how absurd he must have appeared in his wind-breaker, sneakers, and *"Imagine Dragons"* t-shirt. After all, it was the middle of a Russian winter night in 1933. As the kitchen quieted, Vsevelod clapped him on the shoulder.

"But, now to business. We have much to discuss." He inspected Willoughby's plate, which was only half empty. "You must finish your, your dinner, which seems suspiciously like breakfast." He looked up at Zinaida who gave a nonchalant shrug. She stood and walked over to the stove, refilling her cup with steaming liquid, then left the room, the hint of a smile still on her face. Willoughby seemed to notice the steaming cup in front of his own plate for the first time. He picked it up and sipped. The hot liquid—brown like coffee, but with a distinctive barley taste—felt good going down. Vsevelod looked back to him.

"Cooking is not one of Zinaida's strong points, but still—eat! You need your strength. Now, to business." In one swift movement, the man peeled his coat off and hung it on a peg near the stove. He grabbed a chair, spun it around so the back faced the table, and plopped down onto it, his arms resting on the chair back as he watched

Willoughby eat, the spark of amusement gone from his eyes now.

"I was able to meet with Dimitri in a private audience. We spoke for over an hour. He had an…interesting tale to tell."

"Did it include a girl with long, black hair?"

"Yes—hair that shined like the starlight. I think he referred to her as an angel." Vsevelod leaned back, gripping the chair with thin but strong hands. "It happened almost two years ago, he says. He was walking past the Miriiski Theater after midnight on his way home from a late night with friends. He heard music—music like he had never heard before. Its beauty and perfection intrigued him. He was working as a musician in the stage ensemble at the time and had a key to the back door. So, he unlocked it and went in to see who was playing so beautifully at such a late hour. He saw what he thought to be an apparition, in strange clothes, playing her violin in the flickering footlights of the stage. 'She was pure vision,' he told me. 'Her skin was bone white. Her features were delicate and sculptured. She was lost in her music, her body swaying with a grace and rhythm that was not of this world.'"

"That sounds like Sydney," Willoughby mumbled, shoveling in another fork full of eggs and finishing off the bacon.

Vsevelod watched him a moment. "Dimitri recognized the music she was playing. It was music that had been passed down in his family from father to son. It was forbidden music, heard once long ago in a far country, when angels sang it in the skies. He had been forbidden by his father to write the music down. It was never supposed to be played all the way through, not until the end of days.

He was told simply to memorize it, to remember it, to pass it on to his son when the time was right."

Willoughby stopped chewing. He narrowed his eyes. "But he did write it down."

Vsevelod raised an eyebrow. "Yes. He played it all the way through to himself, and nothing happened. The world did not burn. That is part of the reason he did not hold to the superstitious nature of his people. He did find the music incredibly beautiful—too beautiful not to write out. He had recorded the score on rough parchment and hidden it on his person, telling himself he would decide later when and how he would share it.

"Now, he was hearing this vision or angel play it. He wondered if God had found him out, if this angel had been sent to punish him. He stepped forward onto the stage, interrupting the angel's playing. 'Are you here for me?' he asked. It took her a moment to untangle her thoughts from her music. She seemed confused. 'I heard you playing the forbidden music,' he told her. 'I thought it was because you knew I had written it down.' She commanded him to explain. He recounted the edicts of the elders, telling her of the origins of the music, and the command that it never be written down. She replied, boring into him with fiery eyes that she played only music that *had* been written down. Dimitri knew then that his great mistake was known. She knew that he had disgraced his fathers and himself. He had thought the written music would someday make him rich—that it would bring him good luck."

"But it didn't."

"Well, it certainly did not bring him fortune. His father once told him that he believed it to be the creation song, sung once at the beginning of the world, once at this world's meridian of time, and once at the end of days—that it was the music of God's heartbeat, that it was to be sung only when God was so near that he could save or destroy man with the merest flick of His hand. According to the stories of his people, the song had heralded the appearance of a strange star in the heavens, one that was there only a short time. He is not sure how many generations the song has been passed down. His people were said to preserve it according to the instructions of *mal'ak ha-mashhit*—the *destroying angel*."

Vsevelod moved toward the stove and poured himself his own cup of hot liquid. Willoughby continued to sip at his.

"Anyway," Vsevelod continued, "now that he was caught in his mistake, he decided the only way to make it right was to destroy the written score. He pulled it out of the breast pocket where it was hidden, walked to one of the theater footlights, and took the last page of the score, holding it up to the flickering flame. The *angel* girl had watched for a moment with mute horror, then had rushed at him, shrieking for him to put the flame out. He did so, managing to save all but the bottom two stanzas of one page. She was furious at him. She told him he had no right to destroy such beautiful music. The score, she told him, should never be destroyed. She made him guardian of it. She told me to guard it with his life, even with his soul. He pointed it out to me. It is hidden in the lining of his jacket. He thinks he is supposed to meet the angel again someday and give the music back. He is desperate for the time when he can meet her again and can be rid of the heavy burden of the parchment. He is convinced that, only then, will he be at peace. He asked if, when you find this girl, you could have her take the score so he can be released. Can you honor his request?"

Willoughby looked away, uncomfortable with Vsevelod's intense gaze. "I, I'm not sure. It's complicated." He thought for a moment and then looked up. "You said your friend interrupted the angel—he kept her from completing the song, the music that the final malak, or whatever, would play to end all days."

"Yes, that is what he said. What does that mean?"

Willoughby studied his plate, tapping his fork absently against the smooth, white porcelain. He thought of Beelzebub's panic, of his last words. "*I know how to control the anomaly—she does not! Time will rip us apart. If I cannot stop her, you have doomed us all!*" Part of this didn't make sense. If this music was somehow the anomaly that his nemesis spoke of, why was he concerned? Sydney didn't have the full score. *Unless the scrap of parchment he had found in the violin and had put in his box WAS the missing stanzas!* But, this Dimitri said he burned the bottom two stanzas when he set fire to the parchment score. The scrap couldn't be the bottom two stanzas. None of this made sense. Had Beelzebub somehow copied these bottom two stanzas before the parchment was burned? *Why?* He seemed to be trying to stop the anomaly. Why had Sydney's whole demeanor seemed to have changed suddenly at the sound of this music, at the sound of this song? *Could Sydney actually be this, this destroying angel?*

He finally looked back up at Vsevelod. "Please think carefully—is this everything that Dimitri told you?"

"No," Vsevelod said slowly. "We spoke of many things. Much does not apply to you." He paused, then his eyes lit up. "But one other thing may interest you—I asked where he thought we should look if we wanted to find this angel or girl again. He started to shake his head, like he had no idea, but then, he stopped. 'There is a monastery,' he told me, 'built on a mountain. It is said to be a place of miracles. Many years ago, a Black Madonna was found in a cave. Some say it was made by Saint Luke. But my people tell a different story. The monastery is called Sumela, and it is located in the northwest mountains of Turkey, near the southern coast of the Black Sea. An old legend among my people claims this is the place where the voice of the angels first sang. It is where we got the song we are forbidden to play. The legend claims that the angels will come back to the same sky to sing for the last time at the end of days. That is where I would go if I were trying to find this angel of my life. I would try to get her to take this score, this scar on my soul. You can't miss the monastery,' he told me. 'It is built right on the—"

"Edge of a cliff," Willoughby completed.

"Yes. How is it that you seem able to complete my thoughts before I speak them?"

Willoughby went suddenly pale. He looked up, his voice seeming far away. "I need to go back to the Mariinsky tonight. I need to jump into the time hole, but there can be no one around to see. Could you get me there and distract the guards?"

It was Vsevelod's turn to pause. He studied Willoughby for a long moment. Zinaida came back into the room carrying her cup. She sat at the table.

"Have you boys finished with your little chat?"

Vsevelod ignored the question. "Willoughby, if that is really your name—I do not know if I should help you. In the end, I am not sure what this is about. There are things you are not telling me and I believe I know why. Perhaps you have good reason. There are also things I am not telling you. I sense something about you. I have not felt this since I was a young boy. I recall a day when a sudden storm came down from the north. Its black clouds were like the shoulders of a giant and it walked on legs of lightning. The thunder shook me in my boots. I should have been terrified, and I was, but I was also fascinated. There was such raw power being wielded. It made me feel at once invulnerable and small.

"I sense terrifying forces at work in your life, wherever you are from. Awesome and wonderful, but at the same time, terrifying. I smell the power of a storm building. I can see it in my mind. I have made a life of digging at the roots of thought, idea, belief, in order to understand the rhythms of the soul. Yours is a new rhythm, a beat I do not know, one I have never heard. I do know this, though. Yours is a life with resonance—one that spills over its borders like a wave breaking over the rocks of a reef. You do, by the nature of who you are, what I do with my science of movement. You wake up minds—you inspire them to see new possibilities, to seek to be the author of their fate and not simply its victim. That is a good thing, though it is not always possible, I warn you of this."

He sat back in his chair, leaving the perfect space for dramatic pause, and then leaned in. "I have watched my world. I think if I had lived in yours, I might have been one of your Observations, Inc. I have learned that power, like motion, is easy to align with, but difficult to control. People of power are like storms—they have the potential to rage out of control. They do not hesitate to annihilate, or perhaps, to absorb. I have worked to create counter rhythm, to carve for myself a space in the confusion of my world, but if the storm is powerful enough, I cannot stand in its way. It is as simple as that. I must face it. You have a uniqueness about you, Willoughby. That, too, is good, but sometimes, the uniqueness of a single voice is not enough. Sometimes, it takes a unity of voices to subdue the coming storm. Do you understand what I'm telling you?"

Willoughby thought of Sydney, of his team, his friends. He considered the thin, gaunt face of Vsevelod Meyerhold, looking past the tired smile, the bright, sharp eyes, the balding head. He looked at Zinaida, her eyes studying his every move. These were new friends, even though they may never get to truly know him, nor he them. They were kindred souls, though, traversing a fog of flowing time, adrift in time's grand sea, swapping stories, gauging impressions, offering absolution. He thought of the musical score Sydney had once written for this man, based upon a single letter Vsevelod wrote to Zinaida. In that letter, Vsevelod had told of the coming of a terrifying, but fascinating storm. He thought of the future of these two he now considered friends.

A storm was coming for them, and yet he couldn't tell them. Even now, it was trickling down upon them. The power of a revolution, so easy to align with, yet so terrifyingly difficult to control, was tightening its grip upon the country, squeezing like a vice. Power, born out of hatred, out of rage, would soon cut them down, bent on full annihilation. Yet a unity born of the mind—of thoughts and ideas—would save their words, their legacy, and would map them into the passages of time. It was a unity of heart that Willoughby most felt in the weight of this moment, though. He and Vsevelod were kindred to the bone, and the man was attempting to pass along a bit of his own uniqueness, the power of his intellect, of his words, to this new friend who claimed to be a voice of the future. Yes, Willoughby did understand what Vsevelod was trying to say. No voice spoken from a place of care and kindness is ever alone.

He felt a sting in his eyes and swallowed hard. "I, uh, I think so. I wish I didn't have to leave just yet, but I do. I need it to be as soon as possible." That was the best he could manage.

"Yes, you do need to leave," was all Vsevelod would say. He finally looked at Zinaida. "I can take him to Mariinsky just past the stroke of 10. The streets will not be completely empty, but enough, and the guards will not yet be on full alert."

Willoughby nodded. Zinaida reached over and stroked his cheek. Only then did he realize that a single tear had escaped his rapid blinking.

"You will find her," Zinaida said softly, confidently. "You are strong. You will find her. Of this I have no doubt."

39

Secrets of Sumela

As Vsevelod led Willoughby toward the Mariinsky Theater, cathedral bells tolled across the oppressive night. St. Petersburgh was bitterly cold—a damp cold that seemed to permeate the inky blackness, thick with chimney soot, lamp oil, and other smells strange and unknown to Willoughby. The ten chimes of the bells were heavy, chilling, resolute, and unerringly complete. As the ringing finally stilled, fading echoes pierced him with sounds he would not soon forget. This was a place lost to time—an echo of something that existed once, but should not exist now, at least, not for him. The echoes fused and were swallowed by the whine of a rising gale. A storm was coming in, and the irony of the fact was not lost to either Willoughby or Vsevelod. His new friend did little more than tap him on the shoulder as they skirted dark corners, moving from shadow to shadow. Their indirect route finally emerged a few meters away from the silent and ghost-like Mariinsky. Willoughby headed toward the theater, giving Vsevelod a tight smile and thumbs up, trying to keep his teeth from chattering. His new friends had allowed him to keep the oversized boots, coat, gloves, and cap they gave him earlier.

Vsevelod barely seemed to notice. He turned abruptly and called to a stout man who had turned in their direction from across the way. The man seemed a friend, and the two hurried across the street to a dark alcove, gave each other a brusque hug, and spoke in hushed tones. Willoughby knew his friend was trying to distract the man, and silently thanked him for it, heading up the icy steps to the front entry of the Mariinsky. The time hole was almost in the same place as when he saw it earlier. It pulsed with a hidden intensity—one that only Willoughby could see—directly across from the theater's left-most bank of windows.

Pausing a moment to get his bearings, he searched the glowing number strings, hoping to determine the heart of the hole where the pull would be strongest. The lines seemed to be thinning, oozing out from an indistinct ball in thin, spidery lines. Their glow seemed to flicker and fade slightly with every passing moment. He was running out of time.

Pushing into a slow jog, he trained his eyes at the center of the indistinct ball. He broke into a flat-out run just before he dove, headlong, into the sea of numbers.

There was a momentary flash, and then a familiar tug. He felt the sensation of being yanked upward. The air around him exploded in a bright array of whizzing, curling number strings, flowing past him. He held an image of Sydney in his mind, and before he even had time to think, a string flashed just to his right. He recognized it and instinctively grabbed it. It spun him around and down, hurtling him through the flow until he tumbled out of the time stream, having been stretched, dissected, and slammed back together, falling from a hole that was at least thirty feet above ground. Luckily, he fell straight toward a stand of thick trees, and after a few botched attempts at grabbing hold of a passing limb, he finally slowed himself enough to hang on, and then climbed his way down to the cold earth. While brushing himself off and checking his cuts and bruises, he noted through breaks in the trees that the sky above was dim and brooding.

It was an unfamiliar landscape. Tall, green pines surrounded him on all sides. He could hear and catch glimpses of a roaring stream far below. He sensed the incline of a hill, and tilting his head up, he caught a glimpse of a solid rock wall that rose to sharp, craggy peaks. He moved to get a better look, searching for any sign that Sydney or the others had been there. Nothing. *Had he come to the wrong place, the wrong time?* Then, his eye caught sight of something swooping low over the trees. It had leathery wings, like a bat, but was far too large to be any species of bat he was aware of. He peered closer. It was an odd-looking creature with a dark, scaly body and a long, thinning tail. His first thought was that he had somehow found his way back to a dinosaur era and this was some sort of pterodactyl, but the head and the body were larger, and it had four stubby legs, like a lizard. Also, the trees and shrubbery around him were too contemporary. It most resembled a flying lizard, or how he might imagine a small dragon to appear.

He stood, awe-struck for a moment as the creature swooped up the sheer rock face, then completed brushing himself off and moved to a small opening to his right. He wanted to catch another glimpse of the creature if he could. He stepped out from the dim shadows of what appeared to be an overcast day and found the sky roiling with black and gray clouds. A storm was brewing here, too. *Was it the same storm?* High up the cliff rock face and

slightly to his left, he saw what he had been hoping for—
the dark stonework of an ancient monastery looming up
from the gray stone. It seemed to hang on a narrow ledge
of rock about two hundred meters up the cliff face,
melding with the wall as if it were part of the rock face
itself. The beast that had swooped over him only moments
ago, must have climbed the cliff face with alarming speed
as it sat attentively, now, perched atop the deep red roof of
the monastery. A second creature of roughly the same size
and shape sat atop one of the right-most roof pinnacles
amid a row of what looked like stone chimneys. It made
itself known by spreading its wings and issuing a highly
unnatural call, followed by a belch of pure flame that
pierced the gray gloom.

The creature on the red roof answered by letting go
its own curl of flame, then launching itself from the roof
and circling the abbey. It rose to only a few feet above the
middle spire, and hovered for a moment, eyeing a row of
chimneys. The two creatures peered at each other,
seemingly locked in a moment of intense communication,
and then the flying creature dropped down to alight just
below the roof line in a high arched alcove. The dragon-
like creature on the pinnacle launched now and circled the
roof top twice. It then swooped in to alight in a stone
alcove on the other side of what appeared to be a narrow
porch. Willoughby studied the porch carefully. He
counted eight stone archways along its breadth, with high
windows forming the back of each archway. There were
several hooded figures on the left end of the porch, and a
single figure far to the right.

He sensed something from the single figure. The
figure was tall, not hooded, but dressed in black. It had
silver hair and pale skin, and Willoughby knew its

profile—it was *Beelzebub*. As if sensing he had been discovered, the single figure stepped out of view, into the dark shadows between two of the high arched openings. The small dragon nearest the spot lunged inward and spat a belch of fire. This seemed to cause a chain reaction that left the entire porch engulfed in an odd flame.

As he watched, however, Willoughby realized that the porch itself was not burning. He was witnessing a trick he had seen before—an intersection of time grids to create an illusion using some point in the past when the porch had burned completely to overlap the present when it wasn't burning at all. There was warmth and visual fireworks, but no real danger to the porch in the present time.

The trick was enough, however, to push the small dragon-creature away, back into an archway, and hold the beast at bay. The other visible figures on the porch froze. *Yes*, Willoughby thought, *he has created a junction*. The junction did not seem to extend beyond the porch, however, and did not affect the dragon-like creatures. Suddenly, another figure appeared, also seeming unaffected. This figure was obviously female. *It was Sydney!* She jumped up onto the ledge of one of the arched openings, close to the center of the porch. Beelzebub stepped out from the shadows. Sydney seemed to be edging precariously close to a point of no return. The sheer drop from the monastery had to be at least two to three hundred meters. Her right hand held high her bow, her left hand held her violin. She lifted the instrument to her chin, pointing her bow and seeming to yell something at Beelzebub, but he could not make the words out.

"*Sydney!*" he screamed, realizing as he did so that he was too far away for anyone in the monastery to hear him. He scanned the full cliff face. There was no sign of anyone else. He could make out no faces in the monastery windows or additional threats near Sydney on the wall. *Why was she so close to the edge?* One stumble and she could fall. He had to get up there, and fast! His mind raced. He was at least a hundred, maybe two hundred meters away from the rock face. A slow, sloping path zig-zagged its way up to the Monastery doors. Even at top speed, Willoughby doubted he could get to Sydney in time. He frantically combed through his experiences with time travel and with this creature who called himself Beelzebub. His mind grabbed hold of the time he had saved Sydney from a Mayan Priest. They were high on a mountain of frozen mummies in Peru, and the Priest had seemed anxious to turn Sydney into yet another of his frozen sacrifices. Willoughby had been half frozen himself, but had seen in the air between he and the Priest, a series of weaknesses in the time grid—a series of budding time holes he could interconnect to create a flow outside the time grid. He had successfully aligned them so he could move his physical presence across the short span through a series of time junctions. The effect was that he disappeared from the spot where he stood and reappeared directly in front of the Priest in the wink of an eye, with no apparent passage of time. This had been enough to scare away the Priest. Could he use the trick to save Sydney again, this time using it to get him to her before she fell?

He focused, concentrating, determined to pull up the mental sense that let him map the time continuum around him. He pushed back all thoughts of the dragon-creatures, of Sydney's strange behavior when she had jumped into the time hole, and everything else. His single thought was how to get to Sydney, how to keep her from falling off that wall.

At first, he saw nothing in the air around him. Then, the air became alive with massive currents of flowing equations. This was the most active spot of ground he had ever seen in the short time he had been able to use his gift. It seemed like there were small holes and larger holes everywhere. He quickly began to chart a way up the side of the mountain in his mind, anchoring the path to a strong hole only a few meters down from the Monastery entrance.

The calculations churned around him as he glanced one last time at Sydney. She was still looking to her right, fury in her gestures and posture. With a twist of his wrist, he snatched at the first equation, and through a barely perceptible mental exertion, he willed his form to flow along the narrow tunnel that led him from one time hole to the next, skimming over them like an air hockey puck skimming over puffs of forced air. In a blink, he was standing on the dirt, stone-riddled path with the entrance to the monastery just in sight, maybe ten meters or so up a steep incline.

A half dozen small out buildings with red-tiled roofs and ruins dotted the path on both sides. He raced up the root entangled trail past the out buildings to a long, narrow stone staircase. It led to a single stone doorway which was the only visible entrance to the monastery. The door was fully ajar.

Panting for breath, Willoughby scanned for guards, or monks, or signs of other people around the doorway. He saw no one. He took the stairs three at a time and ducked in through the open door. He was immediately confronted with another stone stairway. This one led down toward an inner courtyard. He glimpsed buildings on both sides of the courtyard, each with their own terraced entrance. To the left, he saw a stone chapel, built right into the side of the mountain. It was adorned on all sides with faded and weathered frescos.

In a blink, sound suddenly returned to the world around him. There was the whine of the wind, and a sound of scuffling below. Only then did he remember the junction he had seen Beelzebub create, freezing all figures except Sydney and the dragons. For some reason, the junction had been dropped, or had been broken. He followed the scuffling sounds. In an open space, slightly to the left and around a corner, he glimpsed two familiar figures. His heart leapt with relief—it was Hauti and James Arthur. They were fighting a trio of hooded goons, and handling them quite nicely. He bounded down the stairs two at a time.

While racing toward his friends, however, he glimpsed an even more heated battle on a further level, about ten feet below. The contest was taking place directly in front of the stone chapel. A tall, large man in a black cloak was battling four men in brown hooded robes. The brown robes were identical to the ones worn by the three goons fighting Hauti and Dr. J.

Willoughby did not recognize the large man, but his smooth, swift movements and the deft efficiency of his fighting betrayed him as a martial arts master—possibly even a Ninja. Returning his attention to his friends, he called out as he neared the bottom of the stairs.

Hauti, who was holding her own against a tall, thin man, glanced over. She moved quickly out of range as the man swished a knife blade at her, and then used a combination of punches and kicks to send him sprawling. Despite her heavy breathing, she looked back and winked.

James Arthur was worse off. The two goons on him were thick-set and muscled. They had managed to trip him, pinning him to the stone floor of the courtyard. One man forced a heavy club to Dr. J's throat while the other pulled out a long knife.

Willoughby clicked his mind to focus on the time grid in the courtyard. Numbers swam thick all around the fighting figures. This space was obviously unique, a place where many time lines crossed and intersected. Creating a junction would be elementary here. He reached the bottom step just as the man freed the knife from its place in his robe and raised it high.

Just as Hauti careened into the back of the knife-wielding man, Willoughby lowered his shoulder and hit into the man with the club. The goon hit by Hauti fell hard, his knife skittering across the floor. The man with the club cracked his head against a stone support and fell as well. The first goon was up in a flash, scampering after his lost knife. Willoughby quickly knelt next to James Arthur so he was sure their bodies were touching, grabbed two time strings, and forged a junction. Once before, according to Beelzebub, he had forged a junction purely with his mind. He wasn't sure how he had done it, though, and he didn't have time to waste experimenting, so he went with what he knew. A junction created this way was temporary, he knew, but it would do the job, and whoever he was touching when it formed would be fully conscious and unaffected by the time bubble that formed around them. Everyone in the courtyard except for James Arthur froze. Dr. J leaned back for a moment, trying to get his breath. He then slowly rolled over and pushed to his knees.

"Willoughby... You, my friend, have very...good...timing." He gasped, still panting. "Where'd you come from?"

"Long story," Willoughby said, pushing to his feet, and helping Dr. J stand. "I don't have time to go into it. I don't know how far this junction extends, and anyway, I know it doesn't affect Beelzebub."

"He's here? You sure?"

"Yeah. He's here. How do I get to Sydney?"

"She's here?"

"I saw them both on an outward-facing porch. You didn't know she was here? I thought you were here trying to rescue her?"

"Well, we, we are," James Arthur said. He walked over and tried to pick up the club from the ground. The wood club wouldn't budge.

"It's a junction," Willoughby said. "Things from other timelines are frozen."

James Arthur walked over to the man skittering for the knife and kicked him as hard as he could with the sole of his boot.

"You know he won't even feel that when I dissolve the junction," Willoughby said. "It really didn't accomplish anything."

"That," James Arthur said, taking another jab at the face, "is where you are wrong, my friend. It made," he wiped blood from his face and lip, "*me* feel a lot better." He had looked over toward Hauti and seemed torn at whether to station himself by the club and knife on the stone nearby, or station himself to protect her.

"Willoughby," a new, deeper voice spoke. Willoughby looked up to see the tall man with the black robe hurrying toward them. "I will help them. Your task is not here. Sydney is through that door." The strange man with dark marks on his face and most of his head hidden in the shadow of his hood pointed to a door at the top of a narrow set of steps. The steps led from the lower courtyard to a small wooden door. "Through the room onto the porch. I sent the dragons ahead to protect her as best they can, but you must hurry."

"*Dragons?* Who are you?" Willoughby asked, his eyes narrowing. "Why does the junction not affect you?"

"There is no time. You must go," the man repeated.

"He—this is the guy sent by the *friend*," James Arthur said. "You know, the one that hologram of Sam told us about. At least, we think so. He goes by the *keeper*, and he keeps strange creatures…like, like what he said—dragons. He's the one who brought us here. He told us this is where we would find Sydney. He's on our side. I think."

Willoughby looked at the strange man in black robes. The man's eyes seemed to glisten, but the look was earnest and concerned. He looked beyond the tall figure and noted that at least two of the four men the *keeper* had been fighting were down and seemingly incapacitated.

"Can you protect my friends?" Willoughby asked.

The man in the black robe nodded.

"Okay," Willoughby glanced over at Dr. J, purpose in his glare as he started for the lower porch and the stone steps. "I'll dissolve the junction when I reach the door." He barely noted a slight nod of agreement from the face under the black hood. Glancing over toward the stone chapel one last time, he recognized the face of one of the downed men. It was the bloated, bleached face of Woolfer, one of the hijackers from the *Absconditus*. Looking away, he steeled his mind and hurried up the stone steps, stopping one last time near the wooden door for a quick glance back. The man in the black robe had positioned himself near Hauti. James Arthur was at the knife, ready to grab it and then spring for the club. He unlatched and opened the wooden door and, while stepping quickly through, dissolved the junction. He heard the chaos reach a new pitch below as the goons bellowed their frustration at suddenly finding their marks had magically relocated. He closed and latched the door quietly. Best that the goons below not know he had snuck through. He hurried quickly through some sort of study to a back hall. He could hear the dragons now and smell the sulphur of their flame.

Near the end of the narrow hall, a door opened onto the porch. One huge goon lay sprawled onto the floor in a pool of blood, his throat burned and ripped to shreds, his head barely attached to its still smoldering body. Another smaller man was pressed back against the wall just beyond the door—only, it wasn't really a man. The eyes were bleached white and lifeless and the wounds on the thing, some which should have been fatal, were merely oozing a black goo. The being jabbed an iron pike at the small, fanged snout that spit another burst of flame, but the dragon was too fast. The zombie-like being missed and was singed black, but it held to its pike. This was definitely one of Beelzebub's creatures.

As Willoughby cautiously approached, the now blackened figure lunged again at the dragon, thrusting its pike. Wings flapped and sharp talons moved with uncanny speed, grabbing the form, then jerking it from sight. Moments later there was a muffled scream. The whoosh of wings came louder, mingled with a triumphant cry as the zombie's scream faded. Moments later, there was a distant ping and thud as the charred being and its iron pike slammed against the rocks below.

The small dragon had perched itself in one of the open arches of the porch. It turned. Willoughby froze. The beast eyed him a long moment, then seemed to lose interest. Willoughby inched his way forward, stepping over another burnt corpse and continuing out onto the porch proper. Black ooze was dripping from the creature's needle fangs and sharp talons. It cocked its head, its large eyes unblinking, but did not attack.

"Good...Uh, good boy?" Willoughby whispered, trying to move ever so slightly faster. "I'm on your side— I'm here to help," he said. "The, uh, the *Friend*, I mean the *Friend's* friend, the *keeper*, sent me," Willoughby had eased completely past the creature, but wasn't sure he could turn his back to it. Yet he had to. "I'll, uh," he started. "I'll be going now." He turned away, cringing, listening for a sudden intake of air or something to alert him that the creature had decided to roast him. No sound came except a slight clicking as the creature hopped down to the stone floor of the porch. Willoughby glanced back. The dragon creature had cocked its head again, but was turned away from Willoughby now, seeming to guard the porch from any attack on that side. Willoughby quickened his pace. Once he reached a wider section of porch, he caught sight of Sydney. She had put the bow to the strings and started to play.

"*Sydney!*" he called out. He wasn't sure what else to say. Finally, he added, "What are you doing?"

Sydney stood erect in an arch about twenty meters from him. She stopped her movement of the bow for a moment, looking toward him. Behind her, Willoughby could see Beelzebub. He was at the far end of the porch, being held at bay by the other dragon who seemed willing to just corner him and stop him from moving forward. The demon gave Willoughby a condescending smirk but said nothing.

"So, you've come," Sydney finally said, as if speaking from a trance. "You've come just like he said you would." Her tone wasn't grateful, or happy—it was flat and dull. She seemed tired or resigned, letting her eyes train back upward, as if staring at the sky. Willoughby noted streaks of tears on her cheeks. She had been crying for some time.

"I don't understand any of this Sydney."

"No, you don't."

"Whatever it is, though—whatever he's said, however he's threatened you—we can work through it. We can do it together."

Sydney looked down again, and just for a moment, there was a glimpse of emotion, of the Sydney he knew fighting to surface. "I believed that once. That was before I knew. You are the one who needs protecting, Willoughby. Go back to your home, go back to the team, forget about me. Go, Willoughby. There is nothing you can do here."

Her eyes again seemed to glass over, steeled with acceptance and resolve.

"You're scaring me, Sydney," Willoughby said. "Come back away from the edge. Let's talk about this."

Sydney bit her lip. She shook her head.

"Why?" Willoughby shouted. "Why are you doing this? None of this makes any sense!" The wind was rising now, whipping Sydney's hair and dress around her. He continued to creep slowly forward. He was maybe seven or eight meters away now, starting to flex his legs, prepare his hands—ready to leap and try to grab her.

Sydney looked back up at the sky, her eyes filled with what seemed a bottomless sadness. She slowly lifted her bow again.

"I know about the song," Willoughby suddenly blurted. He was trying to throw her off, to distract her, even though he wasn't entirely sure what she was trying to do. "I know about the song—the score. I know there's something about a note. You're not a destroying angel, Sydney! You don't want to destroy anything. *I know you!*"

"*Then try to stop me!*" Sydney shot back, fighting down a sob. Tears were falling freely now. Willoughby could see her arms were taut and strained, as if she were fighting to keep her body from playing the violin tucked under her chin. "Stop me before it's too late... *Take me out of this!* Don't just send me back." Her face was contorting with emotion as she seemed to have to force the words out. "*You can't Willoughby! It's the edict of time! LET ME GO!*"

Willoughby stared at her, bewildered. "Let you go? *I'll never let you go!*"

Sydney had looked away. She had raised the bow and began to play. Willoughby knew the song. It was the one the violinist had tried to destroy—the one Aiyito had given to Sydney. It was the song she had somehow gone back in time to St. Petersburg to play, and that Dimitri Korsakov had warned him she would try to play here. It was the song that was not to be heard in its entirety until the end of days. *Had Sydney somehow found the few stanzas she lacked? Had her skill with composing helped her to divine how the song ended? Was Beelzebub right that she was somehow trying to destroy the world?* It was all a crazy, insane puzzle. Nothing made sense and there wasn't time to try to figure it all out. He had to reach her now. Only ten steps before she was in reach. Nine. Eight. He would jump and grab her and then find the underlying cause of all this. Six. With every inch he pushed forward, Sydney seemed to push further back, until her heels were hanging over the open edge of the archway.

"*Don't do this!*" Willoughby's voice cracked with fatigue and emotion. Four meters away still. He could never clear that distance in a single leap, yet he dared not inch any further. "*You fall and I'm jumping after you!*'"

Sydney did not respond. She continued to play, her eyes shut—her complete focus on the music. The faint strings of equations that Willoughby used to discern the time grid began to appear around her. They were bright, intense, churning like a spidery web, and they became more solid and visible with every note she played. Willoughby crouched, stunned, watching. The numbers were not disparate equations, but rather, one single equation, repeated over and over. The ends of the repeating equation swirled and snaked, snapping at the air as they seemed to cocoon Sydney. The wind picked up, howling even greater through the archways, the sky seeming to darken, and the clouds to churn, reaching down toward the porch, toward Sydney. The air around him began to roil and simmer, crackles of equation striking out like lightning with its own growing rumble of thunder.

"*Sydney!*" he screamed, springing forward.

In that instant, he saw he wouldn't make it. Even with her eyes closed, it was as if she sensed him coming. Her playing took on an added dimension, almost as if the music was stretching, reverberating, encompassing. Willoughby saw faint number strings leaking from her fingers. This was a new equation, one he recognized. It was the equation he had seen in the open time grid that first time, the one that had taken him to see her concert in St. Petersburg. With a start, he realized it was also the exact equation *he had seen escaping the locked box back at Port Arthur!* The number string was flowing from her. *Was she creating this string or somehow pulling it out of time?*

She leaned back, like a child on a feather bed expecting to fall back onto a pillow, only there was no feather bed behind her. There was nothing for hundreds of meters, and then only cold stone.

He hesitated only a moment on the edge of the archway, then dove after her. In his mind, he charted a course. He would skim the time holes as before, only they were larger here—much larger. *Large enough for him to grab her?* He wasn't sure, but he had to take the chance.

He was just over her, their falls matched in perfect sync, when her eyes below the buffeting wind, suddenly shot open. She was expecting him to be there—right where he was. She wanted him to do something. There was determination, purpose, fire in those eyes. Something communicated to his soul.

Suddenly, he remembered something...*How Loa's box was in his pocket!* It was open now. He grabbed it. Somehow, he understood. It had a purpose. It was *empty.* It had to be filled with this very equation, the one still falling from Sydney's own fingertips. He would never be able to reach Sydney. The force building around her was too strong—he would bounce off it. But he could capture these bits of equation. He would seal them somehow in the box, and it would make a difference. He wasn't sure how, but he knew it would. With the box hanging open, he felt the jerk of the time stream, ending almost as soon as it began as he skidded, then tumbled out onto the ground, right where he had first stood looking up at Sydney. The box had broken free of his hand, but he could see now that it was shut tight, and he could see the numbers once again flowing to it. He had targeted Sydney, had held out a hand hoping to somehow snag her, but he had known it wouldn't work. He jerked his head, looking around.

Sydney was gone.

40

Anomaly

The swirling black cut off his view of the castle. He had to
have an end-point in view to skim the time holes, so that
was out. He felt a pain in his leg and looked down. He had
a neat puncture from a bit of jutting rock. It was bleeding
badly, but he determined it was nothing life threatening,
and he could still walk on it. He ripped a bit of his shirt
and tied it around the wound, then picked up the closed
box and began to make his way up the slow rise toward the
monastery. The sky did not change. It looked almost like a
vortex, and the blackness seemed to be growing. Air still
bubbled and crackled around its center as the wind
howled. He found fighting the wind and climbing the rise
therapeutic as the physical exertion allowed him to escape
the sense of dread and loss he felt, if only for a moment. A
huge crack of thunder ripped through the air. It rattled
him to the bone. Willoughby thought he heard voices—
millions upon millions of haunting, piercing voices, lifted
in some macabre song, twining, and intertwining with
strains of music. At one point, he felt he heard the faint
tinkle of Sydney's bracelets, but when he looked, there was
nothing to see. He wasn't even sure if the sounds he heard

were truly in the wind, or only in his mind. He just looked down and hobbled on, up the uneven path.

"You think this is over, boy?" a voice sounded from behind him. He turned. Beelzebub stood there on the path. He gave Willoughby another sardonic grin and spat. Willoughby noted that the Demon Lord had also been injured. His thigh was oozing something black. The ooze came from a slash wound. He was only a few feet away. The being had to yell to be heard over the howling wind.

"This is far from over," he snapped, contorting his full height. "In fact," he gestured, pointing at the vortex above, "it has only just begun." He made a slashing movement with his arm, opening a bright rip in the lively time fabric around him. Willoughby could see strings of equations escaping from his fingers—just as they had from Sydney. They enlarged and then dissipated, like smoky air from a balloon. "I know where the pendant is now. I will have it soon. I will build this anomaly you've created into my masterpiece! You—too late, you will come to know what you have done!"

With that, he gave a hoarse laugh, stepped through the rip, and was gone.

Willoughby stared at the spot where he stood for a moment, trying to understand. *Equations had come from the being's fingertips. They had seemed able to rip through to the fabric of time with a mere touch. Equations—powerful equations—had been escaping from Sydney's fingertips.* What did it mean?

He stared up at the roiling clouds. At some deep level, he sensed more than understood what he had done. He couldn't articulate it, but he sensed the magnitude of what had just occurred. He began walking again. Within moments, he heard a whoosh of large wings. One of the dragons landed in the path ahead of him. The second dragon landed a few meters back. They cocked their heads at him, curious.

"I wasn't able to stop her," Willoughby started, not sure why he was talking to dragons, but the words unlocked all the pain, all the despair, the exhaustion, the sadness inside him. These descended like their own storm, bringing him to his knees, sobbing into his hands. He heard a clutter of footsteps and then his friends were beside him.

"*Willoughby!*"

It was Hauti who dropped beside him first, throwing a protective arm around his shoulders. He tried to say something, but no words came. "There, there," Hauti soothed. "Let it all out. Lord knows you've been holding it in long enough. Just let it all out."

James Arthur came thundering down after her. He stopped a few feet away, leaning over, panting.

"It wasn't your fault, man," he said. "You did your best—I mean, I about lost my lunch when you went sailing over the edge after her."

Willoughby had calmed the emotional deluge that had hit him now. He wiped at his eyes quickly, embarrassed for his friends to see him this way. "You saw me jump after her?" he finally managed. James Arthur had bent down now.

"Yeah, we both did. You didn't hesitate a moment, just—wow—swan dived over! I thought '*that is one brave dude!*'"

Willoughby tried to force a smile. The beasts ahead of them fidgeted. "So, what are those things?" he finally asked. "Are they really dragons?"

Hauti gave a wide smile. "Well, that's what I would call them. They are...they are with the *keeper*. Not exactly pets, but..."

"They're good to have in a fight," Willoughby added, looking over at them.

"You can say that again," Dr. J added.

With a flap, the closest dragon fluttered up and away. The second dragon eyed Willoughby long and hard, then jumped into the air and winged out after its mate, or the *keeper*, or whatever.

Willoughby started to slowly rise. Two things he knew. First, he knew it would be pointless to look for Sydney's body. She had not fallen to her death. She had been taken by the vortex, or huge time hole, or whatever it was swirling about him. He wasn't exactly sure where, but he believed he may have sent her back to the moment in the Port Arthur prison cell when she had started playing and the box had opened. Or, at least somewhere near that time. In fact, it made some sort of weird sense to him now as he thought back on the change that had suddenly come over Sydney when the box opened. *She suddenly knew this had all happened before!* He had sent her into a loop that she kept playing through over and over. And she had somehow become cognizant of what was happening. Was that why time equations seemed to be bleeding from her fingers? Why had she asked him to stop, to let her go? *Stop what?* Stop saving her from a certain death on the rocks below? Stop her from somehow ending the world?

Too many questions, he thought, giving his head a shake. *Too few answers*. His temples throbbed. His leg hurt. He knew that they had to find T.K. quickly, and find that pendant. It seemed to be the key, and he was worried that somehow, despite all the demon's posturing, he had given Beelzebub exactly what he wanted—he had given him *an anomaly.*

James Arthur had just noticed his leg. "That looks bad. You think you can walk?"

"It's not as bad as it looks," Willoughby said. His voice trailed off. Suddenly, he looked up, resolute. "Have you heard from Antonio?"

"Yeah," Hauti answered. "That's a bit of good news."

"He found T.K.," James Arthur continued. "She's alive, but pretty bad off. They flew her to a hospital in New Zealand."

"We've got to get in touch with him. We've got to get that pendant and somehow destroy it, or keep it safe from Beelzebub. Somehow, everything that's happening is part of his plan. I think he's trying to create a black hole, one that will swallow time, the earth, all of us. I don't know why—I don't know what he gets out of it—but it increases his power somehow. I captured a bit of, of, I don't know— I think time—from Sydney when I was trying to save her. I think it created a loop, or an anomaly around it. That's why you won't find Sydney if you look for her. She isn't here. I think I sent her back somewhere."

James Arthur thought for a moment, his face breaking into genuine joy. "*Then you did do it!* You saved her!"

Willoughby shook his head. "I don't know. I'm not sure what I did to her. It was all very confusing."

The group had started down the path. "We need to get you some sleep and some food and then we can talk more about what happened and what we do next. Our SUV is about a half mile this way," Hauti said, gently leading him in the right direction.

"We can't call Antonio until we clear this mountain," James Arthur said. "There's no cell coverage here—I discovered that when I tried to call you from the top of the path."

Willoughby stopped, looking behind him. "Hey, where's the other guy—the *keeper?* Where did the dragons go?"

James Arthur looked over at Hauti. She shrugged. "We don't know about the *friend*," she said. "He just disappeared. One moment he was there, the next, he was not. As far as the dragons, we think they were just leading us to you. We knew they'd probably take off as soon as we found you. They're probably with the *keeper*, wherever he's at. He's a bit of a slippery kind of guy."

Willoughby gave a slight nod. "Yeah, I know the type." James Arthur barked a short laugh, then they all turned and continued down the path.

41

You Buy, She Like

Antonio had dozed some of the way on the flight in, but his concern for T.K., and the fact that the small plane pitched and rolled a lot, meant he had not gotten any real sleep for over thirty hours now. T.K. had been out the entire trip, heavily sedated. The doctors had operated immediately to stem internal bleeding when they arrived, then they had cleaned her up, bandaged her, and put her in Intensive Care. They forbade any visitors for the next eight hours, but said that she responded remarkably well to the surgery, and that they really thought she was out of the woods.

Antonio couldn't help thinking of the girl who fearlessly took on a plesiosaur, and wondered what the full story of her injuries were. He tried to nap on one of the hospital couches, but he couldn't seem to get any quality sleep, even though he now had the chance. He roamed the halls for a while, buying a small breakfast at the hospital cafeteria. There was a brisk wind outside, but the day was otherwise bright and sunny. He pulled out his cell phone and again tried to call Willoughby. No answer. He tried Sydney. No answer. He considered calling Sian, but thought better of it. Instead, he tried James Arthur and

Hauti. No answer. Trying not to swear in frustration, he thumped his fist against a wall. He continued walking. When he finally looked up again, he found he was peering through the glass window into a small hospital gift shop. A tall, bespectacled Asian man was smiling at him, motioning for him to come in. He sighed and mumbled to himself. "What the heck." Then, he followed the glass to the corner and turned into the shop's open door.

"You much look like in distress," the Asian man said. "Maybe you have good loved one, very sick? Maybe you buy something for her? Something very special?"

"How did you know it was a *her*?" Antonio asked.

The tall considered the question. "You bang fist down hall—I saw you," he said smiling. "Most time when man bang fist, there beautiful lady involved."

Antonio had to grin at the logic. He looked at his watch. They would let him see T.K. in a little over an hour. "Okay," he said. "So, tell me my friend," Antonio narrowed his eyebrows, "I am sorry, I do not know your name."

"I am *How*," the man said, seemingly delighted to share his name. "*How Loa*."

"Well, *How*, what do you think a beautiful lady, who is very hurt, but also very special, might appreciate?"

The tall man smiled, taking him to what was surely the most expensive arrangement in the store. "This for you!" he said. "You good customer! I give you special deal! You buy, she like!"

Antonio looked over the arrangement. It was beautiful, full of vibrant flowers, some of which he had never seen before. Of course, he had never been to New Zealand, so maybe there was exotic plant life here he was not aware of.

"It is most beautiful," he said, pulling out his wallet. "It will certainly brighten her room." After the shopkeeper ran the card and got his signature—the "good deal" on the arrangement set him back two hundred and thirteen dollars and fifty-nine cents—Antonio carefully lifted the arrangement and turned to leave.

"You wait!" the Asian man called after him. "You forget best part! I tell you good deal, that mean extra special gift for fine lady! Here, she read, she like!" He held out to Antonio a small book. "Good deal include special book! It just for you, you give to special lady. She like! She like! She like, mean you lucky man!"

Antonio turned, placing the arrangement back down on the counter. He looked up at the odd oriental man, and then down at the thin, leather-bound book in his hand. *How* had bowed graciously as he presented the book, holding it in both hands as if it were very precious. The leather was intricately sculpted and looked old and expensive. A scene was depicted on the cover that included two small, Chinese-style dragons against a mountainous and wild landscape. An odd city sparkled in the distance seeming to rise from solid cliffs of ice. While he wasn't sure if Tainken was much of a reader, this was obviously a beautifully crafted heirloom of some kind. He tried to kindly refuse the gift, but *How* insisted.

"You good customer! I promise good deal—*How Loa* always deliver!"

Antonio finally thanked him, tucked the book under his arm, and once again lifted the beautiful arrangement. This time, *How* let him exit the shop. He stood behind the counter, waving, and sporting a huge smile.

"*Well, well,*" Antonio mused, looking down again at the book. The addition did make him feel a bit better about the exorbitant cost of the arrangement. *How* walked to the shop opening and called after him.

"Tell her, grand adventure at end of trail—got to get to end of trail!" the tall man added, his head bobbing. A broad smile was still plastered to his face.

Antonio smiled back and nodded, but didn't stop. *Trail? What was the man talking about?* When he finally got back to his couch in the waiting room, he carefully set the flower arrangement down on an end table. Others in the waiting room took note and a few commented on how beautiful it was, one even asking what kind of flowers those were. He said he wasn't sure, then settled onto the couch and took a closer look at the leather book.

What had the funny man meant by, *"got to get to end of trail?"* He read the title of the little book aloud, mumbling the words to himself; '*Catch a Dragon by the Trail.*' He scanned the cover for the author line. The author of the book was listed as *The Fifth Friend*. He cocked his head. This seemed like an odd title for a book, and hadn't he heard that name before? The Fifth Friend...

Catch a Dragon by the Trail? He raised an eyebrow, letting a slight grin creep across his face. *Maybe T.K. will want a bit of light fantasy and adventure to take her mind off things,* he thought. Except, what was fantasy to other people tended, for them, to turn all too real.

Frighteningly real.

Coming Spring, 2019

Cryptic Spaces
Enigma

Empty. It's more than just a word. It's a state of being. To Willoughby, it's like being trapped in a hall of mirrors. All around, he can see himself, but only from the outside-in. The images that fill the hall have no weight, no substance. They're ghosts, dancing through a life that has lost its meaning. Every time he closes his eyes, questions crash down like thunder. *Why did she do it? Why didn't she talk to him, warn him? How deep are the secrets she's hiding? Does he even know her at all?* Memories of piercing eyes, silky hair, the soft ping of bracelets clinking, the brush of satin skin on his lips burst upon his mind, burning like bolts of white-hot lightning. But there is no rain—no relief. Sydney is gone. He doesn't know where, or how, or why. He doesn't even know if she's still alive. He only knows that his life can never be full again unless he finds her.

Determined to risk everything, with Aiyito's full financial support, and the team as determined as ever to see this through, he plunges headlong into a nail-biting journey across time and space. From the shining spires of Atlantis, to Brazil's lost city of *Z*, from Kubla-Khan's ghost-fleet, to the sky caves of Nepal, the team finds old friends, new enemies, and uncovers deeper mysteries as they track down the elusive *Fifth Friend*, a shadowy figure who seems as old as time itself. Get ready for courage, sacrifice, and betrayal; for angels, giants, zombies, artificial intelligence, alchemists, ghosts, time-traveling vampires, and of course, dragons—an entire hidden lair of dragon-kind. The forces of light and dark are gathering. Time itself begins to fold and divide. Willoughby sees his world crumbling. Can time be healed? Will what *was* ever be the same again?

WE LOVE YOUR FEEDBACK! (You can email us at crypticspaces@gmail.com.) We also appreciate reviews online!